D1274459

PRAISE FOR **TO BE WOLVES**

"**To Be Wolves** might appeal to those who enjoy reading fast-paced, plot-driven novels with a flavor of sensational headlines of significant events from classical antiquity."
—**Historical Novels Review**

TO BE
WOLVES

OTHER BOOKS BY DEBRA MAY MACLEOD

VESTA SHADOWS

Brides of Rome

To Be Wolves

Empire of Iron

A NOVEL OF
✦ THE VESTAL VIRGINS ✦

TO BE WOLVES

DEBRA MAY MACLEOD

**BLACK
STONE**
PUBLISHING

Copyright © 2021 by Debra May Macleod
Published in 2022 by Blackstone Publishing
Cover and book design by Alenka Vdovič Linaschke
Forum Romanum illustration by Ana Rey
Book logo by Jeanine Henning

Printed in the United States of America

First large print edition: 2022
ISBN 979-8-200-80993-6
Fiction / Historical / Ancient

Version 1

CIP data for this book is available
from the Library of Congress

Blackstone Publishing
31 Mistletoe Rd.
Ashland, OR 97520

www.BlackstonePublishing.com

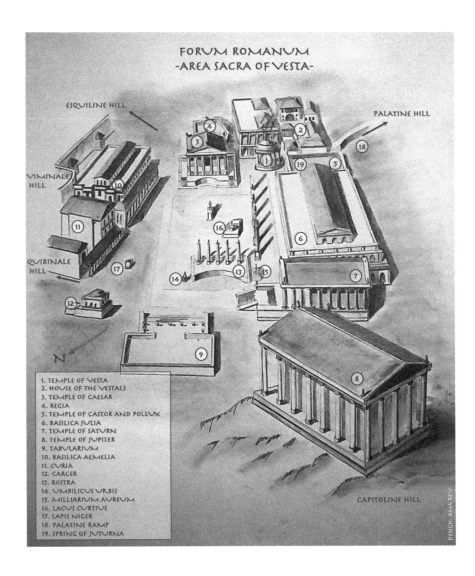

FORUM ROMANUM
-AREA SACRA OF VESTA-

ESQUILINE HILL

PALATINE HILL

VIMINALE HILL

QUIRINALE HILL

N

CAPITOLINE HILL

DESIGN: ANA REY

1. TEMPLE OF VESTA
2. HOUSE OF THE VESTALS
3. TEMPLE OF CAESAR
4. REGIA
5. TEMPLE OF CASTOR AND POLLUX
6. BASILICA JULIA
7. TEMPLE OF SATURN
8. TEMPLE OF JUPITER
9. TABULARIUM
10. BASILICA AEMELIA
11. CURIA
12. CARCER
13. ROSTRA
14. UMBILICUS URBIS
15. MILLIARIUM AUREUM
16. LACUS CURTIUS
17. LAPIS NIGER
18. PALATINE RAMP
19. SPRING OF JUTURNA

AUTHOR'S NOTE

At the front of this book, you'll find a simplified illustration of the Roman Forum and the structures mentioned in the story.

At the back, I have included a dramatis personae, or cast of characters. You'll also find other reader-friendly resources there, including the names of the gods and mythical figures mentioned in the book, a glossary of Latin and other important terms, and several illustrations that tie into the story line and which I think you'll find fascinating.

Thank you for reading.

PROLOGUE

Extremis Malis Extrema Remedia
Desperate times call for desperate measures
−A ROMAN ADAGE

PICENUM, 72 BCE

General Marcus Licinius Crassus secured his formed leather cuirass around his torso and then placed his deep purple cloak over his shoulders, fastening it at one shoulder with a large gold **fibula**. It was cool in his large officer's tent despite the fact that it was made of insulating goatskin and a decent fire had burned all night. He exhaled tiredly at the thought of what was about to happen and saw his breath form an icy cloud in the air.

The Roman legionary soldiers that stood outside his tent heard him approach and pulled the flaps open for him to exit. He stepped out to an even cooler morning. Multiple snapping fires were burning in the dismal tent camp, and he could hear the banging of pots as a sprawling troop of cooks cleaned up after the monumental task of feeding three legions, nearly fifteen thousand men, their breakfast of gruel. Crassus hadn't eaten. He had no appetite.

The thick fog that had settled over the camp and the nearby hills of the Apennines in the earliest hours hadn't lifted but seemed even heavier as day broke. Yet to Crassus it wasn't thick enough. It could never be thick enough to obscure the haunting sight that every soldier knew was still there on the high edge of one of the hills before them.

He inhaled a chestful of the cool air and looked up at them: the bodies of six Roman soldiers hanging from crosses, their heads now dropped forward in what Crassus hoped was the mercy of death and not just exhaustion. He blinked. In the fog, they looked like ghosts suspended in the deathly mists of Hades.

But they weren't ghosts. They were his men— the bravest of his men—captured in battle by those filthy followers of the rebel slave leader Spartacus and crucified in full view of the great Roman army. Or at least what was left of it.

Before the rise of Spartacus's slave army, it had been centuries since the Roman military had had to contend with desertions. Sure, the odd fool still tried to make a run for it now and then, but it wasn't a serious problem. Roman soldiers were the most courageous, skilled, and well paid in the world. They were also the most successful. Many enemies surrendered without a fight; such fear did the tactics of the Roman military machine put in their hearts.

The problem for Crassus and other generals was that Spartacus knew those tactics. He had served in the army before a charge of insubordination had seen him reduced to slavery. After subsisting for years as a gladiator, he had escaped and gathered his own army. Now, he used Roman psychological warfare tactics against its own soldiers. He knew what scared them. He knew what made them run. And it was the ghostly sight above them.

Crassus heard footsteps behind him. He turned and nodded a somber greeting to the young general that Pompey had sent to help him crush Spartacus, a particularly capable man by the name of Julius Caesar. Caesar offered him a piece of bread. He accepted and took a single bite, then tossed the bread aside. Four or five crows descended upon it, cawing and croaking at each other as they ate.

"The men are ready for you, General," said Caesar.

Crassus didn't move.

Caesar's sharp features, which always gave him an air of seriousness, appeared even more severe against the dreariness of the morning. He cleared his throat. "Sir, my **exploratores** estimate that over half of Spartacus's men, perhaps as many as twenty thousand, are no longer moving northward. They have turned, and are heading south—"

"To Rome," said Crassus.

"To Rome," echoed Caesar. "After the defeat of so many of our legions, they are emboldened. They aren't content with escape. They want to conquer." He threw his own half-eaten piece of bread to the crows. "We cannot lose any more cohorts to desertion."

"Spartacus cannot reach Rome," said Crassus, as much to himself as to Caesar. "He will take the city if he reaches it."

"Yes," said Caesar, "he will." The young general squared his shoulders. "The men are ready for you."

Crassus turned on his heel and walked past his tent, past the cooks, past the tethered horses that neighed and shook their manes, waiting impatiently for their morning barley.

The entire Fourth Roman Cohort—five hundred soldiers dressed in helmets and full armor—stood at attention, arrayed in five manageable, well-spaced rows of one hundred men each.

They were surrounded by even more men from Crassus's newest legions—fresh legions, soldiers brought in from the provinces and pulled from other campaigns. And still more were on their way.

It's about bloody time, thought Crassus. Every time Spartacus's army of slaves won a battle, every time they made it a mile closer to Rome, the Senate took Crassus's warnings a little more seriously. At least now Crassus had the manpower to put up a real fight—that is, providing his men didn't break and run.

Unfortunately, that's exactly what many men in the Fourth Cohort had done. Not all of them—some had held their ground and fought Spartacus's wild mob, even after defeat was certain—but that didn't matter. A chain is only as strong as its weakest link. An army is only as strong as its weakest soldier.

As centurions walked up and down the rows of soldiers to maintain order, their red cloaks flowing behind them and their hands on the hilts of their daggers, Crassus mounted his white warhorse, placed his helmet on his head, and rode before his men. Caesar did the same, moving his horse alongside Crassus's.

"Desertion is the plague of our army," Crassus

shouted. "It is a contagion that our legions do not often suffer, but it has returned as a sickness that threatens the life of Rome itself. Today, we will cure that sickness before it can spread to one more Roman soldier."

Crassus hesitated. He had a reputation for being harsh . . . but was this going too far?

He glanced over his shoulder, into the distance. The fog was clearing. The six crucified soldiers on the hill seemed to hang in the air above them.

Crassus imagined Spartacus's men breaking through the gates of Rome. He tried not to imagine what they would do to the women and children they found there. He tried not to imagine what they would do in the streets, in the temples, in the Senate house. They would lay waste to the Eternal City the way they had laid waste to every village they moved through: thieving, beating, raping, and tearing down what greater men had built up.

They would inspire every slave in every household, no matter how rich or modest, to rise up against their master and join their mutinous army. It would no longer be just a military loss. It would be the loss of a civilization that Romulus and the gods themselves had founded.

Crassus lifted his head. "You are the sons of Rome," he shouted. "You are the wolves that tear out the throats of our enemies." He moved his horse to stand in front of the Fourth Cohort, Caesar still at his side. "But some of you have forgotten yourselves," he said. "I am here to remind you." He looked down at the centurion who stood before the first row of one hundred men and gave the order. "Decimation."

The centurion balked. Had he heard that correctly? He opened his mouth, closed it, and then asked, "Should they draw lots, General?" Despite his long career, he had never seen this done. No one had. It was an archaic form of discipline that the Roman army had abandoned hundreds of years ago.

"We don't have time for theater," said Crassus. "Count them off."

"Yes, sir."

The centurion straightened. It was better he did it without thinking. He began to walk along the row, counting each man as he went. "One, two, three, four . . ." When he reached the tenth man, he said, "Take two steps forward." The centurion continued along the row like this until every tenth man had been singled out.

"Remove your armor," the centurion shouted at the ten men.

The men exchanged looks of disbelief. Was this really happening? Decimation was just a ghost story. Yet as the reality of it descended upon them, they did what Roman soldiers were supposed to do. They followed orders. Of the ten men, Crassus recognized only the first one. Was his name Gaius? He frowned. He doubted this man was a deserter. Crassus had seen him drag two of his wounded fellow soldiers off the battlefield and then return to it himself, even while others fled into the surrounding forest.

He thought for a moment about stopping it, about making an exception, but he knew he could not. **There can be no weak link**, he reminded himself. Decimation was an effective, albeit desperate, way to deter soldiers from deserting, yet it only worked because everyone in the offending cohort was equally vulnerable: courageous or cowardly, young or old, soldier or officer. No exceptions. Every tenth man— **decimus**—selected at random.

Ignoring the doubts in his mind and the cramping in his gut, Crassus compelled himself to keep his chin up and his eyes on the man named Gaius. After all, thousands of legionary soldiers had their eyes on him. He needed to look like he was certain about what he was doing. He was the man in charge.

Slowly, Gaius removed his helmet. He held it in his hands for several long moments and then turned around to face his fellow soldiers.

They all had their eyes to the ground.

"Lucius," he said to one of them.

One of the soldiers looked at him. "Gaius, my brother," he said, "I am sorry."

Gaius tossed his helmet at the man. "Make sure my son gets my armor," he said. "Tell him I died on the battlefield."

"He will be proud of you," said Lucius. "I will see to it."

As if he were doing nothing more than undressing for the bath, Gaius unpinned his red cloak and let it fall to the ground. He unfastened the leather belts of his iron armor, set it down a few steps away, and then returned to stand in the same spot. Now wearing only a simple red woolen **tunica**, he dropped his arms to his sides.

"Begin!" the centurion ordered.

Not a man moved.

"Begin," the centurion barked again, "or we'll take every **fifth** man!"

Gaius nodded at his friend. "Do it. Quickly."

The other man's nostrils flared. He raised his club and struck Gaius on the skull. The soldier stumbled backward and fell to the ground as other men joined in, some crying out prayers to the gods and others shamed apologies to the man they bludgeoned.

It was a disgrace to die by decimation. It was an even greater disgrace to survive.

Gaius's fellow soldiers—his friends, the men with whom he had marched under the Eagle to foreign lands and back, men who knew his dreams and the names of his children—raised their clubs and beat him as hard as they could, hoping that each strike of the club would end their friend's suffering and their own shame.

Within two minutes, Gaius's mangled body lay bloody and broken on the ground. Lucius forced himself to look at it, but what lay before him was un-recognizable as his friend. Gaius's skull had collapsed inward: white splinters of bone and red chunks of brain were draining out of it, like wine spilling slowly out of a cracked cup. His jaw jutted out at a gro-tesque, stomach-churning angle, and his arms and legs twitched as the nerves continued to fire.

It happened that way, exactly that way, another

forty-nine times that day. Crassus watched every decimation from atop his horse. After the fiftieth soldier had stopped breathing and the weary soldiers had stepped back into line, the general galloped his horse to stand before the vast swaths of his legions. He put his hand on the hilt of his sword, one side of which boasted a gold medallion of the legendary Roman she-wolf, the other the fiery goddess Vesta.

"What you have done to your brothers today, on this battlefield, is nothing compared to what Spartacus will do to your sons, your wives, and your mothers if he reaches the gates of Rome. You are Romans," he shouted and thrust his sword into the air. "You were raised by a wolf to be wolves! Now go tear out some throats."

CHAPTER I

Graviora Quaedam Sunt Remedia Periculis
Some remedies are worse than the disease.
—PUBLILIUS SYRUS

ROME, 21 BCE
Fifty-one years later

Two Vestal Virgins stood before a white marble pedestal in the dimly lit bedchamber of the emperor Caesar Augustus, their palms up to the goddess in somber prayer. On top of the pedestal sat a wide bronze bowl within which burned the sacred fire of Vesta. It crackled and snapped, consuming the consecrated kindling the Vestals had placed in its orange flames.

Only steps away from the fire, Octavian lay drenched in sweat on his bed. The priestess Tuccia looked down at him and frowned at his drawn and pale face, the raspy sounds of his shallow breaths. It wasn't that long ago that he had ridden around the Circus Maximus and the streets of Rome in the jeweled chariot of his joyous triumphal procession, a gilded crown of laurels held over his head by a slave who whispered into his ear, "Remember, thou art mortal."

At the time, he had hardly seemed it. The grand parade and the spoils of war, the masses of cheering spectators—they had all seemed endless. Tuccia remembered the look in Caesar's cool gray eyes as he had stood on the Rostra and gazed down on his people, more god than man, as the look-alikes of General Antony and Queen Cleopatra were killed before him.

But the slave was right. He was mortal after all.

Livia emerged from the shadows to stand beside Tuccia. Her hair was pulled back into a loose bun and her face, though as appealing and regal as ever, looked tired. She sighed and stared down at her failing husband. His fingers and his mottled flesh twitched in a perverse fashion that made her skin crawl as if it were covered in beetles. She put her hands on her hips and turned to her husband's Greek physician, an irritatingly tall man named Antonius Musa.

"We send Mercury himself to retrieve you from that cesspit Athens, and you can't even stop a simple spasm?"

"The spasm is a good sign, Empress," he replied.

"**The spasm is a good sign?**" Livia raised her eyebrows. "Did you hear that, Priestess Nona? The spasm is a good sign. Well, in that case, Musa, let's have one of the stable boys sit on his chest. Weak breath is a good sign too, nay?"

"Lady Livia," said Nona, "make another offering to Apollo."

As the physician mouthed a silent "Thank you" to the elder priestess, Livia crossed the expansive floor of the bedchamber and stopped at the sacrificial altar to Apollo that had been hastily erected in Caesar's room the day before. A priest of Apollo stood beside it, murmuring soft petitions to the god of healing.

Livia took a pinch of loose salted flour and sprinkled it into the thick flame of a beeswax candle that sat in the center of the altar, at the base of a golden statue of Apollo. Twin baby goats—they looked like they had been pulled from their mother's womb early—lay dead-eyed on either side of the statue, the blood from their opened throats now sticky and rank. Beside them sat a **patera** of oil for libations.

Livia placed her hands on the edge of the altar and knelt before it, looking up into the sapphire eyes of the god. The low voices of Apollo's priest and Vesta's priestesses in prayer mingled in the space behind her.

In prayer for Caesar's life. Her husband's life.

A flickering shadow moved across the frescoed walls of the firelit room, and Livia sensed movement behind her. A moment later her son Tiberius appeared at her side. He placed a small terracotta statue of Asclepius next to one of the fetal goats, gripped the edge of the altar, and knelt beside her. He looked sideways at the priest of Apollo as if to say, "Leave us," and the robed figure slunk away.

"Mother," he whispered, "Octavia has succumbed."

Livia exhaled through her nose. She wasn't surprised. Octavia's son, Marcellus, had died months earlier from the contagion and she had never fully recovered. Neither had Octavian, for that matter. The death of his nephew and heir had left him a weaker man. She heard him groan behind her. "If he dies, we're as good as dead." She put her head in her hands. "Gods."

"Aegroto dum anima est, spes est." Tiberius tossed some salted flour into the flame. Where there is life, there is hope.

"What a stupid thing to say."

"Mother, he may yet live."

"He must live. Agrippa was named second in his will."

"Even if he lives, he will never name me his heir."

"He must and he will," said Livia. "There is no other way. If Agrippa becomes emperor, we will be exiled. He hates us both." Another heavy exhalation. "Agrippa may yet have use for Drusus if he ever sees fit to bring him home from Germania, but we'll be carted off with the worn linens to Pandateria. Just you and me, Tiberius, on a tiny island without even wine to numb the displeasure of each other's company—"

"Mother, stop." Tiberius wiped his brow with the back of his hand. "Will you tell him about his sister?"

"No. Make sure the slaves know to keep their big mouths shut for a change too. He wouldn't survive the shock of it."

A rustle of bedsheets made them both turn around. Octavian had one hand in the air, his finger pointed as if he were about to command a legion. "Wife," he sputtered.

Livia moved to his bed and sat on the edge.

"Husband, be still." She took his hand and rested it at his side, fighting the urge to wipe his cold sweat off her hands. That would look bad in front of the Vestals.

Octavian gestured weakly to Tuccia and she approached his bedside.

"Yes, Caesar?"

"Has Priestess Pomponia left Tivoli yet?"

"Yes, she will arrive in Rome today."

"Do not allow her to visit me. The **Vestalis Maxima** cannot fall ill."

"There has been no trace of the disease in Tivoli, Caesar. Pomponia's physician says it is because the region is less populated and the water supply is uncorrupted. She is strong and shall remain so." Octavian opened his mouth to say something, but a sputter of mucus caught in his throat. "Rest now," said Tuccia. She touched his chest gently. "The goddess keeps you."

Once the priestess had stepped away from the bed, Livia reached into a glass bowl of cool water on a nearby table and wrung out the cloth inside. She wiped away the thick fluid that ran out the corner of Octavian's mouth.

He blinked up at her. The emperor of Rome, too weak to wipe his own chin.

"I hope to live, wife," he said.

"Hope is powerful medicine, Octavian," she replied. "Sometimes it is all the gods leave us."

Octavian managed a weak smile. "Tell me the story of Pandora. It comforts me."

Livia smiled back. On the outside. Inside, she felt a swell of annoyance. She was the empress of Rome, not a coddling nurse. Octavian usually had his daughter, Julia, tell him a story, but he had forbidden her to visit him after his sickness had taken a more serious turn. Strange he had not shown such caution for his wife.

"Pandora was the first woman," Livia began as matronly as she could. "She was created out of clay by the Greek god Zeus as both a gift and a punishment to man, to be his companion and to make him at once a better and a worse being. When Zeus put Pandora in the world, he gave her a closed jar and this one command: "Do not remove the lid.""

"But she did . . ." whispered Octavian.

"Of course she did. What kind of tedious woman would she be if she did not? Pandora found a lovely stream to sit beside, and when no one was looking, not even Zeus, she slowly took the lid off the jar.

"To her horror, out flew every misery the gods

had fashioned for us—death, pain, cruelty, sorrow, worry, fear, and disease. Pandora knew none of these things by name, for they had not existed in the garden of life before. Yet as each one flew out, she felt it for the first time, like a blade in her heart. She tried desperately to catch these evils and put them back in the jar, but it was not to be. Full of despair, she replaced the lid as quickly as she could, but it was no use. The world was afflicted."

Octavian closed his eyes. A tear rolled down his cheek.

"But Pandora was as keen and quick as she was curious, and she had been able to trap one thing in the jar. One thing that humans could always hold on to—"

"Hope," said Octavian.

"Yes, husband," Livia replied. "And that is why wherever there is life, there is hope."

* * *

As she stepped out of the house and into the fresh air of the peristyle that surrounded the open court-yard of Caesar's home, Livia pushed as much air out of her lungs as she could and then inhaled deeply, repeating the process, out and in, until she felt light-headed. It was no use. She couldn't get the stench of Octavian's illness out of her nose.

He had fallen sick suddenly three days earlier. He had been at his desk signing a document, when all at once, he had doubled over in pain and rushed off to the toilet. Such dramatics were nothing new to Livia. Her husband had developed an increasingly weak constitution. This time was much worse than usual, though, and it soon became apparent that the devastating disease that was sweeping through Rome was also sweeping through the emperor's royal guts.

Within hours Octavia was also bedridden, overcome by fever and dysentery. Despite being in better physical health than her brother, she had deteriorated just as quickly and had fallen into an unresponsive state earlier that day.

Although Livia had often resented the close bond Octavia shared with her brother, she couldn't help but feel what she suspected was a trace of true sadness. The contagion was a merciless one, and Octavia, who had always been kind to Livia, and even Tiberius, had suffered horribly. Octavian would reel at the loss. If he lived long enough to learn of it.

His physician, Musa, was offering none of his

usual lofty reassurances and was silent with worry. Livia wondered whether his concern was only for his own fate—at best he'd be banished to some miserable northern outpost if Caesar died—or whether he was truly concerned for the emperor's well-being.

Then again, she wondered the same thing about herself. She honestly didn't know whether the fear she felt was only for her own life or for her husband's.

Livia passed by a large water fountain, at the center of which stood a tall marble statue of Triton blowing a conch shell, his arms raised to hold the heavy shell and his lower body morphing into a muscular fish tail. As if in obeyance to the god's trumpeting command, the water around one side of the fountain rose and flowed like rough waves on the sea. Livia indulged in a long look at Triton's strong chest and muscled arms, feeling her spirits lift. **I must commission that sculptor again**, she thought.

Moving further into the courtyard, she surveyed the house slaves who had been gathered there and who now stood silently in single file before a crimson colonnade. Their heads were bowed in both deference and dread.

It was one thing when their master summoned them like this. It was another thing entirely when their mistress did.

The chief house slave, Despina, greeted Livia. "**Domina**, all is as you have asked."

"If all were as I have asked, Caesar wouldn't be begging Apollo for breath in his bedchamber, Despina." Livia strolled nonchalantly before the row of slaves and servants, letting her eyes inspect each one in turn until she came to a leaning rest against one of the garden's large rainwater cisterns. The coolness felt good against her bare arm. Even for July, the heat was exhausting.

"Last month," she began, "on the kalends, I stood in this very spot and addressed all of you. Do you remember what I said?" she asked in a tone that discouraged answering. "I said that an epidemic was ravaging Rome. I said that any person—man, woman, or child—who brought contagion into this house and exposed Caesar to the affliction would suffer worse than he."

As if on cue, two soldiers emerged from the back of the colonnade. One struggled to hold a long pole, its other end affixed to the neck of a squat but strong wild dog, snapping and growling and contorting itself in an effort to break free. The other carried a large heavy sack, at the bottom of which some unseen creature twisted and turned on itself. A snake. A big one. Both soldiers nodded to Livia and then stood beside her on the grass.

As the reality of what was about to happen struck the slaves, a few pathetic whimpers emerged from the row, and several put their hands over their faces as if to shield themselves from the inevitable. **Poena cullei.** The penalty of the sack.

"As you know, the sack is the penalty for patricide. But Caesar is **Pater Patriae**. He is the father of our country and the father to all. He is your father." Livia pushed herself off the cistern and strolled casually to face one of the slaves—a young, pretty girl with waist-long black hair and even blacker eyes. "You are the little **cunnus** who infected Caesar, are you not?"

"Domina . . ." The girl's voice cracked and she stared at her feet, her body now visibly trembling. She had been warned this would happen. Despina and others had told her to avoid being in Caesar's presence, that being his favorite bed slave was a position that brought more risk than reward, but she didn't listen. Now it was too late.

"Well, get it over with," Livia said to the soldiers. "I'm melting in this heat."

"Yes, Empress," said the soldier who held the wild dog. He dragged the snarling animal toward the other soldier who had set the sack on the ground. He was fighting to open the mouth of the sack while at the same time preventing the sizable snake inside from slithering out. It was hard work, but after a few minutes, the soldiers managed to shove the dog inside as well.

The sack instantly erupted into a writhing, shrieking horror show as the wild dog and the viper viciously bit and tore at each other inside.

While one soldier labored to hold the sack upright, the other grabbed the slave girl's wrists and pulled her forward. She dropped to the ground and screamed, kicking up at him in desperation. He responded with a quick blow to her head. It didn't knock her out—he knew his mistress wouldn't want that—but it was enough to stun her into submission. He gathered her up in his arms. As he did, her high-belted tunica lifted to reveal her swollen belly.

If anyone present still believed the girl was being punished for infecting Caesar with disease, they now knew the truth. Caesar's wife was executing his pregnant bed slave and sending a clear message to the remaining female slaves in the process. **Either you end your pregnancy or I will do it for you.**

With a level of exertion that would have been comedic in any other circumstance, one soldier braced his legs to hold open the sack while the other stuffed the girl headfirst inside, shoving her legs in after her.

The horror show grew louder and more grotesque. Whatever was happening inside the sack was somehow made worse by having to imagine it. The violent intermingling of the bodies within—the thrashing girl, the snapping dog, the coiling snake—and the sinking of teeth into soft flesh. The ear-piercing screams and stomach-churning snarls.

As spots of blood began to soak through the heavy cloth, the soldiers secured the mouth of the sack with a thick rope and then half dragged, half carried it the few steps to the large cistern, doing their best to avoid having their own legs and arms bitten in the process. They lifted the sack and dropped it unceremoniously into the wide water barrel with a loud splash.

The shrieking and biting sounds became muted. The sides of the cistern shook, and it looked for a moment like it might topple over, but the soldiers each pressed a shoulder to it to hold it upright, not seeming to mind the cool water that splashed over them.

It went on like that longer than Livia would have expected. She felt the sun baking the top of her head. "Get back to work," she said to the row of slaves, and then turned to leave without looking back. She strode through the courtyard and sat on a cushioned chair beside the fountain of Triton.

"Despina, bring me some lemon water and cold meats."

"Yes, Domina."

Livia felt shade cover her face as a slave held a canopy above her. **Why rush back to Octavian's bedside? He's not going anywhere.** As she looked up to admire Triton's chest, an image of her husband's gangling limbs and blotched, loose skin crossed her mind's eye. She sighed at the marble god. **Vita non aequa est.**

Life's not fair.

CHAPTER II

Praevalent Illicita
Things forbidden have a secret charm.
–TACITUS

The fresh water from Tivoli was being unloaded from horse-drawn carts and carried by slaves through the **posticum** into the House of the Vestals when Pomponia and Quintina's litter arrived at the main portico of the luxury home in the heart of the Roman Forum. The priestesses slipped out of their **lectica** and headed straight for the ornate wooden doors. This was no time for a ceremonial homecoming. These days, Rome had little stomach for ceremony of any kind.

It had all started months earlier during the rains: first the Tiber had flooded, and then some sickly legions had returned from Germania. The gods only knew what pestilence they brought with them, but within weeks the vile waste that normally ran along the cobblestone streets of Rome had grown even more foul and malodorous. One could smell the acrid sickness as it ran down the streets in brown, weeping rivulets.

The disease had first appeared, as diseases typically did, in the poor, gang-ridden Roman district of the Subura, a lower-class neighborhood both socially and topographically. The waste from upper elevations and upper-class neighborhoods ran downhill to collect and stagnate in its streets and clogged sewers. It was yet another reason wealthier and more resourceful Romans lived on the higher hills of the city, even building a wall between the Subura and the rest of Rome. Out of sight was out of mind.

Yet the Subura had its place in Rome, and it also had a voice in the Senate, even if it wasn't always listened to. Throughout the winter and spring months, the Senate had been besieged with angry demands from Subura residents—Roman shoemakers to Jewish shopkeepers alike—to do something about the worsening epidemic, but no action had been taken.

As the spring months had drawn to a close and the heat had arrived, things started to hit a little closer to home for the upper classes. The kept prostitute of one Senator Gaius Junius Silanus had fallen sick and died. A week later, the senator himself barely recovered. Yet it was the week after that when things really started to change. Silanus's wife unexpectedly succumbed to the scourge that had been passed to her secondhand by her husband's whore.

When news of that particular insult reached the garden parties and frescoed triclinia of Rome's rich matrons, the outraged wives of senators issued their own collective decree to their husbands—no more visits to the whorehouses of the Subura until the disease was under control.

The Senate immediately ordered the placement of more freshwater fountains in the district and the building of several new bathhouses. Sanitation crews had the unpleasant task of cleaning the streets, unclogging the sewers, and clearing the dead from crowded **insulae** and back alleys.

But it was too little too late. Just as the disease had flowed downhill to the Subura, it now spread uphill on the bottoms of sandals and the surfaces of cart wheels to reach the Quirinal, Capitoline, and Palatine Hills, spreading even to the home of Caesar Augustus himself.

The sights, sounds, and smells of the sickness had been evident to Pomponia from miles outside the Servian Wall, and things only got worse once she and Quintina had passed through the gates of Rome itself. Gone were the fresh, dewy breezes of her villa in green-treed and sedentary Tivoli, replaced by the dirty hustle and the dry, oppressive heat of the busy Roman Forum.

Even so, as Pomponia took a few quick steps over the cobblestone of the Via Sacra—it had been scrubbed to a hygienic shine by temple slaves—to step through the doors of the House of the Vestals, she knew she'd returned to her true home. Gone were Medousa, Fabiana, and the little white dog Perseus. Gone was Quintus. Yet all their ashes had been put to rest here among the marble of Rome. Even the green fields of Tivoli could not compete with that.

As she and Quintina moved through the vestibule to enter the atrium, Pomponia heard familiar voices approaching. Tuccia and Lucretia, her sister Vestals. They smiled and held out their arms to her.

"Pomponia, welcome home," said Tuccia. She embraced the chief Vestal and Quintina in turn, and then stood back to let Lucretia do the same.

Pomponia studied Tuccia. The last several months had taken their toll on the normally carefree and eternally youthful priestess. Her skin was still fair and smooth, her amber eyes still bright, but she looked tired. "I'm sorry you have been burdened so," said Pomponia. "It's not been fair. I should have come back sooner."

"Nonsense," said Tuccia. "You have accomplished more from Tivoli than I have here in Rome. Anyway, Caesar was adamant that you remain in Tivoli, away from the contagion."

"Now that his life hangs in the balance, he seems to have changed his policy," replied Pomponia.

"He thinks your presence in Rome will save him." Tuccia grinned, and Pomponia saw a reassuring flash of her usual spiritedness. "He thinks you dine with Vesta herself and that you will ask the goddess to spare his life while you share a pudding."

"If only it were so, Tuccia." As they began to walk deeper into the house, Pomponia eyed Tuccia more seriously. "Tell me, has he changed his will?"

"No. Agrippa remains his heir."

Pomponia nodded, content for the moment. "Then if the Fates have decided he is to die, let us pray it happens before Livia's hand is felt. We may have a worse contagion to deal with if her son becomes emperor."

* * *

Although the return of Rome's long-serving Vestalis Maxima from Tivoli was significant enough to warrant a celebration, the most Pomponia would permit under the circumstances was a mundane notice nailed to the door of the Senate house, one that was quickly covered up by other mundane notices about water quality, upcoming elections, canceled festivals, and postponed chariot races. These days, Rome was all business and no pleasure.

Yet since many Romans could not read and most foreigners at least could not read Latin, the newsreader also spread word from his speaker's platform in front of the Rostra.

"By order of the Senate and Caesar," he began, reading from a long scroll, "our blessed Vestalis Maxima has returned to Rome. She will lead special offerings to Mother Vesta in the temple today to pray for the health of the emperor. Also by order of the Senate and Caesar, new statues of the Dii Consentes, the twelve sacred gods, are to be erected near the Temple of Saturn"—he gestured to the enormous temple behind him—"so that all citizens may plead with the gods for Rome's health." He rolled up the scroll. "The treasury reminds all citizens to leave coin." He passed the scroll to his assistant, who handed him another, this one shorter.

"Last, auspices have been taken, and the heat will continue for at least another two weeks." The crowd that had gathered around him mumbled and shook their heads in frustration. July was always hot, but this year it was unusually and unrelentingly so. And more heat meant more disease. The newsreader continued. "Any freedman or slave found polluting the public water system or soiling in the streets will be crucified. Citizens will be fined and lashed."

He stepped sluggishly off his platform, wiped the sweat from his neck with his toga, and, as usual, set off for the Basilica Aemilia and a cup of wine. "Rome is the Caput Mundi," he said to his assistant, "the head of the world. Yet we still have to remind people to shit in the toilet." As he neared the basilica, he heard a swell of voices and activity coming from the direction of Vesta's temple. **News item one**, he reflected, **the return of the Vestalis Maxima**.

Pomponia pushed open the embossed bronze doors of the round Temple of Vesta and squinted into the hot sun. She and five other priestesses—Tuccia, Lucretia, Caecilia, Sabina, and Quintina—wore their white stolas, red woolen headbands, and white ceremonial veils. Pomponia had insisted that a formal appearance was needed during the day's special offering into the sacred fire. Yet she privately cursed her own choice. As if it wasn't hot enough outside, Vesta's ever-burning hearth made the sanctum of the marble temple feel like the inside of a brick oven. The extra layers and weight of the Vestals' religious attire didn't help.

Stepping into the harsh sunlight, Pomponia looked down at the faces of her two guards, Caeso and Publius, as well as the less familiar faces of additional soldiers. Since the outbreak, the temple's guards had been doubled to keep the Vestal Virgins well away from the public's reach. Untouchable even in times of peace and health, it was especially important during times of conflict and contagion that those who protected the eternal flame were themselves protected. The sight of the soldiers dressed in their full armor, red-crested helmets, and scarlet capes, their fingers always near the hilt of a dagger, said **Keep back** better than any public decree.

As her eyes adjusted to the bright light, Pomponia saw the elder Vestal Nona working alongside Rome's newest full Vestals, Marcella and Lucasta, as well as a few novices, at one of the firebowls along the cobblestone near the sacred area of Vesta. They were blessing baskets of sacred wafers and handing them out to a well-controlled crowd of people on the street—people who would later crumble them into their household hearths as salty offerings to fiery Vesta.

Like the soldiers, the crowd looked up in reverence at the Vestals. They were a powerful sight, one that brought a sense of comfort, constancy, and hope, especially now that High Priestess Pomponia had returned. Instead of staying away from the danger, she had returned to its center to be with them and to pray for Caesar. Surely she could secure the great goddess's protection of Rome. Surely the purity of the priestesses could wash away the blight of disease.

Tuccia leaned into Pomponia. "The last time I saw the people this desperate for blessings, Antony and Cleopatra had stopped the grain shipments to Rome."

"We survived that, and we shall survive this too, sister." Pomponia did not share her suspicion that it was Caesar who had kept the bulk of the grain from Roman bellies—sinking countless shipments at sea—to help justify war against Egypt and rid himself of Antony. In her experience, Caesars preferred to rule alone. She turned and spoke over her shoulder to Lucretia and Caecilia, the two priestesses who were on watch and therefore had to remain in the temple to tend the sacred fire. "I'll send in one of the novices with fresh tunicas and water," she said.

The other four Vestals descended the temple steps and then passed through the portico of the House of the Vestals. Once inside the atrium, their slaves removed their veils and headbands, undressing them down to the simple tunicas they wore under their stolas so they could quickly cool off. Sabina left for her office on the second floor, while Pomponia, Tuccia, and Quintina remained.

"More water is coming today from Tivoli," said Pomponia. "We will drink and bathe in that—all of us: priestesses, novices, even the slaves—until the aqueducts and springs have passed their latest inspections."

Tuccia nodded. "Any word on Caesar?"

"I consulted with Agrippa early this morning. He stood on the street and spoke to me through my office window"—she smiled wryly—"like a forbidden suitor. He says Caesar is unchanged. In better news, he says that construction is almost complete on the Aqua Virgo aqueduct, thanks to this civil engineer Vitruvius."

"I have heard of him," said Quintina, "from my tutor. He is becoming quite famous. He studies the proportions of the human body and applies them to architecture."

"Well, he'll have a lot more bodies to study if the water isn't fresh. I'm told the source of the Aqua Virgo is as pure as the goddess, though."

"We will pray to Neptune that it stays so," said Tuccia.

"Ah, about that," said Pomponia. "Caesar has canceled most public festivals on the advice of his physician. Musa says mass gatherings spread the sickness. Nevertheless, Lepidus and I asked Agrippa to permit a sacrifice for the Neptunalia this month, and he agreed. Now is not the time to anger the god of water."

Quintina perked up. "Will it be held at the temple?"

"No, the old temple is still being restored. It's a mess. And the Forum Augustus isn't ready. Agrippa tells me the contagion has swept through the building slaves. More are being brought in from Gaul and Africa. For now, we'll use the basilica that Agrippa dedicated to Neptune after Actium. It's a bit unusual, but the altar is consecrated, and at least the public will know that a sacrifice has been made."

Quintina nodded. "I see."

"Tuccia," said Pomponia, "I would like you to help Nona oversee the mills. We need to increase production of **mola salsa** and sacred wafers to keep up with demand. We've already dispensed twenty percent more than we did last year at this time. If Caesar lives, we'll need even more in the stores for thanksgiving sacrifices to the gods."

"And if he dies, we'll need more for Agrippa's crowning," added Quintina.

Pomponia frowned. "Do not test the gods."

"Agrippa is our friend," said Quintina. "It would not be so bad."

"Oh, you can predict the future now, Quintina? We should send you at once to the Oracle at Delphi. You have missed your calling as a soothsayer."

Tuccia winked goodbye to Pomponia and left for her duties. It was better to let the chief Vestal chastise the order's young and most headstrong priestess in private. Even as she left, she could hear the edge of defiance in Quintina's voice.

"You said it yourself, Pomponia. Things would not be worse under Agrippa."

"I said no such thing, Quintina. You hear what you want to hear." She clenched her jaw. **Just like your father.** "I said that Agrippa was preferable to Tiberius . . ."

"Close enough."

". . . but Caesar is preferable to both. He is a longtime friend of our order. His policies are predictable, as is his character. Such a status quo is preferable to change."

"Not everyone is fearful of change, Pomponia." Quintina raised her eyebrows. "You know that, right?"

"**Via trita, via tuta**," replied Pomponia. The beaten path is the safe path. "Go cool off in the **frigidarium**. You have watch in the temple soon."

The younger priestess kissed Pomponia on the cheek, and the chief Vestal smiled. Quintina had been an agreeable child and a brilliant novice; however, as a full Vestal now in her twenties, she was growing more like Quintus every day. Contrary as Dis one moment, sweet as a honeyed fig the next. Perhaps it was inevitable.

"Come with me?" Quintina asked her.

"No, I have too much work. I need to go to my office. I will see you at supper."

"All right." The younger Vestal turned on her heel

and started toward the elaborate indoor baths of the House of the Vestals—baths the empress Livia had recently paid to make even more luxurious. It sometimes seemed that the emperor's wife was competing with her husband to see who could expand and embellish the home of the Vestals more.

Quintina loosened her sandals and peeled them off without stopping and then struggled to remove her tunica, dropping each item on the marble floor as she walked. Her body slave, who was rarely more than a few paces behind her, quietly gathered up each piece of clothing, leaving her mistress to enter the baths wearing only a thin chemise.

She passed into the fragrant humidity of the **apodyterium**, the undressing room, and squirmed out of her sweat-damp chemise. It fell to the floor.

She walked naked through the heat of the **caldarium** and **tepidarium** rooms—the last thing she needed was a hot soak—and headed straight for the cool waters of the frigidarium.

As she entered the low, vaulted room of the cold-water bath, Quintina felt a merciful chill run over her bare skin. **What relief!** She dipped a toe into the rectangular pool and then stepped into the turquoise water until it came to her waist.

A soft gasp escaped her lips. That sound, and the sound of the water gently lapping against the sides of the pool, echoed off marine-blue walls covered in richly detailed mosaics of fish, seahorses, and shells.

Feeling her breath quicken with the coolness, Quintina raised her arms to loosen her braids. Her long black hair fell in curls over her shoulders. She took a deep breath and lowered herself deeper into the water until first her breasts and then her head were submerged.

Within moments, the chill was too much and she came back up, all the way up, pulling herself out of the water to sit naked on the edge of the pool. She dangled her feet in the water.

She loved being alone like this in the baths. And whenever she was, her thoughts always turned to him. To Septimus.

He had returned to Rome months earlier after his father, a former commander in Caesar's Fifteenth Legion, had succumbed to the contagion. Yet despite assuring Quintina that he would only be gone a week or two for the funeral, he had not returned to Tivoli.

She had wondered what excuse she could use to see him again or to summon him to her. But an excuse wasn't necessary now. Pomponia had unwittingly provided an occasion for her to see Septimus again. The Neptunalia. As a member of the priesthood, he would be expected to attend the sacrifice. It was his duty. The status quo was useful for some things.

Quintina leaned back, resting on her arms. She and Septimus had walked together many times on the grassy path behind Vesta's temple in Tivoli. At first he had annoyed her, but soon she found herself waiting for him by the tall cypress tree in the garden.

Yet it seemed the more she waited, the less he came.

Her pulse quickened in anger as she remembered their last conversation. It was on the eve of his trip to Rome. He had wept over the loss of his father, but when she placed her hand on his thigh, he pushed it aside.

The risk is too great, Quintina.

She could see his face as clearly as Narcissus saw his reflection in the water. Dark eyes, almost as dark as his black hair, and full lips that parted when he smiled to reveal a jagged eyetooth. She remembered the day it had happened. They had been standing by the edge of the falls when a slave had brought them refreshments. Septimus had taken a large olive and bitten into the pit. He had spat it out—the pit and the shard of tooth—as if he couldn't have cared less, as if he knew that she would find him appealing even if every tooth in his mouth fell out.

She sighed and leaned farther back until she was lying flat on the cool tile floor, her arms at her sides and her feet still dangling in the cold water.

So, he felt she wasn't worth the risk? Was his affection so weak, so cowardly? She had assured him that there was little to fear. Tivoli was not like Rome. There were quiet rumors that past Vestals had taken lovers, but the people simply looked the other way. Life was good in Tivoli. The goddess was good.

And anyway, Pomponia had Caesar's ear. Even if an accusation of **incestum** was made, she could protect them. She had protected Tuccia years earlier. Quintina wasn't sure how, but she knew it was so. That business with the sieve? Maybe the people believed it, but Quintina was there. She had seen Pomponia. The Vestalis Maxima had been up to something.

Her dark eyes narrowed. There was much she didn't know about Pomponia, especially about Pomponia's relationship with her father, Quintus. But again, she had her suspicions. Lovers? Perhaps not. But certainly **in** love. She remembered well the way her father used to look at Pomponia when he would come to the stables to watch Quintina, then only a young novice, learn to ride. He never looked at her mother, Valeria, that way. Then again, who could blame him? The woman was mad.

Still lying on her back, Quintina wiped water out of her eyes and then brought her arms to her sides again, slapping her palms against the tile floor. If Pomponia had known love, then why did she still cling to the status quo? Why did she refuse to challenge the thirty-year vow of chaste service that priestesses of Vesta had to take? Every time Quintina brought it up, Pomponia dismissed it without even hearing her out.

Yet as a respected Vestalis Maxima, Pomponia had the standing and the reputation to spark a change within the order. The people loved her. The Senate and the religious collegia listened to her. Caesar respected her, even consulted her at times. General Agrippa did too.

Rome had changed much in the last few years. Fallen was the Republic, risen was the Roman Empire. And if the Eternal City could adapt to that kind of change, surely the eternal fire could too.

* * *

"A message from the house of Caesar, Domina." The temple slave bowed as she entered Pomponia's office.

The Vestalis Maxima was sitting at her large desk, scrolls and wax tablets spread across its surface. On the blue walls around her, colorfully painted gods and goddesses supervised her work. She looked up from the document she was reading and held out her hand for the scroll.

"Not a word of this to anyone," she said.

The slave backed out of the office deferentially as Pomponia uncurled the scroll. It was written in the hand of Despina, Caesar's most senior slave.

High Priestess Pomponia,

Musa cares well for Caesar, and the emperor's condition remains unchanged. He has consulted with a number of Greek and Roman physicians, and they all agree that letting his fever rage, even to the point of spasm, is wisest. I overheard them this morning comparing case studies, and they seem confident in their approach. When Caesar is lucid, they give him small doses of opium. Musa said that an absence of

pain and feelings of pleasure are essential to combat disease.

The empress is often at her husband's bedside and is protective of him. I am sorry to tell you that Caesar's sister, Octavia, succumbed to the contagion yesterday, as you and I both feared she might. Lady Livia has forbidden a public announcement, lest Caesar hear of it. She fears the shock of it will send him into despair. She has threatened to kill any slave who speaks of it.

Also, yesterday Lady Livia killed another house slave that had been impregnated by Caesar. Her blood continues to come each month. She still consults weekly with various physicians, astrologers, and priests but has been unable to conceive.

Tiberius continues to relay messages and news from the Senate between General Agrippa and Caesar and, from what I have overheard, conveys all information accurately and without bias. Caesar still refuses to see Agrippa for fear of passing on the contagion.

I regret I could not inform you of

Octavia's passing yesterday, but I knew you were leaving Tivoli, and I did not want to risk someone else at the temple receiving my letter in your absence.

I also regret that I cannot welcome you back to Rome with better news. We were all saddened at the loss of Lady Octavia. She was a loving sister to Caesar and a kind mistress to us, and I know she was a good friend to you.

I praise the goddess for your safe return and continued health. You will receive my letters daily, and I will use the same messengers as always. As you know, they are kin to me and can be trusted.

Despina

Pomponia rolled the scroll back up tightly. She dipped the edge of the papyrus into the flame of the beeswax candle at her desk and held it while it burned, looking sadly into the deep orange flame and saying a silent prayer for her friend Octavia.

Warm, lovely, exploited Octavia.

She let the ashes fall into a polished silver bowl on her desk and caught her reflection in it. Even at forty years old, her face was still soft and round, still youthful, and her hair a rich chestnut brown. Yet for the first time, she noticed some gray strands along her temples.

I'm in Rome for not yet a full day, she thought, **and already I am years older**.

CHAPTER III

Extrema Primo Nemo Tentavit Loco
No one tries extreme remedies at first.
—SENECA

CAPUA

"He's not for sale."

"Why not?"

Mettius shrugged and drained the wine from his cup. "I'm superstitious. Or sentimental. Maybe both. Scorpus has made me the richest games man in Capua. I've owned him for fifteen years and can't remember the last time he lost a chariot race. Five years ago, maybe?"

"You could still get decent coin for him."

"Not really. He's nearly past his prime. Anyway, I promised him years ago that the richer he made me, the sooner he'd have his freedom. His woman too."

"You're a fool, Mettius."

"I've been called worse." Mettius manipulated a handful of cooked pheasant into his mouth and then

50

lazily pushed the platter toward his friend Soren who reclined on an adjacent couch in Mettius's triclinium. The two men could not have appeared more different from one another. Mettius—round, overindulgent, and nearly bald. Soren—solid and sharp with cropped dark hair combed forward in the style that Julius Caesar had made fashionable. Mettius flicked some meat off his fingers. "You sound like my wife. She thinks with her purse."

"She is wise."

Mettius shrugged again. "The wise keep their word. Anyway, if you're looking for performance slaves, you'll find better deals. My friend Lucius Bassus may soon be selling a pair that has great celebrity throughout Campania. Thracius and Anchises. They're both dainties—lovers—but if I weren't getting out of the business, I'd buy them myself." He paused and thumped his chest with a fist, clearing a piece of meat from his throat and then immediately pushing more into his mouth and chewing loudly as he spoke. "Thracius is a boxer, but a versatile one. I've seen him fight in the arena with a **gladius** and wrestle too. Anchises is a virtuoso who sings with the voice of Orpheus himself. I've heard him." He raised his eyebrows. "I tell you, take your wife to one of his performances and she'll be running wetter than Volturnus by the time you get home. Gods, the last time I took Aelina to—"

"I have no wife."

"That slave girl you're always buying trinkets for, then."

"I don't need to seduce my slaves, Mettius."

"Oh, you're as romantic as a three-legged boar, Soren." Mettius laughed.

Soren allowed him an indulgent smile.

"So tell me, will you settle in Capua? This is the place to be." Mettius sniffed and pointed absently behind his head. "Marc Antony had a nice estate just south of here. That's where they found the copy of his will, you know. The one that brought him down. He spent a small fortune in Capua. The bastard probably stole it from the treasury but, oh well, what's done is done, eh? The man loved the gladiator matches, though, I'll tell you that much. Always at the arena. I met him once, did I ever tell you? I didn't think he was all that. The gods know what took the emperor so damn long to finish him. He wasn't any taller than you. Once, I watched him walk right under a low scaffolding without even bending his head. And since we're talking about dainties, everyone knew that his favorite boy lived just—"

"I'm going back to Rome."

"Ah, Rome." Mettius clucked his tongue. "Hard market to break into. You have to know someone."

"My brother is a senator. And I have a cousin who is a priestess of Vesta."

"Oh, what I could've done with those connections! Yes, performance slaves are the way to go, then. Just think of all those parties on the Palatine Hill! Not to mention the festivals—"

"I want to go back to Rome with Scorpus," Soren said flatly. "I want to race him in the Circus Maximus."

Mettius tried to nibble the last bit of pheasant meat from a small bone and, failing at the attempt, put the whole thing in his mouth. "Soren," he said, working his tongue around the bone and seeming out of humor now, "he's not for sale."

"Name your price."

Mettius sat up with a quick, angry intake of air. As he did, his eyes widened and again he thumped his chest with a fist. He set his feet flat on the floor and leaned over, trying to cough the bone out of his throat, trying to breathe. He looked at Soren, who remained unmoved, and then rose shakily to his feet, advancing toward the door.

Something appeared under his feet, and he fell to

the floor. He felt Soren's hands on him—**Finally, some help!**—but the larger man's hands suddenly covered his mouth while the weight of his body pressed into his back from above, holding him down. Mettius's movements and thoughts dispersed into a painful panic and what he knew, somewhere in the last remnants of his consciousness, was an unwinnable fight for his life.

As Mettius's body went limp, Soren slipped the crook of his elbows under the man's armpits and began to lift him back up onto the couch. At the same moment—**What a perfectly timed moment!** thought Soren—a house slave strode casually into the room. His eyes popped, and he ran toward Soren to help heave Mettius's body onto the couch.

"He's choking," said Soren. "Do something."

The slave bent over his master and opened his mouth, sticking his fingers down Mettius's throat to retrieve the bone and open his airway. It was no use.

Two more slaves appeared in the doorway and then rushed to the couch.

"What happened?" one of them asked Soren.

"A pheasant bone." Soren shook his head and looked down at the lifeless form of his friend. "Dying over such a little thing . . . What a shame."

CHAPTER IV

Dies Caniculares
The dog days

ROME

Gods, it was hot. Even at night—late at night, when the sun had been down for hours—the radiant heat never let up. Livia stood outside on the balcony of her bedchamber and looked up at the moonless night sky over the Palatine Hill. The stars were scattered brightly and thickly over the black canopy of the heavens, like shards of shining silvery gems spread haphazardly over a vast ebony marble floor.

She heard a rustle and looked over her shoulder. Octavian, reclining on a low couch a few steps away, was rousing. He had spent the better part of his recovery dozing on the balcony, even taking most of his meals there. During the day, a small desk was brought in for him to attend to the most important state affairs.

"Livia," he said, stopping for a moment to clear the phlegm from his throat, "did I ever tell you about the dream my mother had when I was in her womb?"

She turned to face him, leaning against the balustrade. Of course he'd told her about it. He'd told her about it a thousand times. The same stupid dream, the same stupid retelling.

"I think so, my love," she answered. "But tell me again. I do love to hear it."

"She dreamed that her womb stretched to the stars," he said, "and the next morning an astrologer told her that I was sired by Apollo and would one day rule the world. This all happened under the sign of Capricorn. Help me up."

A slave noiselessly emerged from the shadows, the way they always did when summoned, to help Octavian off the couch. He shuffled to Livia's side and leaned against the balustrade, looking up at the starry night sky.

"Can you see Capricornus?" he asked.

"It is not the right time of year," replied Livia. "Now is the **dies caniculares**, when the dog star is brightest." She pointed overhead. "There. Sirius and Canis Major. They bring the heat."

"And some say plague."

"It is not plague, Octavian. Musa has been studying those miserable old medical scrolls of his. They smell like the unwashed Chimera! Anyway, he says the symptoms are not those described during the plague of Athens. The Black Death is different. Worse, if you can imagine."

"I can always imagine worse."

"That is why you are a good emperor."

"You flatter, Livia." Octavian managed a grin. "What is your purpose?"

Livia lowered her head and closed her eyes. She waited a long strategic moment and then, keeping her head lowered, raised her eyes to look up at Octavian as if she were overcome by her vulnerability and his greatness. Octavia used to look at him like that all the time, and he never denied her a thing. Livia did her best to improve upon the performance, taking his hands and looking up at him with such adoration that her eye sockets throbbed.

"Pluto stood by your bedside, husband. The god of death was here, in our bedchamber. That is how close you were. It was only the relentless prayers of the Vestals and the mercy of Apollo that saved you. If you had died, what would have become of Rome?" She pulled his hands to her breast. "What would become of me?"

"You have nothing to fear, Livia."

"Not while you are emperor."

"Ah."

"Octavian—"

"Tiberius will never be emperor."

"Why not? Why do you distrust him so? He has done nothing—"

"That is true. He has done nothing. He has not yet distinguished himself in any way, political or military. Agrippa is the better choice."

"Agrippa will tear down all that you have built, Octavian. He will restore the Republic and return power to the Senate. The memory of you as emperor—your very empire—will be forgotten. He has been a loyal ally to you in life, but in death he will forsake you. You will not become a god as your divine father did."

Octavian shuffled back to the couch and sat. Livia knelt on the floor before him and put her hands on his knees. "Tell me I'm wrong."

"You are not wrong."

"Tiberius has always admired you."

Octavian didn't seem to hear her. "Drusus may be an option."

Livia sat back on her heels. Drusus was not an

option for her. He was her son, yes, but who was his true father? Her former husband, Tiberius, or that hairy Greek pig Diodorus? If Drusus were named Octavian's heir, that would give Pomponia, who also questioned Drusus's parentage, too much power. All Pomponia would need to do was whisper a rumor in Octavian's ear and the suspicion would take root. Drusus, the bastard half blood, would lose favor.

Worse, Octavian would divorce her. Julius Caesar had divorced his second wife for a lesser matter, declaring that the wife of Caesar must be above all suspicion. Octavian was even more moralistic. For all Livia knew, he was already looking for an excuse to divorce her and her barrenness. No, it could not be Drusus.

"Drusus has always served you best on campaign and in the provinces," she said. "He is needed in Germania, and he knows little of politics in Rome. Plus, it is against custom to favor the second son," she said.

"They are not my sons."

"They love you. You are their adoptive father. As the adopted son of Julius Caesar, you should know the weight of that."

Octavian's face tightened. Livia licked her lips and stood up. She had gone too far.

"I am tired, Livia. I must rest for the Neptunalia tomorrow. Leave me now."

"As you wish, husband."

Octavian said nothing as she left, but even as she closed the door of the bedchamber behind her, she could hear him asking for a bed slave.

She suppressed a wave of anger. Perhaps it didn't matter. Her hands moved down to her belly. She had sacrificed to Fortuna Virilis and thrown enough coin at her temple to reach the gods. With any luck, she could soon tell Caesar that she carried his pure-blood heir inside her.

The dog days, she ruminated. **Pray Fortuna they bring forth a pup.**

* * *

The ride in the horse-drawn carriage from the Temple of Vesta in the Roman Forum to the Basilica of Neptune in the Campus Martius, the Field of Mars, was a stifling one; and Pomponia was relieved when she, Quintina, and Lucretia finally arrived.

She pushed back the heavy red curtain before her guards or slaves could even get to it and stepped down. It was no cooler outside the carriage, but at least the open air felt less claustrophobic. She inhaled and glanced up at the red banners affixed to the buildings and columns around the basilica. They hung down, long and heavy, unmoving in the breezeless air, as stabs of sunlight flared off the golden Roman Eagle in their center.

Blinking away sunspots as a slave adjusted her **suffibulum** veil, Pomponia noticed more banners hanging from the Corinthian columns near the basilica's entrance. Solid gold in color with a raised black emblem of Rome's legendary she-wolf in the center, they reflected even more sunlight. They also made a statement: Remember you are a Roman. Stay strong, do your duty, and Rome will get through this crisis as it has every crisis since its founding.

Although not a particularly large structure by Roman standards, the Basilica of Neptune was nonetheless impressive with its wide columns and wall fountains that sent a constant flow of water down the building's marble facade to spray cool mist into the air. Pomponia had always admired the intricate marine-themed relief carvings that decorated the length of the basilica's frieze on all sides: dolphins, seashells, octopuses, exotic sea plants, and of course Neptune's trident.

A memory pushed its way into her thoughts: Ankhu had told her that Quintus had always prayed to the ocean gods when sending one of his messages to her across the sea from Alexandria. She forced the memory from her mind and focused on duty. On Rome.

The chief Vestal hadn't been to this area of the city for some time and was surprised to see Agrippa's latest building project was well underway. The Senate had sent the plans to her in Tivoli: a round temple with a soaring dome and a wide oculus in the center to let in the sunlight. The design was not unlike the Temple of Vesta, but the scale of the new temple, to be called the Pantheon in honor of all the gods, was massive.

No structure in the world, whether within or beyond the empire, boasted the size of dome this temple's architects were building. Only Roman ambition paired with the Roman invention of concrete made it possible. Yet considering the temple was to house statues of the twelve Dii Consentes, including Vesta, such a grand initiative was only fitting. So was the timing. With the contagion showing no signs of abating, and the heat even less so, Rome needed its gods.

The Vestals Lucretia and Quintina stepped out of

the carriage after Pomponia, Quintina's eyes already scanning for Septimus among the senators, priests, and various magistrates who were passing through the colonnade and portico to enter the interior of the basilica.

Quintina spotted the tall bulk of General Agrippa surrounded by a group of politicians and officials. They were all motioning toward the nearby building site of the Pantheon and nodding their heads. Agrippa looked as serious as ever with his heavy brow furrowed in conversation. Although he preferred to wear a soldier's uniform to such events, he was today dressed in an ivory-colored toga with a deep reddish-purple border that denoted his status. The emperor had recently ordered that all respectable citizens wear traditional Roman clothing in public: togas for men, stolas for women. The order was part of Octavian's larger legislation to restore moral decency and tradition to Rome.

Behind Agrippa, Roman soldiers held the public at bay. The soldiers looked as they usually did when relegated to civic crowd control instead of foreign battle. Bored. Irritable. Insulted. They scanned the moving masses around them, eager to spot a transgression—anything that would allow them to justify hauling some poor soul out of the crowd and beating him to within an inch of his life on the cobblestone. Most in the crowd knew better than to test them. Those who didn't know better were too fatigued by the heat to cause any real trouble.

Alerted to the Vestals' presence by a sudden wave of excitement that swept through the crowd, Agrippa excused himself from his companions to cross the street and greet the priestesses at their litter. He lowered his head as he arrived. "Priestess Pomponia."

"General Agrippa," replied Pomponia.

He bowed to Lucretia and then to Quintina. "Lady Quintina," he said, "Caesar's daughter, Julia, will be happy to see you again."

"Thank you for saying so, General. I've missed our friendship while in Tivoli."

Pomponia felt her scalp itch from the woolen **infula** on her head and the heat of her veil. Trying to ignore it, she looked beyond Agrippa to watch the imperial litter approaching the basilica. She raised her eyebrows at the sight of the emperor walking before his grand lectica instead of riding within it. After weeks of being weakened by the contagion, not to mention the rumors of his death that continuously circulated, the message was obvious: Caesar is stronger than ever.

A number of toga-clad lictors cleared a path for Caesar, carrying their ax-headed fasces and looking as official as ever. A soldier held the Aquila atop a staff as if it were an immortal. In many ways it was, for it looked down on Rome and its people, its wars and peace, its health and disease with the unflinching gaze that only an immortal could master.

Pomponia leaned into Agrippa. "Fabiana loved to tell the story of how Julius Caesar tore the Eagle off its staff and hid it in his cloak to save it from enemy hands during battle. She once wrapped a gold wine cup in her palla to mock him."

Agrippa grinned. "Blood is thicker than water," he said. "She could get away with it."

Pomponia let her arms drop to her sides as the imperial litter stopped at the entrance to the basilica and the well-muscled **lecticarii**, dressed in impressive knee-length red tunicas, set it down. Empress Livia quickly exited the lectica, no doubt as keen to escape the closed-in heat as Pomponia had been. Tiberius stepped out after her.

Agrippa glanced at Livia without expression and offered a respectful head bow to Pomponia, Quintina, and Lucretia. "I will take my leave, Priestesses."

"By all means, General," Pomponia replied without

looking at him. She, too, was watching Livia, who now stood on the cobblestone as two body slaves straightened the bottom of her white stola. **White, like a Vestal. Good.**

With Lucretia and Quintina following behind, Pomponia walked toward the basilica's portico to naturally fall into step beside the empress. "It is good to see you again, Lady Livia."

"And you, Priestess. My, the Aniene waters have done wonders for your complexion."

"I shall have some sent to Caesar's home," said Pomponia. "May they do the same for you."

Octavian emerged from behind his lictors and took Livia's hand, a welcoming smile on his face for Pomponia. "High Priestess. It is good to see you again."

Pomponia and the two other Vestals bowed. "**Ave, Caesar.**"

Octavian waited just long enough for all present to see the Vestals bow to Caesar before bidding them to rise.

Pomponia knew the dance. She would prostrate herself before the emperor, and he would bid her to rise, as if rejecting the show of subordination. He was no king, no tyrant. He was a good emperor, the father of his country, merely the first among equals.

It was how Octavian moved in all circles, whether religious, social, military, or political. He had calculated, so far correctly, that such a show was the best way to keep the senators' daggers out of his stomach and live longer than the Caesar before him. But it was a show all the same. Pull back the curtain, even a bit, and it was clear that Octavian—the emperor Caesar Augustus, son of the divine Julius Caesar— was a king in all but name.

"I was saddened to hear of your sister's crossing," said Pomponia.

"I know you share my grief," Octavian replied. "You were a true friend to Octavia. I will always be grateful for the affection you showed her and for the many times you gave her wise counsel. I know she relied upon your discretion. As have I."

A soldierly horn-blower sounded the **cornu**, and Octavian moved on to ascend the steps of the basilica, stopping at the top to salute the crowd who cheered back at him. He turned to pass through the portico and into the basilica, followed by Livia, Agrippa, Tiberius, the Vestals, and other pontiffs, including a man named Laelius who had been appointed the new **Flamen Martialis** after the previous high priest of Mars had died of old age.

A selection of magistrates, senators, and wealthy citizens followed, all having been handpicked to observe the sacrifice.

Pomponia took a last look over her shoulder. Tuccia was supposed to have arrived by now in her own lectica. It was against protocol for a priestess to arrive this much later than her sisters, and she felt a flare of irritation. Tuccia had plenty of help at the temple, especially now that Marcella and Lucasta were no longer novices. Perhaps she was getting too accustomed to being in charge.

Following a step behind Livia, Pomponia resisted the instinct to sigh in relief as she passed through the marble walls of the basilica and into the relative coolness of its expansive interior. She blinked and felt her eyes relax, now mercifully sheltered from the glaring sunlight outside. She was thankful that Caesar had requested the sacrifice be performed inside. Even when he was in full health, he was never one to fare well in the heat.

The basilica was rectangular and bordered by a fairly narrow covered colonnade on all four sides. Its walls were painted in vibrant deep blue and its floor covered in turquoise tile, outlined by a red meander pattern. In the center of the floor was a giant glass mosaic of Neptune in his chariot, pulled by seahorses and holding his trident like a spear. Red crab legs and fish tails in yellow, orange, and green poked out of his full beard and the thick, wild hair on his head.

At the far end of the basilica was a semicircular recessed apse, within which stood a marble altar to Neptune. On top of the altar, Vesta's sacred flame burned within a bronze firebowl, ready to receive the offering of the animal's innards. Next to the firebowl sat a patera of oil and a **simpulum** of wine for libations. The Pontifex Maximus, Lepidus, was already muttering sacred words to Neptune and waving incense in the air. Pomponia stood beside him.

An arm's length away from her was the sacrificial white bull. Draped in ribbons and flowers, its horns gilded in the finest gold, it was restrained by two handlers. Restraint was hardly necessary, though. The beast eyed the musician playing the pipes near the altar and seemed more interested in lying down on the cool floor than on escaping its fate. It chewed its cud contently.

Lepidus held up his arms. "**Favete linguis**," he called out. Everyone fell silent. "**O divine Jane, divina Vesta**," he said, beginning the ritual with the customary prayer to Janus and Vesta. He poured a libation of oil over the altar, sprinkling a few drops into the flames of the firebowl.

Lucretia passed Pomponia a bowl that held the sacred wafers. The chief Vestal crumbled two of them onto the animal's white head, purifying it for the god. "**Vesta te purificat.**"

"**Deis**," said Lepidus. To the gods. He lifted the simpulum of wine off the altar and took a sip, then held it out to Pomponia—and suddenly shook his head.

His body swayed, and Pomponia saw his face blanch to a shade of white she had never before seen on a human being. She grasped his robed arm, and he clung to her even as he slowly crumpled onto the marble floor, spilling red wine across Neptune's mosaic face.

The contagion.

As the shock of it hit her—**The Pontifex Maximus has the contagion?**—she felt strong hands grip her shoulders. It was Agrippa, forcibly pulling her away from Lepidus, now retching at the feet of the sacrificial bull. Pomponia scanned the crowd of faces gathered along the colonnade and spotted Livia holding Octavian's face in her hands, speaking words of reassurance. It seemed an uncharacteristically compassionate act for the empress.

After Agrippa had all but dragged Pomponia to the middle of the basilica, he stopped and looked sternly at her. "Return to the temple, Priestess. At once."

She nodded and turned to walk quickly out of the basilica as Lucretia and Quintina rushed to catch up. As the three of them passed through the portico to step into the furnace of the air outside, Pomponia nearly gasped to see that Quintina's face was almost as drawn as Lepidus's had been.

"Are you unwell?" Pomponia asked, holding her breath.

"No," said Quintina. "But I have a message. Musa is at our home . . . Tuccia is ill."

Pomponia's shock dissolved and re-formed into a barely containable rage. "Gods almighty," she muttered. She gathered the bottom of her stola so that she could walk even faster across the cobblestone to the stifling heat awaiting them in the carriage.

Quintina was about to step inside after her, when she was distracted by a familiar voice calling out to her.

"Sister!"

Quintina spun her head to see her younger sister, Tacita, waving to her from the crowd that was still gathered along the street. It had been over a year since they'd last seen each other.

And the moment Quintina laid eyes on her, she remembered why she hadn't made any attempt to change that.

For Tacita—grinning, self-satisfied Tacita—had her elbow hooked tightly around the arm of none other than Septimus.

CHAPTER V

Silent Enim Leges inter Arma
Laws are silent in times of war.
—CICERO

It was Soren's good fortune that the wife of Mettius didn't share her husband's penchant for altruism. The day after Mettius's death, she had sold Scorpus to Soren for half his worth, throwing in the champion charioteer's longtime female partner for free.

Soren had immediately shipped Scorpus to Rome and then set out to return to the city himself. He hadn't been to Rome in some time. Then, the streets had been alive and joyous as people celebrated the triumph of their new Caesar and the promise of peace. Scarlet and gold banners hung from every building and the cobblestone, cleaned to a near shine, was littered with white flower petals and green laurels.

Now, the streets of the Eternal City ran wet with brown sludge as sanitation officials struggled day and night with clogged drains and an overwhelmed sewer system. Soren could see them working by torchlight, pointing to that drain and this one and shouting orders to their weary, overworked crew.

As Soren neared the portico of his large, lavish home on the Esquiline Hill, any sentimentality of homecoming was lost as he stepped into a fly-covered pile of waste, prompting a black, buzzing cloud of the insects to swarm his face. He coughed and waved them away, then stepped inside.

The house was unchanged and had been well tended by his slaves. Three came to greet him in the atrium: he could hear the others busy in other rooms—cleaning in the triclinium, shaking out linens, clinking pots in the kitchen. Oil lamps affixed to the walls sputtered but nonetheless burned with thick flames that lit the space well enough.

"Where is Dacia?" he asked.

"Domine," replied a male slave, "she arrived yesterday and has retired for the evening. We did not expect you until tomorrow morning. Shall I wake her?"

"No." **I will wake her**, he thought. He could picture her curled into the very corner of the bed as she always was, burrowed under the covers even on the hottest of nights. He could feel her stir and wake, already reaching for him. It was remarkable that he longed for her so deeply after only a few nights apart.

He pointed his chin at one of the house slaves and then jerked his thumb toward the female slave standing behind him, the one who hadn't spoken a word since they had left Capua. **Get her sorted out.**

As the house slave reached out to take the arm of Scorpus's woman, she rounded on Soren.

"Where is Scorpus?"

Soren ignored her and walked tiredly toward the **balineum** and the cool washing basin that awaited him there, still thinking of Dacia. Soon, however, his thoughts turned to something else. Someone else.

Scorpus.

It was an understatement to say that the renowned chariot driver hadn't taken the news of his master's death or the transfer of his ownership well. He had expected to be freed in his master's will, not sold by his master's widow.

Still, his bad attitude was nothing that a little retraining wouldn't fix. Soren had arranged in advance for Scorpus to be housed—perhaps contained was a better word—in the barracks of the large gladiatorial **ludus** in the Campus Martius.

Located near the huge amphitheater that staged

gladiatorial combats, wild animal hunts, and all manner of creative executions, the ludus was perfectly situated to school, store, and supply Rome's human and animal entertainment. It had exactly the type of facilities that someone like Scorpus needed to be reminded of his station in life.

As the primary benefactor of both the amphitheater and the ludus, the emperor's friend Taurus was positively giddy at the prospect of containing the notorious Scorpus the Titan. The only downside was that Scorpus would draw such numbers to the amphitheater that an expansion—or more likely a new and even bigger arena—would soon need to be constructed in Rome. People were already petitioning the Senate for one. For the time being, however, he could charge a client and get free advertising for his facilities at the same time.

Although Scorpus was celebrated for his skill and successes on the racetrack, there was more to it than a near-perfect track record. The slave owed part of his celebrity to the shocking size of his frame, one that required the platform and axle of his chariot to be secured with extra reinforcements. Hence the name: he was Scorpus the Titan, larger than life, larger even than the gods.

It turned out that extra reinforcements were necessary to contain him in the ludus too. And extra reinforcements meant extra cost. As Soren washed the grime of the road off his face and hands, he wondered how much more Taurus would try to scam him for. He hoped his new acquisition wouldn't turn out to be more trouble than he was worth. Literally.

A familiar pressure throbbed inside his skull. Anger. He cursed Mettius. It was his fault for indulging the charioteer so much over the years, even allowing Scorpus to live with his so-called wife in a separate house on Mettius's land, as if he were a citizen or a freedman and not a common slave. The special treatment had gone to the slaves' heads.

He hastily dried his hands and threw the towel on the floor, turning on his heel to march through the house until he reached the stone steps that led down to the servants' quarters. He squeezed through the doorway and descended the steps to the basement, reaching the dirt floor and tasting a dank mustiness on his tongue.

It was a dim, almost cave-like space, lined on both sides with small doorless rooms, each one furnished with nothing more than a hard mattress on the floor and a dripping candle. Soren sniffed loudly, and the few slaves that weren't in their rooms quietly disappeared into them. They didn't want any part of whatever had brought their master into the bowels of the house.

The sound of Soren's heavy footsteps on the dirt—**crush, crush, crush**—echoed off the narrow stone walls as he walked past the rooms, glancing in at each cowering slave and reeking of an aggression they knew too well.

She was in the last room on the left. Soren sniffed again and leaned against the rough wall to study her. Either oblivious to or in defiance of convention, she spoke first.

"I belong to Scorpus," she said. "It has always been that way. There is a special **ne serva** clause in my ownership papers. I am not to be used sexually. Our former master honored it."

Soren didn't care about the law and wasn't particularly attracted to the female slave. She was skinnier than he liked, and she had a hard face. She was nothing like his lovely, soft Dacia.

But then he pictured Scorpus locked behind bars in a small brick cell in the ludus. He knew what would be going through Scorpus's mind. He would be wondering, worrying, what his new master was doing to his woman. He would be imagining the very worst things possible, the most degrading and dehumanizing things, and he would know that he was powerless to stop it.

Soren felt his groin come alive. He grabbed the slave woman by the head and pushed her against the stone wall.

And then he did to her all the things he knew were in Scorpus's very worst imaginings.

* * *

Scorpus felt a thud on his back. The **lanista**, head trainer of this second-rate gladiatorial school, grinned at him from the shade of the octagonal colonnade that enclosed the open-air training arena.

"Your lunch," he said.

Scorpus looked down at the apple. He thought about kicking it at the lanista, but his hunger got the better of him, so he picked it up, brushed the sand off, and bit into it. The first swallow almost came back up, so upset was his stomach with an acrid mixture of worry and rage plus cramps arising from his new, forced exercise regime—one he was compelled to carry out under the sickening heat of the blazing sun. He swallowed again to keep it down and studied the lanista who had now been joined by three other men.

He recognized two of them: one was Taurus, owner of the ludus, and the second was the doctor who had examined him upon his arrival. His incarceration. The third man he didn't recognize but suspected was his new owner—a man named Soren. He tossed the apple core aside and bent down to again lift the sack of sand at his feet, grunting with effort to raise it above his head and blinking away the sand that fell into his eyes.

"How soon until he's fit to race?" Soren asked the lanista.

"I'd give him at least four months."

"That's three and a half months too long."

Taurus spoke. "He hasn't trained properly in ages, Soren. He's grown soft. Unless you want his arms to be pulled out of their sockets before he clears the starting gate, he needs time to regain his upper body strength."

"**Upper body strength?**" Soren gestured toward Scorpus, who stood at least a foot taller than the next tallest man in the training arena. "He's Scorpus the Titan."

"Well, he's going to be Scorpus the Armless if you're not patient," said the doctor. "It takes time to build or rebuild muscle."

Taurus nodded in agreement. "Have you not heard of Milo of Croton?"

"I have not, Taurus, but I suspect you are going to tell me."

"I am. Milo was a famous Greek wrestler who was so strong that he could carry a full-grown bull on his shoulders. But he didn't come about this Herculean strength in one day. It was a process. He started by lifting a newborn calf and he continued to lift the beast every day as it grew, growing stronger himself as each day passed. He grew so strong that he was an Olympic champion six times in a row. If you want your man to be a champion again, you must give it some time."

"I want to talk to him."

"As you wish."

The lanista and doctor took their leave as Taurus caught the eye of a guard and pointed at Scorpus. "Take him to his cell."

The guard, himself a retired gladiator, casually waved Scorpus toward the rear colonnade. They passed under an archway that was decorated with monumental busts of famous fighters. Scorpus glanced up just as he passed under the marble head of Flamma, the most celebrated of Roman gladiators.

The guard followed Scorpus's eyes. "If you're lucky, maybe your head will be up there one day."

"I prefer my head where it is, brother."

The guard chuckled. He didn't bother to shackle the charioteer. After a lifetime in one ludus after another, he knew when to use force and when not to bother. Scorpus might boast the size and reputation of a Titan, but he wasn't the type to start anything. He probably thought he was above it all. It was almost disappointing. Then again, the man was used to holding the reins, not the gladius.

Chariot drivers have it too good, he thought. **Easy glory. We fighters earn our keep.**

Scorpus wiped the sweat off his brow and walked with his chin in the air along the row of cells until he reached his. He swung the metal-barred door open to the sight of a naked woman lying on the thin straw-stuffed mattress on the dirt floor.

The guard pushed him in. The door swung closed, and the sound of the key securing the lock sent a heavy **click** echoing down the long, narrow brick passage. Scorpus spun around to face Soren on the other side of the bars. The slave master crunched an apple.

"I hope they're feeding you more than fruit," Soren said. "For what I'm paying to keep you here, you should be eating like the emperor." Scorpus said nothing, but Soren could see the air of superiority in the slave's eyes. He hated it. He smacked his lips together and eyed the naked woman behind the charioteer.

"The lanista says that you're not really putting your heart into your training. That disappoints me. So I thought you could use some motivation."

"And you think giving me a whore will motivate me?"

"I know that women motivate me. For example, your woman motivated me last night. Several times."

Scorpus felt the blood drain from his face. He stared at Soren, and although he tried to stop them, images of his new master on top of Cassandra—behind her, below her, inside her—flooded his mind. He sensed his body sway ever so slightly as his breathing became shallow.

"I admit it was a bumpy start. She's not really my type. But once I got some momentum, it was actually quite pleasurable."

Scorpus searched for words. How to respond? **I**

will kill you. Do you have any idea who I am, you piece of shit? Please don't hurt her. Why are you doing this? Bring her to me, and I'll win every race you put me in.

"Bring her to me," he said, as if brokering a deal that he had the upper hand in, "and I'll win every race you put me in."

"The Titan rises!" exclaimed Soren. "Praise Jupiter, for a Titan will do anything with the right motivation. Cronus devoured his own children, no? You must only win a race."

"Bring her here, and I will."

Soren spat out some apple seeds. **That sounded too much like an order.**

"Fine living has gone to your head, Scorpus. I will not bring her here. I will keep her in my house, and I will keep doing to her what I did last night until you do in the Circus Maximus what you've been doing for the past ten years in Capua." He threw the apple core between the bars of Scorpus's cell and turned to leave. "Use the whore," he said as he disappeared down the dimly lit brick passage. "I hate to see good money go to waste."

CHAPTER VI

Omnes Vulnerant, Ultima Necat
All hours wound; the last one kills.
—A COMMON INSCRIPTION ON SUNDIALS

Tuccia sounded like she was already breathing the air of Hades, so disturbing were the gasps and strange mutterings slipping from her blue lips.

Pomponia glanced down at the dying Vestal's hands. Even by candlelight, she could see they were the same color as her lips. The same blue she so vividly remembered seeing the evening that Fabiana had died, when Pomponia had kissed her cold hand and wept at the loss of someone who had seemed as immortal as the goddess herself.

But Fabiana's hands had been old and wrinkled, her fingers bent with age. Tuccia's hands were smooth and soft, with slender, straight fingers. They twitched as the priestess gasped again in her restless sleep and released a slow, breathy whimper.

"Can you give her anything else to ease her suffering?" Pomponia asked Octavian's physician, Musa, who stood at the end of Tuccia's bed.

"There is only one thing left I can give her . . . but there is no going back, if you understand, Priestess."

"Is there any going back even if you don't give it to her?"

The physician shook his head. "She will not see sunrise."

The words didn't seem real to Pomponia. It was impossible that he was speaking these words about Tuccia. Surreal and impossible. The hour intensified the feeling of unreality. It wasn't nighttime and it wasn't morning—just that strange, sleepless place between the two, when life feels almost dreamlike.

The door to Tuccia's bedchamber opened, and a slave peeked into the room. "Domina," she said to Pomponia, "Caesar has ordered that Priestess Tuccia be moved from the house, for your health. She will be taken to the Temple of Apollo with Musa."

Pomponia looked up at the physician. "It must happen here, near the living flame."

Musa nodded somberly and retrieved a vial from his physician's satchel. He moved to Tuccia's head and poured a dark liquid between her lips. Some spilled down the side of her face, but he held her jaw closed until she swallowed. Almost immediately, her body relaxed. Her breathing softened.

She opened her amber eyes and looked up at Pomponia, as if just realizing she was there. She was alert and clear. The goddess and the medicine had gifted her a final moment of life.

"Pomponia . . ."

Pomponia lowered her ear to Tuccia's lips.

"My cousin wrote to me. He bought Scorpus the Titan. He is to race for the Blues in the Circus Maximus."

Pomponia turned her head to look into Tuccia's eyes. "I did not know that, Tuccia."

"When I am better, I will bet on him."

"How much?"

"Half a million sesterces."

"That is scandalous, Tuccia."

A faint smile. A spark of what was, only three days ago, a strong flame. "We are no strangers to scandal, sister."

She slipped into a strange, breathless sleep.

Pomponia whispered into her ear. "**Vesta te remunerabitur, Sacerdos Tuccia.**" Vesta will reward you, Priestess Tuccia.

Pomponia stood up, paused a moment to smooth the front of her long white tunica, and then walked out of the bedchamber. She had to go quickly, without thinking, before the impact of it could hit her. It was a familiar feeling. A sickening, disorienting feeling.

With every death, she felt less grounded, less tethered to the earth itself. All the people of her youth were gone now. Gone, as if they had never existed at all. As if that part of her life had never existed.

She made it some twenty steps from Tuccia's room before the sound of Quintina's and Sabina's soft prayers filled her ears and the grief welled up behind her eyes. She took two more steps into the waiting arms of Quintina and, this time, didn't bother to fight the tears. She knew that she would only lose the fight in the end.

* * *

Sunrise. The physician had been correct. Tuccia would not see it. Pomponia sat at her desk in her office and looked out the window. Daybreak in the Roman Forum. The sky was losing its last shade of gray and a vivid blue was already forming. She could hear birds chirping outside, although that sweet sound was soon replaced by the sound of the sanitation crews scrubbing the cobblestone along the Via Sacra. She rubbed her temples. Why did they have to shout so?

At the elder priestess Nona's insistence, she took a bite of bread and washed it down with some warm honey water. The sweetness of the water caused a wave of nausea, so she took another bite of the bread. It helped a bit.

Nona leaned against her doorway. "Caesar wishes a meeting."

"When?"

"Now. He's halfway down the ramp."

Pomponia set down her bread. "When he built the Palatine ramp, I assumed it was so he could move up and down the Palatine Hill, from his estate to the Forum, more easily. But you'll notice that he rarely exits directly to the Forum. He stops here to feed the fish in the courtyard first. It's like our homes are now connected and he is a permanent houseguest."

Nona tiredly pressed her fingers against her eyes. "I know, but the ramp is an improvement on that old staircase. My knees couldn't take it anymore. Now I can ride in my lectica. The ramp is better fortified too. If there is a fire or an attack we can quickly escape up to Caesar's estate."

"Yes, you are right . . ."

"But the fish are getting fatter," Nona admitted. She shrugged. "We are all creatures of habit, even Caesar."

"Thank you, sister. I'll go meet him in the garden."

As Nona left, Pomponia placed her palms flat on her desk and lifted herself. She was exhausted. She thought about having a slave check her appearance or apply a cold compress to her swollen eyes but didn't even have the energy to do that. She was still wearing the same informal tunica she'd been wearing when Tuccia had passed. **Oh well.**

Caesar didn't seem to notice. He was dressed similarly in an early-morning tunica, hair uncombed, stifling a yawn. He and Pomponia entered the courtyard at the same time, with the Vestal descending the stairs from the second floor and passing through the peristyle, and Octavian emerging from the richly decorated vestibule at the base of the vaulted passageway of the Palatine ramp.

Octavian held out his arms, and he and Pomponia clasped hands. "I am so sorry for the loss of Priestess Tuccia," he said. "As a **Virgo Vestalis**, she was one of the great sentinels of Rome. She was also a great comfort to me when I was ill." His words—raspy, exhausted—were nonetheless sincere.

As they sat near one of the decorative pools in the courtyard and the emperor of Rome fed the fish, Pomponia remembered the first time she had met Octavian, now the great Caesar Augustus. It was shortly after the assassination of Julius Caesar. She had gone to the Carcer to petition for the life of Quintus and his father.

She remembered Octavian's cool gray eyes and young, sharp voice as she had faced him wearing her ceremonial Vestal attire. What a fool she must have seemed.

But she had been little more than a child. The same as Octavian, really. Like her, he was still finding his way at that time. Still gaining strength and an identity, still trying to fight for and figure out his place in the world of Rome.

He seemed to read her thoughts. "Do you realize that we have been friends for twenty years?" She smiled and he continued. "We have risen as high as any two people can rise in this world, but it hasn't been without loss. I miss Octavia. I know that since her death I have relied upon you even more for counsel. I am sorry if it has been a burden."

Pomponia suddenly regretted her previous

irritation with Octavian. "It has been a blessing, Caesar, not a burden."

He squeezed her hand and then let go to rub his chin. "How shall we handle the passing of Tuccia?"

"Quietly," said Pomponia. "We performed the sacred rites after she passed, and I have already sent her to her family. They will cremate her and return her ashes. Despite her stature, I do not believe a state funeral is wise right now. It will dishearten the people."

"We will honor her when the time is right," said Octavian. "Will this change the roster of priestesses?"

"Yes, Caesar. This morning I sent my freedman Ankhu to the temple in Tivoli to fetch Priestess Cossinia. There are nine senior priestesses there, three more than they need, and three novices who will soon be ready, so they can certainly part with her. She will take over Tuccia's duties for now. I need more experienced priestesses in Rome. Nona in particular needs help with the mills."

Octavian nodded in agreement. "With the death of Lepidus, I will be taking the office of Pontifex Maximus."

"Of course."

"I want the religious collegia to renew the Pax Deorum by updating the codification of all religious rites, including the **libri pontificales**. I will be doing the same with the **fasti**. I fear we have fallen out of favor with the gods. The contagion still spreads."

"I will begin going through the archives today." When he didn't respond, she added, "Is there something else, Caesar?"

"What is your assessment of Agrippa?"

Pomponia knew the question was coming; however, the way Caesar asked it was unexpectedly blunt. She could tell he wanted her answer to be equally blunt. Twenty years had to count for something.

"While you were in your sickbed, Agrippa all but ruled Rome. He did so competently and prayed continuously for your health. Yet if you walk by the Rostra, you will see it decorated with the prows of Cleopatra's navy ships, the same ships Agrippa defeated at Actium. If you pay for a fish in the market, the coin has your portrait as Caesar next to Agrippa's head as general. Agrippa's basilicas and temples fill the Campus Martius, and his aqueducts water Rome. The legions nearly worship him, and he has shown himself aggressive in battle. I have no doubt that he is loyal to you as emperor, but . . ."

"Continue."

"But our history is full of friends turning on each other. The parallel between you as Caesar and Agrippa as Brutus cannot be ignored."

"You echo Maecenas. He says that I have made Agrippa so powerful that I must now either kill him or make him family."

"Which will you choose?" Pomponia asked, as if she did not already know the answer.

"Family. Agrippa has been the only brother I have known since I was a child. I need him. I will marry him to Julia." He straightened his back and looked at Pomponia. "How will she respond?"

"Dutifully at best. Agrippa is much older."

"Then I will be content with **dutifully**."

"What else does Maecenas advise?"

"Money and marble," Octavian said with a huff, "and lots of both. The Temple of Mars Ultor will be completed soon, as will my mausoleum." He turned his eyes upward. "May the gods keep me out of it for a while longer. Maecenas will find a good sculptor for my Ara Pacis too. It is to be a grand marble altar that will celebrate the peace of my reign."

"Long may that peace last," said Pomponia. "The last time I spoke with Maecenas, he was also looking to commission a poet to write an epic. Something 'legendary,' as he put it. I may have the man for him. Virgil. My brother, Pomponius, knows him."

"Is he in Rome?"

"He arrived with my brother yesterday, but with Tuccia's illness I couldn't step away. It's been years since I've seen Pomponius. He is like Ulysses without a Penelope, always traveling, always headed to the next shore. It will be nice to know he is living in our family home on the Caelian Hill again. I have it all ready for him, staffed with slaves and everything."

"I look forward to meeting him."

"You will like him," said Pomponia. "Pomponius is a gentle soul, but also a simple one. Yet what he lacks in skill himself, he makes up for by recognizing it in others. He is forever befriending those with exceptional talent. He knows your engineer Vitruvius and has referred some fine painters to senators. He says that Virgil's writing is poetic but also politically persuasive, so Maecenas will no doubt approve. I will arrange a meeting between them."

"Good," said Caesar. "I am glad I kept Maecenas in Rome, then. He sent his wife to the country to avoid the contagion, but I refused him permission to go. He is needed here."

Pomponia nodded but said nothing. Maecenas may have sent his wife away to protect her from disease, but that was only half the reason. The other half was to avoid Octavian's advances. It was common gossip that the emperor regularly bedded his closest adviser's wife, the beautiful Terentia, right under the noses of both Maecenas and Livia.

Again, Octavian seemed to read her thoughts. As if not wanting her to think any further on the matter, he offered another sincere sentiment at Tuccia's passing, sprinkled more fish food into the pool, said a pleasant goodbye, and then exited the courtyard to take the ornate Palatine ramp back up to the manicured grounds of his estate. She could hear his slippers shuffling over the tiled floor as he left.

The emperor of Rome returning to his palace, like a houseguest returning to his room.

CHAPTER VII

Caveat Emptor

Let the buyer beware.

–A LEGAL PRINCIPLE

In Rome, it wasn't **what** you knew but **who** you knew. And since Taurus knew the emperor, he was able to arrange for his client's celebrity charioteer—Scorpus the Titan—to race for the Blues at the Circus Maximus at a time when most games had been postponed because of the contagion. Not that Soren had shown any appreciation for Taurus's efforts. He had only complained that it had taken too many months and that he was tired of paying for Scorpus's keep at the ludus without seeing any profit.

Escorted by guards, Pomponia and Quintina moved through the arched walkway that led to the emperor's box. The marble balcony was located in the curve of the bullet-shaped stadium to afford the imperial family and their patrician guests the best possible view of the racetrack below. As always, it was bustling with the usual array of senators and nobles, all mixing business with pleasure while ingratiating themselves to Augustus and Agrippa.

Julia was there too, a piece of cold meat in one hand and a wine cup in the other. She had become pregnant almost immediately after her marriage to Agrippa and, despite her obviously distended belly, was not refraining from wine. She scowled at her new—old—husband as he looked over a scroll with her father, but her mood lifted at the sight of Quintina, and she waved her over.

"Go ahead," permitted Pomponia. "I'm going to sit with my brother."

As Quintina made her way to the front of the emperor's box to sit beside Julia, she offered the chief Vestal's brother a warm smile. Pomponius had chosen an unpretentious seat a few rows back from the viewing balustrade and was exactly as Pomponia had described him: likable enough, but utterly devoid of the kind of shrewdness typically seen in Roman elites. **His sister must have gotten it all**, Quintina thought wryly.

Pomponia sat down next to her brother, and he

received her with a kiss on the cheek. She laughed. "Always the little brother."

He offered a crooked smile in return, and Pomponia marveled at how little he had changed. The same disheveled mess of brown hair, the same hazel eyes, the same pockmarked chin from a childhood illness, and the same nose that, if you looked closely, wasn't completely straight, due to a fall from a tall tree—and a solid landing on his face—when he was six years old. It had happened the day before she'd taken her vows as a novice Vestal.

"I spent some time in the gardens outside the track before I came in," said Pomponius. "The statue of Priestess Tuccia is a fine one. Excellent craftsmanship. There were many flowers at its base."

"No one loved the races more than Tuccia," said Pomponia.

Without asking for an invitation, Livia took the empty seat next to Pomponia. As always, she knew it pleased Octavian to see her cozying up to Rome's Vestalis Maxima.

"Hello, Priestess."

"Lady Livia."

"I suppose your money is on the Blues," said Livia, an obvious reference to the team that Tuccia so fanatically adored. And then, as if suddenly realizing the weight of her words, "I didn't mean it like that." It wasn't quite an apology, but close.

"Not to worry."

Following the dutiful introduction of the empress to her brother, which Livia could not have seemed less interested in, Pomponia settled in her seat but refused the food and drink offered to her by a slave. She had no stomach for either. She had been dreading the chariot races for days, so inseparable were they from the memory of Tuccia.

From the memory of Quintus too. She couldn't bring herself to look at the two nearby seats where all those years ago they had so awkwardly sat together.

Which man do you favor, Priestess?

I favor no man in particular.

Even as a skull-rattling roar went up from the crowd, Pomponia was struck by a silent thought: she could no longer picture Quintus's face with the clarity she once could. She had a small painting of him that Ankhu had made and a lock of his black hair, but his finer features were lost to time now. She caught Livia looking at her sideways and steadied herself, admiring the decorated, elongated center of the racetrack.

"I see Caesar has adorned the **spina** with his spoils from Egypt," she said.

"Yes," said Livia. "Years later, and the shipments still arrive." She tilted her head. "I think it's a bit much, don't you? Two towering obelisks, four golden thrones, and no fewer than eighteen beast-headed statues of Egyptian gods. My husband becomes less subtle with age."

"We all do, Lady Livia." Pomponia shifted her eyes to Livia's slightly rounded belly. The empress had her hands strategically folded over it.

Then again, Livia's pregnancy was no surprise to Pomponia. She had known about it since the day Livia's blood was supposed to come but had not. Despina's daily letters from Caesar's house kept her informed of everything, including Livia's determination to deliver a male child before Julia could do so.

A flourish of horns. Another swell of cheers as the restless crowd waved blue banners embroidered with black scorpions, shouting, "**Scorpus, Scorpus, Scorpus!**" until it sounded like thunder rolling across the cloudless sky.

Pomponia settled back in her seat for the opening performance. Taurus was standing below the emperor's box, his arms outstretched and his head up, ready to deliver yet another rousing speech, not just to Caesar, but also to the thousands of spectators seated around the massive track. Unlike the gladiator games or wild-beast hunts, which often saw women relegated to the upper levels of the arena, women—as well as plebeians, freedmen, and even well-connected slaves—were allowed to watch the chariot races from the lower levels.

The wealthy Taurus was known for his pre- and postgame theatrics, particularly in the amphitheater that he had built years earlier in the Campus Martius. Whether it was a black-robed Charon entering the stadium to usher a fallen fighter to the afterlife or a winged Cupid lamenting the plight of lovers forced to hack each other to death before a cheering and merciless mob, he seemed to prefer Greek tragedy over Roman games. It made for a great show.

"All of Rome is in the Circus today!" he exclaimed, and at that, yet another mad cheer of excitement went up. "And why not? It is where we should be! Think back, dear Romans, to our earliest days . . ."

On cue, a large group of performers flooded into the arena. Men on white horses rode circles around one another, encouraging their mounts to gallop and rear up as dramatically as possible. Across from them, women gathered to mingle and talk among themselves as if oblivious to the men and horses.

Between the two groups stood an imposing, regal-looking figure dressed in full Roman armor and striking a particularly self-important pose.

Taurus gestured to him. ". . . And behold! The divine Romulus, father and founder of our Eternal City!" At that, even the normally cool Octavian seemed dazzled and joined in the fervent applause.

"Transport yourself back, dear Romans, back to the dusty centuries before our temples, before our aqueducts, before our roads and the law of the Twelve Tables, back to the time when Rome herself was newborn. On this land where we now celebrate Roman triumph and excellence, imagine nothing but a bare field. Imagine nothing but Romulus and his band of followers—brave men, but alas, **only** men! And, dear Romans, not even our great father could bring forth issue in such a world!"

A roar of ribald laughter moved through the audience.

The actor of Romulus thrust his sword into the air and shouted, "Rome must be peopled!"

"Yes!" cried Taurus. "And so, the divine Romulus

played a trick on Rome's neighboring tribe, the Sabines. He invited their men into the city to watch his warhorses race each other." At that, the white horses began to run in larger circles, kicking up sand and neighing into the air as if determined to outperform their riders. "And while the Sabine men were captivated by the races, Romulus's soldiers captured their women!"

A whistle blew, and a shouting band of men burst out of the starting gates to surround the women. Some threw the women over their shoulders and pretended to make off with them, while others tossed them to the ground and lay on top of them, thrusting with such exaggerated flair that even Pomponia couldn't stop herself from laughing.

Out of the corner of her eye, she saw Quintina look back at her and smile. She knew that smile. It was the same one she used to give Fabiana when she knew the elder Vestal was enjoying herself.

"Now look closely, dear Romans," shouted Taurus, pointing at the antics going on all around him, "for you may see the faces of your parentage here!"

Another wave of laughter.

"But do not despair for these ill-treated women," continued Taurus, "for these were the first women of

Rome, and they learned to love these brutes—" At this, he opened his arms as if embracing the men in the crowd, who applauded at the gibe. "—so these pretty peacekeepers from the Sabine Hills united our tribes and became the mothers of our empire."

After a few more moments of indulging the cheers and stamping of feet, Taurus raised his arms to mark the end of the performance. The actors gave a quick bow and exited the arena. "Friends," he boomed, "today's hero comes not from the Sabine Hills and not even from the seven hills of Rome! He comes to us from Capua! I bring you . . . Scorpus the Titan!"

It was everything Pomponia could do to not cover her ears with her hands. Her seat shook with the vibration of thousands of stomping feet and shouting voices.

Scorpus burst out of the starting gate like a bolt of lightning from a cloud. The metal that covered the front of his chariot was a piercing ocean blue, and in the sunlight, the iridescent black scorpions affixed to it gave the illusion of either swimming or crawling across its reflective metallic surface. His four black horses looked like massive harnessed scorpions themselves, pulling the reinforced chariot at a speed that seemed insane even for the unparalleled track of the Circus Maximus.

The celebrated driver wore a rich blue tunica, both it and his helmet inlaid with gold. He gripped the reins with one hand and held the other high in the air, waving banners of blue and green: blue for his new team, green in respect for the team he had ridden for over the course of his career in Capua.

In all her years attending the Circus Maximus, Pomponia had never seen a show like this: she hadn't seen the crowd this fevered since Caesar's triumphal procession had lapped the racetrack years earlier. Her throat tightened. **Tuccia would have loved this.**

She contented herself with her starstruck brother's enjoyment. He shouted to her over the applause and pounding feet. "I saw him race in Capua once, but it was nothing like this!"

As Scorpus completed his exhibition lap—it was Taurus's idea, just to get the crowd **really** going—he spared a glance up at the owners' box and caught a brief look at Soren. There was a woman beside him. Not Cassandra. He snapped his whip and passed under the box, refusing to salute his master, and exited the track to make his way back to the starting gate.

As the gleaming blue chariot disappeared from view, Soren licked his lips at the public insult. No matter. The crowd was on its feet. Even Caesar was cheering. And he, Soren, had made it happen.

The pregame show and celebrity round now over, an onslaught of vendors made the most of the brief lull before the blast of the starting horn. They moved through the crowd, selling figs, pears, wedges of bread, and even luxuries like pickled fish, cold sausages, and cheese for those who could afford it. They moved quickly, exchanging as much food for coin as they could during the last moments before the race.

A horn blew, and a row of the teams' colored banners dropped from the top of each starting gate. Even before they had fully unfurled, the earsplitting cheers of the crowd merged into a single wave of sound that swept through the stadium.

An even louder horn sounded, and the starting gates flew open. Four chariots burst out—green, red, white, and last, blue. Even through the clamor of the cheering crowd, Soren could hear the rhythmic drumming of the horses' hooves on the sand.

As the chariots neared the critical point of the first turning post, the crowd's cheers turned to gasps and shouts as Scorpus seemed to lag too far behind, but then, in one smooth motion, he pulled ahead and took the lead.

Soren felt a hand on his shoulder. It was Taurus, returning to his seat after his rousing display of showmanship. "Your man harnesses a team led by Pegasus, Soren."

A gloating grin spread across Soren's lips.

The chariots rounded the track once, twice, three times, four times. With each pass, one more lap counter—in the form of a dolphin to represent Neptune, the god who created the horse—tipped over to signal another completed circuit, the crowd's energy surged, renewed by the excitement of Scorpus's skill.

At every turn, the star charioteer either maintained the lead or strategically hung back to save his horses and keep his wheels on the track. What a shame that such an awe-inspiring athlete had been squandering his talent in Capua! He should have been in Rome all along.

On the fifth lap, an act of desperation.

Scorpus was still in control of the lead, but a battle was underway between the green and the red driver for second place, both men convinced they could overtake the champion and eager to gain position to try.

The red driver whipped his horses so hard that

even from his seat Soren could see the flesh on their flanks separate and split open. A rain of blood flew back into the eyes of the green driver and his horses to create a stinging mixture of blood and sand, compelling the horses to shake their heads and neigh loudly.

The green chariot looked like it might go off course, but the driver corrected it. The red driver would have none of it, though. Gripping the reins with one hand, he reached to grab a metal pole affixed to the outside of his chariot and, just as the green horses gained on him, jabbed it into the eye of the horse nearest him.

That did it. The horse instinctively lowered his head and turned away, upsetting the balance of the racing chariot so quickly that within a single blink of the eye the chariot went from being upright and intact to airborne and then upside down and torn into an unidentifiable pile of wood, metal, and body parts. A "shipwreck," as the Romans called it.

The sixth lap, and Scorpus was still in the lead.

The race was now only between the blue driver and the red. The green driver was off the track and already in the afterlife. The white was close behind, but not enough to pose a threat either in terms of victory or dirty tricks.

The seventh and final lap.

Soren leaned forward in his chair as Taurus slapped him on the back. Scorpus's chariot thundered over the sand, in command of it all—the race, the crowd, seemingly the world itself. Soren turned his head to see the emperor of Rome on his feet. Standing beside him were General Agrippa and the most influential senators and magistrates in the empire, all cheering Soren's chariot driver on.

As the chariots passed under the owners' box toward the final dash for the finish line, Soren could see the determined concentration on the celebrity charioteer's face. He allowed himself a smile. As if sensing it, Scorpus looked up at him.

Soren knew what the bastard would do next.

Time and momentum seemed to inexorably, unexplainably shift. Even as the chariots moved at breakneck speeds, it all seemed to happen in slow motion. Soren stood up.

Don't do it, you prick.

The red chariot gained, or rather, the blue chariot slowed. The crowd descended into madness. Skirmishes and fights began to break out, even in the upper-class sections. The red charioteer passed the finish line nearly a full horse's head in front of Scorpus.

Without even waiting for his chariot to come to a full stop, the victorious red driver leaped out of it and ran around to the heads of his horses, embracing them, kissing their flared nostrils, and wiping the glistening sweat off their necks while shouting thanks to the gods and waving at his fans in the stands.

Scorpus seemed unmoved by it all. He stepped out of his chariot and pulled off his helmet as if he had just finished a simple training run and not lost the biggest chariot race that Rome had seen in ten years.

"Jupiter Almighty." Taurus turned to Soren. "If I didn't know any better . . ." But Soren was already halfway across the owners' box, heading for the exit. **I wonder how much he paid for him**, Taurus wondered. **Caveat emptor.**

In the adjacent emperor's box, the mood was a similar blend of adrenaline-charged disbelief and amusement. Caesar, Agrippa, and the other men of rank stood and converged in a group to excitedly compare wins and losses, to congratulate themselves and offer gibes to their losing counterparts.

Quintina again turned in her seat to check on Pomponia. The Vestalis Maxima seemed to be enjoying herself well enough in the company of her brother and was even partaking in what looked to be pleasant small talk with the empress and some other noblewomen. With Tuccia's death still so recent, it was the best she could have hoped for.

She felt a nudge on her arm. "Look at him, Quintina," said Julia. Caesar's daughter jabbed a finger toward Agrippa as he conversed with the other men but made no effort to lower her voice. "He fancies himself Neptune, but he's more like Proteus, the old man of the sea. And that's with his clothes **on**. Merciful Juno, I pray this child is a boy so I don't have to endure the sight again."

Quintina stood up. She did not envy her friend's compulsory marriage to the older general, but she could not be seen gossiping about it either. Julia kept talking. "I guess there's one good thing to come out of it, though." She shot her stepmother, Livia, a glare. "At least I don't have to live under the same roof as her and Tiberius anymore."

"Take care," Quintina gently scolded her friend. "Your looks could wound Typhon."

Julia huffed. "If only." She stood and fell into step beside Quintina, the two of them making their way toward the front of the balcony to chat idly and watch the cleanup on the track below. They were just about there, when a voice made Quintina's stomach drop.

"Priestess . . ."

Quintina took a stabilizing breath and turned around as casually as she could. "Hello, Septimus." She looked squarely at his face, refusing her eyes permission to move to his companion—Tacita, her elbow again hooked tightly around Septimus's arm. Quintina would not give her sister the satisfaction of acknowledging her first. Anyway, she didn't care to see Tacita's delicate, perpetually childlike face and flawless olive skin any sooner than she had to.

"My dear sister Quintina," said Tacita. She forced an embrace upon the Vestal and then returned to Septimus's arm. "I have missed you."

Quintina did not return the sentiment but simply asked, "How did you gain entrance to the emperor's private balcony?"

Septimus raised his eyebrows at Quintina's un-expected coolness toward her sister. He removed Tacita's arm from his own.

"General Agrippa let me in," said Tacita. Her eyes jumped from Quintina to Julia. "He owes me a favor," she whispered.

Septimus cleared his throat and bowed to Cae-sar's daughter. "Actually, it is my doing, Lady Julia. I am proud to say that my father was a commander in your father's Fifteenth Legion at Actium. He died recently of the contagion. Caesar has been kind enough to arrange some distractions for me while in Rome."

Tacita giggled. "Distractions? Is that what you call it?"

Her three companions ignored her.

"Ah." Julia nodded. "Septimus, was it?" She had heard the name before from Quintina. There was little the two young women didn't share. "Welcome," she said to him before turning to Tacita and adding, "Will you excuse us?"

Tacita delayed for a fraction of a moment, quickly running through her options. Realizing she had none, she bowed her head to the emperor's daughter. "Of course." She turned to Quintina. "Perhaps we can catch up soon, sister."

"Perhaps."

With Tacita safely disposed of, Julia looked toward Agrippa and sighed. "Oh look, Proteus summons his nymph. I must go. He may need my help descending the steps." She leaned into Quintina. "His knees snap like branches of an old oak tree."

After they kissed cheeks in parting and Julia was out of earshot, Septimus put his hands on his hips and tried not to laugh. "I didn't know your sister was Empusa," he said. "A woman one moment, a man-eater the next."

Quintina laughed. **Damn him.** She felt her face flush and tried unsuccessfully to move her eyes away from his. He licked his lips and squinted in the sunlight. Septimus squinted all the time, even when there was no sun, even on the cloudiest days or when they were standing in the shadow of the tall cypress tree in the temple's garden in Tivoli.

"How did you meet her?"

He squinted again. "At my father's funeral feast. Don't ask me how she gained entrance to that."

"On the arm of some fool, probably."

"Probably," Septimus allowed. "She seemed to know of our acquaintance."

"I made the mistake of mentioning it once in passing. That would be enough for Tacita to catalog it forever."

"Well, no matter. How are you?"

"How am I?"

"Quintina . . ."

"Why did you not return to Tivoli when you said you would? No letters, no messengers. No word at all. Nothing until I see you at the Neptunalia wrapped around my sister like—"

"Like nothing, Quintina. Lower your voice."

"Why? What are you afraid of, Septimus?"

"I'm afraid of losing the skin off my back to a scourge in the Forum. And if you had any sense, you'd be afraid of worse things."

"Did you couple with her?"

"No."

"You're lying."

"I'm not lying. I . . . I didn't know she was your sister until afterward. She didn't tell me until afterward."

Quintina stared down onto the racetrack and locked her eyes on the efforts of the undertakers to collect what remained of the green charioteer and his horses. She wished she could drop down onto the track and just run away. Away from the sickening feeling of betrayal in her stomach, away from the knowledge that Tacita had been intimate with Septimus in a way that she could not be. Away from the feeling that she was powerless to do anything about it.

"I'm sorry," Septimus whispered. Then he shook his head. "Or maybe I'm not. We are not together, Quintina. I did not know she was your sister, but the truth is, I can be with anyone I like."

"Leave now, Septimus."

It wasn't Quintina who had spoken. It was Pomponia.

Septimus offered an apologetic head bow to the chief Vestal and quietly slipped away.

Pomponia leaned her shoulder against Quintina's and followed her stare into the arena.

Below them, on the racetrack, a man—presumably the losing charioteer's owner—was yelling obscene threats at Scorpus the Titan. He grabbed a whip that was lying in the sand and began to strike the defeated driver on the back with it. Scorpus accepted the lashing without flinching. Spent, the other man threw the whip aside in frustration.

"I know how he feels," said Quintina.

"Which one?" asked Pomponia.

"Both."

CHAPTER VIII

Tantae Molis Erat Romanam Condere Gentem
A great task it was to found the Roman race.
—VIRGIL

Octavian slouched back in his chair and accepted a cup of wine from his slave Despina. He wrapped his hands around it and squeezed, as if that would release his frustration.

"Was it a boy or a girl?" His eyes were bloodshot, although Musa could not tell if it was from grief, fatigue, or anger. He suspected it was all three.

"A boy, Caesar," the physician answered.

"**Futuo**," cursed Octavian. "My daughter will have a son before I do."

Musa wiped his blood-covered hands on a cloth. He worried that was true. Julia's firstborn child to Agrippa had been a healthy baby girl, and he had no doubt that Caesar's daughter would conceive again quickly.

"The empress is in her late thirties, but I have seen many women conceive at this age," said Musa. "Although . . ."

"Do not tiptoe."

"Sometimes too many terminated pregnancies can cause permanent damage. Lady Livia's previous marriage was an unhappy one. Perhaps she had tried to limit issue?"

"She was with child when I met her."

"Yes." Musa furrowed his brow. "Perhaps it was the combination of terminations and the last delivery . . ."

"You take aim in the dark, Musa."

The weary physician sat on a low stool in front of Octavian's chair. "She is healthy, Caesar. You have both conceived progeny in the past and she has successfully carried to term. There is no obvious reason." He rubbed the back of his head, leaving a streak of blood on his ear. "I can bring in another physician from Athens, one that specializes in—"

"I don't need another physician. I need a son." Octavian stood up quickly and threw the cup in his hands against the wall. Red wine ran down over one of the painted panels: a nature scene of olive trees against a bird-filled sky, the birds raised in stucco relief as if emerging from the wall to fly away. "**Rome** needs a son." After a long moment of tense silence, he waved his hand at Musa. "Go tend to Livia. Send in Maecenas and Agrippa."

Musa left, and the advisers entered the room. Their eyes were questioning, hopeful.

"Stillborn," said Octavian, "and too early. A boy."

"We grieve with you, Caesar," said Agrippa.

"Grieving with me is as pointless as coupling with her," replied Octavian. The emperor's uncharacteristic harshness made the men exchange glances. It was not like him to speak about Livia that way. He gestured impatiently for them to sit down.

Agrippa braved it first. "You have options."

"What are they?"

"You can divorce her. You could have another wife with child by the kalends."

Octavian shifted his eyes to Maecenas.

"It won't look good," said the more politically minded adviser. "It will look hypocritical. Your morality laws discourage divorce."

"Caesar is above the law," said Agrippa.

"Of course he is," replied Maecenas, "but he cannot **look** like he's above the law. We all know how Caesars fare in the Senate when they do that. He'll be wearing armor under his toga for a year."

Agrippa dug in. "The masses have a short memory. **Panem et circenses.**" Bread and circuses. He shot Maecenas, who had started to say something, a warning glance and continued speaking directly to Octavian. "Divorce her. Put on another chariot race in the Circus Maximus—**Scorpus the Titan Returns to Avenge His Loss!**—and the people will soon forget. Grant a few tax breaks in the Senate. Those self-serving old men will look the other way."

"You allow your dislike for the empress to taint your advice, General," said Maecenas. "This Caesar's reign is about virtue and stability. Leading by example."

Frustrated, Octavian poured himself a new cup of wine so hastily that half of it splashed onto the floor. "Leading by example," he muttered. "How can I be the Father of Rome when I can't even be the father of a son?"

Maecenas spoke with certainty. "Julius Caesar did not have a son, yet he did have a blood-related heir. You. And now he is a god." He pointed to Agrippa. "If the general and Julia can produce a male issue, he will be **your** blood heir. You will adopt him as your son."

Agrippa said nothing. The idea of having a son that would be Octavian's as much as—more than—his own was a duty he was still coming to terms with. Despite their long friendship, in his darkest moments, Agrippa had to wonder about Octavian's endgame. He always had one, but Agrippa wasn't always privy to it. Surely Caesar took no pleasure at the thought of his oldest friend bedding his young daughter, and Julia herself missed no opportunity to voice her displeasure to her father. It was a matter of pure necessity. Agrippa was the only man Octavian trusted enough to father his heir. It was a choice driven by political survival. Caesar's survival.

Maecenas continued, indifferent to the impact of the arrangement on Agrippa. It was irrelevant. "With a male blood heir established, we can go on to secure you as the father of our country in other, more lyrical ways. I have commissioned the poet Virgil. He has begun work on an epic that will raise the name Caesar as high as that of Romulus."

"Propaganda," said Octavian.

"Legend," Maecenas countered. "It's what Rome was built on."

* * *

The moon was a high white sliver in the dark night sky by the time Agrippa's horse-drawn carriage arrived back at his home. He walked into the house slowly. He was in no hurry for what was to come.

"Domine," a house slave said, bowing. "Is there anything you require?"

He shook his head and proceeded to his bed-chamber. He opened the door to find Julia sitting up in the large bed, drinking wine and licking food off her fingers. By the soft light of oil lamps, he watched her push a glistening finger between her lips and pull it out again, eyeing him with distaste. He hated her for being so young, so desirable.

She hated him for the opposite reasons. "Must you sleep in here? The mattress sinks like a warship when you lie down." The disgust in her voice was palpable.

After a slave unfastened his sandals and helped him remove his tunica, Agrippa approached the bed. She scowled at him. "Don't even think about getting under these sheets until you've washed. Clean your teeth too."

He did as instructed and then returned to stand uncertainly by the side of the bed. A female slave refilled Julia's cup with wine and then looked at him. "Wine, Domine?"

"No." He hesitated by the bedside a moment longer, calculating how best to get in without prompting more complaints from Julia. Finally, he sat on the edge. "Livia miscarried tonight," he said.

"She's a hundred years old. What do you expect?"

"You know what your father expects of us."

"I know what both of you expect of me. I also know I'm in no position to do anything about it."

"Julia, I've been hearing rumors . . . about other men. Men that you coupled with while pregnant with our child."

"**Our child?**" she said. "You mean Agrippina? The daughter you've already forgotten about? The one you had whisked away to live in some country home so that I can focus on pumping out a boy for you and my father?"

Agrippa tensed. "If your father hears of your behavior . . ." He stopped. He knew he sounded more like a scolding uncle than a husband.

Julia knew it too. She sighed with irritation, set her cup aside, and wiped her fingers on the sheets. "Let's just get it over with." She snapped her fingers at the female slave. "Do as I told you."

The slave walked around the bed to stand before Agrippa, who was still seated on the edge. She bent down and placed her hands on his knees, spreading them apart to expose his genitals below his loincloth.

As the slave took him in her mouth, Julia kicked off the covers and positioned herself on all fours, facing away from Agrippa. "Make sure you're ready before you start this time," she said. "And make it quick. I'm tired."

* * *

The messenger handed Pomponia the scroll from the house of Caesar.

"Sit there and wait," the Vestal said.

The messenger sat obediently on a chair at the far side of Pomponia's office as she pushed aside the wax tablets at her desk and uncurled the scroll.

High Priestess Pomponia,

The empress's pregnancy ended last hour with a stillborn male child. Lady Livia had some bleeding, but Musa was able to stop it, and she now does well, although she weeps inconsolably and broke several cups and medicine jars by throwing them against the wall.

After the stillbirth, Caesar was angry. He did not visit his wife but rather met briefly with Maecenas and General Agrippa. Agrippa told Caesar that he could divorce Lady Livia and have a new wife pregnant by the kalends.

Maecenas advised differently. He said that Caesar must lead by example to maintain stability. He said that Caesar will adopt any male issue of Agrippa and Julia's and that child will be his blood progeny and heir. He also indicated that he has commissioned the poet your brother recommended, Virgil.

Soon after, Agrippa and Maecenas left. They were gone only moments before Maecenas's wife, Terentia, arrived. I saw her and Caesar embracing, and then Caesar took her to his bedchamber. That is all for now. I will send another messenger if anything else of note happens this evening.

Despina

Pomponia took a fresh piece of papyrus and wrote.

Despina,

Go to Caesar's bedchamber when he is with Terentia and watch what happens between them. Take note of what Terentia is wearing and how she performs when they are intimate. I do not trust that woman, and we cannot allow Caesar's passion or affection for her to deepen any more than it has.

You know your master's desires better than anyone, even better than his own wife does. When Lady Livia's health has returned, you must ensure that she inflames his desire again. Caesar still has love for her. Once he recalls his passion for her, Terentia will be of no concern.

VMP

Pomponia curled up the papyrus and sealed it with wax. She handed it to the messenger. "Take this to Despina immediately."

"Yes, High Priestess."

The messenger ran off, and Pomponia poured herself a cup of water from the small, spouted amphora on her desk. She took a few thoughtful sips and then reread Despina's letter before curling it up tightly and burning it in the flame of a candle.

There was no doubt in Pomponia's mind that Terentia was grooming herself to be Livia's replacement. It wasn't enough that she was wife to one of Caesar's closest and most powerful advisers; she wanted to be the empress of Rome.

But Pomponia was content with the current empress. **Nota res mala optima.** A known evil is better than an unknown one. Pomponia knew Livia. She knew how to manage her for the good of the Vestal order. No noblewoman in Rome's history had donated as much money or marble to the temple as Livia had or done as much to advance the order. No, they didn't like each other, but as chief Vestal and as empress, they had an unspoken agreement: you support me and I'll support you. That mutual support was to their mutual benefit.

If Octavian were to divorce Livia and marry Maecenas's backbiting wife, Terentia, things would be less certain. Pomponia would struggle to manage Terentia. She had already shown herself to be an overreaching wife, and as empress, she would undoubtedly interfere in the relationship between Caesar and Pomponia as chief Vestal.

It will be a bright day in Hades before that happens, thought Pomponia.

She was confident that Despina would be able to spark Caesar's passion for his wife again. He loved her, and Livia was still a beautiful woman. Not as beautiful as Terentia, but more interesting. And from what Pomponia had been told of Caesar's desires in bed, that was just as important.

Meanwhile, she would pray, along with all Rome, that the union between Julia and Agrippa would produce a male blood heir for Caesar. Rome needed its prince.

Pomponia's head throbbed. Conniving women, stillborn babies, potential heirs. She poured the water in her cup back into its amphora and reached for an amphora of wine instead, noting to herself that she tended to drink much more wine in Rome than she did in Tivoli.

CHAPTER IX

Lupus Non Timet Canem Latrantem
A wolf is not afraid of a barking dog.
—A ROMAN ADAGE

Scorpus tried not to grimace as he pulled the woolen tunica off over his head. The rough fabric scraped against the still open lashes that ran down his back and both sides of his body, and he muttered a silent curse. The lashing he had received from Soren had been a bad one, and the wounds had refused to heal.

"Serves you right, you damn fool," said Taurus. "You're fortunate he didn't hang you from the starting gate."

"Yes, Fortuna smiles on me."

"No need to get pissy with me, Scorpus. And if I were you, I'd watch my mouth. The gods are almost as vain as chariot drivers."

The doctor's room in Taurus's ludus smelled like a pungent mixture of blood, wine, vinegar, and boiled cabbage. Every time Scorpus came in to get his bandages changed, he had to fight the urge to gag.

The doctor tapped Scorpus's elbow, and he lifted both of his arms over his head, linking his fingers together and resting his hands on his head while the doctor busied himself with the wounds, pulling off the old dressings and applying fresh ones. The new poultices stung even worse than they smelled.

"Funny thing is," said Taurus, "that whole shitshow you put on in the Circus Maximus has created an even bigger demand for Scorpus the Titan. I couldn't have set it up better myself." He lifted an arm with his trademark dramatic flair and spoke into the air. "**The champion avenges himself against that upstart driver for the Reds!**" He chuckled and bit into an apple. "It was brilliant. We get paid for two big races instead of one. I'm telling you, Scorpus, you earn your freedom and maybe we'll go into business together someday."

"I should already be free. My former master—"

"Ah well," Taurus mumbled through a mouthful of apple. "Who among us is truly free, my friend?"

"Philosophizing doesn't suit you, Taurus."

The doctor finished his handiwork and helped Scorpus pull his tunica back down, taking care not to disturb the bandages. "Try not to move around so much," he instructed. "You keep ripping them back open. That's why they won't heal."

"They won't heal because this prick insists I train for eight hours a day. They rip open every morning. What do you expect?"

"Don't blame me," said Taurus. "I'm only following orders. I told Soren you needed to rest. My lanista told him so too, but he'll have none of it. He accused me of making your life too cushy."

"That's what I thought when I woke this morning to the sound of a guard pissing on my sandals. 'Scorpus,' I said to myself, 'your life is too cushy.'"

Taurus shrugged unapologetically. "The boys get bored. After breakfast, go shave. You look like a savage Parthian with that hair on your face. I'm taking you to the amphitheater for a special appearance today, so try to look civilized." Again, a dramatic wave. "**Scorpus the Titan rides again!**" Another crunch of his apple. "Just to keep you in the public eye. Ride around the arena a few times and scream like Jupiter stuck a lightning bolt up your ass. They'll love it."

"Soren agreed to that?"

"Sure, after I agreed to cut your housing fee in

half for the next two months. So don't expect your gruel to reach the edge of the plate for a while. You're an expensive tenant."

Taurus left and Scorpus did what he had to: shaved his face, polished his helmet, and cleaned his leathers. Soon afterward, the lanista and several guards loaded him and a number of gladiators into a caged horse-drawn cart for transport from the ludus to the massive amphitheater in the Campus Martius.

Scorpus crouched at the back of the cart, staring out the bars in an effort to avoid being noticed by the fighters around him. It was no use.

"Aren't we blessed by holy Minerva herself," said a man who was missing his left hand. "Here we are, packed balls to assholes in a slave cart with Scorpus the Titan!"

The other men laughed.

Scorpus offered a conciliatory grin. "Well, not to worry, friend. There'll be a lot more room in here on the way back."

The man's smile melted, and he flicked an obscene finger gesture at Scorpus.

"I'd keep that hand close to the chest, if I were you," Scorpus added. "You can't afford to lose another one."

The laughter shifted from Scorpus to the one-handed man, who angrily sat down and slid a piece of dirty straw he found on the floor of the cart between his teeth. He chewed at it dejectedly as the cart rolled on, and the mood within turned suddenly somber. After all, these men were about to fight each other to the death in the most grotesque ways the officials at the amphitheater could dream up. And they tended to dream big.

The streets of Rome did not impress Scorpus. The smell was intolerable, especially as the cart passed by sanitation crews who busied themselves unclogging drains and sweeping up the filth and excrement that hid in doorways and ran down the ruts in the road.

Despite the contagion that he had heard was ravaging the city, the streets seemed to be as packed as the caged cart he rode in. He spotted a meaty hornet clumsily making its way up one of the bars of the cart, and he crushed it with his palm, offering a silent prayer to Hades that the contagion would do a better job of clearing the Roman streets of Romans.

Finally, the cart packed with gladiators and one celebrity charioteer arrived in the area of the grand amphitheater. As he had done upon first seeing the Circus Maximus, Scorpus tried to be unimpressed by the scale of the structure that appeared before him. He tried not to look at the gleaming marble facade and multicolored columns—blue, red, and yellow—but the amphitheater was so large it intruded into his peripheral vision. He tried to ignore its impossible height and width and the huge banners that hung down heavy in the breezeless air, blood red and boasting the gold letters **SPQR**. Scorpus hated those letters.

As the cart drew closer to the amphitheater, he allowed himself a glance upward to blink at the elaborate cloth canopies that extended over the roof of the arena to shield spectators from the sun. He looked away just as quickly. He wouldn't give whatever architect designed this beast the satisfaction of his awe.

The cart came to an abrupt halt next to a heavy wooden door that led to the lower levels of the arena. There, gladiators and other trained fighters were held alongside common criminals, the city's unsightly homeless that needed culling, worn-out slaves sold as arena kill by owners who just wanted to get rid of them, and of course wild animals including bears and various exotic species of big cats.

What looked to be a full cohort of soldiers

surrounded the cart as a guard unlocked and opened it. The gladiators jumped down one by one, passing through the wooden doorway toward whatever fate awaited them, be it victory or violent death. To Scorpus, they seemed relieved. The waiting was always the worst part. Too much time to think.

Only one of them needed to be persuaded to exit the cart. The youngest, who looked no more than sixteen or seventeen. Scorpus hadn't even noticed him in the midst of the veteran gladiators. A guard pulled him out by his hair, holding him at arm's length to avoid the boy's urine-drenched tunica.

Scorpus stood up and steadied himself against the bars. A different guard, one with the Eagle tattooed on his forearm, pointed at him. "Are you the Titan?"

"I am."

The guard did a quick check over his shoulder and then stuck his head in the cart. "Tell me honestly, did you throw the race at the Circus Maximus?"

"Why would I do that?"

"You tell me," said the guard. "But like I said to my wife, if Scorpus lost that race, I'm Helen of Troy. He either threw it or those goat-screwing Reds sabotaged his chariot."

"Should I come out of the cart?"

"Oh—yes. Come out."

Scorpus lowered his head and turned sideways to squeeze out of the cart, and stepped—he didn't have to jump—down onto the ground to stand at least a foot taller than the guard, who immediately called over three additional armed sentries. Just in case.

The four of them escorted the charioteer some hundred meters to a wider and higher entrance that led to a stable used to house horses until showtime.

Scorpus followed the men through the dusty stables toward a large sliding door that opened directly into the arena itself. The light of day shone through its metal bars, and the sound of the shouting, stomping spectators pulsated through.

A small Nubian man dressed in a tunica that seemed far too clean for the surroundings greeted Scorpus. His Latin was perfect, although spoken with a thick accent.

"Greetings, Scorpus," he said. "The performance is a reenactment of your recent lo"—he stopped short of saying **loss** and continued—"**appearance** in the Circus Maximus. You will ride around the arena seven times. Keep the lead until the last lap, and then fall back . . . The other drivers have their instructions."

The giant door to the arena slid open with a great groan, and the light stabbed at Scorpus's eyes. The Nubian walked beside him, escorting him to a blue chariot drawn by four tired-looking horses.

The crowd erupted at the sight of the charioteer. His name echoed off the walls. "**Scorpus! Scorpus! Scorpus!**"

The Nubian shouted in his ear. "On the floor of your chariot, you will find a sword. When the race is over, you will take it and kill the driver of the red chariot."

"When you say the other drivers have their instructions," Scorpus shouted back, "does that include the red one?"

The Nubian raised his hands as if to say, "Who knows, who cares," and Scorpus stepped up into the chariot, nudging the sword with his foot to make sure it was secure, and then positioned his feet, ready to ride. The Nubian pointed to the starting gates behind him. "The other drivers will emerge from back there after"—he rolled his eyes—"a brief opening performance."

As the crowd continued to thunder and Scorpus gripped the reins to hold the horses steady, a chariot that looked to be made of solid gold emerged from the starting gate. It was pulled by four of the most beautiful white horses Scorpus had ever seen and was driven by a man who was nearly as beautiful: he was naked, wearing only a crown of gilded laurel leaves and a scarlet-red cloak.

The actor drove his golden chariot to the center of the arena and spoke in a voice that Scorpus felt certain would rattle the ears of every man in the stadium.

"It is I, the sun god Apollo, come on my golden chariot to witness the avenging race of my star charioteer"—at that, he opened his arms wide in the direction of Scorpus—"Scorpus the Titan! And you, dear Romans, are now as blessed as the sun god himself, for you, too, shall witness this speedy vengeance!"

Scorpus spat into the sand and did his best to ignore the sun god, instead doing a last-minute check of his leathers. After several more minutes of the naked thespian's monologue, the actor drove his chariot around the arena in a dazzling lap and then disappeared through a doorway that was strategically recessed into the arena's encircling wall.

A loud horn blew, and the starting gates behind Scorpus's chariot flew open. He looked over his shoulder to see three chariots burst out—red, green, and white.

His eyes instantly locked on the outside black horse that pulled the red chariot.

Ferox.

He'd recognize the horse anywhere. He'd recognize him from the top bench in the arena. And he certainly recognized him as he ran past him only a chariot away.

His heart dropped, and a wave of dizziness struck. How was it possible? Ferox was his champion horse, the reason he had won race after race in Capua and been catapulted to stardom. Ferox was himself a star; however, no one in this filthy crowd would know that. They had no way of knowing that the limping, dirty horse pulling the red chariot was one of the most accomplished horses in the entire racing world. Why wasn't he back in his stable in Capua, chewing fresh hay and sweet syrup? Mettius had agreed to retire him three years earlier, when the first signs of age had started to show. Ferox had earned it.

The sinking feeling in Scorpus's heart was suddenly replaced by a rising rage. **Soren.**

As the red chariot pulled ahead, the driver whipped Ferox hard, too hard, and a rivulet of blood streamed down his flank. Scorpus drew in a chestful of air and charged after them. He didn't know what he was going to do yet, how he was going to stop it, but he had to do something.

Scorpus pushed his weary horses until they ran alongside the red chariot. He shouted across to the driver, "Pull over!" But the red driver either didn't hear him through the screams of the crowd and the clamor of the chariots, or he thought it was all part of the show. His face curled into an exaggerated sneer, and he whipped Ferox again.

Without thinking, Scorpus reached down to pull the sword from its fasteners on the floor of the chariot. He slammed the side of his chariot into the red driver's so they were nearly within arm's reach of each other and then, in one motion, swung the sword with all his strength at the driver's neck. The man's head flew into the air behind the chariot and landed in the sand with a solid thud.

The crowd exploded into a wild, collective cheer.

For a moment, it seemed to Scorpus that the worst was over. Ferox and the other three exhausted horses pulling the red chariot ran toward the relative safety of the arena's center, avoiding the green and white chariots that raced by as if oblivious to what had just happened.

They began to slow somewhat as they reached the

center—although not soon enough to avoid the trip rope that suddenly tightened before them.

Ferox stumbled first, dragging the other three horses down with him. All four animals crashed to the ground, their legs and necks seeming to blend into a single twisting, whining beast. The chariot flew into the air, breaking apart and sending shards of metal and wood into the closest spectators.

Scorpus leaped from his moving chariot and ran to the fallen Ferox. The champion horse was still alive, but one of his eyes bulged grotesquely from its socket and a white bone protruded from each of his forelegs.

Scorpus dropped to his knees and put his hands on the horse's head. He leaned over and spoke into the animal's ear, "Go in peace, my friend," and then stood up, retrieved the sword he had dropped in the sand next to him, and stabbed Ferox through the skull.

He did the same for the other three horses, each of which was languishing in its own hopeless agony.

Without stopping, he moved methodically toward the men who had positioned the trip rope. Their jaws dropped as they realized he was serious, and they tried to run, but he quickly caught up to them and decapitated them both as smoothly as he had done to the red driver. The walls of the arena shook so hard with the shouts and stamping feet of nearly twenty thousand spectators that the sand at Scorpus's feet began to vibrate.

He dropped the sword and leaned his head back on his shoulders to stare up into the sky. For the first time since learning of his previous master's death, Scorpus really understood it. He felt it. His old life was over. Soren could do anything.

He could hear the man's voice in his head. **Your woman will be next.**

The Nubian appeared before him, and Scorpus slowly realized the small man was speaking to him.

"Can you hear me, Scorpus?" The Nubian's voice cracked with effort as he screeched to be heard over the crowd. "What a show! Come on, time to go. Leave them wanting more, you know?"

Without looking back at the body of Ferox, Scorpus kicked the sand at his feet and followed the Nubian out of the arena. He passed through the giant sliding door to join the same four guards who had led him through the stable. They escorted him back to the cart that would return him to the ludus. Scorpus stepped into it and sat down on the dirty, straw-covered floor.

The guard with the Eagle tattoo grinned and

brought his face to the bars. "I didn't get to see it," he said. "Did you beat the Red?"

"I did."

"Aha, of course you did!" The excitement made him cough, and he wiped the sputum off his mouth with the back of his hand. "Hey, my son is a big fan of yours, you know. He has a painting of you on the wall of his bedchamber."

Scorpus removed one of the black leather cuffs he wore around his wrists and held it out to the guard. A drop of blood fell off the bracelet's silver scorpion medallion and landed in the straw on the floor of the cart. "Tell your son that Scorpus the Titan says hello."

* * *

Scorpus wasn't sure, but he thought he'd drifted off into a hot, strange sleep as the horse-drawn cart moved down the cobblestone street back to the ludus. Something had jarred him back to his senses. He squeezed his eyes tightly to help clear his focus as the muttered obscenities of the guard with the Eagle tattoo filtered into his ears.

Although it now carried only a single

occupant—the sole survivor of the day's games—apparently the cart had borne too much weight over the years, and a neglected wheel had chosen this moment to break. Scorpus shaded his face from the relentless sun as the guards, red-faced and sweating from the heat, loudly debated what to do about it.

"That was Ferox, wasn't it?"

Scorpus turned his head to see a man with a pockmarked chin peering through the bars of the lopsided cart. Despite his uncombed hair and the slightly crooked nose, despite the way he dragged his feet as he approached the cart, he was clearly patrician. You could always tell. It was more than the expensive toga; there was just something about the way they spoke.

"What did you say?" asked Scorpus.

"That was your horse Ferox in the arena. I saw you race him in Capua." The man stared quizzically into the air. "Maybe seven or eight years ago? I can't remember exactly. But that was him, wasn't it?"

"Yes, it was."

The man took a momentary step back as one of the guards brushed by him to check the damage to the back of the cart, but then he came close again. "You didn't know they were going to do that, did you?"

Scorpus stood up and sighed in irritation. "No, I didn't."

The man looked up at him. "It wasn't right that they did that."

Scorpus felt the man's eyes move over him to survey his squalid conditions—cooking in a prison cart, covered in blood and sand, half-starved and obviously abused. His lash marks had opened yet again, and blood from his back and sides was snaking down his legs to pool in the straw around his ankles. The man seemed offended and looked judgmentally at the guards.

For their part, the guards took no notice. It was late in the day, and their shift was supposed to have already ended. The broken wheel was delaying supper. They stood at the front of the cart negotiating with a passing street carpenter who had offered to fix their problem, although for a price that the guards clearly felt was taking unfair advantage of their situation.

"What do you boys care?" asked the carpenter. "The boss will pay."

"Do it," said one of the guards. "And do it fast. I'm hungry, and it's getting dark."

The carpenter scratched his chin. "I don't know if

my hoist will lift it. You might have to get more men. Get that giant out of the back for starters. I'll see how many blocks I have." He disappeared into the back of his covered cart to retrieve the tools of his trade.

The guard with the Eagle tattoo exchanged frowns with his companions. The idea of removing the Titan from his cage did not appeal to any of them.

Nonetheless, they were all still very displeased to find that, while they were not looking, he had somehow removed himself.

CHAPTER X

Culpa Enim Illa, Bis ad Eundem, Vulgari Reprehensa Proverbio Est

Tripping twice over the same stone
is a proverbial disgrace.

—CICERO

It was the oldest temple in the Roman Forum and the most important one. Centuries earlier, Romulus's successor, King Numa, had built the first temple to Vesta, goddess of the home and hearth, goddess of the eternal flame that protected the Eternal City. That temple had been a simple round wooden one. Round, like the huts of Rome's first homes. Round, like the life-giving sun and the earth. Round, like the stones that encircled the earliest fires of humankind. Numa had appointed a revered order of priestesses to care for the sacred fire and ensure it never went out, for Vesta's flame was the red lifeblood of Rome.

The temple that now stood in that holy spot was no longer made of wood but of the finest white marble. It no longer stood lonely in the marshy valley of the early Forum but was now surrounded by other temples, two-story basilicas, colorful monuments, and soaring arches.

Pomponia loved this temple with all her heart.

She loved every fine white and black shape on the beautiful mosaic floor, every chip in the ancient marble pedestal of the hearth, every soot-stained iron stoker, every tiny imperfection in the wide bronze bowl within which burned the crackling fire that Mother Vesta lived in.

The chief Vestal watched Quintina whisper a prayer over the sacred fire, her palms held up to the goddess. It was a prayer that only full Vestal priestesses knew. It was kept hidden from the novices and other pontiffs, hidden even from the Pontifex Maximus. Pomponia remembered the first time she had heard it. She had been standing here, at this same hearth, with High Priestess Fabiana. Fabiana had handed her a small clay pot of incense and whispered it into her ear. Pomponia's heart had felt like bursting in reverence for the goddess.

But in that same moment, a certain gravitas had

settled upon her. What if she displeased the goddess in some way? What if she misspoke the prayer or a petition or made an error when offering into the flame or performing a sacrifice? Would Vesta cease to protect Rome?

That gravitas had never lifted and was shared by her sisters. It had prompted them, especially in the months since the contagion had worsened, to undertake a meticulous review of the Vestal order's rites. They had consulted countless scrolls in the library and archives, as well as the ancient scrolls stored in the underground vaults, the ones that even Pomponia and her oldest tutors struggled to interpret because of their antiquated Latin, all to ensure their protocols respected the Pax Deorum.

On the morning Tuccia had died and the emperor had descended the Palatine ramp to the House of the Vestals like a common houseguest, Octavian had instructed Pomponia to undertake that very task. At the time, she hadn't seen the value of responding to Caesar's instruction with a "Yes, we've already been doing that." She found it was often better to let men believe they had come up with the good ideas. That was doubly so for Caesars.

Quintina placed a smooth piece of kindling on

the sacred fire as Pomponia sprinkled fragrant incense into the flames. While offerings of loose salted flour or sacred wafers, and libations of wine, olive oil, or milk were standard, Pomponia hoped the sweet scent of frankincense would please the goddess. It had worked during previous times of crisis.

And if it didn't work, at least the smoke that escaped the temple through the oculus in the domed bronze roof would make the surrounding area of the Forum smell better for a while. The sanitation crews were doing their best, but the drains were not always cooperative.

Pomponia added her voice to Quintina's. Together, they prayed for the health of the emperor and his family and then for the health of the Senate, the soldiers, and the people of Rome. They prayed in whispers and then with clear voices, using the exact same words—the **certa verba**—that had been used by generations of Vestals over the centuries.

The bronze doors to the temple opened, and sunlight streamed into the fiery sanctuary. Lucretia and Cossinia, the latter being the Vestal that Pomponia had brought in from Tivoli to replace Tuccia, slipped inside. Like Pomponia and Quintina, they wore long, sleeveless white stolas and simple veils on their heads.

After delivering their report on how the fire had behaved over the preceding hours, Pomponia and Quintina descended the steps of the temple and headed through the portico of the House of the Vestals. It was blissfully cool inside the atrium. Quintina dipped her fingers into the **impluvium**, but jumped as she noticed a ringed snake, a harmless one, cooling just below the surface of the water. "That is a good sign," she said.

"Yes," agreed Pomponia. "We will leave it." Snakes warded off evil. If one had taken the trouble to break into the House of the Vestals and protect them, they would leave it be.

Quintina took off her sandals. "What are you doing now, Pomponia?"

The Vestalis Maxima removed her veil and ran her fingers through her hair. "I am going to finish some work in my office. I have to schedule some **lustrationes**, and then I have a meeting with the empress. And no, you don't have to attend."

"Ha! Thank you, sister. Julia invited me to supper."

"Quintina . . ."

"I know, Pomponia. Agrippa is out of Rome, and I am quite familiar with Julia's activities."

"When the cat's away . . ."

"I know," Quintina repeated. "It will only be the two of us."

"She has a reputation."

"Yes, **she** has a reputation. It isn't contagious."

"Foolish girl," said Pomponia. "Nothing is more contagious than a reputation."

"It is decent that I dine with Caesar's daughter," Quintina replied. She kissed Pomponia on the cheek. "But I hear your words, Pomponia, and I take them to heart."

The high priestess wasn't convinced, but there was little else she could do. Quintina was no longer a child, and she was right; it was decent—even duteous—that she socialize with the emperor's daughter. As the wife of Agrippa, who was Caesar's heir, Julia was positioned to be the next empress of Rome. It was essential that the close friendship between the two young women, a friendship that had started in childhood, continued.

Quintina knew that. After her slave had bathed her and dressed her in a fresh white stola with embroidered purple flowers, she put on a pair of emerald-studded gold earrings. The emperor's daughter had given them to her years ago, when they were both still in their teens. They were a gift for the Vestalia. Or was it the

Lupercalia? Either way, the choice of accessories was good politics. Quintina smiled to herself. Pomponia would be impressed.

By the time she arrived at Julia's home, Quintina's stomach was rumbling. The house slaves escorted her through the atrium and into the triclinium, where Julia was lying on her back on a couch. She was crying.

"Blessed Juno," said Quintina, rushing to her side. "What is wrong?"

"What is wrong? I'll you, my friend." Julia put her face in her hands. "Old man Proteus has impregnated me again." She wiped her eyes and inhaled deeply through her nose. "At least, I think it was old man Proteus . . . Only the gods will ever truly know."

Quintina turned to the slaves. "Leave us." When the last one had gone, she took Julia's hand and squeezed it. "You must never speak that way again, Julia. Not to me, not to anyone."

Julia blinked. "I know."

"Perhaps it is a blessing," said Quintina. "Maybe it will be a boy this time. Then you will have done your duty, nay?"

"**If** it is a boy," said Julia, "and if it doesn't look too much like that blue-eyed Syrian that runs the pig butchery in the Forum Boarium."

Quintina's eyes went wide, and Julia coughed out a laugh despite her tears.

"That's it," said Quintina. "Laugh through your tears. You will make an excellent mother to a son."

A kitchen slave cautiously entered the room to deliver the first course. Quintina gestured for him to leave the tray on the low table in front of Julia's couch. Baked flamingo with vegetables. It smelled delicious.

When the slave was gone, Quintina patted the back of Julia's hand. "**In nocte consilium**," she said. The night brings counsel. "A good night's sleep will help you feel better."

"So will stuffing myself with food." Julia rolled onto her side, reached for a piece of meat on the tray, and bit indecorously into it. Eyeing a stalk of asparagus, she picked it up and waved it at her friend, her usual spirit beginning to return. "You know what this looks like, don't you?"

"Yes. Trouble."

Julia snorted in agreement. "Do you know what's funny, Quintina? I am unhappy because I'm forced to be with a man, and you are unhappy because you are forced to be without one."

After three more courses of food and as many

hours of conversation, Quintina found herself yawning. It wasn't that late, but she had woken early. As Julia walked her toward the atrium, the sound of a distant, muted shout from somewhere in the house caught Quintina's attention.

"Who else is here, Julia?"

Her friend smiled widely, displaying her straight white teeth; they were a rare blessing that the emperor's daughter accentuated by always wearing lip color. "Agrippa is in Campania on state business," she said. "There is no reason I cannot have houseguests while he is away."

"You have people staying here? Who are they?"

Julia put a finger to her lips. "Come and see for yourself."

Quintina followed Julia back through the house and toward the palatial home's elaborate baths. As they drew closer, Quintina heard giggling and splashing. The sounds echoed off the marble walls and mixed with different sounds: moans and the rhythmic movement of bodies. Quintina instinctively slowed her step, falling several paces behind Julia as they passed beyond a heavy purple curtain.

Just before turning the corner into the bath, Julia stopped. She retrieved two red bejeweled masks that hung on the wall, pulling one down over her face and holding the other out to Quintina. "Put it on," she said. "No one will know it's you." When the Vestal hesitated, Julia winked. "I promise, it's completely safe."

Compelled by her curiosity, Quintina slid the mask over her face and followed Julia around the corner. A large rectangular pool filled up most of the space in the bathing room. The steam-filled room was uncomfortably hot and smelled strongly of rose petals.

Inside the pool were perhaps fifteen people, men and women, all of them naked except for the red masks they wore. They were doing things to each other that Quintina had only imagined during her most private moments. Those moments when she thought about Septimus.

But this—she didn't like this. She would never want it to be like this between them. Turning quickly, she walked out of the bathing room, removed the mask, and threw it onto the floor so hard that it broke in half and the jewels scattered. Julia appeared at her side. "You should not show me such things," said Quintina. "It is disrespectful to the goddess. You will make an offering for forgiveness tonight and a private **supplicatio** tomorrow."

Julia's expression fell. "I will. I am sorry."

Quintina marched back toward the atrium, not waiting for Julia to escort her. "It is dangerous for me to be near people like that."

"You are right. I wasn't thinking. We are friends, and sometimes I forget your station. Forgive me, Quintina, please."

The Vestal turned and took Julia's hands in her own. "It is dangerous for you too."

"Quite the opposite." Julia flashed her friend a sly, yet somehow sad, smile. She put her hands on her belly. "The ship is already full. There is no danger of taking on a new passenger."

* * *

Livia dragged her feet as she walked slowly back up the Palatine ramp. At one point she had stopped for several minutes to absently watch a small green lizard with a pointed nose dart back and forth in front of her, climbing the sides of the passageway in frantic search of an escape route and finally finding one through a section of delicate latticework that opened to the outside.

Oh, if only it were that easy, she thought. She peered outside the latticework and realized that she had been standing in the same spot long enough for the light to have changed from day to twilight. The lizard was long gone. She remained trapped.

She had spent as much of the late afternoon and early evening as she could in the House of the Vestals going over various matters with the priestess Pomponia, who, mercifully, did not mention the loss of the baby.

The Vestalis Maxima had been more patient and accommodating than usual. She had even poured Livia's wine herself instead of having a slave do it. Livia suspected it was as close to sentimentality as the two women would ever get.

She would've done almost anything to have remained in the Vestal's company for the rest of the evening rather than return home to yet another dinner party where she and Maecenas would helplessly lock eyes over a plate of seasoned dormice while Octavian's eyes undressed his adviser's wife, recently returned to Rome from the country.

Arriving home after a walk that took far longer than it should have, she nonetheless forced herself to float carefree through the atrium and into the triclinium where the second, or perhaps third, course was already being served.

"I am sorry, husband," she said to Octavian. She then turned to Maecenas and Terentia. "My business with the Vestalis Maxima took longer than expected."

Maecenas looked at her over his wine cup as if to say, "They don't care, and I don't believe you."

She mouthed a silent "sorry" to him as she took her seat next to Octavian. She really shouldn't have abandoned Maecenas for so long. He had been working tirelessly to persuade Octavian to remain married to her.

They both had a vested interest in the continuation of her marriage, for if it ended, they both knew that Octavian wouldn't have to look further than the nearest couch for his next wife. The affair between him and Terentia was becoming a bolder one every day.

Moving as casually as she could, Livia caressed Octavian's arm and then reached across the table for an oyster. Its unexpected slipperiness made her fumble until it landed on her dress with a small but solid thud, leaving an oily stain on the fine fabric.

"Oh, Livia!" Terentia made a little sniff of laughter.

Not **Empress** Livia. Not **Lady** Livia. Just Livia.

At least it gave her a good reason to leave. "Will you excuse me," she said as she stood.

"Where are you going?" asked Octavian.

Livia gritted her teeth. Had he not noticed what happened? Was he so focused on his adviser's wife that he no longer noticed his own, even when she was basically sitting on his lap? "I am going to change dresses, husband," she said as sweetly as she could.

Octavian eyed Terentia. "That gives me a stellar idea," he said. "Let's have you both change dresses. What do you say, Maecenas? We'll have our wives put on a beauty contest for us."

Maecenas opened his mouth but, not knowing what to say, closed it again. His wife leaped up from the couch. "How fun," she said with far more exuberance than the occasion called for. "Caesar, you command a party as well as you command an empire."

Livia gaped at Maecenas, but he looked as astounded as she felt. She turned back to her husband. "Octavian," she said softly, "I don't think our guests—"

"Oh, do be a good sport, Livia," said Terentia. She took Livia by the hand and started to pull her in the direction of her dressing chamber—How did she know where that was?—while at the same time snapping her fingers at Despina, who stood silently against the wall. "Assist us," Terentia ordered.

The slave nonchalantly adjusted a silver bracelet

on her arm, ignored Terentia, and looked to Livia for direction. Her status in Caesar's household afforded her some latitude, even with patrician guests.

Although Livia wasn't in the habit of feeling anything toward her slaves, she was grateful for Despina's gesture of allegiance. "Set out my finest dresses," she said.

"At once, Domina." Despina signaled to another female slave, and the two of them moved quickly out of the triclinium, scurrying ahead to Livia's dressing chamber. Arriving several moments before the two noblewomen, Despina hurriedly gathered Livia's wedding dress, finer gowns, and family jewels and stuffed them unceremoniously into a dirty laundry basket. There was no way she'd let Maecenas's biting little wife wear her mistress's most precious items.

As the two noblewomen entered the cyan and poppy-red painted walls of the sumptuous dressing room, Terentia glided straight to the empress's wardrobe and began rooting through her stolas, knocking rich wraps and beaded fabrics to the ground. Livia had the sudden image of a pig rooting in the mud.

Despina stepped in. "Is there a color you prefer?"

"Find me a green one," said Terentia.

"And you, Domina?"

"Yellow," said Livia. She had always looked best in yellow.

Despina instructed the other slave to dress Terentia while she tended to Livia, only a thin dressing screen between the two women.

She draped the yellow silk dress on the empress, arranging the folds at her waist in an appealing manner and then wrapping a gold, braided rope belt around Livia's midsection. She fussed with the belt until it slid into a position that disguised the still present bulge of her mistress's failed pregnancy.

Retrieving a sapphire-blue palla from the wardrobe, Despina wrapped it prettily around Livia. The contrast of the yellow with the rich blue was a striking one. Livia was pleased. But as she stepped out from behind the dressing screen and saw Terentia, her pleasure faded.

It was painfully evident why Maecenas's wife was widely believed to be the most beautiful woman in Rome, and the benefit of Livia's fine dress made her look even more so. She wore a seafoam-green stola with a deep pink palla on top, a combination that would have looked gaudy on any other woman, but that only accentuated Terentia's exquisite complexion and made her soft, full pink lips look like flower petals.

The slave that had dressed Terentia kept her eyes

on the floor. She had tried to make the fabric bunch or sit unflatteringly on the woman's frame, but it was impossible.

Terentia spun around and ran her hands down the fabric. "He will love this," she said, and then too quickly, "my husband, I mean."

"I know what you meant," said Livia.

Terentia flitted to the jewelry table to greedily scan Livia's selection of bracelets, earrings, and necklaces—all made of the most expensive gold and rare gemstones. Noticing a gold box adorned with brilliant lapis lazuli stones, she grabbed it without asking and opened the lid.

Despina drew in an audible gasp. She had forgotten to hide that.

"Oh my!" Terentia set down the box and pulled out a gold Egyptian diadem, in the center of which was set a ruby-eyed cobra. "Is this what I think it is?" she asked. And then, without waiting for an answer, she lifted it toward her head.

For Livia, it was a Rubicon. She reached out and took it from Terentia's hand. "This is for the heads of royalty."

Despina spoke. "Domina, would you like to wear it?"

Thank you for asking, thought Livia, then answered, "No. It would be uncouth." She inspected Cleopatra's crown with affection, turning it over in her hands. "I remember the day Octavian returned from Alexandria and gave this to me," she said as if reliving a fond private memory.

"Shall we go?" asked Terentia.

"By all means."

Livia strode in front of Terentia, trying to maintain the deportment of queenliness. She was the first to enter the triclinium.

Maecenas clapped his hands as he saw her. "Venus wears yellow this evening," he said good-naturedly.

"Lovely, my wife," said Octavian. He tilted his head, looking past her expectantly. Livia spun around just in time to see Terentia, who had been strategically delaying her grand entrance to maximize its impact, enter the room. She moved over the mosaic floor like a swan moving over water.

Stopping directly in front of Octavian, she twirled girlishly and then twisted a rope of her hair in her fingers. "How do I look?"

"You know how you look," said Octavian. The two of them held eyes.

"But is it enough to win the beauty contest?

Come, Livia, stand beside me. Let us allow the emperor to be Paris and judge between us. Tell us, Caesar, who is the fairest one of all?"

Maecenas coughed and then said, "I'd call it a draw. Who could choose between such beauties?"

"Or perhaps we just need a second round," said Octavian.

"Splendid idea!" said Terentia. Another girlish twirl followed by an equally girlish giggle, and she was off toward the dressing chamber again, all but skipping as she went.

Livia remained standing in front of her husband until the moment became tense and insistent enough that Octavian was forced to look at her. Maecenas busied himself by pretending to select the best grapes from a new bunch that had been set before him. Whatever Caesar and his wife were silently saying to each other, it was their private battle.

Yet after several long moments of tension, it was evident that Livia had lost. Conceding, she followed, subdued and resigned, in Terentia's footsteps.

Back in Livia's dressing room, Terentia had already stripped off the seafoam dress and pink palla. The expensive fabrics were lying in a heap in the middle of the floor, as if she had slipped them off while she walked. The slave was already fitting her in a new dress.

Livia stepped behind the dressing screen. When Terentia turned the other way, she craned her neck and peeked over it. She was being draped in a purple dress. Purple. The color of royalty. The little trollop just wouldn't give up.

"Give me another yellow one," Livia instructed Despina. "A deeper yellow. More color."

Despina shook her head. She held up a simple white stola. "Less color," she whispered.

"Give me the damn yellow one," said Livia.

Again, Despina shook her head. She hooked the white stola on the wall and began to undress Livia.

Why not, thought Livia. Trying to cling to whatever fight she had left in her, she waited while Despina fitted her in the stola. The slave then held out a cloth. "I am going to remove your makeup," she said quietly. Livia nodded.

This time, when the two women stepped out from behind the dressing screen, it was not a war of color. The war was over, one side having surrendered mid-battle. Terentia was a vibrant rainbow in her royal purple stola and shimmering orange palla. Livia was a white cloud, soft and unadorned.

Terentia blinked at Livia and then leaned over, a puff of half surprise, half laughter escaping her lips. A sudden thought occurred to her—**Enter first this time!**—and she shouldered her way in front of the empress, her stride becoming more confident, more alluring, with every step.

She was the first to arrive in the triclinium this round, and she made the most of it. More twirling and giggling. To this, she now added a touch of mischievousness as she toyed with Octavian, pretending to lift her dress and then quickly lowering it again. He played along for several long moments, his arousal evident.

But then, as he had done before, he tilted his head past this woman and looked for the other one. Terentia spun around just in time to see Livia entering the dining room.

Dressed in her immaculate white stola, she looked like a Vestal Virgin entering the temple, the very picture of purity and virtue. Her clear skin and stately beauty, both preserved by an upper-class lifestyle, seemed somehow amplified by the simplicity. She kept her head lowered, modest and demure, and simply stood in the doorway.

"Come here, wife," said Octavian.

She moved slowly, almost apprehensively, until she stood before him. Just as he extended an arm to her, she knelt before him and placed her hands on his knees. Keeping her head lowered, she raised her eyes to gaze up at him as if overwhelmed by being in the presence of such greatness, as if overcome by awe and reverence for him.

"My wife and I will be retiring now," Octavian said to their guests, his voice husky with desire.

Standing, he reached down and took Livia's hands in his own with a gentle softness, sweetly urging her to her feet and then leading her out of the room, toward their bedchamber, as if it were their wedding night and he were a lovestruck groom about to discover his bride for the first time.

Maecenas crunched a grape and stared at the back of his wife's head. She didn't turn around to face him but only stared after Caesar and Livia. He crunched another, this one more loudly. It tasted sweet.

* * *

Livia pulled her palla tightly around herself and rested against the back of the cushioned chair in the open-air courtyard. She blinked up at the statue of

Triton. She heard Tiberius enter but didn't have the energy to look his way. He sat next to her.

"You look tired, Mother," he said.

She poked a finger out from underneath her palla and pointed up at the statue. "I want to replace this."

"With what?"

"A statue of Tantalus."

"Tantalus? Mother, that is hardly inspiring."

"No? I think it is very inspirational. I am like Tantalus, you see. Cursed to stand dry-throated for eternity in the same pool of water, always trying to cup his hands in the water to quench his thirst, but always seeing it recede before he can reach it. It is no different being Caesar's wife." She let her palla drop and held her hands out in front of her. "I am forever trying to grasp onto him, but he is forever drifting away. Yet, I keep trying."

Tiberius spoke softly. "Why don't you just let him divorce you? There is no shame in it. You will want for nothing."

She looked at him incredulously. Although Tiberius had been cursed with his father's blockheadedness as a child, as a man he had grown to acquire Livia's patrician features: large eyes, angular chin, thick hair. If he chose to use them, they could serve him well.

"I will always want one thing," she said to him. "It is the same thing I've wanted since the day Octavian first bedded me right under your idiot father's nose. I want my son to be crowned Caesar."

"And for you to be crowned Caesar's mother."

"Better the mother of Caesar than the wife," she said. "Even Caesar cannot take a new mother."

Tiberius pulled his mother's palla back up around her shoulders. "Julia is pregnant again with Agrippa's child. They may have a son this time. No doubt they will have more children after that. More heirs."

"Heirs die, Tiberius. They have accidents. They eat bad fish or rancid figs. They take ill. Children are especially vulnerable."

"And every one that dies will be replaced by another."

"It doesn't matter," said Livia. "I am like Tantalus. I keep trying."

CHAPTER XI

Cave Canem
Beware of the dog

The Esquiline Hill was the largest of the **septem montes**, or seven hills of Rome, and it had its own history and identity. While the citadel of the Capitoline Hill looked down into the Forum and dazzled those below with its many altars and massive temples, including the temples of Jupiter and Juno, which almost appeared to be suspended in the heavens, and while the Palatine Hill boasted the emperor's domus—and the prestige of being the hill upon which Romulus founded Rome—the Esquiline under Augustus was becoming an increasingly fashionable district for upper-class citizens to build their luxurious urban garden homes.

While the Esquiline Hill hadn't escaped the effects of the contagion, gravity had given it an advantage. Sewage ran downhill, not up. That meant it was better off than many locations in the densely populated city. Moreover, its wealthy residents—including Maecenas, who had built sprawling gardens over an old gravesite—had taken extra steps to keep the area clean. They employed privately owned bands of cleaning slaves rather than relying on state-owned sanitation crews. City workers were too lazy.

But Scorpus the Titan didn't care about any of that.

He didn't care about the sewage or the clogged drains or even the contagion. He didn't care that the emperor's poet, Virgil, had just bought a house by that fountain or that Maecenas often entertained Horace and other great artists by that elaborate library and bathing complex. He only cared about one resident, and that man's name was Soren Calidius Pavo.

After spending weeks in total hiding, Scorpus had been venturing out for the last several nights under the cover of darkness and his own barbarian beard to study Soren's activities and property.

It was good and bad.

Good because Soren's home was lit even less than the homes around it. There were a fair number of torches affixed to the high wall that surrounded the residence, but for whatever reason, Soren's slaves were in the habit of only lighting two or three of them at night.

Good also because the thick padlock on the barred iron gate of what was either a gardener's or slave's entrance—it led directly into the home's courtyard—was so old and abused that Scorpus could see the rust flakes on it from across the street. The slave who was in charge of locking up struggled to do so nightly and half the time didn't double-check to make sure the shackle had caught in the locking latch.

Bad because of the dogs. Soren had two of them—big ones—both of which looked as miserable and hungry as any dog he'd ever seen. A mean-looking sign that read **Cave Canem** hung from the iron gate. Yet Scorpus was far more worried about the dogs' bark than their bite. While a dog that barked during the light of day in an upper-class neighborhood like the Esquiline might be rewarded with a rock to the head, in the dead of night that same dog would be rewarded with a nice piece of meat for its vigilance.

Bad also because of the **vigiles**. Rome's state-funded watchmen worked in shifts from sundown to sunrise, patrolling the streets of the Esquiline just as they did the streets of the other hills and districts of Rome, including the lower-class Subura that lay at the foot of the Esquiline.

The vigiles weren't usually too concerned about things like robbery or rape. People were mostly on their own when it came to such things in the Caput Mundi. If a decent citizen—that is, someone with money—wanted to stay safe at night in Rome, he or she had two options. The first was to venture out with his or her own private retinue of heftier slaves for protection. The second was to not venture out at all. In fact, unless a particularly good dinner party was to be had elsewhere, wealthy Romans didn't leave their houses after nightfall. **That's good**, thought Scorpus. **Soren will be home.**

For the vigiles, the bigger concern was fire. Regardless of the district they patrolled, most of their shift involved ducking into narrow alleys, sifting through piles of garbage, inspecting horse stables and animal barns, and of course keeping an eye on the crowded wooden insulae that most ordinary Romans called home. All it took was one forgotten burning candle, one cracked oil lamp, one neglected brazier, and—**whoosh!**—all Rome would be on fire within a couple of hours. It had happened before. Many times before. Everyone knew it would happen again, but no **vigil** wanted it to happen on his watch or in his patrol area. It was a reliable way to receive a public lashing.

But tonight, Scorpus had a plan for both the dogs and the vigiles.

Shortly before staking out Soren's house this evening, he had started a number of small fires in a row of sheds near the base of the Esquiline, and also in some of the Subura's insulae that stood closest to it.

It was far enough away that wealthy homeowners living in the higher residential areas of the Esquiline, including Soren, wouldn't be alarmed, yet still close enough that the district's vigiles would be called away to help extinguish the flames.

Scorpus hid behind the wide trunk of a leafy tree across the street from Soren's house. There was only one vigil patrolling the winding street where Soren lived, but he was keen and alert and moved efficiently from one residence to the other, poking piles of pruned vegetation with his long stick and peering into storehouses looking for any troublemakers who were ambitious enough to walk this far up the Esquiline.

Scorpus was such a troublemaker. He began to look for better cover as the vigil neared the tree.

Just then, a breathless messenger emerged from a smaller side street and ran up to the vigil. He coughed out a few words and then pointed down the hill to where several fires were burning. They weren't out of control, but those fighting them would need all the help they could get. Both men quickly took off running in the direction of the blazes.

To Scorpus, it was like they were playing their parts in a Greek drama he had written. Keeping low, he crossed the dark, quiet street. He ran along the wall that surrounded Soren's house until he reached the iron gate that led to the courtyard. He bent down and peeked through the bars of the gate, willing his eyes to adjust to the darkness.

As they did, forms came into focus. Both of Soren's very big dogs were staring directly at him, so close their noses almost touched the bars. One remained completely still. The other shook its head, gave a wet sneeze, and then took a step back. It lifted its head, about to bark.

"**Shhh**," whispered Scorpus. "I've got it here." He thrust his hand into the sack he was carrying and gripped the meaty pig leg inside, tossing it through the bars of the gate just as he'd done last night and the night before that. The dog sank its teeth into the bone and then fled into the darkness of the court-yard with it.

The other dog waited patiently. Scorpus retrieved the second pig leg and held it out to the animal through the bars. The dog lowered its head and slowly stepped forward. As gentle as a mother dog picking up her newborn pup, it took the bone in its mouth, turned away, and trotted off to find a private spot to fill its belly.

Scorpus pulled a metal bar from the sack. He slipped it under the shackle of the gate's rusty padlock and broke the locking mechanism with one easy twist of his wrist. He caught the lock before it could hit the stone walkway and felt dusty flakes of rust fall on his sandaled feet.

He crouched down and rummaged through the sack. This time, he pulled out a length of rope and secured it to his belt. Still crouching, he gently pushed open the iron gate. It squeaked—he knew it would—but not loudly and not constantly and, finally, smoothly and silently, as the courtyard opened up before him. He slipped through the gate and then secured it behind him, hiding the sack and broken lock behind some bushes.

Staying low but moving quickly, he crept into and

across the narrow courtyard, past the square pool and fountain in its center, until he reached a pair of fluted columns that stood on either side of a heavy wooden door to the house. He didn't bother to try the door. He knew it would be secured from the inside with a drawbar that would be impossible to break through without waking the gods themselves.

Instead, he edged along the side of the house, still keeping low, and craned his head to look up at the row of windows above him. They were large enough for him to get through, so he kept moving until he came across one that had been left unshuttered.

Slowly, he stood up to his full height and peered inside the window. The kitchen. Probably why it had been left open. To let out the heat of cooking and the smell of whatever supper Soren had stuffed into his stomach.

Or at least that was what Soren wanted him to think. Scorpus knew it was a trap. But Cassandra was inside, somewhere. He had no choice but to step into it.

Poking his head through the open hole of the window, Scorpus strained his eyes. There were no lights anywhere, not a burning candle or torch or lamp. He closed his eyes and listened as intently as he could. No sound either.

He gripped the edge of the window and lifted himself, suddenly appreciative of the training regimen that Soren and Taurus had subjected him to in the ludus. As smoothly as a salamander slipping into a stream, Scorpus slipped into Soren's house.

Once inside the kitchen, he took a few deep breaths and tried to get his bearings. He assumed that, like most Roman houses, all the rooms in Soren's domus—kitchen, bedchambers, dining room, bath room, guest and slave quarters—would be arranged on one level. He wouldn't know for sure until he'd had a chance to look around, though.

But there was an order to doing things. One had to complete the first lap before the second. Before he found Cassandra, he had to kill Soren.

He cleared his mind and proceeded with calm, soundless footsteps across the kitchen floor, extending his arms to avoid bumping into any ill-placed cooking or cleaning items. It was so dark. He exited the kitchen and then wandered around the house, sensing a somewhat unusual layout, until he arrived in what appeared to be Soren's office. A candle had been left burning on a desk. Below the desk, a man was asleep on a straw mat. A knife was balanced on his leg.

Scorpus drew his own blade from his belt and crouched down. Gently, he picked the knife off the sleeping man's leg so it wouldn't fall to the floor with a clatter, and then he slit the man's throat open with it. Blood pulsed out of the man's neck and pooled under his chin to soak into the straw mat below him. The man's eyes opened wide for a moment but then fluttered closed.

Now holding two blades, Scorpus took a step forward to immediately meet eyes in the dark with a second man. This one was pulling down the bottom of his tunica, no doubt just having returned from the latrine. His jaw dropped at the sight of Scorpus, and they stared at each other, frozen, as if they'd both just seen Medusa and been turned to stone.

Then, without really thinking about it, Scorpus threw the dead man's knife at the man standing in front of him. It landed squarely in the middle of his chest with a solid **thump**. The man grunted and looked down at the knife sticking out of his chest. As he put his hands on the hilt to pull it out, Scorpus tucked his own blade into his belt and rushed forward. He grabbed the man's head between his large hands and twisted hard. The bones in the man's neck broke with a muted **pop pop**, and Scorpus silently eased the slumping body to the floor.

The candle on the desk was just bright enough to illuminate the space a few feet in front of Scorpus. Knowing he had no choice but to move forward, he slunk around a corner and into a colonnaded hallway. The narrow space was lit with a few oil lamps hanging from the ceiling. They cast a strange yellow glow. Animal heads and skins, hunting weapons, and bronze statues of the gods lined the walls.

Scorpus's eyes fell upon a certain short sword with a crimson hilt that was displayed proudly above a statue of Hercules. He pulled it off the wall and turned it over in his hands. Beautiful. Perfect.

He sensed movement and looked up to lock eyes with a man standing at the other end of the hallway. He hadn't been there a moment ago. Exploiting a rare moment of hesitation on Scorpus's part, the man shouted, "He's here!"

In an instant, the colonnaded hallway came alive as men emerged from unseen doorways to surround Scorpus. He heard footsteps behind him and instinctively aimed an elbow to his rear, making solid contact with the nose of a man who had somehow gotten close. He heard the man's nose crack and quickly wrapped an arm around his neck, yanking him forward, tripping him over his right knee, and slamming his head into the floor, knocking him unconscious.

He looked up to count two . . . four . . . five more men, all carrying weapons.

The tallest of them rushed clumsily at him. Scorpus backed up, grabbing a fistful of the man's hair and throwing him to the floor in one motion. He tried to scramble to his feet, but Scorpus stomped the man's head into the tile floor, knocking him unconscious.

Two more men charged at the same time, both wielding heavy clubs. They swung at him in unison. Scorpus dropped to one knee to avoid the clubs, then struck back with swift but deep stabs to each man's gut with the crimson-hilted sword. One of them collapsed. The other grimaced and pressed one hand against his wound as his other hand again swung the club. Scorpus rolled out of the way, and the man's club hit the wall, forming a crater in the plaster. Weapons and trophies of various animal parts fell off the wall and scattered noisily across the floor. As the man grunted and struggled to dislodge his club from the wall, Scorpus kicked his legs out from under him, and he crashed onto his stomach, onto his wound, crying out in pain.

Scorpus stood, breathing heavily. Suddenly, he felt his breath leave him as cold, strong hands gripped him from behind and threw him onto his back. He landed heavily, painfully, on his spine. The back of his head throbbed from hitting the tile floor. He blinked at the man standing above him: his face had deep holes along his jawline. Scorpus had seen those before in the arena. They were scars from a spiked club, the type used in gladiator fights.

He heard a voice shouting from somewhere down the corridor. "Stop pissing around and kill him!"

It was Soren.

Scorpus blinked again to clear his vision just in time to see the man above him raise an ax. As it came down, the charioteer rolled his body. The ax shattered the tile only inches from his head. Before the man could raise his weapon again, Scorpus tucked in his legs and shot them out, breaking one of the man's kneecaps. He buckled forward with a grunt and collapsed on top of Scorpus. Yelling madly in a language that Scorpus didn't understand, the downed man began to claw at Scorpus's face, going for his eyes, using his weight to his advantage.

But Scorpus the Titan had pushed horses off his body, never mind a retired gladiator. He wrapped his legs around the man's body and with both hands pushed his chin upward. Clenching his jaw with the effort, Scorpus fought to roll on top of the man and, finally successful, began to mercilessly strike his face from above, over and over again. The man coughed and spat blood as Scorpus stood up, his chest heaving and his muscles burning.

He reached down to retrieve his blade from the floor, when a man's arms unexpectedly tightened around his chest, forcing air out of his lungs and cracking his ribs with an audible **snap**. Scorpus gritted his teeth and slammed his heel bone down on top of the man's bare foot, then lifted a leg and kicked backward, hard, into his groin. The man stumbled backward.

Scorpus held a hand against his broken ribs and looked down the yellow-hued hallway. He opened his mouth to suck in some air, but that made the pain in his ribs flare, so he focused on taking shallower breaths. There was still one man ahead of him: the man's eyes narrowed as he targeted Scorpus, raising a dagger and throwing it with the precise aim of a marksman. Scorpus ducked, and the dagger flew directly into the skull of the limping man behind him.

Straightening, Scorpus eyed the weapons and animal parts that hung crookedly on the walls and lay strewn across the floor. He reached out and pulled a long, sharp animal tusk off the wall. As the man who had thrown the dagger turned to flee, Scorpus rushed him and stabbed him in the back with the tusk. He slumped to the floor.

Scorpus sucked in a few painful breaths and then staggered down the hall, holding his broken ribs with one hand and clutching the bloody animal tusk in the other.

He pushed open a half-closed door and stepped inside a candlelit bedchamber. Soren was there, standing by an open window, holding a dagger. A woman was behind him.

"Cassandra!"

Soren laughed.

As his eyes adjusted to the candlelight, Scorpus saw the woman's face more clearly. It was not Cassandra.

"Where is she?" Scorpus breathed.

Soren said nothing. The Titan dropped the tusk and felt for the rope hanging from his belt.

Amazingly, it was still there. Keeping his eyes fixed on Soren, he began wrapping the rope around his knuckles, the pain in his ribs lessening with every slow, deliberate step toward his master.

Scorpus expected Soren to come at him aggressively, maybe with a wide punch or an indiscriminate stab of the knife. Instead, he leaped out the window. Scorpus jumped out after him, still clutching his rope.

In the dark of night, Scorpus could see the form of Soren running ahead of him across the courtyard, heading toward the iron gate and the relative freedom of the open street. Soren reached the gate several moments before the injured Scorpus did; however, he could not get it open. He shouted an obscenity, shaking the gate as hard as he could. **Why won't it open?**

Soren spun around to face Scorpus. The Titan was smiling and winding the rope menacingly around his hands, advancing slowly but confidently. Even in the darkness, Soren could see the thick muscles of his forearms and the silver scorpion medallion on his black leather wrist cuff.

Cornered, Soren finally attacked. He swung at Scorpus with a wide punch, but Scorpus easily knocked it aside and slipped around Soren's back, wrapping the rope around his neck and kicking his feet out from under him. Soren fell to his knees. His fingers clawed at the rope.

Scorpus sensed light and heat approaching from behind him. Five or six of the house slaves stood behind him, holding torches. "Cassandra!" Scorpus shouted over his shoulder. "Cassandra, hurry!"

"He's come for his woman," said one of the male slaves. "Where is she?"

"I think she's locked in the basement," another replied.

"Who cares?" yelled a third slave. "Do you know what will happen to us if he kills the master?"

Scorpus tightened the rope and felt Soren's body spasm. It would only take another moment.

But then he felt, or rather heard, a solid **thud** on the back of his head. He had been struck with something. Something hard. And sharp. A thick stream of warmth flowed down his back and he opened his eyes wide, trying to prevent his vision from fading.

He had felt this sensation only once before. Years before. Ferox had taken off so fast from the starting gate that Scorpus had lost his footing and struck his head against the side of his chariot. He was dazed until the sixth lap. Had it not been for the instinct and sheer speed of that black horse, he would surely have lost the race.

Scorpus let the rope slip from his fingers. As the slaves closed in around him, as his consciousness faltered, he grasped for the small blade he had fastened to the side of his sandal and used it to quickly cut through the rope he had used to secure the gate.

"Grab him!" he heard one of Soren's slaves shout. "We can't let him get away!"

Scorpus heard more voices, saw more torches. All the commotion had woken the neighbors, who were coming out to investigate. Someone blew a horn to call the vigiles.

Scorpus knew this race was lost. His only hope now was to escape with his life and find another way to get to Cassandra. Even in his panic, even as he scrambled to get away, he began formulating another plan.

He kicked and twisted his body to pull his tunica out of the grasping hands of the slaves closest to him and then stumbled through the iron gate and ran down the street in the dark, quickly dodging the few neighbors who were ambitious enough at this hour to give chase.

The fires lower down the Esquiline had been mostly

extinguished. Only a few orange spots glowed in the distance. Scorpus ran toward them. Bolts of sharp pain shot through his ribs every time his feet hit the ground, and his head throbbed with a deep, disturbing sort of pain that he could feel and hear throbbing in his ears, pounding rhythmically with every beat of his heart.

He ran for a long time, clutching his ribs and fighting to stay conscious, until he finally reached the streets of the Subura. Nearly slipping on some sewage, he slowed to an unsteady walk. There were more people on the streets here. They all carried buckets of water. Some were crying over what they'd lost, others were celebrating what they hadn't. All of them looked as shaken and exhausted as he did. It was easy to blend in.

Feeling the last of his strength drain away, Scorpus turned sharply into a narrow alley that ran between two rows of tall insulae. Laundry hung down from the windows above. A baby was crying somewhere. He thought he heard someone playing a high-pitched pipe but then realized it was just the ringing in his ears.

His steps gradually slowed until they stopped altogether. Ignoring the blood pouring down his back, he fell against the exterior wall of an insula and slid down it until he was sitting on the ground. He lowered his head and pressed his wrists against his forehead.

A few moments later, he heard someone enter the alley, breathing hard as if in pursuit. The dragging footsteps grew closer until the man was standing directly above him.

Without looking up, Scorpus said, "It was a stupid thing to do."

Pomponius crouched down in front of him, gasping for breath and shaking his head in anger. "I've never been accused of being a smart man," he said, "but even I know that."

CHAPTER XII

Dura Lex, sed Lex

A hard law, but still the law

—AN AXIOM OF ROMAN LAW

It was mornings like this one that reminded Pomponia why she was lucky to be a natural early riser. It was so quiet in the House of the Vestals that she could almost hear her own thoughts. Not that she was thinking anything in particular. She had enjoyed an uninterrupted sleep for the first time in weeks and had woken refreshed. She had forgotten what that felt like.

The rejuvenating rest had allowed her to rise hours earlier, even before most of the household slaves. She had taken advantage of it by spending a silent, solitary morning in her office reviewing some documents that Livia had sent regarding Caesar's updating of the fasti.

This Caesar was more fastidious about religious rites than his predecessor. Then again, this Caesar was also still alive and still in power. Those were two conditions that always required the support of the gods. Octavian's meticulous devotion to the Pax Deorum was paying off. And anyway, it was work that Pomponia loved doing. Important work. What could be more important than ensuring the goddess's protection of Rome?

Having accomplished so much so early, she was looking forward to passing some idle time with her brother. She had earned it. She stood up from her desk, adjusted the rope belt tied around the waist of her long white tunica, and headed off to meet him.

Pomponius was already waiting in the atrium when she arrived. She had to smile when she saw him, his nose nearly pressed against the wall as he inspected the intricate design of a fresco. It was a painting of an orange fire burning in a bronze bowl, its flames shooting upward as red sparks transformed into red flower petals before fluttering back down. It was a representation of the sacred fire that burned in the temple's sanctum, and it was as close to seeing the real thing as most men other than the Pontifex Maximus would ever get.

"What is the name of the man who painted this?" he asked.

Pomponia bit her lip. The mural was an old one, having been salvaged and then restored after a fire two centuries earlier had all but destroyed the previous temple. Even then, the artwork was considered ancient. "Hmm, I can't remember right now," she said. "He was Greek."

"Of course he was Greek," said Pomponius. "The best artists are."

"Your friend Virgil is Roman."

"There is an exception to every rule," he said, kissing her on both cheeks and affectionately brushing her hair off her face.

"Does he make progress on his epic for the emperor?"

"Yes, but slow progress. It is his practice to write no more than three lines per day."

"That will drive Caesar mad," Pomponia said, laughing. She slipped her arm around his. "Let's go into the—"

She was interrupted by a temple messenger entering the atrium with a polite clearing of his throat. "High Priestess," he said, "I have a message for you from Senator Pavo. He regrets he cannot attend himself, but Senate is in session and he is needed for a vote."

"What's the message?"

"He asks that you give audience to his brother."

"Certainly. I will send my scribe out with my schedule."

"Senator Pavo was hopeful you could meet with his brother now. He suffered some kind of domestic crisis overnight, and apparently, time is of the essence. The senator regrets that he has not had time to inform himself of the details."

Oh, and I do? thought Pomponia. She sighed inwardly. She wouldn't let this interruption ruin what had so far been a delightful morning. "Show him to my office," she said. She squeezed Pomponius's arm. "Why don't you visit the library and then meet me in the courtyard. I won't be long."

"Of course, sister." As Pomponius wandered off to the library—since his return to Rome, he frequented it often—Pomponia went ahead to her office. It would take a few minutes for the guards outside the house to be satisfied of the guest's identity and to conduct a search of his person to make sure he wasn't hiding any weapons. Although new visitors to the house would be accompanied at all times by two armed guards, every precaution was taken to protect the Vestals, and the guards never deviated from their security protocols.

Pomponia busied herself reviewing another scroll from Livia—she had to remember to praise the empress for her work—until her two guards, Caeso and Publius, appeared in her office doorway. They stood on either side of a hard-faced man. Pomponia tried not to react at the sight of the thick, red, raised welt that ran around his neck like a tight collar. His eyes were bloodshot, as if every vein in them had burst.

Some kind of domestic crisis . . .

She stood and the man introduced himself.

"High Priestess, my name is Soren Calidius Pavo. I am brother to Senator Pavo and cousin to Priestess Tuccia."

"What is your matter, Soren?" asked the Vestal. Pomponia was surprised by her own curtness. There was just something about him that was instantly off-putting. Perhaps it was the way he had entered the room just a half step ahead of the guards.

The guards had noticed it too. Caeso flashed Soren a look that said, **That's as much as we'll take from you**.

"I am the owner of Scorpus the Titan. The chariot driver."

Ah, that's where I've seen you before, thought Pomponia. This was the man she and Quintina had watched whip Scorpus in the Circus Maximus after his unexpected loss. "And?" she prompted.

"He escaped last month from a prison cart. It was believed that he fled the city . . ."

She looked directly at Soren's neck and raised her eyebrows. "Can I assume that he didn't?"

"He broke into my house last night and attempted to take my life. My slaves were able to fight him off."

"How fortunate for you," said Pomponia.

"Yes and no," Soren replied. "The praetor has said he will use the servile law." He pressed his lips together. "All the slaves in my household are to be crucified."

"Ah." Pomponia suddenly realized they were both still standing. She walked out from behind her desk and sat down on a blue-cushioned chair, gesturing for Soren to do the same. He seemed uncertain for a moment but then did so. "I am sorry to hear that," she said. "No doubt it will create a hardship for you."

"It will. Many of my slaves are highly skilled, and I contract them out. Tutors, mostly. I will lose that income. Plus, I will have to buy new ones."

"I am not unsympathetic, Soren. But if you are here to request a pardon for your slaves, I cannot provide one."

"I'm not asking you to pardon all of them, Priestess. Just one. She is very important to me. Her name is Dacia. If my cousin were still alive, I would ask her. I am certain she would do it."

"I knew Tuccia well," said Pomponia, "and I am not so certain." She leaned back in her chair. "May I ask," she said, "why are all your slaves to be crucified? According to the servile law, if a household slave attempts to murder their master, every slave in that household is to be killed. It is a deterrent law. But Scorpus was not living in the house, correct?"

"The praetor believes there was collusion in the household," said Soren, "but there was not. Several of my slaves have children, so if they knew what he was planning they would have told me. I know he acted alone."

One of the guards snorted.

Pomponia looked at him. "Do you have something to add, Caeso?"

"Yes, my lady. I was informed of this at first watch. It was the opinion of the vigiles that slaves within the household granted Scorpus access to the property after dark. A kitchen window was left open for him, probably by a female slave that had been his wife of sorts while in Capua. There was collusion." He looked at Soren. "It's in the official report."

"Where is Scorpus now?" asked Pomponia.

The guard spoke again. "Most likely escaped through the city gates, Priestess. Search parties have been sent out along the Viae Labicana and Tiburtina. But he's miles from Rome by now, I expect."

"I expect so too," Pomponia agreed. Then turning to Soren she said, "I'm sorry, but I cannot pardon your slave . . ." She tried to remember the name.

"Dacia," said Soren. "Priestess, I ask you to reconsider. She is innocent and had no part in this. She has been my slave for years and has never given me any trouble. She is loyal. I had plans to free her so that we could—"

"It is unfortunate you did not do it sooner," said Pomponia. She began to rise from her chair, glancing at the guards as she did so. **We're done. See him out.**

"My brother would disagree with your decision," said Soren.

It was the tone that set Pomponia off. So much for her delightful morning. She leaned back in her chair and met Soren's antagonism with a measured dose of her own.

"Senator Pavo would not have wasted my time with this had he known the details," she said. "He will be standing in the portico by midday apologizing. There is no precedent for a Vestal to pardon a slave. In fact, High Priestess Fabiana specifically forbade it, and I will defer to her authority. And her experience. She lived through the Spartacus uprising, you know."

"Perhaps that biased her."

"Of course it did. Her nephew was a legionary soldier of Crassus. He was captured by Spartacus's men. They crucified him on a hill in full view of his fellow soldiers, including his general and his own cousin, Julius Caesar. The poor man hung on the cross for two days until the crows began to eat him alive, like Zeus's eagle ripping apart Prometheus bound to the cliff."

"No man deserves that."

"Some do. But he didn't. Neither did the other Roman soldiers who were crucified by slaves, always in sight of the army when it was at its weakest. You're an educated man, Soren. You know your history. Crassus had to resort to decimation to gain control of the legions. The servile law and crucifixion are not so different from decimation. The fear of them maintains order. You know what would happen if the slaves who walk our streets, who serve in our homes and even our temples, didn't live in fear of the law."

"My slaves are no threat to Rome or to anyone."

"We wouldn't be having this conversation if that were true." Pomponia contemplated the wound around his neck. Soren tried not to react. "All slaves are a threat to Rome," she continued. "They may lower their heads when they bring your supper, but who knows what is in their hearts? Spartacus's men were as evil as any enemy Rome has faced. There are countless slaves in the empire, and each one is a potential enemy to his master and his master's family."

"With respect, isn't the sacrifice of my other slaves enough? Cannot one be spared?"

"How many are to be killed?"

"Eighteen in the household, nineteen including Dacia."

"So, by this time tomorrow morning, nineteen crosses will stand along the Appian Way outside the city walls. Once Scorpus is caught, it will be twenty, although I suspect his will be the one most visited. That is good. The people need to see that he is no

Titan. He is no god, no legend. He is only a man. And twenty crosses is not so big a number. Six thousand crosses stood along the Via Appia after Crassus defeated Spartacus. They ran for over a hundred miles from Capua to Rome. We cannot encourage a second Spartacus because you have fallen in love with your bed slave. I would not spare a slave of Caesar's, never mind one of yours. It would be a debasement of the Vestal privilege and an insult to the legions that fought and died for Rome." She exhaled tiredly. "Out of respect for Tuccia, I've taken the time to explain my decision. But we are finished now. Good day, Soren."

As she stood, Soren leaned forward, and his hand reached out for her. In the blink of an eye, before she could even process what had happened, Caeso and Publius had lifted him out of his chair and were holding him against the wall. Caeso's hand gripped Soren's already raw neck.

"I meant no harm." Soren looked bewildered. His face contorted in pain as Publius bent one of his arms at an unnatural angle. "You misunderstand . . ."

Caeso looked at Pomponia. "The Carcer?"

The Vestal shook her head. Soren was desperate. He was aggressive. But it was unlikely that a nobleman, even one such as he, would attempt violence against her. Plus, Senator Pavo was a respected politician. He didn't need the scandal of a brother in prison.

"Go home, Soren," said Pomponia. "You have the means to recover from this. You will rebuild your household soon enough."

He seemed to calm himself. "Thank you for your time, Priestess."

Pomponia didn't respond. With a glance at Caeso, she instructed the guards to escort Soren out of her office and the House of the Vestals. She suspected it would not be a pain-free journey for Soren. So be it. Who was she to tell the guards how to do their job?

Trying to swallow her irritation, she poured herself a cup of mint water from the green glass jug on her desk, drank it all at once, and tucked her hair behind her ears. She left her office and headed for the courtyard.

Pomponius was already there, sitting in the same chair he always sat in when he visited, and looking the same as he always did: absorbed in some scroll he had found in the library, an untouched tray of food and drink sitting on the table beside him.

She all but collapsed into the chair next to his. "What are you reading, brother?"

"Aristotle," he said. "An exceptional copy."

Pomponia looked at the scroll. "We may have an original in the vault," she said. "You will have to ask the librarian. And probably bribe him as well." She smiled.

"Money well spent." Pomponius smiled back at his sister. "What was your business, Pomponia? Not pleasant, obviously."

"I don't know how apprised you are of the latest gossip," she said humorlessly, "but Scorpus the Titan—you remember, the chariot driver we saw—well, he escaped from a prison cart last month. The man I just met with was his former master. Scorpus tried to kill him last night. I can understand it too. I felt like strangling him after two minutes."

"What did he want from you?"

"The praetor is going to apply the servile law. Seems that a number of his slaves were in on it, including one that was Scorpus's wife of sorts. He wanted me to spare his bed slave."

"Are you going to?"

"No."

Pomponius rolled up the scroll and took a sip of water. "So, all his slaves will be killed?"

Pomponia nodded absently as she eyed the food

tray. "Yes, all of them." She picked up a bowl of pear slices and began eating them with her fingers.

"That's a hard law," he said.

"Maybe," Pomponia replied, crunching a pear slice between her teeth. "But what good does a soft law do?"

* * *

Soren didn't sleep that night. Dacia was gone. While he had been in the Forum begging that bitch of a priestess to spare her, soldiers had come to his home and removed her and his other house slaves.

Soren had never been in his home without the presence or sound of his slaves. It felt like a different house entirely. He didn't eat lunch or supper and didn't take any wine. There was no one to prepare it or serve it. He hadn't bothered to light any lamps, but had let the night descend unchallenged to fill each room with blackness.

As the first light of day broke through the open window of his bedchamber, he got out of bed and struggled to dress himself, without the aid of his dressing slaves, in a toga. He gave up and put on a tunica instead. He shaved himself and combed his hair.

The streets were busy, and it took him longer than he expected to reach and then pass through the Esquiline gate and finally the less crowded outskirts of Rome.

When Soren arrived at the execution site, he found that a long row of thick wooden posts was already erected and secured to the ground in postholes. These were actually permanent structures as this particular stretch of road just outside the city limits was often used for mass crucifixions.

Crucifixion was, as the Vestal had said, a deterrent. At least that was its overarching purpose. Yes, it could be a source of entertainment. Yes, it could be a just punishment for criminals. But those were just bonuses. The act of crucifying a person, or even better, hundreds or thousands of people at one time, was ultimately a political statement: Rome is in charge. Follow our rules, or this is where you'll end up.

There was just something about the way a body hung on the cross, so exposed and degraded, that worked really well. There was something about the expression of agony on a crucified person's face, about how long it took them to die, that was phenomenally effective.

Try as they might—and they had tried—Rome's

executioners had failed to come up with any other punishment that inspired so great a fear response or such a macabre reputation. The whole process was even more memorable when the crosses were placed at eye level. This let people get nose-to-nose with a kind of pain that stirred a guttural response in even the most numb-to-violence among them.

Nonetheless, crucifixion could be a labor-intensive job for the soldiers who had to carry it out, so they had created some shortcuts. Having permanent posts along the execution route was one time-saver. That way, the condemned, who would be nailed to the crossbeam while on the ground, could simply be hoisted up by a couple of soldiers, and the crossbeam's center hole slipped over the tapered top of the post. Even a single century of soldiers, led by one keen centurion, could have hundreds of crosses standing by midday. It was Roman efficiency at its best: minimum manpower with maximum productivity.

Yet, before the main event of placing the crossbeam onto the post could happen, each of the condemned had to be scourged. This didn't just add another layer of pain to the experience, it also put them in shock, subduing them so they were easier to deal with. That also helped to keep things moving.

It was this phase of the execution that Soren saw upon his arrival. The first slave he recognized was his dressing slave—he could have used him this morning—who had been stripped naked and was now tied to a scourging pole, his arms pulled high over his head and his legs nearly dangling below.

A soldier carrying a mean-looking, leather **flagrum** strolled casually to the pole and was just about to strike the slave's back when he noticed Soren. "Might want to stand back a bit, sir," he said. He held up the whip and then eyed Soren's good tunica. "It splatters."

Soren kept walking. There was only one slave he was here to see. It didn't take much longer for him to spot her—or rather hear her, first. Her voice, soft and pleading, soon rose to a panic-stricken scream of protest.

He passed by two more scourging poles, including one to which Scorpus's woman, Cassandra, was tied. Her back was covered in blood, and she was hanging limp by the wrists. A soldier reached around to slap her on the face, and she jerked back into consciousness.

Soren kept walking until he reached Dacia's pole. She had also been stripped naked, and her hands were tied over her head. Her beautiful, shapely backside was fully exposed to the soldier who stood behind her, although he didn't seem overly impressed. He was too busy chatting idly with the soldier next to him. Their centurion walked by, and both soldiers snapped back to their duties.

As the soldier raised his flagrum and aimed it at Dacia's smooth backside, Soren took a step back. The soldier snapped his whip, and it struck her body with an audible **crack**. Deep red lines appeared across her lower back and buttocks. A moment later, the flesh parted and a fountain of blood poured down her legs. A moment after that, the pain registered, and she let out an excruciated scream, twisting wildly from her tethered wrists until her body spun around and she faced the soldier—and Soren.

"Soren!" she cried out. "Help me!"

He stood like a statue in front of her, unmoving and emotionless.

The soldier glanced at Soren for a moment—this was intriguing—but then spotted his commanding centurion returning and pulled back his whip again, this time striking her across the front of her body, slicing into her bare breasts and midsection. Her eyes went wide and her mouth fell open. Soren counted three seconds until she screamed.

Her left breast had been all but ripped open. Soren looked down at the soldier's flagrum. Like all of them, it had long strips of leather; however, this soldier had gone through the trouble of attaching chunks of lead and shards of bone to them, just for extra impact. No doubt scourging could become a boring job after a while. Innovation kept things interesting.

Dacia opened her mouth to cry out again, but she saw the soldier pull back his whip and take aim for a third lashing. In a pitiful attempt to protect her torn breast, she tried to spin around and present her back to the soldier. The whip caught the side of her body this time. Another stream of blood coursed down her buttocks and over both legs. Another delayed scream.

Soren was grateful she was facing away from him again. There was nothing he could do for her, anyway. He didn't know why he was here. To comfort her? No. To see it through and prove to himself that he could watch it? Perhaps.

The soldier snapped his whip a fourth time, and Dacia's head fell back. Drained of the energy to scream, she instead fell into strange low sobs. It sounded like she was trying to form words, but Soren couldn't be sure.

The soldier was about to whip her again, when he

glanced over his shoulder to see how many bodies still had to be lashed. His shoulders slumped. More than he'd thought. Another cartful had just arrived: overflow from the games the day before, a large huddle of men and women who hadn't been needed in the arena. He'd be here all day if he didn't get a move on.

He curled his whip and attached it to his belt, then approached Dacia and reached over her head to untie her. "Got one for you," he shouted to his colleagues. Two soldiers quickly came to get her, as a third soldier pushed another slave against the scourging pole in her place.

The pair of soldiers dragged her, naked and dazed toward the row of upright wood posts that ran along the roadside. Ten or twelve slaves had already been raised up on crossbeams, and Soren could see Dacia stare at each one in wide-eyed horror as she passed.

A few of the smaller slaves, three youths in their teens didn't warrant the full post-and-crossbeam treatment. Instead, their wrists were wrenched above their heads and hastily nailed to the post, leaving them to hang by the arms. One of the youths was convulsing silently, his eyes fixed straight ahead as if looking at some horror only he could see. The other two were weeping uncontrollably and trying to catch gurgling gasps of air between sobs. With their arms extended above them, they could not take a breath without first lifting their entire body weight using only their impaled wrists. Their faces contorted with the torturous strain of each inhalation.

Pulling her to the first available wooden post, the soldiers pushed Dacia facedown onto a heavy crossbeam that lay near its base. They stretched her arms out to both sides until her palms were pressed against the splintered wood of the beam and her breasts were pushed into the muddy ground.

Soren stood back but Dacia somehow managed to turn her head and spotted him. "Soren, do something! Pray gods, save me! I don't want to die!" He took two steps to the side so she could no longer see him. "Please stop, please stop," she begged the soldiers.

Unmoved, the soldiers worked in unison. Each man knelt on an outstretched arm to hold it in place while leaning over to retrieve a thick rusty nail from a basket.

From where he was standing, Soren could see the soldier who knelt on her left arm position the tip of the nail against the back of Dacia's wrist. She must have felt it and known what was to come, because she cried out "No!" with a force that Soren wouldn't have thought she was still capable of and almost wished she wasn't.

The soldier picked up the hammer that was lying next to him and, with the skill of someone who had performed the action a thousand times, drove the nail through the bones of her wrist with one hard pound.

Dacia pushed her face into the wood of the crossbeam and a guttural cry came out of her throat. Her naked backside lifted and her feet dug into the mud while she writhed, desperately trying to twist free, as the nail's shaft made every nerve in her wrist fire nonstop.

Another pound of a hammer, and the nail was through her right wrist as well. The lower half of her body thrashed against the ground. Her crying stopped for a moment, but then a low groan grew into a sort of howling sound that was so grotesque it made Soren feel physically ill.

He turned around and vomited on the ground.

He turned back just in time to see the soldiers exchange amused grins.

After the nails were in place, each soldier wound a rope around Dacia's wrists and forearms to help support her weight. There was nothing more irritating than having to renail someone to the crossbeam.

The soldiers stood up. Each one grabbed an end of the crossbeam and lifted it high enough that Dacia dangled from it like a fish dangling from a hook. They hoisted it up and then lowered it on the post so that it sat securely in the cross position, with the front of Dacia's body pressed against the post: although both crucified men and women faced the road, the latter were often secured to the back of the post to at least partially obscure their breasts and genitals. This wasn't done out of decency. It was done to make sure the horror of crucifixion didn't descend into a peep show. Gawkers were bad enough. It would be intolerable if the perverts started showing up too.

Their work almost finished, at least for this cross, one of the soldiers retrieved two more rusty nails from the basket. As his colleague pressed Dacia's left ankle against the side of the post, he drove the nail through the bones of her ankle.

She tried to scream—Soren could tell by the way her lips parted—but like the youths hanging from the posts near her, she now struggled to breathe. There was simply no air to waste for crying or calling out. As her lips opened and closed, Soren was again reminded of a fish hanging from a hook, its mouth gaping open and closed.

The soldiers shifted and drove a final nail through her right ankle so that both of her feet now straddled the post. Without bothering to check their work, they turned to head back to the scourging area and their next victim.

Their departure left Soren and Dacia face-to-face, him standing an arm's length away from where she hung reversely on the cross. Her head was hanging to the side, and he could tell by the look in her eyes that she was silently calling out to him, begging him to reach out—he was right there!—and pull the nails out of her wrists, out of her ankles, gather her in his arms, and carry her home, where the pain and the horror of this could stop.

He could also tell by the look in her eyes that she knew he wouldn't do it. He could tell she wanted to scream at him, to say that she hated him, that it was his fault this was happening to her. He was relieved that she didn't have the breath or energy to say it.

As he stared into her eyes, he saw her eyelids flutter as she began to faint. Her body slumped, and her head rolled back. A moment later, the weight of her sagging body snapped the fine bones and ligaments in her wrists and she jerked back into consciousness with a howl of pain. Her breath came in short gasps as she tried to alleviate the strain on her impaled wrists by tightening her knees around the post and pushing her body upward. That effort made a stream of blood spurt out of her left ankle, and she froze. She was quickly realizing that if she tried to relieve the pain and pressure in one area, it only amplified the pain and pressure somewhere else.

As Soren stood before Dacia, two soldiers passed behind him dragging a large male slave toward the post next to hers. This condemned was a lot more trouble, and the soldiers struggled to lay him down on the crossbeam. He yelled and bucked up with muscular legs as his wrists were nailed to the wooden beam. One of his knees just missed hitting a soldier in the groin.

Irritated, the soldier grumbled, "Oh, for the love of Juno." He picked up his hammer and bashed the man's kneecaps until jagged bits of bone flowed out with the blood. He and his colleague waved over two more soldiers, and the four of them lifted the man's crossbeam onto the post. He let out a long, high-pitched scream. The irritated soldier rolled his eyes.

Soren looked at the slave's face. He couldn't remember the man's name but recognized him as one of his more skilled slaves, a Greek geometry tutor.

Soren's nostrils flared in anger. The slave had made him a fortune. As he stared at the man's blanched face, an image of Scorpus's smug face flashed across his mind and he felt his rage rise.

As the soldiers beside him finished nailing the tutor's ankles to the post and headed back to the scourging pole—the Roman machine never stopped—Soren tapped one of them firmly on the shoulder.

The soldier looked at him as if to say, "I wouldn't do that," but then noticed the gold coin in Soren's hand and grew more accommodating.

Soren said nothing but nodded his head toward Dacia. The soldier glanced at her without reaction, plucked the coin out of Soren's palm, and then headed in the other direction.

"Where are you—" began Soren.

The soldier looked back, irked. "I can't do it now," he said under his breath. He pointed to the road, and for the first time, Soren noticed how many people had gathered to watch the mass execution. "There are no games on today," the soldier added, "so it's busier out here than usual. But don't worry, they'll get bored soon enough."

Soren stood where he was, in front of Dacia as she

faded in and out of consciousness, as she whimpered and gasped, as her face contorted beyond expressions of pain, as she constantly tried to adjust herself and find a position that offered some relief, even for a moment, only to find that the effort itself revealed yet another stratum of suffering.

Hour after hour, Soren stood there. His bladder ached to be emptied. Muscle spasms shot through his back, down his legs. He didn't move.

Dacia's gasps didn't stop. They were always the same. Each one a sharp intake of air, as if she were constantly surprised by where she was and what was happening. Her groans didn't stop either. It was wrong of him, that much he knew, but he was almost growing impatient with her. Irritated. For a moment, he understood where the soldiers were coming from.

Morning turned to midday, which turned to afternoon. The crowds hadn't thinned. Each time the soldier who had taken Soren's gold coin walked by, he shrugged as if to say, "It's not my fault. I'll do it when I can."

As afternoon turned into early evening, Soren heard a murmur suddenly running through the crowd of spectators that lined the road.

Within a few minutes, the crowd had thinned to half. A few minutes more, and the road was all but empty. Soren watched the last of the spectators depart, some crying, some murmuring prayers, some consoling each other, all of them visibly upset. Not by the crucifixions. Something else.

The soldier with the gold coin appeared at Soren's side.

"What's happened?" Soren asked.

"News from Campania," said the soldier. Even his face looked drawn and somber. "General Agrippa is dead." The soldier chewed his lip for a moment as he thought about this. He turned to go and then, remembering why he was standing there in the first place, pulled a dagger out of his belt and sliced Dacia's throat open. As Soren took a shocked step backward, the soldier flicked the blood off his blade and then pointed it at the deserted road. "See? I told you they'd get bored soon enough."

CHAPTER XIII

Cui Bono
Who stands to benefit?
—A LEGAL PRINCIPLE

Accompanied by her two guards, Pomponia entered Caesar's home and was greeted in the atrium by Livia.

"He is in his library," said the empress. "I've had Musa give him a mild tonic for his nerves, but he is alert."

"I will try not to upset him," said Pomponia.

"There is no stopping that," Livia replied. She looked at the guards. "Leave us." When she and the Vestal were alone, she took a step closer to Pomponia. "He collapsed when he heard the news. Knocked over an oil lamp and nearly set the dining room ablaze." She looked at the fine emerald-studded scroll box in Pomponia's hands. "He needs time to rest. You know he is frail when it comes to such things. I wish it could wait."

"As do I," said Pomponia. "Truly. I am only following the orders given to me."

Livia sighed and led the Vestal deeper into the house. "Try to get him to take some drink. Musa's mystery Greek potion be damned. A cup of Roman wine will do his nerves more good."

"We are agreed on that," said Pomponia.

They reached Caesar's library, and Livia opened one of the carved, gold-inlaid wooden doors. It was quiet inside, lit by candles and an oil lamp, and Pomponia squinted until Octavian came into view. He was alone, sitting upright on the far edge of a couch against the wall. He could not have looked more grief-stricken if he'd been sculpted by Proserpina herself.

"Husband," Livia said softly, "Priestess Pomponia is here." Octavian nodded and waved the Vestal inside. Livia quietly closed the door and left them alone.

Pomponia walked across the mosaic floor of the library, along a deep yellow and Pompeian-red wall appointed with masterful frescoes of architectural elements. She had been in this room many times with Caesar, Maecenas, and Agrippa. She tried to dismiss the feeling of surrealism, of disorienting loss, that she always felt when someone close to her died.

"Emperor Caesar Augustus, it is my duty as Vestalis Maxima of Rome to deliver to you the authentic last will and testament of General Marcus Vipsanius Agrippa." She opened the bejeweled scroll box and removed the document inside, placing it directly in Caesar's hands. "The general instructed me to put this in your hands immediately upon notice of his death, without delay or ceremony."

Octavian grinned humorlessly. "Without delay or ceremony," he echoed.

"How else would it be with Agrippa?"

"Come, sit, Pomponia."

It was one of the rare times she could remember Caesar using her name without an honorific before it. He did not invite her to call him Octavian. To her knowledge, only Livia, Maecenas, and Agrippa had ever held that level of intimacy with the emperor.

Octavian looked at the scroll in his hands. "How many friends must we say goodbye to?" he asked her.

"Only the gods know that number, Caesar."

"Perhaps it is best that way." He fumbled with the wax seal on the scroll, but his hands shook, and Pomponia heard him swallow hard. "I did not expect this," he said. "Not so soon. Not so suddenly. I thought I would have time to prepare . . . to prepare the . . ."

"All will be done," said Pomponia. "Surely you can take a few moments before reading the will." She poured him a cup of wine from a nearby table, and he took a sip. Then another.

"What should I do first?" he asked himself, as if alone in the room. "Who will I . . ."

"All will be done," Pomponia repeated. "Maecenas is on his way and will already be at work. You can rely on him."

"And who else?"

"The Senate and all Rome. You are a Caesar with many friends and few enemies."

He nodded, but Pomponia knew her words brought no reassurance. Octavian hadn't just lost his best friend. He had lost the man who had helped him build the world's greatest empire. Agrippa had literally fought Octavian's battles for him, and the latter's relative cowardice on the battlefield was well known. It was rumored that he had once hidden behind a bush while Agrippa had roared his legions ahead to victory, all under the red banner of the new Caesar.

To Rome's relief, the friendship between the politician and the soldier had continued beyond the civil war years to lay the foundation for the Pax Romana, the longest period of peace that Rome had enjoyed for generations.

Octavian tapped his fingers against the scroll. "I was no more than a boy when I met Agrippa," he said. "Neither of us yet wore the **toga virilis**." Tilting his head in thought, he turned to look at Pomponia, suddenly sharp and serious. "But we are not so old. Agrippa was healthy as Apollo . . . indestructible as Achilles. How could he have died?" His cool gray eyes moved back and forth, searching for an answer.

Pomponia wondered whether he'd ever find the same one that she had.

She spent the rest of the hour sitting with him, their soft conversation jumping between anecdotes of Agrippa and matters of state. At his request, she prayed to Vesta Aeterna for Agrippa's soul, and then, when he began to nod off, she quietly called for Livia and two slaves, who took him off to bed with the general's will still in his hand. Musa's tonic was doing its work.

A house slave escorted Pomponia back to the atrium and through the portico, out into the cool air of evening. She had just stepped into her lectica—she had been too tired to make the trip to Caesar's house on foot—when Despina poked her head into it.

"I am sorry for the intrusion, Priestess," she said. "May we speak briefly?"

"Of course, come in."

Despina stepped into the lectica and pulled the curtain closed. "I have not had a chance to write you since we learned of Agrippa's death this evening."

"What is the matter?" asked Pomponia, and then added, "Or I should say, what else is the matter?"

"Caesar took a new mistress last night," said Despina.

"Who?"

"Lady Tacita."

Pomponia slumped her shoulders. "Tacita? Priestess Quintina's sister? Are you sure it was her?"

"Yes, I am certain, Priestess. I saw her myself."

"All right," said Pomponia. "Keep doing what you're doing, Despina. Watch them together, especially when they are in bed. Tacita is even worse than Terentia. She is younger, more fertile." She sat back, dejected. "They don't stop, do they, Despina?"

"No, they don't," replied the slave. "But we will not stop either."

* * *

It had taken two full days for the body of the great General Marcus Vipsanius Agrippa to be brought home to Rome. On its way, the somber procession had stopped in Casinum where Agrippa's body was kept overnight in the Temple of Apollo on the citadel.

Inside the temple, priests prayed nonstop for the general's spirit. Outside the temple, fires burned as soldiers and citizens of all ages and classes stood watch, all night long, as if protecting the body of the general who had spent his life protecting them.

Long before daybreak, the procession departed. Road and municipal officials had quickly marshaled their resources to arrange for fresh horses and supplies to be stationed at every fifteenth milestone along the Via Latina, a road that had for centuries connected Campania with Rome. Romans were nothing if not organized.

News of the general's death had spread fast, and in addition to the old cypress trees and elaborate family tombs that lined the Via Latina, crowds of mourners had flocked to the roadside to watch the procession pass. Vendors moved among them, selling everything from sweets to wooden toy soldiers with the name Agrippa carved into the armor. Children dressed as young Agrippas battled each other with wooden swords.

It was after nightfall by the time the procession arrived at the Via Appia and passed through the Porta Capena to finally enter the city of Rome. To the lictors, priests, and soldiers that had accompanied the procession from Campania to Rome, this last stretch through the city itself seemed to be the longest part of the journey, their pace having slowed to a crawl as Agrippa's body—now raised on a bier—inched its way through the crowds and the mourning stops that had been scheduled along the way.

At last, the procession entered the political and religious heart of the Roman world: the Forum. It moved along the cobblestone street and passed through the shadows cast by torches affixed to the monumental temples and basilicas until it reached the Milliarium Aureum, the Golden Milestone. All roads in the empire led to Rome, to this very spot. The procession then continued to the nearby Rostra.

Although the Roman Forum was usually closed to the public come nightfall, the emperor had instructed that Agrippa's body be placed on the Rostra upon its arrival in Rome and that the Forum remain open, albeit heavily guarded, so that the people could look upon their general. Despite a rise to power that was second only to Caesar's—some might say nearly equal—Agrippa was a plebeian by birth and had always remained a man of the people. Octavian knew how to pick his battles; had he closed the Forum, he would have had to contend with a virtual riot.

The fires that burned on and around the Rostra had been lit from the **viva flamma**, the living flame from the nearby Temple of Vesta. Caesar passed a sleepless night staring down into the Forum from his estate on the Palatine Hill above, his eyes fixed on the distant orange flames as the songs and prayers from the Rostra floated up to him.

As the first red of sunrise painted the sky, the emperor and empress walked down the Palatine ramp to and then through the House of the Vestals. As they emerged from its portico to step onto the Via Sacra, Caesar smiled sadly at the sight of the young Vestal novices kneeling before him on the cobblestone street, black pallas wrapped around their small shoulders.

The imperial couple continued to walk along the Via Sacra to the Rostra. Although he hadn't donned armor since Actium, Octavian had chosen to forgo his imperial purple toga and to instead wear a military uniform. Livia wore a deep purple stola with a black palla, while the Vestalis Maxima who followed behind her wore the ceremonial white stola and headdress of her station, a black mourning palla replacing her usual white one.

Led by lictors and accompanied by priests and centurion soldiers, they all walked with lowered heads to the Rostra, where Agrippa's widow, Julia, sat soberly on a plain wooden chair. Decorated or cushioned chairs would have been disrespectful. It was not proper to focus on comfort while grieving the dead. Julia's hands rested on a noticeably distended belly. Tiberius sat on a wooden chair near her with an empty seat reserved for the empress between them.

The Rostra itself was surrounded by a somber gathering of even more soldiers, priests, senators, and noblemen. Fires burned on the great marble platform; red banners with **SPQR** in gold hung from tall posts; and the Aquila, the golden Eagle of Rome, perched high above the general's body.

Dressed in full military attire, Agrippa's gold-plated armor shone in the early morning sun. A newly minted gold coin had been placed in his mouth to pay the ferryman Charon to cross the River Styx and take him to the afterlife.

Caesar ascended the Rostra to the sound of beating drums. As he did, Pomponia poured a small libation of oil into one of the bronze firebowls that burned along the front of the platform. She then lifted the bowl by its two handles and carried it onto the Rostra after the emperor. She stood well behind him, between two black-robed priests of Pluto, god of the underworld, and placed the firebowl on a white pedestal. A horn sounded, and the crowd fell silent.

Octavian stood near the edge of the raised platform and opened his arms. It had been years since Pomponia, the Senate, or the people of Rome had seen him like this: dressed in his gleaming armor, a purple cloak embroidered with gold hanging from his shoulders, a gladius at his side. The formed muscle cuirass around his torso was embossed with ornamental stars and figures of the gods. In its center, a snarling she-wolf made of black hematite gazed out at the world. The message was clear: Agrippa was great, but Caesar is greater.

As Pomponia looked into the crowd of mourners, she noticed Mae-cenas. He assessed the crowd's awestruck reaction to the sight of Caesar on the

Rostra and nodded approvingly. She had been correct. Octavian's adviser was on top of things.

A horn blew again, and then the only sound was Caesar's voice, strong and clear, echoing off the marble around him. "My fellow Romans, it is proper that we bid farewell to our general here on the Rostra, surrounded by the rich spoils and rare treasures of his many victories, under the eyes of Father Jupiter on the Capitoline Hill and near the Senate, the symbol of lawfulness and order that Agrippa always upheld." He took the few steps to where Agrippa's body lay strewn with flowers on a bier, placing one hand on the general's head and raising the other in the air. "General Agrippa, by decree of the Senate and the people of Rome, the highest powers were bestowed upon you. It was made law that no one in any province of the empire would have greater imperium than you." He looked down at the body. When he spoke again, his voice quavered but quickly recovered. "You were raised to a great height by our friendship, but mostly through your own extraordinary accomplishments, which all men acknowledged."

After reciting Agrippa's many military achievements and honors—all from memory—Caesar held out his hand and a soldier slapped a scroll into his palm. Octavian held it up high. "This is the last will and testament of General Marcus Vipsanius Agrippa, kept unmolested and true by the Vestal priestesses in the temple. In it, he leaves to the emperor of Rome the entirety of his personal fortune and also all monies, materials, and slaves connected to the building of the Pantheon, bridges, aqueducts, and the expansion of the Cloaca Maxima. To the Senate and the people of Rome, he leaves the Basilica of Neptune and his extensive gardens and properties in the Campus Martius. Consistent with the love General Agrippa had for the people of Rome, I, Caesar, pledge to distribute four hundred sesterces to every citizen from the general's estate."

Handing the scroll back to the soldier amid a mixture of cheers and shouted prayers of gratitude—it was a very generous amount—Octavian again put his hands out to command silence.

"As Caesar and as friend to General Agrippa, I also pledge to continue his good works of infrastructure and to complete construction of the Pantheon in his name." He turned to Pomponia who held her palms up over the firebowl. "Our Vestalis Maxima prays to Mother Vesta that our protecting goddess's sacred flame will light Agrippa's way to the afterlife. May he who served Rome on the red fields of battle now take rest in the green fields of Elysium . . ." His voice quavered, more this time. "He was a wolf of Rome . . ."

For a moment, no one was sure whether Caesar would keep speaking or not. In a move that impressed Pomponia as much as it surprised her, Tiberius stood up, thrust his arm out in a soldierly salute, and shouted, "Hail, Caesar!"

A roar of "**Hail, Caesar!**" moved through the crowd. Octavian looked down at Tiberius and returned the salute. It was exactly the backup he needed, and he could not have looked more the master of the world, dressed in his armor, standing high above the masses with his soldiers at his feet, all against a backdrop of Rome's magnificent buildings and flowing scarlet banners.

Caesar waited on the Rostra while six legionary soldiers who had served under Agrippa raised his body on the bier and carried it off the platform. It was time for the funeral procession to the general's final resting place. The mausoleum of Augustus. It didn't matter that Agrippa had built his own mausoleum. If the emperor wanted his general's eternal resting place to be in his imperial mausoleum, where his own ashes would one day rest, that was how it would be.

The soldiers carried Agrippa's body at shoulder level through the streets of the Forum, exiting it to continue to the mausoleum among a parade of soldiers, priests, dancers, and music makers. It was a spectacle that all Rome had come out to see, and soon the cobblestone was covered in flowers and fresh fruit that mourners tossed to sweeten the general's journey.

Octavian and Livia, as well as Tiberius and Julia, followed close behind the bier. Behind them followed the chief priests, including Pomponia as chief Vestal. After the priests came Agrippa's extended family, as well as actors who wore masks molded from the actual death masks of Agrippa's ancestors. Romans never forgot their dead, and certainly not the dead of their own family. It would be a sacrilege.

It was midday by the time they arrived at Caesar's massive mausoleum complex not far from the banks of the Tiber. An expansive circular structure, it had required the clearing of several city blocks to accommodate its ambitious plan: a central, round structure, built in layers, overlaid with the finest white marble and topped off with a gleaming bronze roof and a colossal bronze statue of Augustus, one arm raised in command, high enough to be seen from far away. Around the perimeter of the roof, a small forest of cypress trees had been planted to give the illusion that the great mound of the mausoleum was at once above and below the ground.

The bier carrying Agrippa's body stopped before a circular iron fence as if saying its final farewell to the people of Rome. The gate opened and the bier moved through it to the sound of beating drums. Only the imperial family followed it inside the gates.

Stocked with towering black poplar trees and flowers of every color and variety, the private garden space inside the fence was alive with chirping birds and fluttering butterflies. It was a man-made version of the Elysian Fields and a natural, if not poignant, location for the **ustrinum**—the imperial funeral pyre—which stood near the mausoleum.

A powerful fire was already burning. Octavian approached the body of Agrippa and with Tiberius's help removed the dead man's armor, gladius, belt, and boots so that he wore only the soldier's red tunica. Octavian looked into the face of his friend, his partner in all things, for the last time.

"I don't know where the years have gone," he said to Livia. "So many battles, so many plans . . . although at this moment I cannot remember any of them."

"Your memories will return to comfort you, husband." Livia took his hand.

As soldiers hoisted the body of Agrippa on top of the pyre, Julia removed her jewelry and threw it into the fire. More riches to pay Charon.

The general's young wife had not said a word nor cried a tear this day, yet not even those closest to her would have been able to read her thoughts: **He left Rome to get away from me. I should have been kinder. He did not deserve this. Now my father has no one. Now my children will be fatherless.**

The flames roared up and engulfed Agrippa's body, snapping and crackling and sending out so much heat that those present had to take a step back. It burned strong and loud for a long time as it reduced the general to bone and ash.

At long last, the fire abated, and four black-robed priests of Pluto doused the burning embers with wine. One of them held out a gold urn as the emperor and Julia went through the remains of the fire, scooping out wet ash and bone and placing it in the urn.

That done, the priests led Octavian, Livia, Julia, and Tiberius past two wide pillars and into the heart of the enormous cylindrical mausoleum. As they moved deeper into it and neared the chamber where the urn would be enshrined, Livia took Octavian's hand. The ashes of Marcellus and Octavia were already here, contained in similar gold urns and housed in marble niches. Life-size statues of them stood behind the urns. Octavia's features in particular were so real that it seemed she would part her marble lips and speak at any moment. Octavian looked at it for a moment and quickly looked away.

Finally, a priest placed Agrippa's urn on a pedestal in the niche next to Octavia's. Three other niches remained empty: they awaited the remains of Octavian, Livia, and Julia.

Julia stared into the niche that would one day contain a gold urn of her ashes, the vessel that would so silently and finally enclose everything that she had ever been or said or felt or done. In the midst of her musings, she felt eyes on her and looked up to see Livia staring at her.

For whatever reason, Julia suddenly felt herself becoming more protective of her husband in death than she ever had been in life. She held Livia's stare. **I know you did this**, she said with her eyes. She put her hands on her pregnant belly. **And yet an Agrippa may still be Caesar's heir.**

CHAPTER XIV

**Bene Qui Coniciet, Vatem
Hunc Perhibebo Optimum**
I shall always think the best
guesser is the best prophet.
—CICERO

". . . So anyway, my brother wants me to speak for him in the assembly and support him in his bid to be aedile. It will be a good appointment for my family. You don't have any objections, do you?" The young priestess Lucasta stoked the hearth fire within the sanctum of the Temple of Vesta and looked at Pomponia, who was on watch with her.

"Not at all," the chief Vestal replied distractedly. "I wish him success."

Lucasta stoked the fire again. She was tired, but not because of the late hour. Everyone was tired. The unexpected death of General Agrippa had affected the whole city, especially those who knew him personally. That included the Vestal priestesses.

"What do you think killed the general?" asked Lucasta.

"The same thing that kills all of us," Pomponia replied. "Living."

Although her station as Vestalis Maxima meant that Pomponia could appoint another Vestal to take her late-night watches, she usually didn't. She didn't want the other priestesses to think she was getting lazy. Plus, she found them peaceful.

Pomponia stood on her tiptoes to reach a flickering oil lamp affixed to one of the columns that encircled the sanctum. She refilled it with olive oil, and it sputtered back to life, making the temple grow a little brighter.

"That is no answer, sister," said Lucasta.

"Do not ask questions I cannot answer," replied Pomponia. She leaned her back against the cool marble of the temple's wall. "I am sorry, Lucasta. I do not mean to snap."

"Would you like me to fetch you something to eat? I didn't see you at supper."

"I will tell Caeso to have a novice bring us something," said Pomponia. "We will both eat." She crossed the floor of the temple and pushed open a bronze door, nearly knocking the Vestal Cossinia off the top step outside.

"What is the matter?" Pomponia asked.

"Caesar has sent for you," said Cossinia. "A messenger has just arrived from Carthage . . ."

"Oh gods," Pomponia replied. Messengers who arrived at night never brought good news. She closed her eyes for a moment and steadied herself against the wall, not quite ready to take the brunt of another blow.

"A number of temples in the city were attacked by a marauding tribe. They snuck into the forum to steal gold and . . ."

"And?"

"And Priestess Corina was killed. Her guards left their post during the onslaught, and tribesmen entered the temple. She died trying to protect the sacred fire."

"**Mea dea**," said Lucasta.

Pomponia pulled the veil off her head in frustration. She had sent Priestess Corina to the Roman colony of Carthage several years earlier, not long after Corina had become a full Vestal. "Stay with Lucasta," Pomponia said to Cossinia. "Pray. I will consult with Caesar and see what is to be done."

Pomponia left the temple as Cossinia entered it. She ran down the steps where Caeso, Publius, and Ankhu were waiting for their instructions.

"Ankhu," she said, "go prepare for a journey. When I return from seeing Caesar, I will write letters to the other temples. They need to know what has happened and how it will change the roster. You will leave tonight to deliver them. Take what you need."

"Yes, Domina." The Egyptian freedman was gone in an instant. **He is winged Mercury**, thought Pomponia. **He always was.**

She decided to forgo her lectica and instead walked briskly alongside Caeso and Publius up the passageway of the Palatine ramp and through the walled imperial grounds to Caesar's house. The exercise would help her think.

Despina was waiting in the portico and escorted her into Caesar's library where he, Tiberius, and Maecenas had been having a late-night strategy meeting. They were still dealing with the complicated consequences of Agrippa's death: from his public works that targeted the contagion to the foreign military campaigns he oversaw, the general's death had left a void.

All three men stood to greet Pomponia. She was suddenly aware that she was not wearing her veil, but no one seemed to notice or care. They had bigger things to worry about.

"Please sit," she said while taking the empty chair between Maecenas and Tiberius. Caesar sat across from them at his desk.

"The killing of a Roman priestess is a sacrilege," said Octavian. "The proconsul in Carthage has already dispensed two cohorts to hunt down the tribesmen. Our priority right now is to reaffirm our commitment to our temples in the province."

Tiberius consulted the wax tablet on his lap. "Just last month, we settled an additional six thousand veterans in the region, all of them receiving fine land grants. The province is entirely Romanized, from architecture to administration. Trade has been uneventful. Despite this unfortunate incident, the legions there have good control. Handled properly, this won't create any larger issues."

"I understand, Tiberius," Pomponia replied. "I will be sending Priestesses Nona and Sabina. They will relocate there permanently."

"Why those priestesses?" asked Maecenas.

"They are well balanced," said Pomponia. "Nona's

age will command respect. And all three of you know how Sabina is. She is sunshine. The people will love her, and she has the best chance of appeasing the native people there. Some of their traditions, especially regarding the religious nature of fire, are not so different from our own."

"That is wise," said Maecenas. He looked at Octavian. "This should not affect Rome's policy of religious tolerance in the region. If they can keep their gods and traditions, they will be easier to rule."

"As long as they pay their taxes," said Caesar, "they can pray to whatever crude gods they wish. When will the priestesses leave?"

"The day after tomorrow," said Pomponia. "I will need a day to prepare their orders and brief them. They will not be surprised by the posting. They already knew they were the priestesses to be dispatched should a crisis happen in one of the provinces."

Octavian sat back in his chair and dragged his fingers through his hair. "My divine father was proud of the work he did rebuilding and Romanizing Carthage. We need it for everything from olives to lions, but Tiberius hits the mark. I need the land for veterans. They want a Rome in Africa, and they shall have it. That includes our temples and our priestesses."

"Yes, Caesar," said Pomponia.

Tiberius uncurled a scroll, read it, and then said, "Apparently three marauders managed to enter Vesta's temple. The guards were able to protect one priestess, but Priestess Corina was slain trying to prevent"—his face hardened—"trying to prevent one of the marauders from pissing on the sacred fire. Her guards returned shortly thereafter and are pleading mercy, saying they only left their post to defend another temple they felt was under more imminent threat. What shall we do with them?"

"Have them lashed and executed," said Pomponia.

Tiberius nodded.

"Is there anything else you require?" Octavian asked the Vestal.

"Not urgently. But there is something I've been meaning to speak with you about, and it does touch on this."

"Go ahead," said Octavian.

"Before General Agrippa died," she said, "he had spoken to me about improving the drain and expanding the section of the Cloaca Maxima that runs underground near the temple. He said it could be used as an escape route for the priestesses in the event of invasion or fire. As you know, the drain is very big, big enough that Agrippa himself could stand up inside it. If we needed to, we could escape through it, all the way to the Tiber or any spot before that, with embers from the fire, other sacred objects, and important documents, including your will."

Maecenas waved his stylus in the air. "That is easily enough done," he said. "We could build a secret drain in the House of the Vestals and a tunnel that connects to the Cloaca Maxima. It's a small matter for the engineers. And, Caesar, it does give you and the empress an additional escape route as well."

"I would like to do this here in Rome," said Pomponia, "but I would also like to see whether we could do something similar in other temples, starting with Carthage."

"I will have monies allocated and send an engineering team to consult with you," said Octavian.

"Thank you, Caesar. That is all."

"Very good. Let us meet again after the priestesses have been dispatched."

The men bade Pomponia good evening as she rose from her chair and left the library. Despina met her in the antechamber and walked her back to the atrium and outside into the portico of Caesar's home, where Caeso and Publius awaited her.

"Where is the empress this evening?" asked Pomponia.

"She turned in early tonight," Despina replied. "Lady Julia is still awake and had intended to greet you, but she is in the bath, trying to get some relief."

"Is it anything to be concerned about?"

"No, only the effects of this late-stage pregnancy," said the slave. "The baby is due any day, and Lady Julia is quite uncomfortable at night."

"Poor girl. Give her my best."

"Yes, Priestess. I am sorry to hear what befell Priestess Corina. I remember her, although still as a novice."

"Me too, Despina. Time seems to stop at a certain point when we think of someone, does it not? Very strange. Anyway, thank you for your kind words."

"**Bonam noctem**, High Priestess."

Bonam noctem, thought Pomponia. **Good night.** There was nothing good about it.

Accompanied by Caeso and Publius, Pomponia walked purposefully across Caesar's estate, down the Palatine ramp, and back to the House of the Vestals. She entered the vestibule to find her sister Vestals

Nona, Sabina, Lucretia, and Caecilia waiting for her. A moment later, Quintina arrived with Marcella.

"Who is on watch?" Pomponia asked.

"Lucasta and Cossinia," said Nona.

"Oh yes . . . of course . . ."

The elder Nona embraced the chief Vestal. "Sabina and I are ready to do our duty," she said.

Pomponia wrapped her arms tightly around Nona. "You have been a mother to me all these years. You and Fabiana. I do not know what I will do without you." The chief Vestal pulled back and wiped her eyes.

Sabina reached out to touch her shoulder. "It is all right, Pomponia," she said. "It is as the goddess wishes. It will be an adventure."

"Sabina," said the high priestess, "you may think of yourself as a grown woman, but I will always see you as a small child stepping on the rosebushes and trying to catch the fish in the pool." She put her hands over her eyes, trying to withstand the memories washing over her. "I feel like I am losing a mother and a daughter on the same night . . . and yet, it must be done."

"Yes, it must," said Nona. She stroked Pomponia's hair. "This is why Fabiana made you the Vestalis Maxima. You always do what must be done."

CHAPTER XV

In Vino Veritas

In wine there is truth.

—A ROMAN ADAGE

CAPUA

Soren put his hands behind his head and looked up at the bare breasts of Mettius's widow, Aelina, as they bounced above him.

"Slow down," he said.

She moaned, and he grinned. The woman was as eager as any prostitute he'd had in Pompeii, but he doubted Mettius had enjoyed her enthusiasm very often. He slipped a finger between her legs and she shuddered and screamed in the way she always did when she climaxed. He reached up and clutched the back of her hair, pulling her off him and then directing her head to his groin. He dug the back of his head into the pillow until his release came in waves.

She collapsed next to him, kicking the covers

away so they both lay naked and exposed. Her hand caressed his chest as his breathing returned to normal.

"That was amazing," she whispered in his ear.

He sat up and drained the rest of a wine cup that was sitting on a table next to the bed. "Mettius once told me about two performance slaves that are very well known in Capua. One is a boxer, the other a singer."

She put her arm over his lap. "Thracius and Anchises."

"I want to buy them. Do you know who owns them?"

She nodded playfully and looked up at him. "Of course. I know everyone in Capua. You're lucky to have me." She sat up next to him, not bothering to cover herself. "Do you know who else has been lucky to have me? Thracius the boxer. My friend's husband owns him. She sent him to me last year for the Lupercalia."

"I thought Mettius said they were dainties."

"The singer Anchises is. But Thracius is a boxer. He'd penetrate anything you put in front of him."

"Do you think her husband will sell them?"

"He **is** selling them. They're having an auction on

the ides." She nuzzled into his shoulder. "Why? Do you want to bid on them?"

Soren tensed. "No, I don't want to bid on them. I want to buy them."

Aelina ran her fingers through his hair. "Now, now," she said, pacifying him. "I am sure you can afford to place a winning bid."

"I don't like taking chances," said Soren. "I want to own them. I want to take them to Rome to perform." He reached for a gold cuff on the table beside the bed and fastened it around his wrist as he spoke. "Do you know who else will be bidding on them?"

"I know four or five who will bid, but if you're serious, there's only one who would be real competition. Manius. His wife has been begging him to buy them for her." She nuzzled into him again. "She tells the fool that she can't live without the voice of Anchises in her home, but everyone knows it's Thracius she wants under her roof." She giggled. "So to speak."

"Can you find out from her what her husband will bid?"

Aelina bit her lip. "She doesn't trust me . . ."

"Oh? Why not?"

"Try to guess," she said mischievously, sliding down onto her back.

Soren slid down and forced himself to put his arm around her affectionately. "You're a pot of honey," he said into her ear. "I'm sure you could tempt Manius to dip his fingers back in." Soren moved his hand down, between her legs.

She giggled again. "Say please."

Soren moved his fingers, and she sighed. "You say please," he said.

* * *

It had taken two costly amphorae of Soren's best **vinum atrum**, red wine from the expensive vineyards of Caecubus, before Aelina could coax Manius into a pliant-enough state to reveal his bid. But she had done it. Soren couldn't stand her—she was nothing like Dacia—but he had to admit she was useful enough, both in and out of bed.

Manius's bid was a serious one. For this auction, all the bids had to be for both slaves. Their current owner, Lucius Bassus, knew they commanded a much higher price together than apart. He had made a large part of his fortune touring the two of them throughout the wealthy Campania and Bruttium regions: Anchises would open with a song, and then Thracius would knock some unfortunate soul into Hades. For years, Bassus had touted them as Apollo's Pair, Apollo being both the god of music and the patron god of boxing. As a marketing strategy, it was equal parts pious and profitable.

Soren rolled Manius's bid around in his mind. One and a half million sesterces to buy Thracius outright, and a lease to own Anchises for half a million sesterces a year for three years, with a penalty-free option to break the lease and return Anchises in the event that Thracius was killed during a boxing match.

It was a price that would make Midas think twice. But Soren wanted them. Even as he raged at the amount, even as he beat Aelina's slaves out of frustration, even as he shattered her fine bowls and statuettes against the wall, he knew he would outbid Manius.

And so he had arranged for the coin to be brought from Rome. He had Aelina's slaves dress him in one of his finest togas and the two of them rode in a litter to the auction house which, to his surprise, wasn't an auction house at all but rather Manius's palatial home.

As Aelina hung on his arm and introduced him to her intensely unlikable friends, Soren tried to ignore the mind-numbing small talk of Capua's patrician classes by downing yet another cup of wine. It was excellent wine. At least he couldn't complain about that.

"Is this not the most pleasant slave auction you've ever attended?" Aelina asked him.

"It's the cleanest," Soren replied. "And the quietest. Usually, you can't hear yourself think for all the crying and screaming."

After what seemed like the twentieth course of meats and a variety of slave performances, including a mock orgy that Soren found altogether uninspiring, the host and seller, Lucius Bassus, stepped into the center of his colorful triclinium and raised his arms in the air.

"Friends and associates," he said charmingly, "my wife and I would like to thank you for your friendship these past years in our beautiful Capua. As you know, we are retiring to our estate in Capri and so will be selling our entire slave inventory, except our personal house and business slaves. We are here today not just for the sale but also for the celebration of Apollo's Pair, two performers you are all well acquainted with. First, the incarnation of Orpheus himself, the voice that every lyre longs for, the virtuoso Anchises."

The gathering broke into fervent applause as a

fair-haired, middle-aged man wearing an indigo tunica with a gold border joined his owner in the center of the room. Had it not been for the letters **LB** tattooed on his forearm, Soren would have been unable to tell which man was the master and which the slave. Anchises smiled warmly at those around him, clearly on familiar and friendly terms with many of them.

"Second, the mortal rival of Hercules, the fists that Father Mars himself would duck to avoid"—at that, everyone laughed and Bassus happily continued—"the boxer Thracius."

Soren inspected the boxer as he walked across the room. He had half expected—dreaded—that this athlete might resemble Scorpus, but Thracius could not have been more different in appearance or demeanor. He was bulkier and younger than Scorpus was, not nearly as tall, and had none of the charioteer's sharp, shrewd features. Like Anchises, he wore an indigo tunica and had the letters **LB** tattooed on his forearm. He moved humbly amid the applause, his head almost down, even as men patted him on the back and women cooed admiringly. He stood next to Anchises and gave him an uncertain look. The singer took his hand. **It will be fine.**

"Friends and associates," said Bassus, "this is a blind auction, where the single highest bid wins. Each bidder will submit his bid in private to my clerk here. The winning bid will be announced immediately after all bids have been registered and read."

A murmur of excitement moved through the gathering.

"I will remind you of this sale's special terms," the host continued. "Thracius is to be manumitted upon retirement or no more than ten years from the date of purchase, whichever is sooner. Anchises is to be manumitted at the same time as Thracius or no more than ten years from the date of purchase, whichever is sooner."

Anchises raised his eyebrows. "If I live that long," he said lightly, and again the crowd laughed.

"Neither slave may be sold as arena kill. Further, both slaves may be used for intimate purposes by their owner or other authorized persons, but neither may be sold as prostitutes."

Several heads nodded. Those seemed like reasonable conditions. The new owner was not restricted from exploiting Thracius's sex appeal for extra profit, yet the boxer was protected from being sold into a life of forced prostitution, regardless of how much a brothel owner might offer. It was a clause that allowed a conscientious or grateful owner to extend some kind of protection into the slave's subsequent ownership. It was not merely a symbolic clause either, but rather one that a high-profile slave such as Thracius could expect to be upheld under the law.

"Let the bidding begin," said Bassus.

Excited chatter ran through the gathering as the clerk ushered each bidder, one at a time, into Bassus's **tablinum**, where each offer was registered.

The process went quickly: after submitting his bid, Soren barely had time to empty his bladder and finish a fourth cup of wine before the clerk returned to the triclinium with the results. He whispered into his master's ear.

Bassus smiled. It was even higher than he'd expected. "Congratulations are in order to you, Soren Calidius Pavo," he said. "Our new friend from Rome is the new owner of Apollo's Pair."

Instantly, Soren found himself surrounded by a throng of well-wishers congratulating him on his purchase and questioning him: **Will you take them to Rome? Will they perform for Caesar? Will Thracius box in the amphitheater or fight in the Circus Maximus?**

Only the wife of Manius seemed displeased. She gave her openmouthed husband an accusatory glare, angrily fingered the string of fine glass beads around her neck, and then headed straight for the meat table.

As the gathering continued to swarm the successful bidder, the two auction items moved aside to speak privately.

Thracius shook his head. "What happened?" he asked Anchises. "The master said Manius was going to buy us. You said he would."

Anchises's mind was racing. "I don't know . . ."

"But what will happen—"

"Quiet, Thracius," said Anchises. He pulled the boxer into a corner of the room. "We must be calm."

"Are we going to Rome? I don't want to go to Rome. I like it here."

"Just let me think." Anchises pressed his fingers to his temples.

"I like Manius," said Thracius.

"So do I," Anchises replied.

The singer felt a throbbing pain behind his eyes. Manius had assured him that his bid would be the winner. He had joked that his wife would be impossible to live with if he lost, such was her affection for Anchises's voice. Yet Anchises knew, everyone knew—everyone but Manius—that his wife's affection lay with the boxer, not the singer. Manius was often gone from Capua on business, and Thracius would warm the cold spot in her bed quite nicely. That was fine by Anchises. She was harmless enough and had always been pleasant to both of them. They would have been allowed to continue living together, and life wouldn't have changed much.

But now all was uncertain. He had no answers, no leverage, and Thracius looked like a panic-stricken child who had just been pulled from his mother's arms and thrown to the lions. Anchises gripped him by the shoulders and looked into his eyes as confidently, as reassuringly, as he could.

"Rome is the Caput Mundi," he said with a smile. "They say that Apollo makes the sun rise there first each morning. What better place for the two of us?"

CHAPTER XVI

Ave, Caesar
Hail, Caesar

ROME

At first Livia thought the sound that had woken her was coming from outside the open window in her bedchamber: a crow, somewhere in the distance, cawing from a tall tree, crying for its parent to bring food.

Slowly, she realized the sound was coming from outside her bedchamber. It was not the cawing of a crow but rather the raucous cry of a human baby. A newborn. She pushed off the covers and swung her legs out of bed, listening.

More crying.

She tiptoed across the floor of her bedchamber and cracked open the door to peer outside. As her eyes adjusted to the dim light, she saw

Julia standing several meters away. She was holding a child in her arms.

"Oh, Livia," said Julia, "did the baby wake you?"

"Not at all," Livia lied. "I was awake."

The baby kicked and fussed in Julia's arms, and the young mother turned her back to Livia, trying to calm the child.

"Perhaps it is hungry," Livia offered.

"No, he wants to walk," Julia replied.

Livia laughed out loud. "He wants to walk? The little grub can't even hold its own head up yet."

Julia said nothing but bent down to place the baby on the floor. She stepped back and—to Livia's shock—the baby was no longer an infant but a young man of sixteen or seventeen.

He stood straight and sure, dressed as a Roman soldier in full armor and boasting the embossed cuirass of the emperor Augustus around his torso. A royal purple cloak fell down his back. He wore a crown of gilded laurels. At his side hung a sword with the initials MVA engraved into the hilt. Marcus Vipsanius Agrippa.

The boy set his eyes on Livia and marched toward her. His eyes moved up and down her, and then he lifted his chin. "Kneel and swear allegiance to the new Caesar," he commanded.

Again, she laughed. "I will not."

Octavian appeared at her shoulder. "You must, Livia."

"Husband," she said, "I will not."

Octavian moved to stand beside the boy. He took Agrippa's sword from the boy's side and swung it at Livia's legs. She felt her body drop, and she looked down to see that Octavian had cut off her legs at the knees.

The boy took a step closer, now towering over her. "You will kneel, Livia, one way or another."

Livia woke with a start. She caught her breath. It was the same dream, the same nightmare, she'd had for the last four nights in a row.

Her fitful sleeps had annoyed Octavian. Trying to be sweet, she had asked him if he wanted her to sleep in her private bedchamber, and to her disappointment he had said yes. Looking back, she should never have made the offer nor been surprised that he accepted it.

She yanked the covers up to her neck and stared at the ceiling. Octavian had been more distant since Agrippa's death. More distant to her, at least. While he had always fussed over Julia, now that she carried Agrippa's child and possibly Octavian's heir, the two of them seemed closer than ever. They had bonded over their shared loss and the potential within her belly. Livia had never felt more an outsider in her own home.

Even worse, Octavian had started spreading his seed around Rome like a starflower plant on a windy day. If it wasn't some clambering slut of a socialite, it was a slave from the kitchen or the gardens. His current favorite was a pregnant cleaning slave. The pregnancy wasn't his doing, not this time, and not that it mattered to him. It was the novelty that aroused him.

Livia remembered when Octavian used to take her while she was pregnant with the baby of her first husband, Tiberius. The sight of her rounded belly had excited him to an almost frantic state: he had not so much made love to her as pummeled into her, consumed by the perversion of it. She had such power over him back then.

Frustrated, she pushed the covers off her body, sat up in bed, and snapped her fingers. The slave Despina and another of Livia's younger body slaves quickly approached.

"Yes, Domina?" asked Despina.

"I am going to Caesar's bed," she said.

"Domina . . . Caesar is not alone this evening."

Livia threw her body back down onto the bed and put her hand on her forehead. "So, who is it tonight? A girl from the kitchen? A boy from the stables?"

"It is a young noblewoman named Tacita. She is sister to the Vestal Quintina, although I am told there is no affection between them."

"I know the girl," said Livia. "Is this not the second time she has shared Caesar's bed this month?"

"It is the third time, Domina."

Livia groaned. Tacita was young, beautiful, had the benefit of a noble family name, and was probably more fertile than a woodland nymph on the first day of May. On those few occasions Livia had seen her in the company of Caesar and other important men—the last time was at a chariot race at the amphitheater—she couldn't help noticing that Tacita was very much like she had been at that age: bold and ambitious, with little to lose and everything to gain. The similarity was sobering.

Livia pulled the covers back up and began to sulk, but Despina leaned over the bed. The slave remembered her instructions from the high priestess: it was important for the empress to rekindle her husband's desire for her.

"Domina . . ."

"What is it, Despina?" Livia snapped.

"If you will permit me, perhaps you **should** visit Caesar's bed tonight."

"You just said Tacita is in it."

"Yes, I know." Despina sighed. "Caesar will not expect you to join them. Do you understand, Domina?"

It took the blink of an eye, but then Livia understood. House slaves and married socialites were one thing. A fertile, unmarried blueblood who knew her way around all four posts of Caesar's bed was another matter altogether. She could not allow this to go on another night. She had to do something. Something big.

"Help me prepare," said Livia. She pushed off the covers, stood, and stripped as the younger slave brought a warm pot of water and cloth. She cleaned the empress's body while Despina followed behind her, rubbing a perfume made from rose petals onto Livia's skin.

That done, the younger of the slaves approached with a fresh, soft tunica, the type of undergarment most usually worn to bed. Livia held out her arms to be dressed, when Despina cleared her throat.

"Oh, just say it," said Livia.

"Domina, perhaps Caesar would enjoy seeing his beautiful wife in something less familiar." She held out two pieces of white fabric: the first was a **strophium**, a strip of cloth that wound around the breasts. The second was a **subligar**, a delicate, feminine type of loincloth.

Livia nodded and deferred to Despina's suggestion. The slave was often able to predict Caesar's desires. She held out her arms as Despina wrapped the soft fabric of the strophium around her breasts, winding it around her upper torso until her breasts were supported and appealing.

Next, Despina positioned the fine fabric of the subligar around Livia's waist, bringing the sides of the cloth together at the front of her body to make a knot just under her navel, and then bringing the rest of the fabric up, between her legs, to tuck it behind the knot.

Despina took a step back and eyed the empress from head to toe. "Yes," she said. "Most lovely. Caesar will be pleased."

Livia pulled a blanket off the bed and wrapped it around herself. She slunk through the dim house like a thief in her own home until she reached the closed door of Octavian's bedchamber. She had no idea how she would handle the sight of her husband lying naked in bed with another woman, especially a tart in perpetual heat like Tacita.

She pushed open the door and slipped inside, creeping noiselessly to the side of the large four-post bed. They were both asleep. Octavian was propped up and leaning on the headboard. His left hand rested on Tacita's bare backside, as if he'd been rubbing it before he had fallen asleep.

Livia lost grip of the blanket around her. It slipped down to her waist to expose her cloth-bound breasts, and the rustling caused by her fumbling struggles to pull it back up made Octavian open his eyes. He drew in a quick breath when he saw her.

"Livia?"

She didn't know what to say, so she said nothing.

His eyes moved over her, lingering at the sight of her full breasts wrapped tightly in the strophium. He sat up and put his feet on the floor, still staring at her breasts. Livia held her breath as he reached out to push the blanket to the floor and gaze lustily at the cloth between her legs. He slid his palm over the fabric and then moved it up, over her bare midriff, to feel the fabric over her breasts.

Livia could see his chest expand as his breathing became deeper, more deliberate. She took his hands and moved them to the back of the strophium, where it was tied, and his fingers pulled and tugged at the ends of the cloth until it began to uncurl and dropped to the floor. Her breasts now fully exposed, Livia tried not to think about the woman asleep in the bed. Her bed.

Octavian's hands moved to the subligar. His fingers slipped behind the knot fastened below her navel, and he was just about to pull out the cloth tucked behind it to reveal her genitals when Livia heard Tacita stir.

She knew she had to take the lead. She had to control how this went. At least, it had to seem that way.

"Why don't you have your friend do that?" she asked coyly.

In response, she felt Octavian grip the flesh on her hips hard. "You little minx," he said to her. Livia smiled. He had wanted this for years, hinted at it repeatedly, and even asked outright more than once. Now it was finally happening.

"Tacita," he said, not taking his eyes off Livia, "remove my wife's clothing." The young woman sat up and looked around the room for a moment, then did what the emperor told her to do and got up, walked around the bed to stand beside Livia, and unfastened the subligar. It fell to the floor.

Livia's smile widened and she let her fingertips touch Octavian's bare thighs. Then, she took Tacita's hands and moved them over her bare body, over her breasts and between her legs, as Octavian watched, his breathing becoming quicker with every passing second.

Within a minute, he had both of them on the bed: Tacita lying on her back and Livia lying on top of her, also on her back so that her breasts and body faced Octavian. He grabbed Tacita's hands roughly and guided them to Livia's breasts, instructing the young woman to caress his wife from below while he penetrated her from above.

As it went on, as Livia heard Octavian's panting breaths above her, as she felt the woman's hands on her from below, she surmised that this was probably as well as it could have gone. Her back hurt from the awkward angle of his thrusts, but at least she was the woman on top.

When it was finally over, Octavian collapsed onto his back, spent and still breathing hard. Livia rolled off Tacita as gracefully as she could and wedged herself between her husband and his young lover. Octavian put his arms around her.

"I love you, husband," she whispered in his ear.

"I love you, wife," he said.

Out of the corner of her eye, Livia saw Tacita pull the covers up, contented, confident.

But then, as if suddenly remembering that Tacita was there, Octavian lifted his head and cast her an irritated glance. "Leave us."

"Caesar?"

"Go home," he said, "now."

Immediately, three slaves neared the bed. One of them was Despina. Livia hadn't even seen her enter the bedchamber. Despina grabbed Tacita's arm and pulled her out of the bed, throwing a sheet around her and then all but dragging her out of the bedchamber as another slave gathered the woman's clothing off the floor. She could dress in her lectica on the way home.

Livia caught a glimpse of Despina's satisfied face as she dragged Caesar's troublesome young mistress out of the bedchamber. It was like the slave had known all along. The only way to get Tacita out of Octavian's bed, once and for all, was for Livia to get into it with her.

* * *

Julia's screams hadn't stopped all night, and they brought in the dawn. She was having a long and difficult birth. Agrippa had been a very large man.

As difficult as the birth was to Julia, it was even more difficult for her stepmother, Livia. The empress knew that it should've been her, his wife, giving Octavian a child, not his daughter giving him yet another grandchild.

Another scream. It had to be soon. Livia closed her eyes. She prayed to Fortuna and then to Juno that the child would be another girl. Another girl would be next to useless to Octavian. She could not be Caesar's heir and would be sent away to live with her sister so that Julia could try again. At least that would buy more time for Livia.

Octavian paced back and forth in front of the closed door to Julia's bedchamber. He prayed to Juno this child would be a boy. Sighing, he leaned against the wall and thumped the back of his head against a vibrant mural of a peacock. "How can it take so long?" he muttered. "It did not take this long the first time."

"Husband," said Livia. "Come and sit next to me." She patted the cushioned seat next to her, and he moved to sit beside her on the marble bench. She ran her fingers through his hair, and he sighed again.

Livia sighed too. Ever since that night of debauchery with Tacita—Livia could not bring herself to think of the ways she had debased herself—Octavian had shown more interest in her and less interest in his inventory of mistresses. She knew that every time he took her, he was reliving that night in his head. He now touched her the way that Tacita had touched her. Livia cringed. The experience continued to make her feel violated. But at least it had rekindled his desire for her in bed.

Out of bed, not much had changed. He did not ask her opinion on things or seek her support the way that he used to. The one exception, however, was with her work on the fasti. The Vestalis Maxima had told Caesar that Livia's work updating the religious calendar had been exceptional. That had pleased him. He was always pleased by her religious work.

It was ironic, though, that after all these years and their history that the Vestal would help her. Then again, the priestess Pomponia had always been one to favor the predictability of the status quo. She probably didn't want Livia replaced any more than Livia wanted to be replaced.

Octavian turned to Livia as Julia's deep groans of agony pulsed through the closed door. "It is good that her mother is with her, is it not?" he asked.

Of course not, thought Livia. **The last thing I need is Scribonia, your shrew of an ex-wife, sniffing for crumbs around here. It's bad enough your daughter has moved back in.** "Of course it is good," she forced herself to say. "Her mother will be a great comfort to her."

"It is strange that Julia did not want you in the birthing room as well," said Octavian.

"It is not so strange, husband. Women can be modest when giving birth."

Another muted scream from the other side of the door. Octavian stood and moved to stand in front of the life-size statue of Juno that the **obstetrix** had brought with her and placed a few steps from the door. Juno, protective goddess of women and childbirth. He looked into the goddess's powerful, beautiful face and held his palms up to her. Again, he prayed the baby would be a boy. He prayed his daughter would not die in childbirth.

His physician, Musa, appeared and stood beside Octavian. "Praise Juno," he said before the statue.

He handed a cup to Octavian. "Just some wine with tonic. To calm your nerves."

Octavian looked at the closed door. "Why does she scream so?"

"Caesar, I mean no disrespect," said Musa, "but you would not ask that question if you ever had occasion to witness childbirth. A friend of mine once said that he'd rather risk his life three times in battle than give birth once."

Octavian drained half the cup in one swallow. "Is my daughter's life in danger?"

"I do not believe so," Musa replied. "Attica is the best midwife in all Greece and Rome, even better than the midwife who delivered Julia's first child. She has delivered over one thousand living babies. I've been told that she crafts her birthing chairs and instruments herself, doesn't even use a carpenter or a blacksmith."

Octavian lifted the cup and drained the rest of the wine and tonic mixture. "Have you spoken to her?"

"No, she will not leave Julia, and I am not permitted in the room," Musa replied, "but I spoke with her assistant. Attica gave Julia a mixture to speed the labor. She said the child was not positioned properly, but that she was able to manipulate it under lubrication . . . I believe she uses a special blend of olive oil infused with some herb so that she can slip her hand in and move the—"

Octavian put his hand out.

Musa stopped talking, and in the silence that followed Octavian noticed something. Julia had stopped screaming. He pressed his ear against the closed door.

At long last, the door opened and the perspiring face of the midwife's young assistant peeked through. She met eyes with Octavian and bowed her head. "Caesar, please come in."

Octavian pushed past her and strode into the room. A moment later, his eyes became blurry, and the room seemed to spin around him. Musa put his arms around his chest, from behind.

"It is all normal," said Musa, referring to the piles of bloody linens around the room and the vision of a panting, red-faced, sweat-stained Julia in the birthing chair, still gripping the chair's handles as blood trickled down her legs. Her mother, Scribonia, was standing behind her with her hands on her daughter's shoulders. Her expression was a mixture of exhaustion and relief.

The midwife Attica was sitting on a stool

between Julia's legs with her back to the door. Her head was down, and she was inspecting something on her lap.

A shrill cry. A baby's cry.

The midwife stood up and turned around to face Octavian. Tall and statuesque with a strong but feminine face that did not look so different from the statue of Juno in the hall, she smiled as much at her own role in the delivery as the mother's.

"It is a boy," she said proudly, looking at the newborn in her arms. "Living and free of deformity."

The midwife turned to show the baby boy to Julia. Octavian's daughter looked at the child as if she had never seen a creature quite like it. Then she began to weep. "Father," she said, "I wish Agrippa were here. I was unkind to him."

Octavian rushed to her and kissed her forehead. "Agrippa has conquered Elysium by now," he said softly. "He will have Mercury carry him to see the boy." He touched the infant's wet, wrinkled skin as it squirmed in the midwife's arms. "The next emperor of Rome."

The midwife wordlessly wrapped the newborn tightly in a blanket and nodded deferentially to Octavian. "Imperator Caesar Augustus," she said, "**divi fili**, son of the divine Julius Caesar, take me to the shrine of your ancestors."

Octavian led the obstetrix out of Julia's bedchamber. Scribonia followed behind, and Livia fell into step beside her as they moved through the lamp-lit house. Livia still didn't know the baby's gender and didn't want to ask. That would seem too obvious, especially to Scribonia. But the look of awe on Octavian's face was a bad sign.

Octavian led the midwife into the atrium, where the chirping of early birds filtered into the home from the **compluvium** opening in the roof. A slant of warmth from the morning sun radiated into the atrium and sunlight reflected off the water in the impluvium below to dance on the colorful walls. The blessed day was everything Octavian could ever have hoped it would be.

The midwife proceeded to the **lararium**. The family shrine was located in front of a scarlet wall, on which hung the death masks of Octavian's great ancestors, including Julius Caesar, all of them lit from above by the delicate sunlight streaming into the atrium and from below by oil lamps on the altar, which burned with the sacred flame of Vesta.

As was customary, the midwife placed the infant

on the floor in front of the shrine and then stepped back. Her duty was done.

Scribonia stopped a few steps away from the baby and lowered herself onto her knees. She held her palms up. "Juno, queen of Heaven, we thank you for the safe delivery of this child and his mother."

His **mother**, Livia thought. **Futuo.**

It was up to Caesar now. Fulfilling the final duty of the family and his own role as **pater familias**, or male head of the household, Octavian approached the baby on the floor and picked him up, cradling him in his arms and looking up at the death masks.

"In the name of all the gods and the laws of Rome, I claim this child as a son of the Julian clan and the Caesarian family."

He glanced down at Scribonia, and Livia saw a warm smile pass between them. It was their moment.

Livia had to make it hers. She stepped between them and forced herself to look at the baby in Octavian's arms in the same way that she looked at Octavian himself: as if overwhelmed by the presence of greatness. She forced herself to smile into the little grub's wrinkled face, and she forced herself to say the words.

"Ave, Caesar."

CHAPTER XVII

Navis Stultorum
Ship of fools
—AN ANCIENT GREEK ALLEGORY

Pomponia was never one to fuss over babies, but even she had to admit that Julia's infant was pleasing to the eye. His wrinkled newborn skin had smoothed and cleared, and his eyes were bright and round. His soft hair had been combed forward by his doting nurse. Best of all, he hardly cried. Other than a few squawks and grunts, which were quickly stanched by some time at his wet nurse's breast, he was a quiet and content baby.

Because so many infants died in the first few days of life, it was the custom that a male baby was not given a name until he was nine days old. That was today, and Caesar was marking the occasion with a lively gathering of senators, priests, and Rome's most elite couples at his home on the Palatine Hill.

They had arrived with gifts in hand and good wishes that were, for the most part, sincere. A blood heir of Caesar's did smack of royal succession, but if Octavian's heir was half as competent and benevolent as he was, the empire would continue to enjoy peace and prosperity. Even those senators and nobles who had republican leanings had to admit that things could be a lot worse.

The name that Octavian had given to the boy was a banner of the infant's past and future: Marcus Julius Caesar Agrippa Postumus.

Agrippa Postumus paid tribute to his late father. **Julius Caesar** declared his divine lineage as the adopted son and heir of Octavian as well as his destiny as the next emperor of Rome.

After spending most of the evening in very pleasant small talk with the emperor's poet, Virgil, Pomponia reclined on a couch in Caesar's triclinium to the sound of chattering voices and happy music—**tibia** reed pipes and the strings of a lyre. She brushed the side of her light veil off her face and sipped wine from a gold cup. Octavian had brought in carts of the finest Caecuban wine to celebrate, and Pomponia was making sure to count how many times the slaves refilled her cup.

Octavian seemed to read her thoughts. "The

sacred fire will not go out if you sleep deeply to-night," he said, grinning from an adjacent couch.

Pomponia bit her lip and laughed and then held out her cup for a passing wine slave to refill. It was a joyous occasion, and they had come together as longtime friends, with the usual formalities and conventions of their respective positions much relaxed.

Although the official reason for the celebration was the birth of Julia's son, Pomponia had her own reason to celebrate. After the bittersweet parting of Nona and Sabina, Ankhu had returned to say that the two women had arrived safely at the temple in Carthage and were quickly settling in. The city had welcomed them with an extravagant ceremony attended by the proconsul, magistrates and officials, priests and crowds of people. Nona's and Sabina's letters to Pomponia sounded genuinely happy. It was a relief and a blessing for the chief Vestal.

Quintina and Julia were sitting on a couch adjacent to Pomponia's. The new mother was cooing at the boy, and Quintina was teasing her. The young Vestal reached out to stroke the baby's soft hair. "He's almost ready for the crown of laurels," she said.

Julia kissed the baby's head. "Yes," she murmured happily.

Quintina laughed at her friend. "You are more changed than Medea under a spell. Who could have imagined that such a small man could possess such power over a woman?"

"Yes, but look at his face, Quintina," said Julia. "See the way he looks about the room? Is it not unusual for a newborn to be so alert?"

"He is Caesar," replied Quintina. "He is already on the watch for any Gauls that might have slipped through the gates of Rome."

Octavian clapped. "Ha!" he said.

Pomponia smiled to herself. Quintina was becoming more politic every day.

The music in the background faded and then stopped altogether as Livia floated into the center of the triclinium with her hands clasped in front of her.

"Dear friends," she said, as if she had never been happier in all her life, "we thank you for coming to share our good fortune. All Rome rejoices at the naming of Caesar's heir." As the guests fell silent and circled around, she looked at Octavian. "Husband, I have a gift for you. In all the empire, there is only one singer whose voice is beautiful enough to first grace our young Caesar's ear. With your permission, he shall perform."

Octavian stood and walked to Livia. He embraced her tightly. "Thank you, wife." He took her by the hand, and they returned to his couch as Despina ushered Anchises to the center of the room.

The virtuoso wore an expensive, emerald-green tunica, the bottom hem and sleeves of which were bordered in gold embroidery. Several in the gathering began to applaud at the sight of him, not even waiting for Caesar's slave to formally introduce him.

"Anchises of Capua," noted an impressed senator. "Outstanding choice, Empress Livia."

Anchises bowed to the senator. "I see my reputation precedes me," he quipped, "although I hope not all of it." The gathering laughed and applauded again.

A natural showman, the singer moved to stand in front of the adjoining couches that Julia and Octavian reclined on. He bowed deeply, first before the emperor and Livia and then before Julia and the child in her arms.

Pomponia was just putting the wine cup to her lips when Anchises's voice wisped into her ears, softly at first but then stronger and with a certain familiarity and poignancy that made her throat tighten with emotion. She had heard the melody before; Medousa used to hum it to her when they were children.

Anchises sang the song in Greek. Like most educated Romans, Pomponia knew the language and recognized some of the lyrics as belonging to an old poem to Poseidon, the name that the Greeks gave to Neptune:

> **Poseidō enépo, halós médonta**
> **krataión,**
> I sing of Poseidon, mighty god
> of the sea

> **ēïónōn t'ánakta kai dē Aigéōs**
> **póntou,**
> Lord of shores and the broad
> Aegean

> **Enosíchthona, Damaíon, neōn**
> **rhutēra,**
> Earth-shaker, tamer of horses,
> savior of ships

> **hos tas tōn nautilloménōn ku-**
> **bernās aísas,**
> Who shapes the destinies of the
> ocean-bound.

**chair', ō Póseidon, gēs
psamáthōn koírane,**
Hail, Poseidon, master of Earth's
sands

**hos tēn Seirēnōn aoidēn hoios
t'ei mónos akoúein**
Who alone can hear the song of
the Sirens

**kai hómōs ep'aktás hikánein
olbías sōs,**
And still safely reach the blessed
banks

**tō nautílō boēthei en nēï
anoētōn!**
Aid the mariner in his ship of
fools.

To Pomponia, the union of the melody with the words felt both nostalgic and new. Nor was she the only one moved by the virtuoso's performance. Rome's aristocracy, who prided themselves on being hard to impress, were unusually dazzled.

That included the emperor. He had been a more openly emotional man since the birth of his heir, and the song had brought him near to tears. He applauded at the end and then looked around the dining room until he spotted his poet.

"Virgil," he said, "perhaps one day Anchises may sing your poem to me?"

"Normally I would descend into an artist's tantrum at the mere suggestion," said Virgil, "but not this time, Caesar."

Pomponia wasn't sure whether the poet was serious or not—he was notoriously possessive of his work—but it was a diplomatic answer nonetheless, and it pleased his powerful patron. Yet, as the gathering returned to small talk and drink, Virgil was the first to find his way to Anchises's side. After several minutes, Pomponia lifted herself off the couch as gracefully as she could under the effects of the wine and joined them.

Virgil did the introductions and then asked her, "Priestess, how is your brother, Pomponius? I have not seen him in some time."

"I was going to ask you the same thing," said Pomponia. "I hardly see him these days. He is up to something, but I will find out what it is." She turned to Anchises. "The song you sang tonight—where does it originate?"

"My lady," said Anchises, "the melody comes from my home island of Delos in Greece."

"Delos . . ." Pomponia thought for a moment. "I will have to check the records, but I believe a former slave of mine was first taken from Delos. She used to hum that melody to me."

"I have never heard the melody elsewhere," said Anchises, "but on Delos everyone knew it. We sang it to praise Poseidon and protect our island from . . ."

"From what?" Pomponia asked, smiling. "Sea monsters?"

"From Romans, Priestess."

"Ah," said Pomponia. "Yes, I suppose so."

Livia stepped into the conversation, catching the end of it. "Still, things worked out for the best for you, didn't they, Anchises?" she asked, not waiting for an answer. "Here you are, singing for Caesar in Rome. Certainly, that is better than singing to the fishes on some wretched island in Greece."

"As you say, Empress," Anchises replied.

"Caesar seemed very pleased with your performance," Pomponia said to the singer. She added to Livia, "It was a thoughtful gift."

"Let's hope my husband doesn't forget it."

"Caesar has a good memory," said Pomponia.

"Lady Pomponia," said Livia, "if I didn't know any better, I would think you were trying to make me feel better."

"Caecuban wine lowers one's defenses," said Pomponia. "But I have stopped drinking now, so I'm sure the weakness will pass."

Anchises clapped his hands together. "This is the most I have enjoyed Rome so far," he said. As he had hoped, both women laughed.

The empress hooked her arm around Virgil. "Now," she said, "tell me how Caesar's poem is coming along." Virgil hesitated for a moment but then let Livia lead him off in private conversation.

The Vestal remained with Anchises. "I would like to have you sing at one of our events," she said. "Who is your owner?"

"His name is Soren Calidius Pavo."

The Vestal's eyes narrowed with curiosity. "And how is life under your new master?"

Anchises clapped his hands together. If he expressed any discontent, it could make matters worse for him and Thracius. The thought of his partner made his chest tighten: **Where is he right now?**

What's happening to him? Soren had separated the two of them upon their arrival in Rome, and Anchises had not been permitted to see or ask about Thracius since.

"It has only been a short while," he replied, "but I hope my master has reason to be pleased with me. I am sure he will treat me accordingly."

The Vestal brushed her white veil off her face and caught the attention of one of Octavian's house slaves. "Prepare my lectica."

"At once, High Priestess."

"I found your song very moving," Pomponia said to the singer. "I look forward to hearing you perform again."

Anchises bowed deeply. "Truly, I thank you, Priestess. It has been my great honor."

By the time Pomponia had said her goodbyes to her hosts and friends—an endeavor that required another cup of wine and several more conversations to successfully complete—she was feeling even more tired and light-headed.

One of Caesar's slaves escorted her through the house, to the atrium, then beyond the portico and outside into the darkness of night, to her waiting litter. Her lecticarii were in position to carry her back down the Palatine ramp to the House of the Vestals. Publius and Caeso were also standing at attention.

She was just about to step into her lectica when Tiberius appeared and politely held the curtain open for her. For the first time this evening, Pomponia realized that he had spent very little time mingling with the guests. She couldn't blame him. The naming of Caesar's heir was no doubt a sore spot for him and his mother.

"Priestess Pomponia," he said pleasantly, and then added with a good-natured smile, "I hope you have enjoyed the wine."

"Is it that obvious?" she asked.

"It is," he replied, "but I am also guilty. And there are worse crimes, nay?" He gestured to a figure that emerged from the darkness. "Priestess, have you met Soren? He is brother to Senator Pavo. He owns that Anchises fellow who sang tonight, as well as a very good boxer. What's his name again?"

"Thracius," said Soren.

"Yes, Thracius," Tiberius confirmed. "He brought them both from Capua."

"Soren and I have met before," Pomponia said to Tiberius, "although under unhappy circumstances." She faced Soren. "I see you have already begun to restock your household with slaves. Your virtuoso was outstanding. I'll be sure to bet coin on your boxer if I see him."

"Thank you, Priestess," replied Soren.

The Vestal's words were flattering enough, but her flat tone sparked a flare of anger in Soren's veins. He imagined how good it would feel to reach out, wrap his fingers around that smooth throat, and squeeze the life out of her. He had hated watching Dacia gasp for breath. He'd give half his fortune to watch the priestess gasp for hers.

The thought was almost arousing, and he compelled himself to pull his eyes off her. When he did, he realized that both of the Vestal's guards had moved a step closer and were staring intently at him. No doubt they recognized him from that day in her office, the day she had refused to save Dacia and his desperation had prompted him to move suddenly toward her, only to find himself thrown against the wall.

The Vestal stepped into her lectica: two small oil lamps burned inside to light the space. The litter-bearers lifted the vehicle onto their shoulders, and Soren watched it travel into Caesar's gardens, heading toward the Palatine ramp that led down to the House of the Vestals in the Forum. One of her guards cast a final glance over his shoulder. Soren quickly looked away.

"Here comes your moneymaker now," said Tiberius, pointing to Anchises, who had just emerged from Caesar's portico.

Soren jabbed his thumb at his own litter, which sat nearby, instructing Anchises to go wait next to it.

"Yes, Domine," said the singer.

Soren offered Tiberius a slight bow. "Thank you for your hospitality," he said. "It has been a successful evening for me. Although, if I may speak boldly . . ."

"Please do," said Tiberius.

"I believe that Caesar has made a mistake by not naming you his heir."

Soren held his breath. It was a risky comment. If Tiberius were truly loyal to Caesar, it could be seen as treasonous.

Tiberius put his hand on Soren's shoulder. "It is good to know I have friends to call upon, should the need arise."

"Very good," said Soren. "Good night."

After Tiberius had disappeared through the portico, Soren proceeded to his litter and stepped into the large lectica. He held the curtain back. "Get in," he said to Anchises.

The singer stepped inside and sat on the couch across from his master. He shifted in his seat as the lecticarii—four in the back and four in the front—lifted it and began to move.

"I'm told you performed well tonight," said Soren. His face was lit by a single oil lamp, giving it an even more sinister slant. He stared into the darkness outside. "That's why you're in here instead of out there, helping to carry this thing."

"It is an indulgence, Domine," Anchises replied. "Thank you."

For a moment, for just a brief, passing moment, Soren thought about closing the curtains and having the virtuoso get on his knees in the small space between the couches. The image of his hands around the Vestal's neck had inflamed his arousal. He closed his eyes. He'd wait until he got home. He had a batch of new female slaves to choose from.

Anchises watched his master nod off, lulled to sleep by the rocking of the lectica as it traveled back to Soren's home. The singer didn't sleep. He never slept these days. He stayed awake until the litter reached the house on the Esquiline. It was a long walk. Other masters might have taken a small horse-drawn carriage to spare their slaves, but not

Soren. He had paid good money for these muscled Africans. They could earn their keep.

The slaves set the lectica down. Soren grunted awake and got out first, immediately pointing to two of the female slaves that had come to meet him and ordering them to his bedchamber. He looked back at Anchises.

"Take off that tunica," he said. "I paid a fortune for it."

Anchises stepped out of the lectica. A house slave handed him a rough tunica and he changed into it where he stood. It irritated his skin, and he scratched his legs as he entered Soren's grand home and headed for the stone steps that led into the dank basement.

Unlike most houses which had the **cellae servorum**—servants' rooms—on the main level, Soren was that breed of master who preferred to have his slaves under him in every way. He had a roughed-in stone and dirt basement, one he often locked, for that reason. Yet in the house of Soren, most slaves were happy for the extra distance from their master.

"Anchises!"

The singer stopped at the sound of Soren's voice. He squeezed his eyes closed—**damn it**—and then turned around. "Yes, Domine?"

"Come with me."

Soren sauntered into the kitchen with Anchises following close behind. He pointed at a table with two rickety chairs pushed against it. "Sit there. Put your arm on the table."

Anchises did what he was told. He knew what was coming. **There is no way to stop this**, he told himself. **Do not cry out. It will be over soon enough.**

Soren reached for a large metal spoon that hung on the wall next to the brick oven: a fire was burning inside. He bent down and put the bowl end of the spoon in the fire for several long moments.

Without any warning, without any expression, he removed the spoon from the hot oven, gripped Anchises's hand to secure it against the table, and then pressed the hot metal against the **LB** tattoo on the delicate skin of the slave's inner forearm.

Anchises smelled his flesh burning before the pain registered. Smoke hissed from the edges of the metal, and even as he watched, he could see blisters forming along its rim. The pain was beyond anything that Anchises had ever experienced or thought possible. When Bassus had tattooed him and Thracius, he had gotten them drunk first. It had been done humanely and had barely hurt. But there was nothing humane about Soren.

Anchises bit down hard on his lower lip. He knew that Soren was holding the scalding metal against his skin longer than was necessary. He lowered his head and shifted on the wobbly chair, his feet scuffing the floor in agony. Finally, he could not stop himself, and he cried out, "Stop!"

Soren laughed. He removed the metal and hung the spoon back on the wall.

Anchises forced himself to look at his forearm. Blisters were forming so quickly that it looked like his skin was boiling water. The areas that were not blistered were charred black, like burnt animal meat that had been forgotten on the brazier and was too blackened to even eat.

He tried to control his breathing, taking deliberate breaths in and pushing them out just as deliberately, but the pain only intensified with each passing moment, and he found it difficult to breathe at all. His forearm had swollen to what seemed like twice its normal size. He bit his lip harder. It was bad enough that he had cried out. He would not let Soren see his tears.

Soren took no notice. He saw a loaf of bread on a

shelf and ripped off a piece. "Clean the wound," he said through a mouthful of bread. "No audience wants to see pus oozing from your arm. The ladies won't like it." He exited the kitchen, heading to his bedchamber and the two female slaves that awaited him there.

When he had left, Anchises indulged in a few weepy breaths before compelling himself to get up and look for a way to treat his wound. He had cleaned many of Thracius's deep cuts and gashes, but never a burn. He found an amphora of water and poured it over the black, blistering burn, hearing groans of agony slip through his lips. Next, he found a clean linen cloth, soaked it in wine, and wrapped it loosely around his forearm. Before leaving the kitchen, he tidied up after himself. Just in case.

Anchises moved slowly through the candlelit house. He descended the steps to the basement and walked tiredly down the dim, depressing corridor—more of a stone and dirt tunnel, really—that he had come to despise over the past weeks.

He located the entrance to his cramped quarters and slumped onto the hard mattress on the floor, cradling his wounded arm next to his chest and letting his back rest against the cold stone wall of the cell-like room.

Earlier this evening, his song had moved Caesar Augustus to tears. He had been sipping Caecuban wine with Rome's elite—the empress, senators, and priests, the Vestalis Maxima and the emperor's poet, the renowned Virgil.

Now he was squatting in Soren's vile basement, praying his wound wouldn't become infected and wondering when the man was going to feed him a meal that wasn't mere crumbs or half-rancid.

But the worst part of all, the part he could hardly bring himself to think about, or rather, couldn't stop thinking about, was Thracius. Where was he? What was happening to him? The pain of worry was worse than any wound. He put his hands on his face and then moved them to cover his mouth.

He didn't want the other slaves to hear him cry.

* * *

The sound of something heavy repeatedly striking metal with a reverberating **bang bang bang** woke Thracius with a start. At least, he thought it woke him. He wasn't sure if he'd actually slept.

The ludus that his new master, Soren, had left him in was a much larger gladiatorial school than the one in Capua, and there was no peace, not even at night. The sound of construction as new wings and structures were being added didn't stop. The food and drink were worse here than in Capua too.

The training was adequate, though. The fools that ran the place at least knew enough to hire an experienced lanista and decent trainers. Thracius thought they might have come from Capua themselves, but if they did, it was before his time, because he didn't recognize any of them. And from what the other fighters had told him, the ludus had managed to avoid the worst of the contagion. All in all, they seemed to know what they were doing.

Thracius lifted himself off the stained, straw-filled mattress in the center of his small cell and stretched his arms. He needed to train. He needed to move and burn off some energy, but there wasn't enough space in the cell to do anything useful. He gripped the bars of the door and tightened his arm muscles.

He hadn't seen Anchises since their new master had carted them off to Rome. It was the longest they had been apart in many years, and Thracius didn't like it. He didn't like anything about Rome so far, Caput Mundi or not. The streets were loud

and filthy, and the people even more so. It was unlikely Apollo made the sun rise here first.

In Capua, he and Anchises had lived together in
a small but private house on the extensive grounds
of the ludus. There were no bars. They could come
and go as they pleased.

They usually went into town, after Thracius was
finished training, to find drink or food that would
satisfy one of Anchises's many cravings or to watch
a show at the amphitheater. They often rode their
horses to Bassus's house in the country for dinner
and parties, or to hunt in the thick trees and fish
in the well-stocked ponds of their former master's
estate.

And then there were the women. While Anchises's desire was only for men, Thracius often enjoyed
the intimate company of his adoring female fans.
Many of them were beautiful, and even the ones
that weren't beautiful were patrician enough to boast
soft, perfumed bodies.

Of course, there was the harder side of things.
The boxing matches. Every few months, Thracius
had to step into the arena and quite literally fight
for his life. Every time he killed a man, he made his
master Bassus a richer man. Every time he killed

a man, he and Anchises were guaranteed another few months of the good life.

Thracius gripped the bars tighter. He felt like an animal here. A caged animal. He was worried about Anchises, and that only amplified his sense of being trapped and helpless. He let his head fall back and looked up at the ceiling, when something caught his eye—letters carved into the wooden lintel above the door.

Scorpo hic erat. Scorpus was here.

Scorpus the Titan?

He spat on the dirt floor and took two steps back from the barred door. He and Anchises had known Scorpus for years in Capua. They had seen him race in the amphitheater and had attended many parties with him.

Thracius didn't like Scorpus. He was a charioteer, and they had it too easy. The horses did all the work: all the chariot driver had to do was not tip over, and lots of them couldn't even get that right. Boxers and gladiators did twice the work at a thousand times the danger. Scorpus had an ego too. He'd spent too many years being treated like he was Quirinus returned to earth.

But the biggest reason Thracius didn't like Scorpus

was that the charioteer had once joked that Anchises's singing sounded like a weasel caught by the ass in a trap. Everyone knew he was going for a cheap laugh and didn't really mean it, but the damage was done. Anchises took it to heart, like he always did, and had moped around for the better part of a month.

Still, Scorpus hadn't deserved what—at least according to the rumors that flew back to Capua—had happened to him when he was sold to a new owner and moved to Rome.

His horse Ferox had been tortured in front of him in the arena, and his woman, Cassandra, whom Thracius did like, had been crucified after Scorpus had unsuccessfully tried to kill their master. Scorpus himself had apparently fled Rome. Soldiers from Rome had come to Capua to see whether he had returned there, but he had not been found.

Thracius knew that he could be slow to figure things out. Anchises said it was from one too many hits to the head. It was all coming together now, though. On the night of their auction, soon after the winner's name had been announced, a nobleman from Capua—a man who frequented Rome—had spoken privately to Anchises. He had looked concerned, and the singer had seemed distracted after the conversation, despite reassuring Thracius that all would be well.

This Soren fellow, their new master, must have been Scorpus's master as well. And his treatment of Scorpus and Cassandra had been bad enough that Scorpus had risked it all to try to kill him.

Thracius's heart hammered in his chest. What if Soren was doing something to Anchises right now? What if Anchises was hurt or suffering . . . or worse?

And then his fears seemed to take form before his eyes. A large man with a ropey red scar around his neck appeared on the other side of his barred door and leaned against it.

"Taurus says you're ready to fight," said Soren. "He says you're in excellent shape."

"I am, Domine," Thracius replied. "Am I permitted to see Anchises?"

"You'll find that Rome is different from Capua," said Soren, ignoring the boxer's question but noting his deference. That was already an improvement on Scorpus. "No more fighting pretty boys to impress the wives of rich fools," he continued. "You'll fight for real in Rome, in front of the emperor himself."

"It doesn't matter who's watching," said Thracius.

"I can crack a man's skull just as fast in front of the emperor as I can in front of a rich fool's wife."

Soren sneered. "We'll see."

"Am I permitted to see Anchises?"

"That's up to you," said the master. "Win in front of the emperor and I'll consider it. Lose in front of the emperor and no. In fact, lose in front of the emperor and I'll make sure your little dandy Anchises feels even shittier about it than I do." He grinned and then said thoughtfully, "You know, I've never had a catamite. The idea crossed my mind the other night, but—"

"Domine," said Thracius, "I will not lose."

Soren shrugged. "I've heard that before."

CHAPTER XVIII

Necessitas Non Habet Legem
Necessity has no law.
−A ROMAN MAXIM

The wet nurse woke up slowly, peacefully. That was her first indication that something was wrong. Usually, Julia's baby boy squawked every few hours during the night for a feeding. He was a little pig, but a delightful one.

She rolled over and peered down into the cradle at her bedside and then sat up with a gasp. Even by the light of the nursery's single burning candle, she could see the infant's skin didn't look right.

She screamed as loudly as she could, and Caesar's house sprang to sudden life. Slaves lit oil lamps and came running into the baby's nursery. Julia was close behind them with Musa on her heels.

"What is wrong?" the young mother asked as she rushed to the baby's cradle.

Musa shouldered Julia and the nurse aside and picked up the baby, placing him on the wet nurse's bed and shouting, "More light!"

Slaves surrounded him with burning oil lamps and candles. The child's skin had a disturbing blue tinge to it. His legs and arms were still and saliva was trickling out of the side of his mouth in a thick stream.

Musa put his ear to the baby's chest. The infant's heartbeat was not detectable. His skin was already cool and clammy. He felt the child's body convulse weakly against his ear and looked down at him— the child was agonal, and his breaths were gone, replaced by faint gasps. His eyes were open, but his pupils were dilated. He had moved past the point of no return some time ago.

Octavian and Livia appeared in the doorway. The emperor's eyes were wide, and his face was blanched. He was squeezing Livia's hand so tightly her knuckles were white.

"Father, he isn't breathing." Julia rushed to her father's side. Octavian let go of Livia and gripped his daughter's arms. They both dropped to their knees where they stood.

"Queen of Heaven, Juno," said Octavian, "we

pray for the life of this child. Save the life of this child, and we will make great sacrifice to you." He repeated the prayer, his voice shaking as if he were standing naked in the cold. "Queen of Heaven, Juno, we pray for the life of this child. Save the life of this child, and we will make great sacrifice to you."

"It is too late for that, Caesar," said Musa.

The prayers stopped.

Julia stood up and walked to the bed. She leaned over the baby and put her mouth to his, catching the last of his breaths, as was the custom. She put her lips to his tiny ear. "Go meet your father now, sweetheart," she whispered.

Other than the sound of a sputtering oil lamp, the room was silent.

Livia spoke first. "It is the contagion," she said. "The contagion, here in our house." She pointed to the wet nurse. "Brought by that one, no doubt."

"Domina!" exclaimed the wet nurse. "I am not sick! And if I were, I would **never** have been near the child!" She began to sob. "I loved the boy."

Julia stepped away from the child. "You are not to blame," she said to the wet nurse. Her voice was emotionless. She walked to the nurse and put her arm around her and led her out of the nursery without another word. As they walked away, Tiberius shuffled past them into the nursery.

"My slave just woke me," he said. "What's wrong?"

Musa met his eyes and shook his head. He glanced down at the unmoving baby on the bed.

"Oh," said Tiberius. He stood uncertainly and looked at Octavian, still kneeling in the middle of the nursery floor. He was about to say something, when Livia caught his eye. **Not now, you idiot.** Quietly, he turned and went back to his bedchamber.

Livia gently placed her hand on the top of Octavian's head. "Husband," she said, "let's return to bed now. There is nothing to be done. You must rest."

Octavian tried to stand but stumbled and fell hard onto his shoulder. Two slaves rushed to his side and helped him to his feet. He put his arms around them, and they half walked, half carried him back to his bedchamber.

Musa watched the emperor disappear from view. He sat on the edge of the bed and stared down at the baby. This was not right. There was no reason for this to have happened. The child was healthy, the household was healthy, the wet nurse was healthy.

He had seen death from the contagion. Many times he had seen it. This was not it. Plus, the contagion had been abating, thanks to Caesar and Agrippa's expansive public hygiene efforts and the cooler weather. The physician's eyes narrowed as he noticed something glistening on the baby's lips, something that wasn't just sputum. He touched it. **Sticky. Like . . . honey?**

A memory came back to him slowly. A case, many years ago on Capri. He had found honey on a dead man's lips. It had been very strange, and there were many suspicions surrounding the man's death. The slaves had been tortured for information, and one had finally revealed that their mistress had poisoned her husband—by mixing hemlock in with honey. That was it. Hemlock poisoning.

Musa stood up quickly and spun around, suddenly realizing that the empress was the only person still in the room with him. She was standing in the doorway and staring intently at him as if assessing his thoughts. He looked at her blankly.

She cocked her head. "Don't just stand there staring like you've caught Venus in the bath," she said. "Make yourself useful and bring Caesar a tonic."

* * *

Pomponia wrapped a black palla around her white stola and met Octavian in the elegant vestibule of the House of the Vestals, the one located at the base of the Palatine ramp. The emperor hadn't walked down the passageway but had instead been carried in a small lectica.

"Caesar," she said, "would you like to go inside or speak in the garden?"

"The garden," he answered.

She led him into the courtyard. It was a cool morning and bronze firebowls were burning in several places. They sat on a cushioned bench next to one of them, and the emperor leaned toward it, letting the heat radiate into his bones. A temple slave appeared with a heavy woolen blanket and laid it across his knees.

"Have you seen Julia?" Octavian asked Pomponia.

"Yes. She has been here every day and often stays the night. Quintina has been offering what small comfort she can." The Vestal nodded to a slave who approached Caesar with a tray, upon which sat a single cup. "Musa has sent your tonic," said Pomponia.

Octavian drank the doctor's medicine in two swallows. "It calms my nerves," he said.

"That is good, Caesar."

"Atrox Fortuna spins a cruel fate," said Octavian. He let his eyes linger on Pomponia's black palla. "Thank you for still mourning my son's . . . my grandson's . . . passing."

"All Rome mourns with you," said Pomponia. "Although that will not make it any easier for you." She pulled the palla around her shoulders to keep out the early-morning chill.

Only a couple of weeks before, she had felt great joy at the naming of Caesar's heir. Now, the grief of the child's loss was even greater than the joy of his naming had been. It wasn't getting any easier either, especially as the shock of the loss subsided, and the reality set in. Caesar was once again without an heir. Rome was without an heir.

More than almost anything else, the Roman Empire needed certainty and constancy to survive and thrive—hence the importance of keeping Vesta's fire burning at all times. The uncertainty of Octavian's succession had left everyone feeling a bit vulnerable.

"Do you know a freedman by the name of Tiro?" asked Octavian.

"Do you mean Cicero's former scribe?"

"The very one," said Octavian. "He came to me a few months back for official permission to publish Cicero's books."

"Did you allow it?"

"Yes. Maecenas and a censor will read them first, but I instructed that only seditious material be removed." Octavian slid his hands under the blanket to warm them. "Tiro didn't just bring Cicero's books, though. He brought many of his personal letters as well. I have been reading them, especially the ones that he wrote after the death of his daughter, Tullia."

"I remember," said Pomponia. "He took it very hard."

"If he were alive, I would consult him about this matter," said Octavian. "You know, he was unfriendly to me in the years after my divine father's assassination. He used to call me **boy** and make me wait for hours for an audience with him." Octavian smiled tightly. "I cannot say I blame him. I **was** a boy. I think that in time he and I would have become friends, though. He would have had words of wisdom for my . . . my grief." His face grew tight with pain.

Pomponia leaned closer to him. "I am sorry for your loss, my friend. You have not just lost a son and a grandson but the heir to the empire that you have built. I had visions of you taking the boy to Senate hearings while he was still in his basket." She smiled sadly. "You must have had many plans for him."

"You understand well," Octavian replied. "I had hoped he would be a second Marcellus." He wiped his eyes with the back of his hand. "In reading Cicero's letters, I have discovered that he had great resentment toward his second wife, who was Tullia's stepmother. She did not mourn for Tullia and did not comfort him. It is why he divorced her." He clutched the blanket and twisted it in his hands. "My wife does not mourn with me. I have spoken to Maecenas, but he says I should not divorce her. He says the people need to see that Caesar is constant. But Julia says . . ."

"What does Julia say?"

Octavian looked Pomponia in the eye. "Do you think that Livia had Agrippa killed? And the child . . . do you think she had a hand in his death?"

Pomponia pulled her palla tighter around herself. Thanks to Despina's letters, she knew this question was coming. She knew most things. Within minutes of the baby's midnight death, she had known about his passing. And since that time, Despina had kept her apprised of everything that transpired in Caesar's home: every one of Julia's accusations, every conversation between Octavian and Livia, every discussion between Caesar and Maecenas, and every decision the emperor was planning to make.

Yes, Caesar, Pomponia thought. **Your wife killed them both—first Agrippa and then his son, your true blood heir. She also killed my friend Medousa, at one time your favorite bed slave. She is a murderous harpy in human form, and one day, if you are not careful, she will kill you.**

How she longed to say those words. They would taste like honey leaving her lips. But she knew she could not. **Nota res mala optima.** The evil you know is better than the evil you do not know.

"No," she said. "Livia would never hurt you so deeply. She wants Tiberius to be your heir and has made no secret of that, but she is his mother, and that is only natural. The deaths are unkind coincidences."

"Unkind coincidences," mused Octavian. "You echo Maecenas." He pulled his hands out from beneath the blanket and folded them on his lap. "Thank you for your counsel, Priestess. I will give her what she wants. I will make Tiberius my heir. Once my will is amended, I will deliver it into your hands myself for safekeeping."

"We shall protect it as we protect Vesta's fire."

He sighed tiredly. "I am planning a number of Senate and funding reforms, and the senators are not going to like it. I need a man I can count on to have my back. Tiberius is the only remaining option. I do not want to wear armor under my toga for the rest of my days. He is the closest male relative I have, even if it is not by blood."

"I understand perfectly," said Pomponia. "It is a wise decision under the circumstances. And if I may speak boldly, Caesar, perhaps Tiberius will surprise you. When you were ill with the contagion, he followed your and Agrippa's instructions to the letter. And remember your speech on the Rostra at Agrippa's funeral? When you wavered from grief, he supported you in front of the people."

"That is true," he agreed. "He may indeed exceed my expectations. That is also my hope." Octavian surveyed the courtyard—Pomponia had the sense he was making sure his daughter did not unexpectedly walk in on them—and then spoke again. "Since he is to be my heir, I must also marry him to Julia."

Pomponia pushed a lock of loose hair under her veil. "Yes."

"I know there is no affection between them," said Octavian. "But Tiberius is close in years to Julia, not like Agrippa was. They will learn to love each other. A baby will help."

"Of course," said Pomponia, knowing the words were Livia's.

"How will Julia react?" Octavian asked her.

"Less dutifully than she did with Agrippa," she replied.

Octavian wrung his hands. "Yes, I know. I am thinking of having Maecenas tell her while I am at the Senate house."

"You will hear her reaction from there," Pomponia replied.

Octavian laughed. It was a sad, tired laugh, but a laugh nonetheless.

"There is one more thing," he said. "A personal matter. In one of Cicero's letters, he mentions that High Priestess Fabiana had given him a special oil lamp for his daughter's entombment. Do you know anything about this?"

"Not specifically, but Cicero did visit Fabiana several times after Tullia's death. I suspect she gave him a perpetual lamp. It is a rare and very old custom that comes from Alba Longa. There is a certain way to prepare the oil so that it burns indefinitely . . ." Her voice trailed off as she struggled to remember the procedure. "I will consult the archives and personally prepare one for the child."

"His ashes will be entombed in my mausoleum the day after tomorrow."

"The lamp will be ready," said Pomponia. "And the light will stay with him."

"That is some comfort," Octavian replied. "Little children do not like the dark."

CHAPTER XIX

Ride Si Sapis

Laugh, if you are wise.

—MARTIAL

The grand wedding reception of the emperor's daughter, Julia, to her stepbrother, Tiberius, now the official heir of Caesar, was held on the Caelian Hill at the sprawling luxury estate of a wealthy land-owner and merchant named Pollio.

Lively music and even livelier conversation pulsed throughout Pollio's house and streamed into the home's beautiful central courtyard, in the middle of which was a large oval pool of clear water. Rounding the pool were colorful statues of aquatic wildlife—vivid green alligators, purple octopuses, and massive eels with reflective glass eyes and glistening white teeth.

Anchises had never been to such an elaborate or crowded private function. Then again, it wasn't a purely private function. The wedding of Caesar's daughter to his heir was a public matter as much as a personal one.

The famed singer, this time dressed in a rich red tunica with silver trim, had opened the celebration with a song about Jason and the Argonauts and their quest for the Golden Fleece. The crowd had applauded greatly at the end and said it was perfection, but Anchises was still silently fuming at the idiot lyre player who had dropped a note. No one had seemed to notice, but it still irked him. He hated working with amateurs.

After the performance, a number of men had offered him coin, but he graciously declined. Unlike his former master, Bassus, who let him keep his gratuities, Soren was not so generous. Anchises thought of the heavy purse of coin that he and Thracius had saved up and buried for safekeeping in the woods outside Capua. Their plan had been to retrieve it after their manumission and start a new life with it. These days, his only plan was to get through each day without setting his master off.

He had now been in Rome for months and had not seen Thracius once during that time. He had stopped asking Soren about him. Not only were answers never forthcoming but Soren seemed to actually enjoy withholding the information. Anchises wouldn't give him the satisfaction anymore.

As the singer conversed with two senators and their wives, he glanced at his master out of the corner of his eye and saw that Soren was staring at him, judging how he was interacting with Rome's elite. As Soren's property, Anchises's behavior was a reflection on the master himself.

Anchises smiled obligingly as one of the senator's wives continued to speak of her own remarkable singing ability. Her self-praise was interrupted by a toga-clad man with gold cuffs on both wrists who entered the garden with his arms in the air to catch everyone's attention.

"My dear friends," said Taurus, "what a wonderful occasion we celebrate this afternoon! The marriage of the emperor's daughter, Julia, who we have watched grow before our eyes, to the emperor's heir, Tiberius. It is a union that all of Rome rejoices in." Taurus glanced at the bride and groom but, realizing they were the only two people not rejoicing, quickly moved on. "We thank Pollio for his hospitality in hosting this prestigious reception."

Pollio stood and nodded in appreciation as the

gathering applauded. "It is my great honor and privilege to do so," he said. He turned and bowed to Octavian and Livia, seated on one couch near the edge of the oval pool, as well as to Julia and Tiberius seated on an adjacent couch. Octavian and Livia smiled. Julia scowled. Tiberius drained the wine in his cup.

Taurus continued. "Tonight, dear friends, you have already been treated to the unmatched voice of Anchises, but now—prepare yourselves! For you are about to be entertained by the other half of Apollo's Pair, in his very first fight in Rome—Thracius the boxer! Let us see what the Fates hold in store for the sun god's famous fighter here in the Caput Mundi!"

A swell of excitement. Ten or twelve of Pollio's house slaves appeared in the courtyard carrying tall torches. They arranged them in a circle at the far end of the oval pool. As the guests rushed from all directions to gather around the makeshift boxing ring, Thracius entered the garden.

Like all boxers, he neared the ring wearing nothing but a loincloth and a pair of **caestus**—leather straps wrapped around his knuckles and fastened under his palms. His eyes were moving over the faces around him.

Anchises knew he was looking for him. Feeling

his heart race and fighting the urge to call out, he snaked his way through the crowd until he caught Thracius's eye.

The boxer looked fit and healthy, but both of his eyes were swollen from hits: one was healing from a deep cut that Anchises estimated had happened only two or three days earlier. He had some strange bruising on his bare back, and a fresh scar ran the length of his left lower leg, from the back of his knee to his ankle. Whatever training he was receiving in Rome left marks.

Like Anchises, Thracius had had his former ownership tattoo removed from his forearm. A thick, uneven scar was forming over what had clearly been a deep and painful burn. Above the scar, the letters **SCP** had been tattooed to identify the boxer as Soren's property.

Thracius stopped in his tracks and looked at Anchises. He opened his mouth to call out to him, but the singer shook his head emphatically. **No! This is not the time.**

When Anchises looked back at the ring, he saw that Thracius's opponent had already entered it. The man was taller than Thracius, completely bald and naked except for a pair of caestus. Anchises looked more closely—unlike Thracius's pair, his opponent's wound all the way up to the elbow and were outfitted with iron spikes protruding from the knuckles. He swallowed hard. Such unfair gimmicks were frowned upon in Capua.

But if Thracius was bothered by his opponent's advantage, he didn't show it. He entered the ring and pulled off his loincloth, tossing it aside. It was customary for boxers to fight naked, and the women in the crowd seemed pleased. Several exchanged mischievous glances: their female friends in Capua had not exaggerated Thracius's attributes.

Thracius briefly eyed his opponent and again scanned the crowd. He saw Anchises and looked him over as if checking for signs of harm. Seeing none, he smiled. But the momentary distraction meant that he felt his opponent's hit before he saw it—a solid blow to the side of his head. One of the spikes in the man's caestus tore open Thracius's earlobe, and blood ran down his neck, over his chest.

Thracius didn't react to the pain but instead frowned in anger and swung at his opponent, once, twice, three times, hitting the man's skull each time. He was about to swing a fourth time, when the man slumped to the ground. Dead.

The crowd fell silent. They had never seen a match end so quickly. Out of the silence came a chuckle. Taurus, laughing at the crowd's stunned reaction. He stood next to the boxing ring and held up his arms. "Do not worry, friends. The Fates are not through with Thracius yet."

As two slaves dragged the fighter's limp body out of the torch-lined ring, another fighter stepped into it.

This opponent was nearly identical to his predecessor. The only difference, as far as Anchises could tell, was that this one had a strange depression on the very top of his bald head, as if it had been partially caved in by a rounded object. Like the fighter before him, he wore a pair of caestus wrapped to the elbows with spikes protruding from the knuckles.

Thracius narrowed his eyes and raised his fists, readying his muscular arms for battle. His opponent swung first, but Thracius ducked and came back up in one movement, grabbing the back of the man's bald head and bringing it down hard on his knee with an audible **crack**. Blood poured out of the man's broken nose, but he wiped it away and shook his head, stumbling backward. Thracius again glanced toward Anchises, but when he did, his opponent swept his legs out from under him, landing

DEBRA MAY MACLEOD

him on his back with a solid thud. The bald man kicked Thracius twice in the head and then dropped down hard on top of him.

"So, how are you enjoying Rome, Anchises?"

A form moved in front of Anchises, blocking his view of the match. It was a senator he had met at the last event he had performed at. He struggled to remember the man's name as he peeked around him, trying to see what was happening in the ring.

"It is a change, to be sure," he said, "but I am adjusting. How is your son, Senator? Did you not say he was ill the last time I saw you?"

"I did, Anchises. How good of you to remember. Yes, he is much improved. We feared it was the contagion, but a week in the country seems to have cured him."

"Thank the gods," said Anchises. He pointed over the man's shoulder. "Do you not enjoy boxing, Senator?"

"No, not really." He curled up his lip. "Can't stand the sight of blood, to be honest. Who's the dainty now, hey?" He ribbed the singer jovially.

"It is still me," said Anchises. Again, he peered around the senator's head.

"Oh yes," said the senator, "I forgot the boxer is

your boy. Or maybe it's the other way around. What business is it of mine, hey? **Suum cuique.** I'll let you watch the match. I should find my wife, anyway. Oh look, there she is." He winked at Anchises. "By the way she's eyeing up your man, I think I'd better take her inside, for both our sakes."

"Well done, Senator," Anchises said and smiled, praying to the gods the man would move on. When he finally did, Anchises moved closer to the ring.

Both boxers were on their feet now. Thracius had his arms tightly around his opponent's chest as the man fought to twist free. He succeeded and swung around to strike Thracius but missed and took two fast, hard blows to the side of his head. A flurry of rib-breaking strikes to the chest followed. The patrician spectators cheered.

The bald fighter began to fall. As he did, Thracius brought his elbow down on the depression in the man's skull. The cavity collapsed inward to the level of the fighter's brow. His eyes rolled back in his head, and he fell onto his knees, but before he could fall forward entirely, Thracius kicked him under the chin and his head whipped back, the bones in his neck breaking with a loud, crowd-pleasing **snap**. Blood sprayed out of his nostrils.

Two or three of the wives who had been watching only steps away from the action decided that a close-up view of Thracius's manhood just wasn't worth getting blood on their good dresses and made their way toward the back of the crowd.

The bald fighter dead on the ground, Thracius started to unfasten his caestus. He stopped as Taurus rushed to the ring carrying a helmet and followed by yet another boxer. This one wore a shining breastplate decorated with the three Fates—three women standing in a circle around a golden loom, stars floating over their heads.

"Friends," said Taurus, and turning to the boxer, "mighty Thracius! As you all know, our fate comes in threes." He handed the third opponent the helmet. The man put it on and stepped into the ring as if he, not Thracius, were the star of the show.

Taurus continued. "The first Fate, Clotho, spins the thread of our lives. Her sister Lachesis distributes those threads, and then the most feared of the sister Fates, Atropos, cuts the thread . . . But when? That is the question that none of us can answer. Let us hope that Thracius's thread is not cut now, as he faces his fate for the third and final time!"

The crowd laughed at Taurus's dramatics. It was

all very amusing, and they were having a good time.

Anchises's throat was dry. Thracius looked more tired than he should after two quick matches. He looked stressed. Distracted. This was no boxing match, no test of skill. It was a circus of gimmicks. How could a tired, naked boxer fight a fresh man in armor?

The third opponent roared like a lion and thumped his breastplate with his spiked caestus. The **clang** rang out to applause. Anchises slipped to the front row of spectators and met Thracius's eyes. A half smile creased the boxer's lips. Anchises could read his eyes: **It is all right. I love you. Take care of yourself.**

The singer shook his head: **Do not lose. Do not leave me.**

Anchises felt a strong hand grip his shoulder.

"You're not here to watch," said Soren. "You're here to work. There are some women waiting for you over there. Go entertain them."

Anchises balked. He held Thracius's eyes for a long moment, praying it would not be their last, and then turned to go, leaving his lover to his fate.

Anchises weaved through the crowded gardens, past the oval pool and along the peristyle until he reached a group of perhaps fifteen women reclining on several long couches, eating, drinking, and gossiping around a large statue of a swan, the graceful neck of which extended some six feet high.

He forced a smile onto his lips, trying to ignore the sickening feeling in his stomach and the ring of tightness around his throat. Shouts and cheers floated through the air from the boxing ring to the swan statue. Another lion roar from the armor-clad opponent.

"Ladies," said Anchises. "How lovely to see you again."

"Anchises," said the wife of a certain senator, "where did you learn to sing as you do?"

"My father was an accomplished virtuoso on Delos," he said. "He used to sing for Andronicus of Rhodes, the famous philosopher who published Aristotle's works."

"Did Andronicus not teach in Rome some years back?" asked a young voice. Anchises bowed. It was the young Vestal Quintina. "Yes, Priestess," he said. "I am certain Andronicus would have taught some of the men here today, or their fathers."

"And some of the women," said Quintina.

"If there were any justice in this world," replied Anchises, "he would have taught **all** the women."

Quintina rewarded him with a warm smile as the chief Vestal appeared at her shoulder.

Another roar and cheer from the boxing ring.

Another question from the half-drunk wife of an even drunker senator. As Anchises answered her question, he noticed that the emperor had quietly approached and was whispering into the ear of the chief Vestal. The high priestess discreetly excused herself to speak with him in the peristyle.

"Caesar," she said, "the wedding went well, and the reception goes even better. You must be pleased."

"It goes smoothly on the surface," replied Octavian. "Underneath, the current is unpleasant."

Pomponia couldn't disagree. Anyone who knew Julia could tell that she was a heartbeat away from tearing off her wedding veil and strangling her new husband with it. Or her father.

"I hope this was not a mistake," he said to himself as much as to Pomponia. They both looked at Julia. She was drunk and leaning against a column further down the peristyle, speaking too loudly to— Pomponia frowned—Septimus. To the young man's credit, he was trying to calm her.

"Caesar," said a light voice, "your daughter is a lovely bride." It was Quintina's younger sister, Tacita.

She moistened her lips and touched his chest with her fingertips.

Pomponia's frown deepened. She hadn't seen Tacita approach and hadn't even known she was here. The young woman's boldness with Caesar annoyed her.

She wasn't the only one who thought that way. Livia seemed to materialize from nowhere, gracefully hooking her arm around Caesar's and kissing his cheek. He returned the kiss and turned his head away from Tacita, sending an obvious message. **Move on.**

Tacita slunk away—and made a straight line for the arm of Septimus. As Caesar had done, Septimus turned away from her. Again, she slunk off.

That's hopeful, thought Pomponia. **Maybe she won't be able to cause any more trouble.**

In fact, the only person who looked like she was going to cause any trouble at all was the bride. Julia was growing louder and more belligerent by the second.

"Something must be done," Livia muttered.

Pomponia was about to go speak with Julia, when Quintina brushed by.

"Julia," said Quintina, "why don't you come with me and listen to Anchises? He is a very interesting man."

Julia swayed on her feet. "All right, my friend," she said, but then Tiberius strode past and she sneered at him.

Quintina grimaced. Bad timing.

"Oh, Quintina," slurred Julia. "You say that Anchises is an interesting man? Let me tell you, my friend, there are no interesting men. Take this fool my father has forced me to marry. I know I should cry, but I can only laugh. I don't know what the idiot will do a worse job of screwing, Rome or his wife." She leaned in. "You lead a charmed life, Quintina. You and your sister Vestals . . . your chastity is a gift from the goddess. Just for a moment, close your eyes and imagine yourself lying sweetly in your bed . . . now open your eyes and picture Tiberius coming at you in the dark! His stinking breath, his stupid face, his flaccid—"

Julia's body convulsed with a particularly unflattering wine belch. That seemed to calm her down, and she moved to sit on the edge of Caesar's couch. Her eyes went wide, and she pointed into the garden. "I stand corrected," she said. "There is one interesting man left. Oh, how I wish I were spending my wedding night with that one!"

They all turned to see a naked Thracius being toured through the courtyard by Soren.

Both of the boxer's eyes were swollen nearly shut, although it looked as though one of the swellings had been slit open and drained so that he could see well enough to walk. Several open gashes poured blood from his side. He was dripping in sweat. Pieces of dirt and stone were stuck to his flesh from having grappled for his life on the ground.

Anchises reacted without thinking. He ran to Thracius and threw his arms around him. The men embraced tightly.

A wave of emotion and a loud, exuberant cheer washed over the crowd. **Apollo's Pair! What a performance!**

A gloating smile formed on Soren's lips. It faded only a bit as he noted the blood and grime Anchises had gotten on his expensive tunica.

* * *

The applause and accolades for Apollo's Pair continued for some time. As it subsided and the wedding guests returned to their wine, drink, and gossip, Thracius was separated from Anchises and led into a corner of the gardens where three slaves began the task of cleaning him in a tub of water and dressing his wounds.

A small group of women stood nearby and watched as the boxer was washed and outfitted in a fine tunica that matched the one Anchises was wearing—red, with silver trim. Almost immediately, blood spots soaked through the fabric from Thracius's wounds to make his tunica an even deeper red. That didn't dampen the women's interest but, rather, inflamed it.

Anchises knew what was happening. Soren was auctioning Thracius off, for one night only, to the highest bidder. The women that had gathered around him were either widows or wives whose husbands were not at the reception, most likely out of Rome on business while their wives indulged in pleasure.

The singer swallowed hard to suppress the rise of jealousy he felt. Normally, this part of an event didn't bother him that much. He was accustomed to it, but it had been so long since he had been with Thracius, so long since they had been intimate or even able to speak privately, that he almost resented him for the physical pleasure he would experience tonight. He knew he shouldn't feel that way. He knew that Thracius would prefer to be with him and not some leering, rich wife. But it still hurt.

He felt a hand on his shoulder—not Soren's painful

clench, but a softer touch. He turned to face the chief Vestal Pomponia. She was looking at him curiously.

"Come sit with me and my brother," she said. It was as much an order as an offer. Then again, privileged women usually spoke that way.

The Vestal led him to three private couches arranged to face each other in a quiet section of the peristyle around the courtyard. A man was already reclining on one.

"This is my brother, Pomponius," said the Vestal.

"Hello, Domine," said Anchises.

Pomponius sat up and gestured cordially to the couch next to him. Anchises sat down.

"I saw you perform in Capua two or three years ago," said Pomponius. "You were as exceptional then as you were tonight, although . . ."

"Yes, Domine?"

"That lyre player should be run through with a long sword for dropping a note," he said.

"I couldn't agree more, Domine."

Pomponia glanced at the scar and new ownership tattoo on Anchises's forearm. She leaned over the low table that sat in the middle of the couches and filled a plate with meat.

"Eat," she said, holding the plate out to Anchises.

The Vestal passes me food? The breach in protocol made Anchises hesitate. The Vestalis Maxima passing food to a slave? He knew he should refuse, but he was starving. Even the gut-churning anxiety of the boxing match had not stopped his hunger pangs.

"Priestess," he said, "I think I will. Thank you." He accepted the plate graciously but then nervously cast his eyes around the courtyard to see if Soren was watching. If his master saw this, he'd take a bloody beating at home.

"Tell us, Anchises," said Pomponia. "How is life under Soren?" Her voice had an edge of concern that Anchises would not have expected from someone of her standing. Anchises gripped the plate in his hands and said nothing.

"Never mind," said Pomponius. "Just eat."

Anchises chewed slowly. He could be stoic in the face of cruelty. In the presence of sympathetic company, however, he found it more difficult to keep his defenses up, and he could feel a lump forming in his throat.

A loud voice from a nearby set of couches made all three of them turn their heads. Julia was at it again. She was standing in front of the emperor and empress, looking down at them as they reclined on their couches and announcing some discontent to them. Her new husband, Tiberius, was standing beside her, his hands on his hips.

Quintina put her hand on Julia's back. "Let us go in the house now, Julia." The bride glared at her father and then her stepmother. No one was quite sure what she was going to do next, but she only wiped her eyes and went off with Quintina.

Tiberius remained where he stood. He shrugged at Livia, and she shrugged back. It didn't matter. Julia could pout until Atlas dropped the heavens. The marriage was a done deal. The emperor sat up. "Water," he said.

Pollio, the host, snapped his fingers, and a slave moved quickly in front of the emperor to present him with a glass of water.

As Octavian reached out for it, the slave—a teenaged boy whose hands shook at the prospect of serving Caesar—let the glass slip from his hands. It shattered at Octavian's feet.

"You fool!" the host shouted.

"It is no matter," said Octavian.

"Breaking a glass at Caesar's feet is unforgivable," Pollio insisted. He took two angry steps toward his slave, clutched him by the hair, and proceeded to drag him toward the oval pool of water.

"No, Domine!" the young slave cried out in terror. "I meant no harm!"

Pollio didn't listen. As a crowd gathered around, he threw the boy into the still water.

And then the water came alive.

Eels. Hundreds of them. They swarmed the boy so violently, splashing and jumping, that it suddenly looked as though the oval pool were a giant pot of boiling water.

More spectators rushed to the side of the pool. Now **this** was something they hadn't seen before. As they gaped into the water below, tens of spotted brown eels descended on the slave boy. They clamped their teeth onto every part of his body—his arms, legs, face, buttocks—and twisted their snake-like bodies around his.

"Great Jupiter!" exclaimed a woman in a rich orange dress. "He looks like a son of Laocoön, attacked by sea serpents!"

Her companions laughed and raised their wine cups in agreement.

The boy gasped for breath. In his terror and pain, he tried to unclamp the eels' jaws from his body, but soon he was so weighed down by their long, fleshy bodies that it was all he could do to keep his mouth and nose above water.

"Mama, Mama!" he called out.

An older female slave rushed to the side of the pool and collapsed onto her belly, screaming and shrieking and reaching into the water to grab for the boy. Five or six eels instantly latched onto her arms, curling around them and biting hard. She didn't seem to feel the pain, but only continued to grab for her child, even as the water turned red around him.

"How awful," said Pomponius. He tried not to look, but the shrieking and wild splashing, the exclamations of those circled about the pool to watch, were impossible to ignore. He saw his friend Virgil shake his head and wander off. As the poet left, Pomponius spotted Soren next to a girl he recognized as Priestess Quintina's sister, Tacita: they were standing side by side at the very edge of the water, watching the boy be devoured—bit by bit, bite by bite—with open amusement. Tacita vacillated between laughter and disgust. Soren just laughed.

Pomponius wondered if Soren would still laugh if he knew that Scorpus the Titan was hiding in an insula in the Subura waiting to strike again, like an eel hiding in the depths.

Like her brother, Pomponia was also trying but failing to ignore what was happening only a few meters away. But there was just too much commotion. It seemed the only people who weren't watching were Anchises and Thracius.

Anchises was sitting up straight on the couch, clutching the plate in his hands. Pomponia followed his eyes. Thracius was being shackled for transport, and the two men were looking at each other. Even as the screams and splashes continued, the boxer was led away. A middle-aged woman dressed in a rich turquoise dress and yellow palla, long gold earrings grazing her shoulders, followed happily behind him. One of her friends winked at her as she left.

The mother of the boy in the pool of eels let out a particularly horrid scream. "Vesta Mater," she cried out. "Save my son, Goddess!"

Pomponia stood up, nearly knocking over an amphora of wine on the table. She gathered her stola around her and looked for Octavian. He was no longer sitting on his couch, so she moved closer to the pool.

The first person she spotted was Tiberius. He was leaning over the water to get a good look at what was happening. He laughed, and the wine in his cup sloshed out into the water. It was already red with blood, so it made no difference.

A large eel jumped out of the pool and flopped around the blue tile at the sandaled feet of several spectators. Tiberius chortled and kicked it back into the water as the men around him cheered and congratulated him on his bravery.

Finally, Pomponia spotted Octavian. He and Livia were also standing by the pool watching the boy's violent struggle. Livia watched with fascination. Octavian seemed disinterested or, more likely, distracted from his argument with his daughter.

"Caesar," she said quietly as she reached his side. "I am going to end this. Such ill treatment, even of a slave, taints your daughter's wedding day."

"Priestess Pomponia," said Livia, "Pollio is only showing his respect to Caesar."

Octavian nodded slowly. Livia smiled at his agreement, then frowned as he said, "You are correct, Priestess."

"Caesar," said Livia, "it is Pollio's home."

"Pollio's home?" Octavian said with incredulity. "It is my empire!" He searched the crowd for the host and then shouted, "Take the boy out at once!"

Without waiting for a direct order from their master—certainly, one from Caesar would suffice—two house slaves rushed to the side of the pool. They extended a long pole out to the boy in the water.

"Grab it, Felix! Grab it!" they shouted. The boy tried to reach the pole, but it was too short and he was too weighted down with eels to swim to it.

At that, the tide turned, and the crowd began to root for the boy. "Reach for it, young Felix! Swim to it!" they called out. They began to look for more poles, more tools they could use to reach him and pull him to safety.

A particularly inventive senator spotted a tall sapling at the far end of the garden and ran to twist and yank it out of the ground. He ran back to the pool and extended it out to the boy. It was just long enough to reach him, and he grabbed onto it.

The senator pulled back on the sapling, but it wasn't until two other men joined in that the boy and his horrible load began to move through the water toward the edge of the oval pool. The men pulled harder. They heaved the boy out of the water and onto the blue tile that skirted the pool. Several eels still had their jaws fastened on him, and their long bodies coiled around his limbs.

The boy's mother began to peel them off, sticking her fingers into their jaws to unclamp them from her son's body. One of the house slaves jabbed at the eels with the pole in his hands until, at last, the boy was free. He scrambled to his knees—bloody bite marks covering his body—and embraced his mother. Both of them were crying.

The crowd applauded. But the show wasn't quite over.

Octavian pointed at the soaked, shaking boy. "Bring me every glass in this house," he said. "Now."

"Yes, Caesar." The boy's voice trembled from shock and pain, but he stood and ran off to do as he was told, rushing out of the courtyard and into the house, leaving bloody footprints in his trail.

Pollio and the gathering of wedding guests waited openmouthed in the courtyard. Even from where they stood, they could hear the frantic shouts and rustling of slaves inside the house as they hastily gathered every glass they could find.

Within minutes, the boy returned to the courtyard along with two other slaves. They each pushed a large cartful of glasses.

Caesar strode to the boy's cart. He reached into it and pulled out an expensive glass, then immediately smashed it onto the tiled floor. Then he did it again. He looked up. "Everyone," he said.

The wedding guests moved uncertainly toward the carts. But an order from Caesar was an order. They began to throw the glasses against the floor, each one shattering loudly and leaving sharp chunks and glistening shards around sandaled feet. They continued until all three carts were empty and every glass in Pollio's house had been broken.

And then, in an act of violence they hadn't seen from Caesar in many years, they watched him grab the shoulders of Pollio and toss him into the pool of eels.

The creatures reacted no differently to the rich man than they had to the slave. The only change was that no saplings came to the host's rescue.

Octavian stared at Livia. "I hereby manumit every slave in the household of Pollio and claim his estate as my own," he said. "Its assets will be sold off and distributed equally to the former slaves of the household."

As the reality of what was happening descended on the former slaves of Pollio—now freedmen and freedwomen—they lowered themselves onto their knees and began to cry, "**Ave, Caesar!**"

The wedding guests erupted in applause.

Pomponia found that her mouth was hanging open. She closed it. Tiberius—how long had he been standing beside her?—smiled.

"Now, **this** is a party," he said to her. He raised his wine cup to the Vestal and moved on.

While the other astonished wedding guests gathered around to watch Pollio—this was no slave, but one of their own—thrash and gasp before disappearing under the blood-red water, Pomponia returned to her couch. Anchises was still sitting rigidly, but Pomponius was grinning.

"Taurus couldn't have scripted a better tragedy," her brother said to her as she sat down.

Pomponia tried not to smile but couldn't help it. "Look at him," she said, and they all turned to look at the ludus owner. He was applauding the dramatics and dictating notes to his scribe. "He'll be reenacting this in the arena on the Lupercalia," she added.

Anchises placed his wine cup on the table and stood.

"You can ask any slave where the latrine is," said Pomponius, and then added, "Oh, I guess there aren't any slaves left now, strictly speaking. Someone will direct you."

"Thank you, Domine," said Anchises. The singer

excused himself and exited the clamor of the court-yard to enter the calm of the house.

He did not need to use the latrine. He just needed a private space to take a deep breath. He was feeling light-headed. Between Soren's threatening gaze, Thracius's pummeling and prostitution, and the eels—it was too much. He could only keep up the facade for so long before it started to crumble. He had always been that way.

As he entered the empty triclinium, he exhaled loudly, and an unseen form that had been reclining on a couch sat up quickly. It was the emperor's daughter.

"I am so sorry, Domina." Anchises bowed. "I did not see you there. I did not mean to disturb you."

"You are the only person who has not disturbed me tonight." Julia wiped her eyes. "Come, Anchises," she said. "Sit by me, and sing me a song."

Anchises sat beside Caesar's daughter. He had not seen her since he had sung at her son's naming celebration. How cruelly the Fates had dealt with her since. To his surprise, she took his hands in her own. "Do you have a favorite song, Domina?" he asked.

"Sing your favorite."

"Alas," he said, "my favorite song is a sad one."

"Perfect."

Anchises sang of Odysseus, whom the Romans called Ulysses, the great warrior whose wily mind created the Trojan horse that ended the war but whose fate was a plaything of the gods. They cast his ship this way and that upon the sea for ten long years, preventing him from returning home to his beloved Penelope.

He sang of the sad hero's longing for his true love, even as he was forced to be with another, even as he wondered whether her love for him would stay true. And then he sang of the hero's resolve, his strength, and his refusal to let even the gods sink his spirit. His voice cracked—that never happened—and Julia squeezed his hands.

> **What if the gods do wreck me out**
> **on the wine-dark sea?**
> **My heart is hardened to suffering,**
> **and I shall endure.**
> **In my day, I have weathered many**
> **storms. They are not strangers**
> **to me.**
> **And so let this new calamity come.**
> **It only makes one more.**

When he was finished, Julia patted his hands. "You bring me comfort, Anchises."

"It pleases me to hear it."

Julia kept her hands on his. "They will not let me see my daughter, Agrippina," she said.

Anchises lowered his head. "I have also been kept from someone I love," he replied.

Julia gently pulled her hands away. "I can tell by the way you sing," she said. "Bonam noctem, Anchises."

The singer stood. "Bonam noctem, Lady Julia." He departed with a deep bow and was reluctantly heading back to the courtyard, when Soren stepped in front of him.

"What was that all about?" he asked, jutting his chin back toward the triclinium and Julia.

"Lady Julia requested a private song, Domine."

Soren clucked his tongue. "Good," he said. "We're leaving."

"Yes, Domine."

Anchises wished he had the opportunity to say good evening to the Vestal and her brother, but it would not happen. Soren took fast, long strides through the house and atrium, out the portico and over the pavement to his waiting lectica and the slaves who stood by it. Anchises had to move quickly to keep up with him.

When they reached it, Soren said, "You can travel inside with me."

"Thank you, Domine," Anchises replied. **Although, I'd rather have bleeding feet than ride with you**, he thought.

Soren stepped into the lectica and Anchises followed after, sitting on the couch opposite his master. The litter-bearers were just about to lift and move forward, when Soren spotted Tacita coming out of the portico. He held back the curtain, ordered his slaves to wait, and called her.

Giggling, she ran over and stepped inside. She sat close to Soren. Anchises thought about getting out of the lectica but decided it would be safer to wait for instruction from Soren. There was no predicting what his master wanted, so he just stared at the floor.

"Soren, you scamp," said Tacita, "are you sneaking out already?"

"I am," Soren replied humorlessly, "but not without giving you some advice first."

Tacita raised her eyebrows and touched his chest. "Oh? And what might that be?"

"You're wasting your time trying to seduce the emperor."

She pulled her hand away and stopped smiling. "I don't know what you mean."

"It's pointless."

"Is it?" she asked. "And what if I told you that the emperor has already had me?"

"I'd say that half the men in Rome have already had you, and you aren't any further ahead for it. Only a fool keeps making the same mistake." Soren sniffed. "You need to start using your head and not just your tits, as pretty as they are. The empress guards her husband like the Minotaur guards the Labyrinth. And like the Minotaur, she's very skilled at devouring young maidens like you."

Tacita huffed. "I'm not saying you're right, Soren," she said, "but let's assume for a moment that you are. What is your advice for me?"

"All night I watched you flitting from one senator to another, from one high priest to another, from one rich landowner to another, but they're all wise to your ways. So are their wives. You need to aim for someone who isn't used to being targeted."

"And I suppose you have someone in mind?"

"I do," said Soren. "The Vestalis Maxima has a brother named Pomponius. The man is one step above an imbecile, but he is wealthy and well connected.

He has probably never had a woman that he didn't own. If you were sharper, you would've noticed that he was looking at you all afternoon. Cozy up to him and you cozy up to Rome's elite."

Tacita reached out a hand and placed it between Soren's legs, squeezing gently. "How might I show my gratitude for your concern?"

Soren leaned toward her and placed his lips on hers, kissing her deeply. She groaned and pressed her body into his, but as soon as she felt him harden against her palm, he pulled away.

"Keep me apprised," he said as he held open the curtain for her. "Come to me when he's yours."

She giggled and stepped out of the lectica. "Good night."

"Let's move," Soren called out to his slaves. As the litter-bearers lifted the lectica and began to move, Soren closed the curtains.

Anchises kept his eyes on the floor as the lectica gently swayed with each step; even so, he could feel the weight of Soren's gaze on him. He prayed that his master would put his head back and fall asleep so he could finally take a deep breath.

"When you and the boxer had sex," said Soren, "who would penetrate who?"

Anchises felt the blood rush to his head. He licked his lips nervously, desperately thinking how best to respond.

"Who would penetrate who?" Soren asked again. His tone suggested he didn't want to ask a third time.

"Usually Thracius would penetrate me," said Anchises. He could hear his voice trembling with equal parts fear and humiliation. Such information was private. It belonged between him and Thracius only.

"Did you ever penetrate him?" Soren asked.

"On occasion, yes."

"Did you fellate him?"

Anchises felt his chest tighten. "Yes."

"Are you any good at it?"

"I cannot say, Domine."

"Let me put it this way," said Soren. "Did you make him ejaculate?"

"Yes, Domine."

Soren shifted in his seat, and Anchises finally looked at him. He was sitting with his toga lifted and his genitals partly exposed. His loincloth lay in a small heap on the floor.

"Do it," he said to Anchises.

The singer moved off his seat and got onto his

knees on the floor of the lectica. He was determined not to protest—that would only add to Soren's pleasure. He reached out to touch Soren, when the man grabbed his hand roughly and squeezed hard. He pulled his toga back over his genitals and leaned forward, whispering in Anchises's ear.

"The next time I see you talking to that bitch priestess like she's your best friend, I'll penetrate you harder than a nail on a cross," he said.

Anchises held his breath. "Yes, Domine. I am sorry, Domine."

Soren put his head back. Within a few moments he was snoring. Quietly, Anchises lifted himself off the floor and sat on the cushioned seat across from his master. His eyes settled on the red scar that ran around Soren's neck.

If only Scorpus had finished the job, thought Anchises.

CHAPTER XX

Fere Libenter Homines Id Quod Volunt Credunt
Men readily believe what they want to believe.
–JULIUS CAESAR

Pomponius stepped in a pile of fly-covered feces and cursed under his breath. Caesar's public hygiene efforts, which he had continued after the death of Agrippa, had been ambitious and costly. Improved and expanded aqueducts brought unlimited fresh water to nearly a million people in Rome, while additional fountains provided safe drinking water. Countless new **thermae** and public latrines had been built to encourage cleanliness, and the massive sewer system of the Cloaca Maxima had been expanded even more to usher Rome's filth out of the city. Sanitation crews were constantly on the move, cleaning the streets and unclogging drains.

Although there were signs the contagion was abating as fall approached, it often felt like two steps forward, one step back. Despite the efforts, despite the cost, despite the proven efficacy of Caesar's public health policy, people still left shit on the streets.

Well, on some streets, Pomponius reflected with a sigh. **This** is **the Subura.**

Pomponius stopped to scrape off the bottom of his sandal. At least it wasn't an expensive pair. Like most things in his life, he had learned the hard way not to wear his good clothes to the Subura.

The first time he had come to visit Scorpus wearing a fine toga and sandals, he had woken up in a back alley with a goose egg on his head and wearing only his underclothes. He had been forced to walk barefoot to Scorpus's insula, and the charioteer had spent the entire visit doubled over in laughter at him.

Pomponius weaved through the narrow, crowded streets, ducking under clotheslines and keeping a wary eye turned upward to spot any piss pots that might be about to empty on top of his head from an open window in any one of the tall, multi-tenant insulae that surrounded him.

Shops lined the lower levels of the insulae: tables and carts were stacked with loaves of bread, fruits and vegetables, raw fish, slabs of meat, and amphorae of wine. Children ran wild between these carts, stealing what they could. Pomponius had to dodge a flying apple more than once as an angry shopkeeper took aim at a fleeing young thief.

The smell of food cooking from communal braziers filled his nostrils. The insulae in the Subura were packed so tightly that people generally shared cooking facilities. Or they just bought their meals from street vendors. This reduced the risk of fire, the ever-present danger that every urbanite feared. Next to war, fire was Rome's greatest threat, worse even than the contagion.

Pomponius turned the corner onto Scorpus's street. Only a couple blocks ahead, he could see the massive fire wall that had been erected to separate the Subura from the new Forum of Augustus and to protect Caesar's new forum and temples from the fires that so often raged through the Subura.

If a man were ambitious enough to climb the wall and sit on top, he would be able to gaze down upon two entirely different worlds. If he looked down at the poor Subura district, he would see endless rows of multistory wooden apartment blocks built so closely together that there was barely enough room to walk sideways along the bumpy stone and dirt streets that ran between them.

If he turned his head and looked down at the

Forum of Augustus, the view would change dramatically. He would see the monumental and nearly complete Temple of Mars Ultor, with its gleaming white marble exterior and its ornate floors made of purple, red, yellow, and black marble that had been imported from every exotic corner of the Roman Empire.

Pomponius slipped through the narrow doorway of Scorpus's insula block and ran up the creaky wooden stairs to the third-floor hideaway that he had rented for the charioteer. He banged on the door until Scorpus unlocked it.

Pomponius slipped inside and was instantly frustrated. These days, the Titan spent most of his time half-drunk, his barbarian beard sticky with wine. Today was no exception. The charioteer took the sack from Pomponius's hands and dumped its contents onto a rickety table.

"Meat, cheese, bread . . ." He looked at Pomponius. "Where's the wine?"

"You can pray to Bacchus for your wine," said Pomponius. "You're lucky I still bring you food." He sniffed. "It smells like a stable in here."

"I like the smell of stables," Scorpus replied. He shook the sack and heard something jingle.

Reaching in, he pulled out some loose gold coins at the bottom.

"It's more than enough to get out of Rome," said Pomponius.

"I have no intention of leaving Rome."

"Yes, well, why would you?" Pomponius glanced around the squalid apartment. "It has treated you to such good fortune."

"I will make my own fortune. I am not leaving Rome until I kill Soren."

"What do you do in here all day?" asked Pomponius.

"I have been helping a neighbor in his shop. He makes tombstones."

"Is that wise?"

"I can't think of a wiser business," Scorpus said with a grin. "Each day guarantees new customers."

Pomponius sighed. "Is it wise to be seen?"

"Probably not. But he is old and alone and has no one to help him. Anyway, Soren himself wouldn't recognize me with this beard and hair."

"You're a foot taller than any other man this side of the fire wall, and you can lift a slab of stone big enough to make a tombstone out of. You don't think he'd put it together?"

"Even if he did, he wouldn't report me. He'd lose his workhorse. Have you heard anything of the manhunt?"

"They've called it off. They think you're dead. Some soldier in Campania found a rotting corpse stuffed in a drain and said it matched your description. Probably just wanted the reward money." He eyed Scorpus's wiry black beard and unwashed hair. "Although you do look like a man who's spent some time in a drain." Pomponius walked to the small open window and looked down onto the street below. "The contagion seems worse here," he muttered.

"Everything is worse here," said Scorpus.

"What is this?" Pomponius picked up a small vial from the windowsill. It had a thin yellowish liquid inside.

"I bought it from a man on the street. He says it prevents the contagion. It is a sacred mixture from Apollo's temple at Delphi."

"Sure it is," Pomponius scoffed. "Is this how you spend my coin? Making these swindlers rich? This is probably a sacred mixture of rancid oil and horse piss." He sat on a squeaky chair—testing it before putting his full weight on it—and Scorpus sat on a low stool across from him. "When I went to the wedding reception of the emperor's daughter, Julia, I spoke to Caesar's physician, Musa. He has the most fascinating ideas about the contagion."

"Does he?" Scorpus said indulgently.

"He does. He has been consulting an old physician named Varro, and together they have speculated that certain diseases are carried by tiny creatures too small to be seen."

"**Tiny creatures too small to be seen?** And what do they do, carry the disease with them in little sacks that are also too small to be seen? That is crazy. They do not exist."

Pomponius shrugged his shoulders. "You cannot see the gods, and yet you believe they exist."

"So, now you don't believe in the gods? You are insane."

"I don't know if I believe or not," said Pomponius.

"It is a sacrilege to say so."

"Hardly. A man can believe what he likes. I even discussed the matter with Caesar."

"And what did Caesar say?"

"He said that as long as I believed in paying taxes, he didn't care either way."

"You put too much faith in physicians,

Pomponius." Scorpus reached for a piece of bread on the table and spoke as he chewed. "Do you know what the last tombstone I worked on said? It said, 'Here lies my beloved wife, who was strong enough to survive the contagion but not her doctor's cure.' That should tell you something."

Pomponius ignored him. "I spoke with someone else of interest at the reception. Someone you may know. A singer from Capua named Anchises."

Scorpus stopped chewing. "Anchises is in Rome? What about Thracius?"

"Yes, both of them are here. Soren has purchased them. Thracius is at the ludus, but Anchises lives in Soren's home."

Scorpus began to chew again, this time slower. "Then, my prayers are with them both."

"Anchises hates Soren. I sat with him, and I can tell."

"All of Soren's slaves hate him. What is it to me?"

"Maybe they can help us. Anchises seems quite clever."

"Anchises is a coward."

"Perhaps," said Pomponius. "But at some point, hatred becomes more powerful than fear."

"Finally, you speak sense," said Scorpus.

"Thracius is strong, and no more cowardly than you. He will be worried about Anchises. Maybe I can find a way to speak with him?"

"No," said Scorpus. "If you tell him about me, he will tell his master. He will hope that Soren will reward him by letting him see Anchises."

"How do you know that?"

"Because if Cassandra were still alive, that's what I would do."

"Not everyone thinks as you do."

"Thracius doesn't like me," said Scorpus.

"I can't fault him for that. But who do you think Thracius likes less, you or Soren? There is a saying: **Inimicus inimici amicus meus est.**" The enemy of my enemy is my friend.

Scorpus swallowed another mouthful of bread. "Let me think on it."

"Perhaps my sister could help you."

"Your sister? The Vestalis Maxima of Rome?" Scorpus laughed out loud.

"She does not like Soren."

"Not liking him and conspiring to kill him are two different things," said Scorpus. "If your sister finds out I'm alive, she will immediately order my death to cover your patrician ass."

Pomponius thought about it. "You're probably right."

"Just promise me that you won't do anything without talking to me first."

"You should be making **me** that promise."

"Tell me more about Soren," said Scorpus. "Was he at the reception?"

"Yes, he was there. You would smile to see the scar around his throat. He tries to cover it with a high tunica under his toga, but it is always visible." Pomponius scraped his feet on the floor. "I saw him speaking with the younger sister of one of the Vestals. Her name is Tacita. I ran into her in the market yesterday. She seemed kind of interested in me."

Scorpus shook his head. "Pomponius, you confound me. You can be wise and foolish to equal depths. If she is a friend of Soren's, she is no friend of ours."

"I did not say she was our friend. She may be **my** friend, though."

"She is not your friend."

"How would you know? You have not met her. My friend Virgil agreed she was beautiful."

"So what? You have coin. Go rent yourself a beautiful girl for the night and get it out of your system.

Rent three beautiful girls if you like. Or buy a new bed slave. I doubt this girl is truly interested in you."

"Why not? Because I have not raced a chariot around the track? Because I cannot play the big man?"

"Don't be stupid, Pomponius. You are not the type of man that women chase after. How well does she know Soren? Birds of the same feather always flock together."

"I am tired of talking about Soren," said Pomponius. He stood and crossed the floor of the small apartment. "Make the food last. I don't know when I can make it back," he said as he exited the apartment and slammed the door behind him.

Scorpus scrambled to his feet and opened the door, but Pomponius was already halfway down the stairs. "Fine," the charioteer shouted after him. "Don't forget the wine next time!"

* * *

"Domine, there is a Lady Tacita here to see you."

"Really?" Pomponius set the scroll he was reading on his desk and stood up. "Fix my toga," he said.

His slave adjusted the folds.

Pomponius made a conscious effort to stand up

straight—his sister was always after him for slouching—as he met Tacita in the atrium of his house on the Caelian Hill.

She was wearing a lavender dress with a deep pink palla. Small glass beads were woven into her dark hair, and they sparkled as the sunlight that streamed in from the open roof reflected off them. The last drops of the afternoon's light rain shower were falling into the impluvium below, and Tacita was playfully reaching for the raindrops.

"**Salve**, Lady Tacita," greeted Pomponius. "How nice to see you again."

She turned, and a warm smile spread across her lips. She put a wet fingertip into her mouth to taste the raindrop. "I hope you don't mind my stopping by without an appointment."

"Not at all. It is a pleasant surprise."

Tacita spun around, admiring the frescoes in the atrium. "This is my favorite," she said. It was a vivid blue peacock painted against a deep orange wall, with long, full tail feathers that filled most of the wall and fanned out into a splendid aura of green, purple, and gold.

"It is my favorite also," Pomponius replied. "It was painted by the same artist who painted the emperor's walls. This was my father's home, but I have made many improvements since I have taken possession of it. I have hired only the most skilled artists."

"I see." Tacita took a few sauntering steps to lean against a fluted column, also painted in a glistening sheen of green and gold. "I brought you a present," she said.

"Oh?"

She held out a yellow silk wrapping cloth that she had been hiding under her palla. Pomponius took it from her gently, although a little more awkwardly than he would have liked, and unwrapped the gift. A small bronze statuette of the goddess Vesta.

"I was looking at this yesterday in the market," he said happily.

"Yes, I know. I saw you," she replied. "I was pleased when you did not buy it, because I wanted to buy it for you."

Pomponius held up the statuette. "I am familiar with this particular metallurgist," he said. "He is as skilled as Vulcan himself." He turned the statuette over in his hands. "The casting is superb. Just look at the quality of the goddess's fingers . . . And here— the laurel wreath on her head—it is so detailed."

Tacita brought her face so close that Pomponius

could smell her perfume and feel her hair brush against his hands.

"I see," she said. "Very beautiful."

"He claims that he is descended from the Etruscan who made the she-wolf bronze on the Capitoline, but I think that may be overreaching, even for him. Although his bronze alloys do contain a higher copper content than any other metal sculptor I've seen work. He doesn't cheap out. His bronzes will outlast the empire."

"Do not let Caesar hear you say that," Tacita said with a giggle.

"I shall put this on my lararium immediately," said Pomponius. He walked to the shrine that stood against a scarlet wall of the atrium and placed the statuette of Vesta beside a burning candle. "It is a thoughtful gift," he said. "Thank you."

"Not at all," replied Tacita. "We both have sisters who are Vestal priestesses, so I thought it was suitable."

"Yes, we are blessed," said Pomponius. "Although, if I may be so bold, Tacita, it seems that you have strained relations with Priestess Quintina. Am I mistaken?"

"No, you are correct," Tacita said forlornly. "I blame myself."

"Oh no," said Pomponius. "I cannot imagine you are to blame. What is the matter between you?"

"There is a man named Septimus. My sister has always been fond of him, although of course, her sacred vows prohibit her from being with him."

"You are not suggesting that she . . ."

"Oh no," said Tacita. "My sister would never break her vows to the goddess. That much is certain. She is very fond of Septimus, though. The problem is, he has always preferred me to her, and she is envious of that."

"I see . . ."

Tacita clasped Pomponius's hands in hers and held them close to her breast. "I swear, Pomponius, I have rejected all his advances. I love and respect my sister. I would never be with a man that she has any affection for."

"Does she not believe you?"

"I am not sure. To be honest, I just think it is too painful for her, knowing that Septimus desires me more than her."

"I cannot blame him," said Pomponius. "You are . . ."

"Yes?"

". . . quite beautiful."

She lowered her eyes coyly and folded her hands in front of her. "You flatter, Pomponius. I am sure you have had far more beautiful women show up at your door."

Pomponius shifted uncomfortably. "You know, I saw you at the wedding reception of Caesar's daughter."

"My, that was a bad business, wasn't it? That poor young slave . . . and then Pollio thrown to his own monsters! I found the whole thing quite upsetting."

"I noticed that you were speaking with a man named Soren. Is he a good friend of yours?"

"Why do you ask?"

"I have reason to believe that he is a cruel man, Tacita. You should take care around him."

"You are sweet to caution me," said Tacita. She toyed with the long gold chain around her neck.

"I saw him looking at you."

"A lot of men look at me, Pomponius." She reached out to touch his chest with her fingertip. "I saw you look at me." She saw his cheeks redden. "To be honest, I found that Soren fellow rather unlikable. I shall take your advice and avoid him."

"That is good to hear." Pomponius nervously cleared his throat. "I have been uncourteous. Would you like to come in and sit with me? We could take some wine or food."

"I would like that very much," she said. "Why don't you show me around your home? It is very fine. I live at my uncle's home on the Esquiline. It is also very fine, but you have far superior tastes."

"Do you not live at your father's estate?" Pomponius asked as he led her out of the atrium.

Tacita lightly trailed her hands along the painted walls as she followed her host deeper into the house. "No, my sister has ownership of that," she said. "Her Vestal privileges allowed her to have custody of me when I was a child, but she gave **patria potestas** to my uncle, so now I am under his command. I don't mind. He is a good man." She sighed. "I think a much better man than my father was."

"Oh? Why do you say that?"

"My father was quite cruel to my mother, at least from what I can remember. I was young when they died. I did not know my father that well. He was sent to Egypt by Caesar during the war with Antony and was killed there." She shook her head sadly as they walked together. "I've always suspected that he drove my mother mad by his poor behavior toward her."

"That is tragic," Pomponius said sincerely. "I did not know my father that well either. I have always held a private belief that he blamed me for my mother's death. She died in childbirth with me."

"How sad," said Tacita, hiding her delight. Pomponius was the type to find deeper meaning in their similarly strained relationships with their fathers. "People like us must find our own path, I suppose, even without a father's guidance."

Pomponius held out his arm, inviting Tacita to enter his study. Shelves full of scrolls and parchments lined the yellow and red walls. His desk was covered in wax tablets and documents written in Latin and Greek. Tacita touched them gently, admiringly.

"I am surprised to hear that your father was unkind," said Pomponius. "I know that my sister was a friend of his. She does not speak of him often, but when she does, it is with respect. I believe she even freed him from the Carcer during the proscriptions. But there is always another side, isn't there? **Audi alteram partem fabulae.**"

"Yes," she said, "always." She picked up a wax tablet and pretended to read it. "I have always wondered about the friendship between my father and your sister . . ." Tacita proceeded carefully. "Do you think—"

"No," Pomponius said abruptly. He took the wax tablet out of her hands and placed it back on his desk.

That was too far, Tacita scolded herself. "Oh no, Pomponius, I was not going to suggest anything improper. I cannot speak for my father's morals, but I know that High Priestess Pomponia is the very essence of virtue."

He hesitated. "Would you like to see the triclinium? There is a very detailed landscape painting of Diana hunting deer in the woods."

"Show me your bedchamber first."

Pomponius stiffened. Tacita was blinking up at him, bold and appealing. She was so pretty, so petite, with big brown eyes and long eyelashes. He felt a cold, nervous sweat form under his toga.

"It is this way," he forced himself to say.

As Tacita followed Pomponius into his large bedchamber, she spun around in exaggerated awe of its artwork. She put her hands to her face. "What a magnificent painting of Venus," she said, gazing at a fresco of the goddess of love reclining on a sandy shore and looking out at the sea that had borne her.

"Thank you," said Pomponius. "It was done by an artist from Pompeii."

Tacita flitted past the large bed to a statue of Venus that stood next to it. This depiction of the goddess was more sensual. She was nude, holding her arms up as she fastened her hair. Behind her, the muscled form of Mars reached around to caresses the goddess's bare breasts.

Tacita turned to look at Pomponius, and then reached out to touch Venus's bare breasts with her fingers. As Pomponius watched, mesmerized, she let her fingers trace a circle around the nipple.

Pomponius felt like his feet were nailed to the ground. He could not move, but only stood and stared at her as she walked toward him, feeling his breaths become more rapid by the moment. His thoughts tumbled over each other. **What is she going to do? What should I do?**

Tacita didn't leave him wondering for very long. She put her hands on his chest and then slid them up over his shoulders, pulling him forward to kiss him on the lips.

"Have you ever had a woman before?" she asked him. "You seem unsure of yourself."

"I have only had my slaves," he said. "Have you

been with a man before? You are an unmarried no-blewoman, so I assume you are a—"

Tacita cast her eyes to the floor. "I have been taken by only one man," she said, "one I could not refuse." She raised her eyes to again meet his. "The emperor of Rome."

It had precisely the effect Tacita thought it would. Pomponius took her face in his hands and kissed her hard on the lips. She took a small step back, toward the bed, and began to remove her dress. She let it fall to the floor. She was not wearing any underclothes—she had come prepared for this un-veiling—and again, the effect was masterful.

Pomponius hastily undressed. The heavy fabric of his toga fell on the floor, and he was about to reach for her again, when she pushed him onto the bed. He sat on the edge and stared up at her.

Still standing before him, she took his hand in hers and used one of his fingers to trace her nipple, making him touch her the way she had touched the statue. He gasped, and Tacita smiled to herself. **Such a silly thing**, she thought. **And yet all men love it.**

Finally, she grazed his hardness with her finger-tips. Pomponius exhaled and lay back on the bed. Tacita climbed on top and straddled his body: she lowered herself onto him, quickly moving up and down, stroking him.

She felt him release inside her.

She couldn't wait to tell Soren all about it.

CHAPTER XXI

Roma Uno Die Non Est Condita
Rome wasn't built in a day.

It was twilight in the Forum of Augustus. The Temple of Mars Ultor—Mars the Avenger—was finally complete. Octavian had vowed to build it years before in honor of the war god, the vengeful god, the god who had fought on his side and helped him hunt down and tear out the throats of Julius Caesar's assassins Brutus and Cassius at Philippi. It had taken years for the temple to be erected, such was its magnificence and monumental size.

The new forum was closed to the public and guarded in anticipation of the temple's dedication the following morning. After the last of the engineers and clean-up crews had finished their final inspections, only three people remained inside the forum's massive walls. The Vestalis Maxima was one of them.

The others were Laelius, the High Priest of Mars, and Caesar, now the Pontifex Maximus of Rome.

This would be the first major public sacrifice that Pomponia and Octavian would perform together as two of the highest officers in Rome's religious collegia. Pomponia wondered whether the strategic Octavian had foreseen this day twenty years ago, on the day they had first met in the Carcer. Had he decided then and there that she would be useful to him? It was a cynical way to think after two decades of friendship, but she knew it was likely true.

As was customary on the eve of a temple dedication, signs had been taken and the augurs had assured Caesar they were good. The flight of the birds proved that the gods were pleased. Pomponia's cynicism persisted: If the signs were bad, would the augurs really tell Caesar? He had waited years to dedicate this temple. Every able-bodied person in Rome would be there. Celebratory games and parades were planned. Perhaps the augurs considered those signs too.

She walked for an hour or more alongside Caesar and Laelius, meandering through the temple's **cella** and apses, until Laelius took his leave. He still had work to do to prepare for tomorrow. Pomponia remained to admire the bronze statuary in one of the apses. It contained the twelve gods and goddesses of the Roman pantheon, and she was pleased with Vesta's statue. Octavian had shown her five models and had asked for her opinion. She was happy that he had chosen her preference. This statue of Vesta held a firebowl in her hands: inside the bowl, a waning fire burned, and the flames illuminated the goddess's strong but serene face.

She watched the flames for a while and then wandered back into the cella. In its center stood a mammoth statue of Mars, spear and shield at the ready, always yearning for the thrill of battle. She strolled out of the temple, gathering the bottom of her stola to walk down the marble steps. Both sides of the wide steps were lined with fountains that represented the nearby Temple of Venus constructed by Julius Caesar—Venus, born of the water; Venus, the goddess of love, whom the Romans positioned close to Mars to temper the violent nature of the god of war.

Octavian was waiting for her at the base of the steps. "Three lines a day, Priestess," he said as she descended. "That's all Virgil writes of my epic. Three lines a day."

"So I have heard," she said with a laugh. They looked up to again admire the temple's expansive facade: wide and towering Corinthian columns stretched across the front and along each side. Each column's capital was carved with intricate figures of the winged steed Pegasus. The gilded rosettes in the coffered ceiling reflected the last of the day's sunlight, as did the multicolored marbles of the temple's floors. Behind the columns that lined the front of the temple stood a row of golden Roman Eagles on marble staffs. High above, colorfully painted relief carvings adorned the temple's pediment, and above it all was a colossal gold statue of Augustus riding in a horse-drawn chariot as if he were Apollo himself.

Pomponia held her arms out to the temple. "Was this not built brick by brick and only then paved with marble and gold? Poets must lay their bricks one by one too. Greatness takes time. Have patience."

"I will try."

"Caesar, if it is permitted, may I ask about the poem's subject matter?"

"It is about Aeneas, prince of Troy and ancestor of Romulus," said Caesar. "It is Rome's founding story. Our story."

"Ah," said Pomponia. "There is no better story. Virgil's poem will be a monument to you, more

lasting even than this temple. **Aere perennius.**"
More lasting than bronze.

"You may be correct," Caesar replied. "Maecenas
and I have read some of it—the few lines he will
agree to show us!—and it will stand with the **Iliad**
and the **Odyssey**, I am sure of it." He bent down
to pick a stray chunk of tufa off the marble paving.
"Good news from Africa. The proconsul in Carthage
writes that Vesta's temple thrives."

"So do its priestesses," said Pomponia. "I received
a letter from Nona yesterday. The priestesses there
do not live in a single house as we do. Each has
her own house within a complex not far from the
temple. It is unusual, and I was thinking of changing it to conform to Rome, but Nona seems to like
it, so I will leave well enough alone."

"The beaten path is the safe path," said Octavian.

"I have often said so myself, Caesar."

They walked side by side out of the forum to where
their guarded litters awaited. Caesar had arrived in
a horse-drawn carriage, and Livia lay resting on fine
cushions within it. He had asked her to attend the
reading of the signs but had instructed her to wait
inside the carriage while he and the other priests finished their religious duties. She hadn't been impressed.

Pomponia bade farewell and departed in her lectica. She, too, had work to do.

As Octavian stepped into his imperial carriage,
Livia sat up and ran her fingers through her hair to
hide the evidence of her nap. "Were the signs good,
husband?" she asked.

"Very good," said Octavian. "Livia, did I ever tell
you what happened when the augurs read the signs
on the eve before I became Pontifex Maximus?"

Livia forced a curious smile to form on her lips.
**Of course you've told me. You tell me every time
auspices are taken for anything. Twelve vultures
appeared in the sky above you, just as they had
for Romulus** . . . "You may have told me," she said
sweetly, "but tell me again. I do love to hear the story."

* * *

Like most public sacrifices, the one marking the
dedication of the Temple of Mars Ultor would take
place outdoors. It would be held on the expansive
platform atop the temple's high, wide steps, which,
by design, made for excellent viewing.

In the center of the platform stood a blood-red
marble altar. On it sat a bronze bowl that burned

with Vesta's fire plus some incense, a patera of oil, a simpulum of wine, and a silver dagger.

Select senators, members of the religious collegia, nobles, dignitaries, high-ranking magistrates, and of course Tiberius, Julia, and the empress had front-row seats as they always did, with the rest of the masses—thousands of citizens, children, freedmen, and even slaves—filling up the space of the new Forum of Augustus and spilling over into the adjacent forums.

Dressed in her ceremonial white stola, red headband, and white veil, Pomponia stood on the platform at the top of the steps and looked in the direction of the Temple of Vesta in the nearby Forum Romanum. It seemed to her that every column, monument, and rooftop between here and there had a scarlet banner hanging from it, the gold letters **SPQR** emblazoned in the center of each one. She wondered whether Caecilia, Lucasta, and Marcella had forgiven her for leaving them to tend the sacred flame while she took along Quintina, Lucretia, and Cossinia—the last of whom had yet to experience a major Roman dedication.

Pomponia tried not to show favoritism to Quintina, but it wasn't always easy. Yes, she was an unusually bright priestess. But more than that, she was so much like her father. That was good and bad. But lately, the bad had been getting worse. Quintina's preoccupation with Septimus reminded Pomponia of the way Quintus used to regard her. His love for her had bordered on obsession at times, even though Pomponia suspected love had that effect on everyone.

She looked over at the young Vestal. Quintina was speaking with Tiberius, and the two of them were discussing something that was making them smile. Pomponia couldn't help going forward in her mind: now that Tiberius was Caesar's heir, it was very likely that Quintina would one day serve as Vestalis Maxima and work alongside him as Pontifex Maximus.

But for today at least, she and Octavian still had their places in the sun.

The emperor of Rome stood at the top of the monumental steps and, as he always did, gazed down at his people like a god. He was dressed in the white robes of the Pontifex Maximus, the heavy fabric draping around his body and covering his head in sacred respect to the gods. He was the image of Roman tradition and piety.

As everyone took their places, his clear,

commanding voice rang out. "My fellow Romans, we praise Mars the Avenger, who fought on our side in the war against my divine father's assassins. We dedicate this temple in his honor. From this day forward, all senatorial votes concerning matters of war will be cast here, in the house of Mars, rather than in the Senate house. Also, all soldiers leaving on campaign will be blessed here before the statue of the god."

A horn sounded three times, and a swelling cheer—**"Hail, Caesar!"**—moved as a loud wave from the base of the steps, through the Forum of Augustus, all the way to the outlying Forum of Caesar and the Forum Romanum. Pomponia knew the Vestals inside the temple would hear it like a wave crashing against the shore.

The sound of pipes replaced the blaring of horns, and all heads turned to watch the sacrificial white bull being led to the altar by the young priest of Mars, Septimus. The bull's massive head was topped with laurels and flowers. Ivy hung over its back. Pomponia and Laelius stood on either side of the altar as Caesar stood at the docile beast's head.

"Favete linguis," said Caesar. The pipe-player stopped, and a reverential silence settled on the crowd that stretched out before and below Octavian. He poured a libation of oil over the altar and sprinkled a few drops into the flames of the firebowl on top as he spoke. "**O divine Jane, divina Vesta.** O Father Mars, we pray that you strike down our enemies. We pray that you fill the hearts of our sons with courage and vengeance. We pray that you lend your fearsome strength to the people and the Senate and the soldiers of Rome. To you, Mars Pater, we offer this pure beast as a testimony of our will and devotion."

Pomponia took two sacred wafers from the bowl she was holding and set the bowl on the altar. She moved to the beast's head as Septimus pulled downward on the bull's nose ring. It lowered its head and Pomponia crumbled the wafers over its horns.

"**Vesta te purificat**," she said.

"**Deis**," said Laelius.

Caesar lifted the simpulum from the altar and took a sip, passing it along to Laelius and Pomponia, who did the same. Pomponia then held the vessel to Septimus's lips, wondering whether Quintina, who stood behind the altar with the other Vestals, would be focused on the ritual or the young man. She poured a small amount of wine over the bull's head and then placed the simpulum back on the altar, meeting eyes with Octavian. His face was full of pride but also held a trace of sadness. The victory at Philippi was as much Agrippa's as it was his own.

"**Victimarii**," Caesar called out.

In response, two well-muscled men neared the bull's head. One of them bowed to the Pontifex Maximus and took the silver dagger from the altar. Pomponia stepped up onto the elevation along the altar as the other man raised the bull's head.

The **victimarius** was highly skilled, and the bull released only the smallest groan as its throat was opened. It fell onto its side, its breathing slowing and then stopping as blood gushed out of his neck and into the bowl that Septimus held below it. Its blood filled the bowl and then ran down the marble steps in red rivers, its course slowed slightly by the sand that had been placed there to absorb it.

Pomponia knew Caesar would be pleased. The easier the animal died, the more willingly it had accepted its fate and the more impressed the god would be.

The haruspices descended on the animal and opened its belly to read its entrails. They nodded in solemn approval to Caesar, and he accepted bloody handfuls of its hefty innards, placing them in the fire on the altar as a burnt offering to the god of war.

As the familiar smell of the altar sacrifice hung in the air, he sprinkled incense and wine into the fire.

Finally, he held his bloody palms up to the gods. **"Gratias vobis ago, divine Jane, divina Vesta."**

The sacrifice was ended. The dedication was complete.

As Laelius washed Caesar's hands with sacred water, Octavian looked at him and Pomponia. "What is your assessment?" he asked seriously.

"The rites were performed flawlessly," she said. "No **vitia**." No errors.

"Then, the Pax Deorum is honored."

"Most definitely, Caesar," assured Laelius.

Octavian looked down at his blood-soaked sandals. "Then, I'm sure the gods won't mind if I go change my sandals. I shall see both of you at Tiberius's house this evening." His eyes moved to the bull and to the butchers, who were already carving out the choicest cuts. "We shall dine on what Mars has left for us."

* * *

Quintina arrived at Tiberius's newly purchased home on the Palatine Hill before Pomponia did. Lively music was playing, and the house was full of guests already eating, drinking, and congratulating Caesar on the temple's dedication. The Vestal was led into the triclinium by a house slave and greeted by Julia.

"Where is the Vestalis Maxima?" Julia asked as she kissed Quintina on the cheek.

"She will be here soon," Quintina replied. "She insisted on reading some letters before she came. If you ask me, she just wanted to relax a bit. Your parties are intense these days."

"If you're referring to my wedding reception," said Julia, "I'll remind you that they are supposed to be memorable."

"The historians will write of yours, Julia." Quintina felt the fabric of Julia's dress. "Your dress is splendid. But does your father not disapprove? It is on the immodest side."

"At the dedication, I was dressed for my father. You saw me. I looked like an unpaid priestess"— Quintina laughed and Julia continued—"but now, I am dressed for my lovers."

"You tempt the Fates," said Quintina.

"The Fates cannot be tempted," Julia replied. "The Fates cannot be bought or bribed or appealed to. They do as they wish, or they would not be the Fates.

That is why I will not deny myself whatever pleasures I can extract from the life my father forces upon me."

The two friends found empty couches in the triclinium. Even for royalty, it was an unusually large home, and the dining room was two or three times bigger than average. Then again, Tiberius had purchased and expanded the house as a wedding gift to a wife he could barely stand to be in the same room with.

"Your dress is also very pretty," said Julia. "Does Priestess Pomponia not take issue with your wearing color?"

Quintina ran her fingertips over the fine orange embroidery of her white stola. "As long as I am not by the sacred fire or performing a ritual, it is decent enough for the goddess," she said. "Pomponia doesn't like it, but she doesn't forbid it. Sabina sometimes wears color too. At least she did when she was in Rome. I don't know if she does in Carthage. It was Nona that frowned upon it most." She reclined on the couch. "Dare I ask how married life is?"

"This husband is worse than the last," said Julia. "So much worse, Quintina. Really, I cannot stand the man, and believe me, the feeling is mutual."

"Have you . . . how shall I say it?"

"Taken steps to give Rome a new son? No. He has not tried to touch me, thank the gods for that." Julia tipped the bottom of her wine cup toward the far side of the triclinium, where Tacita was clinging to Pomponius's arm. "I see your sister finally managed to pull one to shore," she said.

"Oh no," Quintina replied. "Not poor Pomponius! The man has no idea he is swimming with a shark. Pomponia will not like this."

"Your sister even puts me to shame," said Julia. "She is getting a reputation."

"I'm glad you've opened that door," Quintina said quietly. "People are starting to talk about you, Julia. If your husband and especially your father hear of what you've been doing . . ."

"What can they do about it? Lock me in my bedchamber?"

"Caesar has passed morality laws in the Senate. Adultery is now a crime in civil law, not just a personal matter." Quintina leaned forward. "If your father finds out, you risk embarrassing him, even undermining him."

"My father has shown little concern for my sensibilities, Quintina. Why should I care about his?"

"There is no reason, other than he is Caesar, and we must all care about his sensibilities."

"That's not reason enough for me," said Julia. "My father and I have grown more distant since the loss of . . ." Her voice trailed off, and Quintina did not make her say the words. "Anyway, do not worry about me." Julia scanned the room for another target. "There's your man Septimus. Let's call him over before Priestess Pomponia arrives and wags her finger at you. Septimus! Over here!"

The young man heard his name and looked around the room until he spotted the two women on the couch. He moved toward them, raising his eyebrows and pointing not-so-subtly at Tacita as he passed behind her back.

"That one's at it again," he said as he rested on the couch opposite Quintina. "And Priestess Pomponia's brother too. Quite the victory for her."

"Don't plan her triumph just yet," said Quintina.

Septimus turned to Julia. "Your house is impressive. It's certainly large enough."

"It could never be large enough," said Julia. She gave her husband the evil eye as he walked by. Tiberius raised his wine cup to Quintina and Septimus, but thought better of stopping at his wife's couch.

He joined Caesar and some senators who were heading to the courtyard.

Julia was about to throw an insult after him, but at that moment she spotted Terentia floating beside Maecenas. "You know," she said conspiratorially, "that one was almost my new stepmother. If I had the strength, I'd drag her back into my father's bed myself."

"Sometimes the evil you know is best," said Quintina.

"Perhaps," Julia replied. She eyed another target. This one seemed to make her happier. It was the singer Anchises, standing beside his rather stern-faced master, whose name she didn't remember. "When did Anchises arrive?" she asked. "Excuse me, I am going to speak with him." She left the couch to greet the virtuoso, leaving Quintina and Septimus alone together.

"Lady Julia," Anchises said, bowing. "How good to see you again. I am honored to sing at your new home."

"May you bring some joy to it," said Julia. She put her hand on Anchises's shoulder, and he patted the back of her hand.

The slave's presumptuousness seemed to irritate

his master. "Lady Julia," he said, "I am Soren. I did not have the chance to meet you at your wedding reception."

"Hmm." Julia stepped away from Anchises and looked Soren up and down without pretense. Stern-faced, yes, but there was something about him that she found a little exciting. "You are brother to Senator Pavo, nay?"

"He is brother to me."

Julia smirked at his ego but did not leave. "I am a true admirer of your singer," she said, "but if I'm honest with you, I'm an even bigger admirer of his counterpart. That boxer . . . What is his name?"

"Thracius," said Soren.

"That's right. I've heard a rumor that he is available for private events. That is, **very** private events. Is the rumor true?"

"Most rumors are true," Soren replied.

"Good," said Julia. "I shall have one of my slaves make the arrangements. For now, I will content myself with more wine and wait for Anchises to pleasure me with his mouth. I guess he gets to go first." She winked and made for the wine table, arriving at the same time as Pomponia, who had just entered the triclinium.

"Hello, Priestess," said Julia. "You will want a full cup of wine this evening."

"Thank you for the warning, Lady Julia."

The hostess departed with a polite smile while Pomponia took a cup of wine from the table. She grinned at some friendly noblewomen who were waving at her from across the expansive room and then took a sip from her cup as she made a quick assessment of the room.

The Vestal clenched her teeth. Normally she was very fond of such parties; however, this afternoon's gathering seemed to be a collection of her greatest frustrations.

Soren, looming over Anchises like a storm cloud. Terentia, pretending to fawn over Maecenas while waiting for an opportunity to seize upon Caesar. Quintina, sitting alone with Septimus on a couch, engaged in what an observer could easily interpret as a lovers' quarrel.

Worst of all, there was Tacita. She was wound around Pomponius's arm like a viper in a green dress while, for some inconceivable reason, stealing glances at Soren and clearly jealous of the way his eyes followed the other women in the triclinium. Julia's warning made sense now.

DEBRA MAY MACLEOD

Pomponia's head spun with indecision: Which frustration to face first? A loud giggle from Tacita's painted lips made her decision for her. She took three long strides toward Pomponius. On the fourth, the face of Livia appeared before her.

"Let me guess where you're going," she said.

Pomponia moved to step by Livia, but the empress kept her position.

"There's no point saying anything to your brother," said Livia. "You'll just be playing into her sweet little hands."

"My brother will listen to me."

"He will not. He is only listening to one thing right now, and it is not his elder sister."

"There is no need to be crude, Livia."

"There is every need, Pomponia." The empress narrowed her eyes at Tacita, and even though her voice was low, Pomponia could hear the edge of hatred in it. "I nearly had to break my back to get her out of Caesar's bed."

Pomponia stopped herself from saying, "Yes, I know," and instead asked, "What do you advise?"

"Tonight? Do nothing. Just look at your brother. She feeds him lotus flowers, and you will not break the spell. If you speak against her, he will rise to her defense and refuse to see you. That only works to her advantage."

Pomponia fidgeted angrily with her veil. She knew Livia was correct. "I find it hard to be in the same room with that woman," she said.

"I find it hard to be with half the women in this room," replied Livia. Her eyes landed on Terentia. "But that's only because my husband finds it so easy to be with them."

"Your position is secure," said Pomponia.

Livia faced Pomponia. There was something about the way the Vestal had said the words. With such certainty. As if she had personally seen to it and the matter were settled.

"I am happy to hear you say so," said Livia. Octavian summoned her from somewhere in the crowd of guests, and she moved to join him.

Pomponia forced herself to relax and lower her shoulders. Her anger had brought them nearly to the level of her ears. She took a hasty sip of wine. Over the rim of her cup, she saw Quintina's cheeks softly color as she spoke to Septimus.

A thought came to her. It was a party not so different from this one where Quintus had found her in a private alcove.

Tell me that I'm the only man you'll ever love. Swear it on the Altar of Juno.

How she longed to hear him say those words again. At the time, she had not answered him. She had been too taken aback, too overwhelmed by what was happening. Quintus knew that she loved him. That much was certain. But she still wished he could have heard her say the words. **You are the only man I will ever love. I swear it on the Altar of Juno.**

She heard Livia's voice from the middle of the triclinium.

"Dear friends and family," said the empress, her hands extended in a gracious welcome, "Caesar thanks you for your support today and for your piousness at the temple's dedication. He thanks you also for attending this celebration at the home of his heir, Tiberius, who has arranged for you the finest entertainment in all Rome. Anchises the virtuoso."

As the guests applauded, Pomponia navigated through the crowded space to get a better view of Anchises. They met eyes, but he looked away without returning her smile.

For a moment, she felt offended. But then she caught sight of Soren glaring at his slave, his cold, combative eyes darting between Anchises and herself.

Again, she forced herself to lower her shoulders. Even as the singer's exquisite voice slipped into her ears, she couldn't help thinking that she and Livia were of one mind.

Pomponia couldn't stand half the people in this room either.

* * *

"There are more bedchambers in this house than I can count," Julia said to Tiberius. "You do not need to be in mine."

Tiberius stood in the doorway of Julia's room and swayed on his feet as he looked at her lying in her bed. The last of the guests had departed an hour ago, and he had been fuming in solitude since then; his wife's behavior during the party had been disgraceful. "It is my house and therefore my bedchamber," he said.

"You're drunk."

"I have to be. How else do you expect me to get through this?"

"If you think I'm going to couple with you, you're even stupider than I thought you were." She slapped her palms on the bed. "Look at you! Your head is too wide, and your ears stick out. And you have a very feminine way about you, Tiberius. You are strangely soft. Women do not like to couple with men who have smoother skin than they do."

"Yes," slurred Tiberius, "tonight I learned from a friend that you like things rough."

"What is that supposed to mean?"

"You tried to hire a stud service . . . that boxer."

"Mea dea," Julia huffed. "Can no one in this gods-forsaken city keep a bloody secret?" She threw herself back onto the bed and pulled the covers over her head. "Go away."

Tiberius wobbled to the side of the bed. "You should respect me, Julia," he said. "I have been a great support to your father. He praised me tonight, in front of everyone. Perhaps my mother is right. It will take time for feelings to develop between us."

"My feelings for you are already developed, Tiberius. I hate you."

"No more than I hate you," he replied. He ripped the covers off her. "But love or hate, you need to stop screwing every centurion and senator on Rome's payroll. You are Caesar's daughter and my wife."

"I will screw whoever I want," she shot back, "whenever and wherever." She glared accusatorily up at him as she fought to pull the covers back up. "I don't think you're one to moralize about sexual restraint, Tiberius. You take your slaves at least three times a day. Poor creatures, you're going to wear them out at that rate."

"It is for my health, Julia. Musa says that physical pleasure helps ward off the contagion."

"Musa is as witless as you are. Now, let me go to sleep."

Julia squeezed her eyes closed. A moment later, she felt the mass of Tiberius's body descend on her. She gasped for breath. He was straddling her, her arms pinned painfully at her sides under the bony weight of his knees. He leaned forward, and she twisted her torso, trying to take a breath under the crushing pressure.

"Let's get this over with," he said.

He lifted his body off her, and Julia inhaled the air greedily. As Tiberius pulled his tunica off over his head, she kicked her feet free of the covers and tried to sit up, but he struck her across the face, hard. She felt disoriented. Her eyes went blurry, and her hearing seemed strangely muted. She had never been hit before in her life.

"So, you like it rough, do you?"

Julia heard his voice throb in her head. Her anger had dissipated, replaced by fear and dread. She struggled as best she could, but it was no use. She felt her legs part against her will.

And then she felt much worse than that.

CHAPTER XXII

Fortuna Multis Dat Nimis, Satis Nulli

Fortune gives much to many, but enough to none.

—MARTIAL

The slaves in Soren's house on the Esquiline Hill cowered in their tiny rooms in the musty basement. Upstairs, they could hear their master raging. He beat the slaves who hadn't had time to make it to the basement. He shattered plates in the kitchen. He tore the linen. He kicked at doors. He ripped his animal trophies and rare weapons off the walls. He broke glass against the floor. He shouted out in . . . grief? No.

Soren was not mourning the sudden death of his brother Senator Pavo from the contagion. Rather, he was raging at the lost advantage. Brotherhood with a Roman senator came with a lot of perks. Now, those perks were gone. He was irate. First, his cousin Tuccia had succumbed. That had stolen enough of his prestige. Now his brother—he had always been weak—had died.

Spent from his rage, Soren leaned against the wall to catch his breath. He slid down and sat on the floor. He reminded himself that all was not lost. Not by any means.

He had restocked his household with a number of skilled slaves, which in turn had restocked his purse. Without a doubt, the most profitable of his new slaves were the virtuoso and the boxer. Apollo's Pair. It was a ridiculous name, but the two of them were raking in the coin.

For a passing moment, he thought about taking Taurus's advice and letting the singer visit the boxer at the ludus for a night or two. But the thought passed as quickly as it had come. They were both performing very well. As far as Soren could tell, there was no need to change the status quo.

One of his house slaves approached. Her head was down. "Domine," she said cautiously, "Lady Tacita is here to see you."

"Gods, she doesn't give up," Soren muttered. "What does she want?"

"I do not know, Domine, but she is very insistent and says she will not leave the house without speaking with you. Would you like me to—"

Soren pushed himself off the floor with his hands. He brushed the dust off his tunica. "Clean the damn floor," he barked at the slave as he headed to the atrium.

"Hello, Soren," Tacita said lightly as he arrived.

He grunted a reply, then cupped his hands in the water of the impluvium and splashed it onto his face. It cooled his hot temper a bit. "What do you want, Tacita?"

"I have news."

"Yes, I can tell you're very pleased with yourself about something. What is it?"

"I am with child."

Soren furrowed his brow. "Is it the child of Pomponius?"

"Yes."

"Are you sure? Because . . ."

"I am sure, Soren. Pomponius is the father."

"How do you know?"

She put her hands on her hips and said irritably, "Because you turned me down, and because he is the only one I have been with since my blood last came."

Soren grimaced. Normally, he did not care to

know such details about women, but this was too important. He had to get it right.

"It is his, Soren. There is no question."

"Good girl," he finally said.

"Good girl? I am not a dog."

"No, you are a pretty little wolf." He walked toward her, took her head in his hands, and kissed her aggressively, pushing his tongue into her mouth and moving his hands roughly over her body. He patted her belly and smiled widely as he led her through the atrium and toward his bedchamber.

She followed obediently, thinking it was probably unwise to ask him why his house was such a mess.

* * *

Pomponia sat at her desk, poured herself a glass of cool lemon water, and settled in to read her daily secret briefing from Caesar and Livia's house slave Despina.

High Priestess Pomponia,

Tiberius was here again this morning. He again complained to the empress and the emperor that Julia is coupling with other men. He said that she had been an

adulteress during her marriage to Agrippa and that she often had sexual orgies at his home while he was out of Rome. Tiberius said he suspected the children she had by Agrippa, especially the boy, were not the general's children, but rather the bastards of one of her lovers.

Tiberius was in the middle of an accusation when Julia herself stormed into the house. Tiberius pointed to her and said, "My friend Soren says she tried to hire his boxer for sexual services." Those may not have been Tiberius's exact words, but his words were to that effect.

Julia then took her father's hands and wept. She accused Tiberius of striking her and taking her against her will in bed. Caesar said that such business is between a husband and wife and not to bother him with it again. He scolded both of them and told them to keep their problems private. He said he did not want to hear any more about Julia's escapades and told Tiberius to get his wife under control. Tiberius and Julia left in separate litters.

When they were gone, Caesar moved between anger and worry. First, he was enraged that Agrippa's memory might be tainted by Julia's reputation. But then he became fatherly and asked the empress whether she thought Tiberius would strike Julia or take her against her will. The empress assured him that Tiberius would never do such terrible things to Caesar's daughter. She said, "You are correct, it is a matter between husband and wife."

She told the emperor that even though things looked bad, she felt that the relationship between Tiberius and Julia was improving and that she herself had witnessed soft moments between them at their house party, after the dedication of the Temple of Mars Ultor, and at several other state events. Caesar seemed encouraged by that.

Despina

The Vestal curled the papyrus scroll tightly and dipped its edge into the flame of the burning candle at her desk. Julia was becoming a problem. And not just for Tiberius and Caesar. She was also becoming a problem for the high priestess. It seemed like the more the emperor's daughter challenged her station in life and questioned her duty to Rome, the more Quintina tended to do the same.

It was almost predictable: Quintina would return from a dinner or party with Julia and ask Pomponia the same questions: **Why do we need our vow of chastity? Could we not serve the goddess and the people just as well as married women with families? The other priests marry, and many of their wives have religious duties. The priestesses of Ceres are often married. Do we really rule ourselves?**

Pomponia would give Quintina the same answers: **Vesta is a virgin goddess, and our vows honor her. We must be as pure as her flame. Our vows distinguish us from other women and make the people respect and revere us. A Vestal's first loyalty must be to the living flame and to Rome, not to a husband or family. Perform the duties that the goddess and the emperor have given you. At the end of your years of service, you can rule yourself. You can marry who you wish, even have children.**

Quintina was acquiescent enough but never truly at peace with those answers. Pomponia knew why. She was not content with the idea of marrying some speculative husband years hence. She wanted Septimus, and she feared he would not wait for her.

She was right about that. Pomponia's informants regularly reported on the young man's numerous sexual partners; however, since taking up with a young noblewoman named Cornelia, he had become less promiscuous. Pomponia wondered if Quintina knew of his deepening relationship with the woman.

In any event, Pomponia had to give Septimus credit. He had not bedded Tacita since learning she was Quintina's sister and was probably the only man in Rome who hadn't coupled with the emperor's daughter, most likely out of respect for Quintina. If circumstances were different, Pomponia would approve of him as a husband for her. She almost trusted his discretion and restraint more than the young Vestal's.

As the last of Despina's letter burned to ash, a slave appeared in Pomponia's doorway. "Priestess, your brother is here for his afternoon visit. He is in the courtyard. Is that adequate?"

"Yes, I'm coming now."

Pomponia left her office and greeted Pomponius in the courtyard with an embrace. He wrapped his arms around her tightly, even jovially. It was unlike him. "You are in happy spirits today," she said. "I have a treat for you. Our rooftop terrace is finished. Let's have our visit up there."

She led him through the peristyle and up a pink marble staircase, from which they emerged onto a sizable and very high terrace, also paved in pink marble, that overlooked the entire Forum Romanum and offered a view of the shrines and temples on the Capitoline Hill.

Pomponius walked to the balustrade and applauded. "Magnificent," he said. "The Palatine barely affords a better view. The Arch of Augustus is well seen from this angle. You can see how perfectly it spans the street between the Temple of Castor and Pollux and the Temple of Caesar. And just look at the basilicas." He turned his head to the right. "There is the emperor's statue on the Temple of Mars. And the top of Vesta's temple . . . Incredible! I can see the smoke coming out of the roof. I feel like the Eagle up here."

"The empress built this for us," said Pomponia. "It is similar to the one at her home."

Pomponius ran his hands over the fine marble of the balustrade. "All right, I have admired the terrace. Now, why don't you tell me what is bothering you?"

"Nothing, not really," said Pomponia.

"Is it the contagion? I know it has returned along with the warmer weather."

Pomponia leaned over the balustrade with her brother. "Every time someone coughs, I fear the worst."

"I know that Priestess Tuccia's death still weighs on you."

"It does. In many ways."

"What does that mean?"

The Vestal shifted on her feet and looked out toward the Capitoline. "I keep having the same nightmare . . . about the Evil Field." She laughed humorlessly. "I need to stop reading the archives before bed. I've been reviewing the old scrolls, the ones written during past contagions, past plagues. I have found two cases where Vestals were accused of **crimen incesti** during the outbreak. One was buried alive. The other hanged herself before they could put her in the pit. They were later proved innocent, but during the panic of the plague, the people used them as scapegoats. It is no different from what happened with Tuccia during the war with Antony and Cleopatra. People tried to blame her for the conflict and their own hunger."

"She was proved innocent," said Pomponius. "And if I remember correctly, your letters to me suggested Tuccia's miracle with the sieve actually elevated her and the order's prestige. Who would be foolish enough to accuse a priestess after Vesta herself absolved one?"

"Yes," murmured Pomponia, "the miracle." She pictured Quintina sitting next to Septimus on the couch at Tiberius's house: the way Quintina's face reddened when they spoke. Her feelings for the young man were always painted on her face, visible to anyone who looked closely. "I hope you are right," she said.

Pomponius turned to lean his hip against the balustrade and face his sister. "And more practically, did you not persuade Caesar to change the way an accused Vestal is tried? It will be fairer now."

"That is the hope," Pomponia replied. She affectionately adjusted a fold of her brother's toga. "All right, I will try not to fall into such dark imaginings, especially since you have such a light step today. What is your news?"

Pomponius suddenly seemed so elated that

Pomponia half expected a girlish giggle to escape his lips. "You know that I am acquainted with Priestess Quintina's younger sister, Tacita, correct?"

Pomponia tensed. "Yes."

"Well," he said, "we have become very close. I was going to tell you earlier, but she insisted on keeping things quiet and not bothering you—you have been so preoccupied with your work on the priestly books and the temple and so on." He tried to hold back a smile. "She'd be upset if she knew I was telling you now. But . . ."

"But what?" Pomponia tried to speak casually.

"Tacita is with child," he said. "I have asked her to marry me."

The Vestal stepped away from the balustrade, gripped the back of a chair, and sat down. "Brother," she said, "I wish you would have consulted me earlier about this matter. About Tacita, I mean."

Pomponius sat on the chair next to her. "Why would I consult you about Tacita, sister?"

"**Consult** is not the right word. I did not mean it like that. I only wish you had told me earlier that things were getting serious between the two of you. I did not know."

"You know now," said Pomponius. "I am happy,

sister. I am going to have a child, and you are going to have a niece or a nephew. Does that not please you?"

Pomponia didn't know how to answer that. She loved the idea of having a niece or nephew: she hated the idea of Tacita being that child's mother. It would allow her to wield too much power, even with the law of patria potestas. Whatever meek role Tacita was playing now, Pomponia knew that she would come to dominate Pomponius in every way once the wedding vows were exchanged and the child arrived.

"Sister, does that not please you?" Pomponius asked again.

Pomponia tucked her hair behind her ears. Her shoulders were rising again. Her recurring nightmare flashed before her eyes. A horde of angry, sickly men dragging Lucretia, bound and gagged, through the streets toward the Evil Field, throwing her down into the blackness of the pit. Quintina hanging by a rope around her neck, her face swelling purple and her legs twitching.

And now there was Tacita's complete victory, the effects of which, like the contagion itself, would worsen and spread out like diseased vines to wrap around her brother and everyone else in its path. It was too much.

"No, Pomponius, it does not please me. You are a well-traveled and well-read man, but you are a fool when it comes to women. She plays you like a lyre. This child will bring you no joy, not with her as its mother."

"Pomponia!" Pomponius nearly jumped out of his chair. His face was blanched, and his eyes were wide with shock. With hurt.

Instantly, Pomponia wished she could take it back. The cruelty he would suffer at his wife's hands would be bad enough. He would need his sister's support. "Pomponius," she said and reached for him.

But he was already storming off the terrace and down the stairs. Pomponia sat back down. She could not be seen running through the courtyard after her brother like a cat after a mouse.

She would let the matter settle for a while and then go to see him at his home on the Caelian Hill. She would make this right, even if it took another miracle.

CHAPTER XXIII

Probitas Laudatur et Alget
Honesty is praised and left to freeze.
—JUVENAL

The Senate had adjourned after a full day of tiresome motions and contentious cases. Only Caesar and Tiberius remained in the large central hall of the Curia. The rest of the senators and magistrates had left long ago, but Tiberius was still red-faced with anger.

"You are too permissive to those who speak against you, Caesar," he said, pacing the green and purple tile floor of the Senate house. "Especially that bastard Aelianus. Last month on the ides—and that should be enough of a bad sign for a Caesar—I heard him criticize your foreign policy and your morality legislation in front of eight or nine senators." His booming voice echoed off the white and gray marble walls. He tugged irritably at his red-bordered toga.

"And who is he to criticize? He is made fat with the bribes he takes. I do not think he has cast a vote in his entire career that someone else didn't pay for. He should return to Corduba, preferably carried by his wife in a cracked urn."

"It is no matter," replied Caesar. He leaned forward in his wooden curule chair and rested his hands on his knees. "As long as he uses words against me and not daggers, I am content. You must not allow the ardor of your youth to turn an annoyance like Aelianus into an enemy. The people need to have a voice. It is better than forcing them to whisper, is it not? We cannot hear their whispers."

Tiberius sat on one of the senatorial marble benches. "That is true," he reluctantly admitted. "It makes my blood rise, though. They criticize and complain, but the moment a session adjourns, they flee the building faster than a chariot breaks out of the gates. Only Caesar remains to finish up the paperwork, like a plebeian scribe."

"You sound like your mother," said Octavian.

"Do not say so, Caesar."

The two men laughed, and Octavian stretched his back. "It is not so bad," he said. "At least you are here to help. I have not had support, not the kind I can really count on, since Agrippa."

"It pleases me to hear you say so," Tiberius replied. He fidgeted with a stylus he found on the bench and looked up at the ceiling in thought.

"Speak freely, Tiberius."

"That is difficult to do. It concerns my wife."

"Ah," said Octavian. "Speak freely anyway."

"There are rumors going around. They are the type of rumors that could cause you great embarrassment and that could undermine your efforts to restore morality to Rome."

"You mean that she is coupling with other men?"

"I have tried to keep the matter private, Caesar, as you instructed. But I cannot cover every mouth in Rome. People are talking, and the latest rumor is very subversive."

Octavian rubbed his face with his hands. "Tell me."

"I have been told by a trustworthy source that Julia visits the Forum after dark. That she performs sexual acts on some of the soldiers that guard the temples at night . . ."

Octavian rubbed his face more vigorously. "Go on."

"And that she does this on the Rostra"—Tiberius held his breath a moment—"under the Eagle."

After a long silence, Octavian stood up and began to pace the floor of the Curia as Tiberius had done. "Who speaks these rumors?" he asked.

"Caesar, everyone does."

"Everyone?" Octavian stood in the middle of the floor and looked at Tiberius. "The men who were here today, in the Senate, do they speak them?"

"Yes. It is only their fear and respect for you, and their reluctance to deliver such hurtful news about your daughter, that prevents them from telling you themselves. I would not tell you either, but my duty and fidelity demand that I do what others will not. I believe that Agrippa would have told you and so I have done the same."

"Have you struck my daughter?"

Tiberius sat up straight. "On one occasion, yes. She was trying to leave the house in the middle of the night. I suspected she was going to meet another man. I asked her to stay, but she refused. I said, 'Julia, do not debase yourself. You are the daughter of Caesar. Refrain from such behavior. Do it out of love for your father, if not your husband.' But she would not hear it. I was overcome with fear for her safety and reputation, and so yes, I struck her in a moment of desperation. Not hard, not enough to harm. I just wanted her to do her duty. I regret it entirely."

Another long silence, and then Octavian said, "I regret you did not hit her harder." His voice cracked. "On the Rostra? It is a space as sacred to us as any temple. It is the place where Agrippa and I accepted our honors after Actium, where I was named Augustus, where my great father's body lay after he was murdered. How dare she taint such a place with debauchery? It is no wonder the contagion has returned to Rome, with such disease in the house of Caesar."

Tiberius sat in silence. The disease wasn't as much in Caesar's house as it was in his own, but he saw no need to interject.

"Tell me, Tiberius, do the people laugh at me? What do the senators say?"

"No one laughs at Caesar," said Tiberius. "The people love you. The senators, well, they love no one but themselves and their purses, but they are friendly to you. Rome prospers and is at peace, and everyone knows it is because of your rule. I think people are angry at Julia for not doing her duty or abiding by the morality laws that her own father has passed. But . . ."

"But what?"

"But I do not know how long that sentiment will last. If Julia's behavior continues, I fear it is only a matter of time before the people do begin to question your leadership. They are not laughing yet, but they may soon enough."

"Of course they will laugh," said Octavian. "It is a subject ripe for ridicule."

The emperor chewed his lip. How long could he continue to look the other way and ignore Julia's behavior? His morality legislation—which he had announced from the same Rostra his daughter was fornicating on—condemned adultery, especially on the part of women. How could Caesar's laws condemn the adulterous daughters of other men, but not his own? What senator, what citizen would respect such an emperor? He could hear the voice of Maecenas in his head: **It will be seen as hypocritical.**

"There is also the matter of my reputation," Tiberius said more cautiously. "If the people are to one day call me Caesar, they must respect me. Anything else would taint your legacy."

Yet another long silence before the emperor spoke. "I will not attend the Senate in the morning. Give notice that I will speak from the Rostra the day after tomorrow." Octavian inhaled deeply, as if physically drawing strength and resolve into his body. "I will show my daughter what the Rostra is really there for."

* * *

The newsreader stepped onto his platform in front of the Rostra in the Roman Forum. Despite the warmth of the early-morning sun, he felt invigorated. It had been ages since he had announced anything interesting, anything other than boring decrees from the Senate.

Then again, things were looking up. If the contagion kept getting worse again, at least he had those numbers to look forward to. The more deaths to announce, the more people stopped to listen. That was better than reading the news to no one but the crows that hopped around his feet, pecking the cobblestone street for crumbs.

He extended his arms to the crowd before him: it was the tenth time he had read the same announcement since first being handed it this time yesterday morning, and the crowd grew bigger with each reading. **This is how it should be**, he thought with satisfaction.

"Today, at the eleventh hour," he boomed, "Caesar Augustus will ascend the great Rostra. The emperor has heard the accusations against his daughter, Julia Caesarius filia, now married to his adopted son and heir, Tiberius Julius Caesar. The emperor assures the people and the Senate of Rome that all accusations concerning Julia's nocturnal revels will be answered in all fairness to the laws and the people and gods of Rome!"

By the time the eleventh hour arrived and the emperor stepped onto the Rostra, dressed in a solid purple toga and accompanied by lictors, the square in front of the great marble speaker's platform was packed with citizens, freedmen, and slaves come to hear the news. Alongside the Rostra sat many senators and magistrates, along with Tiberius and Livia.

Pomponia was there too. She knew what was about to happen, and she knew that Octavian would likely never be the same after this day. In a show of support that she knew Fabiana would take issue with, Pomponia and the Vestals Quintina, Caecilia, and Lucretia stood on top of the Rostra at the side of Caesar.

Octavian strode to the center of the Rostra. He glanced at Pomponia, but she remained expressionless, hoping he would interpret it as a sign of resolute support. It was. Mostly.

The emperor stood at the edge of the Rostra, under the golden Eagle and the red **SPQR** banners, and held out his hands. A horn sounded once, twice, and the crowd fell silent.

"My fellow Romans," Octavian called out, "Caesar makes the law, but Caesar is not above the law. Nor is the family of Caesar above the law. **Nemo supra legem est.** Indeed, the family of Caesar must be above suspicion. I am no stranger to the acts of indecency and adultery committed by my daughter, Julia. Yesterday in the Senate, in my absence, I ordered that charges be read against her. I submitted the matter to the judgment of the Senate, instructing them to choose between execution and exile."

Cries of "**No, Caesar!**" and "**Have mercy!**" began to move through the crowd. These people had seen Julia grow up. No one wanted to imagine the execution of a woman they had seen chasing butterflies through this square as a little girl.

Octavian ignored the shouts and murmurs. Grim-looking legionary soldiers began to move through the gathering, scanning for those who called out, and an uneasy hush descended.

"By unanimous vote of the Senate," continued Caesar, "Julia is to be exiled to the island of Pandateria. There, she will live in discomfort and distress, without the pleasure of wine or human company, without any of the luxuries that have bred so thankless a daughter. By imperial decree, I have annulled her marriage to my heir, Tiberius, and I have disowned her as my child. As I stand on the Rostra before you, soldiers are entering the home of Tiberius and arresting her. I will not see her . . ." His voice dropped off, but then he met eyes with Tiberius, and it was roused. "I will not see her again, not as long as I live."

Octavian fell as silent as the crowd. He could not stop himself from remembering.

It is a boy, living and free of deformity.

The next emperor of Rome.

"I am no longer a father to Julia," said Octavian. "I am Pater Patriae, the father of my country. It is a name that you have given me and a name that I honor above all."

At that, Tiberius stood. "**Ave, Caesar!**"

The shouts went up, as they always did. "**Ave, Caesar! Ave, Caesar!**" Octavian straightened his back and thrust his arm into the air, and the shouts came louder. Finally, he stepped off the Rostra and strode toward the Senate house as if it were just another day at the Curia. The senators and magistrates followed him.

Pomponia and the other Vestals stepped down also. "Return to your duties," Pomponia said to Quintina, Caecilia, and Lucretia. They said nothing but turned to walk the short distance to the Temple of Vesta, followed by their guards.

When they were gone, Pomponia nodded at Livia, and the empress approached. She wore a simple white stola. No jewelry. The perfect contrast to Julia's extravagance.

"Thank you for the support you have shown Caesar today," said Livia. "He pretends to be unmoved, but he is not."

"The Vestal order is a friend to Caesar."

"To your mutual benefit," said Livia.

"And to your benefit as well," replied Pomponia. It was perhaps a little more biting than she intended, but as she looked into Livia's face—the woman had cried dry tears during Octavian's speech—she realized just how outmaneuvered Julia really had been. The death of her aunt Octavia and especially her husband Agrippa had left her as vulnerable as a mouse in an open field, with a hungry hawk circling overhead. Agrippa in particular would never have let Octavian exile Julia, regardless of how she behaved as his wife.

If Agrippa were alive today, his young son would be alive too. The speech from the Rostra would have been a very different one. It would have been Caesar and his great general standing side by side, announcing the executions of Tiberius and Livia as co-conspirators who had tried but failed to kill Caesar's true heir.

Then again . . . would it? Or would Livia have sweet-talked her way out of it and persuaded Octavian to defend her, thereby starting a civil war between Caesar and Agrippa? If any woman—any person—had the potential to come between them, it would be Livia.

Pomponia's guards, Caeso and Publius, appeared at her side to escort her back to the temple. She went with them. As she walked along the Via Sacra, she tried to shake off the gloominess of it all. She found herself marveling at Livia. She had to give the empress credit. Through the years, through the adversaries, through the competitors, and through what often seemed like certain defeat, Livia had always prevailed.

Fas est et ab hoste doceri, Pomponia reminded herself. It is right to learn even from one's enemies.

She reached the deep red doors of the House of the Vestals and stared absently at the white and blue rosette carvings until Caeso pulled the door open for her. "Priestess," he said pleasantly as she entered.

"Thank you, Caeso."

Quintina was waiting for her on the other side. She gathered her stola angrily and stepped toward Pomponia before the chief Vestal had even made it all the way into the atrium. "This is not right of Caesar," she said.

"Lower your voice," Pomponia scolded. "Come with me to my office."

When they arrived there, she waved Quintina inside and closed the door. "Practice discretion everywhere," she said, "even here, in our own home."

"I am sorry, but I am angry. Caesar uses Julia as nothing but a vessel for children, all for **his** legacy, not hers. He condemns her for adultery? Him, of all people! He says that Caesar is not above the law? That is laughable. We both know that he has coupled with—"

"Don't be so damn foolish, Quintina," Pomponia snapped. "Julia has no future in Rome. Her behavior was bound to catch up with her, and you should thank the gods that she is out of your life. It was only a matter of time until she did something that incriminated you. And I promise you, once they carted you off to the Campus Sceleratus, once you stepped onto the first rung of that ladder and descended into the black pit, your sympathy for poor Julia would disappear faster than the light of day."

"Banishment is unfair. She did not deserve it."

"Unfair? You are thinking like an indulged child. That's what has Julia on a pox-filled ship to some wretched island no bigger than the Rostra she was fornicating on."

"Why did I have to stand on the Rostra with Caesar? Everyone knows that Julia is my friend. It will seem that I have betrayed her."

"That's exactly why you had to be there. Don't you understand? Tiberius will be the next emperor. He will be the next Pontifex Maximus. When you are Vestalis Maxima, which is my hope for you, you will work alongside him. He needs to know that your loyalty and duty are to him, not to Julia. He must trust you. You must become his adviser and confidant, as I have done for Caesar."

"Maybe I don't want to be Vestalis Maxima. Maybe

I will leave the order when my years of duty are completed. Maybe I will marry and have a child."

"Septimus will not wait for you."

"You do not know that."

"I know many things," said Pomponia. "Too many. It is the blessing and the curse of my position. Septimus has been seeing the daughter of Senator Cornelius. He is going to propose marriage to her. The senator is already preparing her dowry."

"How do you know this?"

"Because my informants have told me as much."

Quintina put her hand on the wall and then slumped into the blue-cushioned chair that sat against it.

"This cannot come as a surprise to you," Pomponia said more softly.

"No, it does not," Quintina replied. She wiped a tear from her eye. Then another. "He tried to tell me. At Tiberius's house. He tried to tell me, but I just got mad, and we quarreled." She pulled the veil off her head and put her face in her hands. "It is very painful, Pomponia . . . It is very painful to imagine him with her . . ."

Pomponia lowered herself onto her knees at Quintina's feet. "I know it is."

"How would you know?"

Pomponia pulled off her own veil and folded it on the floor. "It was painful for me to imagine your father with another woman."

Quintina's body went rigid. She stared at the floor. "Ah, I have always wondered when this dark truth would see light."

"Quintus and I had a . . . complicated relationship," said Pomponia. "I never broke my vows to the goddess, but I did love him, and he loved me. He said that once I left the order, we would marry."

"So, you were going to leave the order? You, of all—"

"I didn't say that. But the words I spoke to Quintus, or didn't speak, never mattered. He heard only what he wanted to hear. You have inherited the trait, Quintina."

She pursed her lips, her eyes still streaming tears. "I cannot argue with that. Are you the reason he was cruel to my mother? Tacita thinks so."

"I don't know," Pomponia said. "Perhaps."

"I do not blame you," said Quintina. "My father chose to treat my mother the way he did. If he did not love her, he should not have married her."

"Marriage is rarely about love, Quintina. Just ask

Julia." Pomponia ran her fingers through her hair. "I am glad you mentioned Tacita . . ."

"Oh no," said Quintina. She took a deep breath and wiped her eyes with the veil in her hands. It seemed to soothe her. "What has she done now?"

"She is with child. It is my brother's. He is to marry her."

"Gods, poor Pomponius! Tacita is like that species of spider that eats her mates alive. I should have warned him when I first saw her circling him."

"He would not have listened. He is a fool for her."

The unexpected news shifted Quintina's focus—how to protect a baby, her own little niece or nephew, from Tacita. "We can manage this," she said. "We will both be aunt to the child. We will watch over her or him as we watch over the sacred fire." The younger Vestal put her hand on Pomponia's shoulder and spoke resolutely. "It will be all right. I will reach out to my sister. I can handle her."

Pomponia's thoughts flew back to her recent argument with Pomponius on the rooftop terrace. "Yes, we will make it right." She pushed herself off the floor. "Go rest before you need to relieve Marcella in the temple. I must finish a letter to Carthage." She moved to her desk and forced a lighter tone into her voice. "Ankhu says he is painting a picture of Nona and Sabina at the temple for us. We will put it in the triclinium so we can dine with them in spirit."

"I did not know Ankhu was so skilled."

Pomponia hesitated but then pulled open a drawer in her desk and removed a small painting. "Ankhu was your father's slave in Egypt. After Quintus was killed, he came to serve me here in Rome. He painted this of your father," she said.

Quintina stood and took the painting in her hand. "I had forgotten what he looked like," she said.

"He had black hair, like in the painting," said Pomponia. "And a scar that reached behind his ear."

"Was he handsome?"

"He thought so."

Quintina laughed. "Did he have a good nature?"

"Not at all," said Pomponia. Quintina laughed again, and Pomponia said, "But he wrote beautiful letters."

"Can I . . . keep this painting for a while?"

"Of course." Pomponia stroked the younger Vestal's hair. "I wish we could help Julia," she said, her thoughts returning to the day's drama on the Rostra. "One day, I will intercede for her. I know Caesar. He will regret this, and he will hear a petition from me. But the timing must be right. Livia and Tiberius will not want Julia to return. We must use discretion."

Quintina nodded. "I know."

Pomponia walked Quintina to her office door. "Now that Tiberius is Caesar's heir, my priority will be to establish a closer friendship between you and him. You will find Tiberius more difficult to manage than I have found Caesar."

"It will be many years before he is emperor," said Quintina. "We have plenty of time."

Pomponia wondered how much she should tell Quintina. Should she share her suspicions about Livia, about the death of Agrippa and his infant son? Should she give voice to her fears? **I worry every day and every night that the knock will come at the door—Caesar is dead!**

Pomponia had already lived through such chaos once. She knew it could happen again. Now that Tiberius was Caesar's official heir, how long would Livia wait to see her son inherit the laurel crown? Tiberius was Octavian's reluctant choice, and the emperor could change his will at any time. Livia knew that as much as anyone.

"Yes, we have plenty of time," she said to Quintina.

Yet as she watched the young Vestal leave her office and walk down the colonnade, Pomponia hoped that her voice sounded more convincing to Quintina's ears than it did to her own.

CHAPTER XXIV

Panem et Circenses
Bread and circuses
−JUVENAL

The novices' study and library took up a good portion of the second floor of one wing of the House of the Vestals. Its walls were painted a rich orange, but instead of being decorated with murals or panels of frescoes, they were covered in marble plaques on which were inscribed the names of Vestal Virgins:

VV · R. SILVIA	VV · FLAVIA
VV · LICINIA	VV · TUCCIA
VV · AMATA	VV · CLAUDIA
VV · POPILLIA	VV MAX · FABIANA
VV · GEGANIA	VV · CAPARRONIA
VV · CORINA	VV · ARRUNTIA
VV · VENENEIA	VV · OPPIA

| VV MAX · TULLIA | VV · CASSIA |
| VV · FABIA | VV · AEMILIA |

and so many more.

The plaques documented centuries of priestesses who had guarded the sacred flame and also reminded the novices of the gravity and grace that came with serving in the Vestal order.

Nonetheless, the study itself was an airy, cheery space with plenty of natural light that came in through multiple windows that overlooked the courtyard and illuminated the desks and scroll-filled shelves. A large fireplace was built into one wall. In the cooler months and most mornings, a roaring fire snapped and cracked to warm the priestesses who taught and the novices who learned.

These days, the priestesses Lucretia and Caecilia spent the most time here with the novices. Under Pomponia's direction, they taught the sacred rites and the Pax Deorum, but also other subjects: philosophy, astronomy, history, poetry, law, decorum, and diplomacy. Influential tutors, writers, and scientists often came to speak.

Vestal Virgins moved in the highest circles of Roman society. They needed to be well educated and well read. A Vestal who could not carry on a learned and engaging conversation with Caesar or an important foreign dignitary was an embarrassment to the order and to Rome. Even young novices were expected to take their studies seriously.

Yet they were still children, and Pomponia knew they sometimes needed a break. She entered the study just as Lucretia was about to ask the novices a question, and she held up a basket.

"I need help," she said.

"With what, Priestess Pomponia?" asked one novice, and a moment later they had all jumped from their desks to crowd around the basket and look inside.

"With eating all this honey cake," she said.

As the novices descended on the basket, Pomponia smiled at Lucretia. "I am off to the amphitheater soon," she said. "I am taking Cossinia and Quintina. Next time is your turn, I promise."

"This morning I prefer honey cake," said Lucretia.

Pomponia said her goodbyes and exited the study. Just outside the doorway, a house slave approached and held out a scroll.

"A letter from the house of Caesar, Domina."

Pomponia took the scroll, moved a few steps away from the study for privacy, and then read it.

High Priestess Pomponia,

Caesar is in good spirits again today. He was up before the sun and at his desk working, as is his habit. Tiberius continues to rise early with him and work late into the evening.

Maecenas was here until after sunset, strategizing with Caesar and Tiberius. They discussed more land grants in Africa for veterans, some owed taxes from Herod in Judea, and some trading matters from Palmyra in Syria. They also discussed the contagion. Caesar seemed contented that since Julia's exile, the numbers of reported deaths from the sickness have decreased. He stated that her banishment and the renewed Pax Deorum have pleased the gods, and both Maecenas and Tiberius were in agreement with this.

During their strategy meeting, they also discussed how to dispense with Julia's various lovers. Maecenas presented Caesar with a list of seven senators, two noblemen, and twelve soldiers that have been confirmed as her paramours. Caesar says he will order the property of the senators and noblemen to be confiscated. The senators are to be banished from Rome and the noblemen will be compelled to commit suicide. I heard him say the soldiers will be flogged, but I regret I was unable to hear their form of execution as I was called away at that moment.

After Tiberius and Maecenas left, the empress and emperor took a late dinner in the triclinium. They discussed Tiberius, and Caesar said he was pleased. He expressed his relief at having a man he could count on (his words) in the Senate and admitted to his wife that perhaps he had been unfair in his previous disregard for him.

Caesar spoke of Julia's banishment without emotion, and the empress flattered him for being a model of decency for his people. He again expressed gratitude that you stood on the Rostra with him during his renouncement of Julia, and the empress assured him that you and the Vestal order were true friends to Caesar.

After they dined on some cold meat, olives, bread, and only a bit of wine, the empress asked Caesar if he wished her company in his bedchamber. He said, "Wife, do you not have a gift for me tonight?"

The empress said she did, if that was his pleasure, and he said it was. The empress smiled until he left for his bedchamber but then threw her wine cup against the wall. She instructed me to send one of the virgin slaves I purchased from the market last week to Caesar's room. She said, "Make sure she isn't too pretty." I did as instructed, and Caesar took the girl in the same way he took the others. The empress stood outside Caesar's door until he was done with the slave and then ordered me to remove her from the room and send her back to the market first thing in the morning (this morning) for resale, which I did arrange.

If you will permit my prediction on the matter, Priestess, I believe the emperor's previous passions are returning, and so I expect more visits to the slave market lie

ahead of me. That is all for now. As I write, Caesar and his wife are departing for the boxing match at the amphitheater, so you will see them there.

Despina

* * *

Pomponia sat comfortably in the ornate box seating reserved for the Vestals within the massive oval of the crowded amphitheater. She offered a polite smile to Livia, who sat not far from her on the emperor's balcony, which also held—among others—Soren and Anchises as well as Septimus and his soon-to-be wife, Cornelia. Pomponia had declined Livia's offer to sit on the emperor's balcony; today, she preferred the privacy and view from the box that Taurus had designed specifically for the Vestals. It gave her and Quintina some breathing room away from Soren and Septimus respectively.

The Vestal Cossinia was also with them. She had been dropping hints that she was ready to return the Temple of Vesta in Tivoli now that Pomponia had matters more under control in Rome, and the chief Vestal was trying to treat her to as many spectacles as possible during the last of her time in the Caput Mundi. Taurus's grand stadium was such a spectacle.

All around were cheers and the sounding of horns, **SPQR** banners and multicolored flags. The people were in a good mood. And when they were in a good mood, they were loud.

To celebrate the recent abatement of the contagion, Caesar had funded public games on a large scale: two months of daily gladiatorial combats, chariot races, public executions, and beast hunts, among other sport, to be held in both the Circus Maximus and the amphitheater. Spectators sat shoulder to shoulder, stomping their feet and shouting for the main attraction: Thracius the boxer.

Cossinia sat back to enjoy a cup of honey-lemon water. "Do you plan to return to Tivoli soon, Pomponia? Our sisters there are wondering." When the chief Vestal tilted her head in indecision, Cossinia smiled. "It is all right. I suspected you would be staying in Rome."

"I will be back," said Pomponia. "I miss my sisters and friends. I miss my estate too. It is so peaceful compared to Rome. And my slave writes that my vineyard has produced the best grapes in years."

"Don't worry about your wine barrels," Cossinia replied. "The rest of us will take care of those."

Pomponia leaned against Cossinia affectionately. "You have been a great help to me. When you return to Tivoli, the temple there will benefit from the way you've helped manage this crisis here in Rome."

"I've already been working on some protocols so that we are better prepared for a contagion should it strike our town," said Cossinia. "The crisis at the temple in Africa has also inspired me to make sure we are prepared for anything. Our sisters may not be happy to see me return, such is the work I will bring with me."

"They will be happy beyond words," said Pomponia. "And you know it. Now look, sisters, Taurus takes the stage."

The wall and the seats in the stadium shook as thousands of spectators jumped to their feet, applauding and shouting excitedly at the appearance of Taurus on the arena floor. He walked with his arms extended and his eyes wide with the drama of it all until he stood before the emperor's balcony.

"Great Caesar!" He bowed and then turned to the private box of the Vestals. "Blessed priestesses, welcome!" His arms and eyes went wider as he spun in a slow circle on the sand-covered floor of the arena to address the masses of spectators that wrapped around him. "My fellow Romans," he shouted, "the great boxer Thracius, having killed all fighting men in Capua, continues his reign of terror in Rome. How will he fare today? Will his luck and his winning streak finally end?"

An earsplitting roar of excitement rose up like a roll of thunder. Taurus pumped his arms up and down, gesturing for the uproar to cease. "We will soon find out! But first, dear friends, we must say goodbye to another great athlete from Capua, one whose scandalous death was as fascinating as his life . . . Scorpus the Titan!"

At that, a Scorpus look-alike charged out of the gate and onto the arena floor, riding the very chariot that Scorpus the Titan had ridden in the Circus Maximus. Its blue metal surface gleamed in the sunlight while the iridescent black scorpions on its veneer seemed to crawl this way and that, depending on how the light struck them.

The look-alike raised one clenched fist to the cheering crowd, while the other gripped the reins to control the four white horses that pulled the chariot. His resemblance to the famous charioteer was remarkable—strikingly tall, muscular, handsome, and confident, dressed in a rich blue tunica and wearing a helmet inlaid with gold.

He could not have looked less like the real Scorpus the Titan who sat on the highest tier of the amphitheater and watched the dramatics below with only the mildest of interest.

His beard was sticky with wine and neglect, and his tunica was in even rougher shape. He sat hunched over to hide his height and that, combined with the loss of muscle and bulk he had suffered over the previous months, stripped away his most recognizable features. His face was drawn, and he looked little like his former self.

The four white horses pulled the brilliant blue chariot in a lap around the arena. As it came to a stop near the spot where Taurus stood, he again pumped his arms to quell the surge of shouts and the stomping of feet.

Suddenly a horn sounded. It was a strange sound, sad and despairing, as if rising from the depths of Hades. Which, of course, is exactly how Taurus wanted it to sound. As it wailed, the black-robed figure of the ferryman Charon—a frequent visitor to Taurus's amphitheater—moved ominously toward the double, approaching the unsuspecting charioteer from behind.

The spectators began to cry out. "**Scorpus, turn around!**" "**Look behind you, Scorpus!**" "**Scorpus, you fool, watch your ass!**"

But it was not to be. Charon gripped the long handle of his death oar and struck the charioteer with it. He howled out in mock pain, then stumbled out of his gleaming blue chariot to stagger a few steps this way and that, faltering and almost falling with every step, his exaggerated dramatics eliciting laughter and applause from the crowd.

As he floundered, another chariot entered the arena from the gate. This one was black, tattered, and pulled by four equally black and tattered-looking horses. It seemed to move on its own, without a driver.

"Oh, what a tragedy!" Taurus shouted as he pointed to the black horses. "What a sad story that you, dear Scorpus, should be called so prematurely to harness the dusky steeds of Pluto!"

The look-alike shuffled through the sand, lumbering toward the decrepit chariot of death. He pulled himself inside, taking care to not step on the dwarf man who held a hidden set of reins within. He gripped the reins and called out, "Mighty steeds of Pluto, take me to your master in the underworld!"

The chariot lurched forward, moving toward a gate in the stadium's encircling wall. The figure of Charon walked behind, waving his death oar threateningly at the crowd. "**Mors omnem ludum vincit!**" the ferryman called out. Death wins every race.

The death chariot disappeared through the gate, and the crowd sprang to its feet, erupting in applause. The real Scorpus scratched his beard and then clapped from the highest tier in the stadium.

Far below, in the private box of the Vestal priestesses, Pomponia also clapped. She risked a glance at Soren. She was curious—what would he think of this? No doubt the scandal with Scorpus was a sore spot for him. To her disappointment, he seemed unmoved and was chatting idly with a magistrate. Anchises sat rigidly beside him, nodding pleasantly to a senator who was standing over him and relating what, even from a distance, she could tell was a tedious anecdote. It was unusual for a slave to be granted access to upper-class areas, but the singer's celebrity among Rome's elite meant that Soren often had him in tow.

And then something in Anchises's demeanor

changed. His back straightened and the accommodating smile on his face fell into a stiff frown. On the floor of the arena just below him, several arena slaves were positioning tall torches in a circle, when Thracius emerged naked from an unseen door in the wall and walked heavily toward the torch-lined boxing ring. His leather caestus were wrapped around the knuckles of both hands.

Behind him followed two women dressed in white stolas and wearing Vestal-like veils. Each pseudo-priestess held a shallow bronze bowl from which incense sent up thick coils of smoke into the air.

Taurus opened his arms. "Caesar, blessed priestesses of Vesta, and my fellow Romans," he called out again, "Soren Calidius Pavo, owner of the boxer Thracius, wishes to pay tribute to his cousin, our beloved Priestess Tuccia, on this day which would have marked the thirty-ninth year of her life."

Pomponia gripped the fabric of her stola and clenched it in her hands.

"With all honors to our Vestalis Maxima Pomponia and with all devotion to the Vestal order of Rome," said Taurus, "Soren Calidius Pavo hereby renames this slave **Ignis**! Ignis, for the fire that the great goddess ignites in our hearts! Ignis, for the sacred fire that Priestess Tuccia guarded for our sakes! Ignis, the name of fire itself!"

The crowd emitted a collective gasp of emotion. Manic applause. And then thousands of voices began to chant "**Ignis! Ignis! Ignis!**"

Pomponia looked at Soren. He was on his feet and standing as smugly as any human being could stand. He stared at her expectantly, and she could read his thoughts: **You have no choice but to stand and acknowledge me before everyone here, before Caesar, before all Rome.**

She felt Quintina's hand on her shoulder. "Keep calm, sister," she said into Pomponia's ear. "Do your duty. We will deal with him later."

Soren saw a gracious smile spread across the chief Vestal's lips. He saw her stand and nod in gratitude to him. He bowed his head to her, and then after she took her seat again, he did the same.

Horns sounded and Thracius's—Ignis's—hulking opponent appeared on the arena floor. He strode with his hefty arms in the air to the boxing ring of fire, within which Thracius stood waiting. Both fighters turned to the emperor's balcony, and Thracius's opponent saluted Caesar shouting, "**Ave, Caesar!**"

Octavian raised himself off the Tyrian-purple cushion of his high-backed chair and returned the salute. "**Avete**," he answered. Fare you well.

Thracius's opponent made the first move. Thracius held his forearms in front of his face to absorb a few fast blows to the head and felt the flesh on his forearms separate. Unlike the caestus around his own hands, his opponent's knuckle wraps were outfitted with some kind of cutting metal inserts. Thracius wasn't surprised. He had yet to fight an opponent in Rome who wasn't given an advantage.

He parried his opponent's wide swings and then, in a move the crowd loved, caught the man's fist in his palm and thrust his arm forward so that the man struck himself in the face. A swell of laughter went up.

The other boxer stepped back with an angry roar and then came at Thracius with his legs, kicking while Thracius backed up and also started to laugh. "Are you a man or a donkey?" he asked his opponent. The audience howled in amusement and stamped their feet. Some pretended to bray like a donkey, while others again chanted "**Ignis! Ignis! Ignis!**"

But then his opponent got serious. He took a step

back and eyed Thracius head to toe. He spat in the sand. He lifted his arms and advanced with a cross punch that had such power behind it that Thracius could hear it move through the air. It landed squarely on his jaw, followed by an uppercut to his chin. The metal inserts cut into his flesh, and blood ran down his neck.

Thracius bit his tongue and cursed himself as he spat out blood. He lowered his head and bobbed around the other fighter, blocking a jab and countering with a series of rapid kidney punches that momentarily knocked the wind out of his opponent.

The other boxer spun and stumbled back but quickly recovered. Fists raised, he sprang at Thracius and bobbed and weaved around him, the two of them exchanging a series of punches and counterpunches that had the crowd of thousands on its feet.

Thracius coughed. His mouth was filling with blood from his injured tongue. He spat a mouthful of blood at the other fighter, who stepped back for a moment but then rushed him, head down, striking Thracius in the midsection with his skull like a battering ram striking a fortified door. Thracius felt the man lock a viselike grip around one of his legs and try to lift it but, before he lost his footing, he managed to bend over his opponent's back and wrap his own arms around the man's neck from above.

With his head pinned down, Thracius's opponent nevertheless managed to land several solid, lacerating punches to Thracius's back and midsection. In response, Thracius kneed him in the face. He felt the man's nasal bone collapse and then warm blood oozing down his leg from the injury.

Thracius pushed the man away and rushed at him with a flurry of straight, powerful punches that he, his opponent, and every spectator in the amphitheater knew would not stop until the man was dead. Thracius's opponent wobbled on his feet and collapsed where he stood to land in a bloody heap on the sand.

He thought he might be imagining it, but to Thracius it seemed like the sand at his feet was almost vibrating, such was the force of the reverberation caused by the shouts and stomping of the stadium's spectators. He spat another mouthful of blood into the sand as the arena slaves dragged the man's corpse from the stadium.

Above him, on the emperor's balcony, Anchises allowed himself to exhale. Soren smirked and looked at Caesar—no doubt he had been entertained. The proud owner frowned, however, when he saw that Caesar wasn't even looking at the boxer.

An elderly magistrate, one Soren had been speaking with earlier, was now whispering into the emperor's ear while pointing at a man who sat in the seats just beyond the balcony. Caesar's attention was riveted to the man. He twisted in his seat and called over a centurion guard.

The centurion nodded as he received his instructions, locked his eyes on the targeted man, and then left the balcony with two other guards.

By now, everyone's attention had shifted away from the arena floor and on to whatever was developing in the stands above it. The three armor-clad guards approached the man. Pushing aside his red soldier's cloak, one of the guards gripped the man by his toga and pulled him out of his seat, dragging him unceremoniously toward the exit.

Caesar stood. "My friends," he called out, "I have been informed that this man, called Eulalius, is one of the many who committed adultery with my disowned daughter, Julia. He will answer for his crime right now!"

As the crowd ruminated excitedly, the three guards appeared below them on the floor of the arena, one of them still dragging the man named Eulalius by his toga. The guard threw him at Thracius's feet before he and the other two soldiers backed away.

Eulalius raised his hand in a feeble defensive gesture and blinked bewilderedly up at the boxer, turning his head slowly to survey the cheering crowd that encircled them. His eyes stopped at the spot where he had been sitting. Thracius followed his stare to see two teenaged boys standing, their mouths hanging open in shock.

"Get up and fight," said Thracius. "You don't want your sons to see you die a coward."

"I don't know how to fight," the man stuttered.

"You've hit your slaves, haven't you?" Thracius asked. "Sure you have. Pretend I'm one of your slaves. Come on, I'll let you land a few so your boys don't remember their father as a sniveling woman." The boxer shrugged his shoulders. "That's all that's left to you, brother."

The man opened his mouth stupidly and shook his head up at Thracius.

The boxer sighed. "If you don't stand up, you'll die on the ground. Don't think about it. Just get up. The sooner it's over, the better."

The man stood. He spread his legs in something

that almost resembled a fighting stance and held his trembling fists in front of his face.

Thracius spat yet another mouthful of blood into the sand—his damn tongue wouldn't stop bleeding—and raised his fists. He bobbed back and forth in front of Eulalius and then threw a fast punch, pulling it at the last second so it landed softly on the man's jaw.

Eulalius stumbled backward. Thracius gave him a moment to recover. He didn't fully, but whatever instincts were within him finally kicked in, and he ran at Thracius, swinging madly and landing punches that Thracius imagined the man's slaves laughed about behind his back.

Thracius leaned his head back and pretended to fall down: he wasn't sure if the crowd was cheering or laughing at his act. Either way, Eulalius began to punch and kick wildly at him while he slowly lifted himself to his feet. And then in one swift motion, he punched the man hard in the face. He fell back like a stiff board, blood spurting from his nose and mouth. He was dead before he hit the sand.

The crowd was in a near frenzy now. The stone and wood boards of the stadium's huge encircling wall vibrated from the noise. The games were always entertaining, but this kind of violent human drama was pure bliss.

Yet it presented Caesar with a problem. A slave had just killed a nobleman. Yes, it was on Caesar's order, but still . . .

He waved one of the guards on the arena floor closer, and the man ran to stand just below the emperor's balcony. He took off his helmet and looked up at the emperor. Caesar shouted down to him, "Kill the boxer."

The guard turned to look at Thracius. **Damn it**, he thought. **I liked him.** He called back up to the emperor. "Yes, Caesar. Do you have a preference?"

Octavian's eyes fell on the burning torches that outlined the boxing ring. "Burn him," he ordered.

The guard put his helmet back on and jerked his head to his two subordinates. **Let's get this over with.**

Each of them grabbed a tall burning torch and cautiously approached Thracius with it. If they thought the boxer was going to put up a fight, however, they were wrong. Thracius was a man who took his own advice. **The sooner it's over, the better.** As the soldiers moved in on him, he simply stood and searched the stands for Anchises.

He stopped searching when the first torch scalded his flesh. Two more followed. The guards stabbed at him randomly, exchanging baffled looks with each other—the boxer wore no clothes and his hair was cut to the scalp. It was hard to actually set him on fire. Instead, his skin just burned and blackened in the areas the torches touched.

One of the guards had an idea. He rushed to the body of Eulalius and fumbled until he had removed the man's heavy toga, leaving him sprawled on the sand wearing only a short tunica.

He returned to Thracius who was now backed against the wall of the arena and dropped the toga at his feet. They all stabbed their torches into the fabric, and it caught fire with a **whoosh**. Thracius cried out in agony.

And then the crowd began to cry out too. Shouts of "Let him live!" rose up to shake the stands. People were on their feet, clutching their heads in dismay and pointing at Thracius, whose lower body had caught on fire. "**Let him live, let him live!**"

Octavian slumped his shoulders. It was a rare occurrence, but he had misjudged the crowd. They liked Ignis. He flared his nostrils in irritation. **I wouldn't have done it if Maecenas were here**

today, he thought. **Maecenas never misjudges a crowd.**

In the Vestal box next to his balcony, Pomponia's chest was tight with dread. Anchises was rising to his feet, and she knew what would happen next: he would cry out and in his panic, maybe even try to jump down into the arena, but he would be caught, and Caesar would have him killed as well. It would be a double spectacle: Apollo's Pair, meeting Hades together in horror.

Yet the crowd's vocal displeasure with Thracius's execution and Caesar's self-reproaching expression emboldened her. She stood up. "Caesar," she called out, "your faithful priestess begs you to spare this man's life."

Octavian swung his head to look at her. **Good thinking**, he thought. **A show of force and then a show of mercy. That'll teach Maecenas.**

The emperor stood and shouted down to the guards. "Let him live!"

They quickly obeyed. One of them removed his soldier's cloak to suffocate the fire, while the others kicked sand onto the flames. Within moments, the fire was extinguished. His chest heaving, Thracius leaned against the stadium wall. His arms and torso showed large patches of pale pink and black burns that had singed away the top layers of his skin, while his legs were covered in raised, oozing, cherry-red blisters and sections of charred flesh.

Medics rushed onto the arena floor with a stretcher. They wanted to catch him before he fell into the sand and packed his burns with debris. They arrived just in time, and with the help of a guard, they guided his collapsing body onto the stretcher.

Taurus ran into the middle of the arena as the medics carried Thracius out of it. He was as jubilant as the crowd, and like them, applauded and shouted, "**Ave, Caesar!** We thank the gods for our merciful Caesar. And Ignis thanks the gods for his blessed name!"

Pomponia gazed at the moving mass of spectators that jumped, applauded, and laughed in the massive oval of the amphitheater. Every one of them assumed it was Thracius's new name—Ignis!—that had moved her to a Vestal's mercy, but they were wrong. Pomponia hated the name. Nonetheless, she smiled graciously at the faithful around her who called out her name and the name of the goddess.

"Next up," shouted Taurus from the floor, "the gladiatorial combats!"

A quick rise of applause, and then the volume in the amphitheater fell with the intermission. Arena slaves scooped up clumps of bloody sand and dragged Eulalius's corpse away. Civic slaves moved through the crowd, handing out free loaves of bread, as they always did during the games. People ate them whether they were hungry or not. They turned to their companions to relive the match or to gossip, or got up to stretch or make their way to the latrines.

"That was well done," Cossinia whispered to Pomponia.

"I think you just earned us a second rooftop terrace," Quintina said with a grin.

"Just what we need," said Pomponia as casually as she could. "Let's make our pleasantries." Cossinia and Quintina followed Pomponia out of the Vestal box, along a well-guarded private colonnade, and directly onto the emperor's balcony, where they each gravitated toward their respective friends.

Pomponia accepted a cup of wine and made small talk with one of her favorite senators. She did her best to appear indifferent to the presence of Soren and Anchises, even as Soren slurped from his wine cup and sauntered up to her.

"I suppose I should thank you for sparing my slave," he said. "**This** slave, that is."

"Not at all," said Pomponia. She neither looked at Anchises nor acknowledged the self-serving tribute that Soren had made to Tuccia. She didn't trust herself to mention it without losing her composure. "Excuse me." She brushed her veil off her face and strolled to the front of the balcony, where the empress was staring absently down into the arena.

"Priestess Pomponia," Livia greeted her, "Caesar is grateful for your judgment today." She spun around to rest her back against the balustrade, when something caught her eye. Pomponia turned to follow her stare. In the corner, Quintina was engaged in a hushed but emotional exchange with Septimus.

"That girl is going to get herself into trouble," Livia said flatly. "The last thing Caesar or the Vestal order needs."

"The very last." Pomponia tapped her fingers on her wine cup. She had hoped that her recent cathartic conversation with Quintina had cooled the younger Vestal's passions, but it had not. The situation could not go on. "Lady Livia," she said, pointing a finger to Septimus, "was that young man not often seen in the company of Julia?"

Livia understood immediately. It was how her mind worked. "Yes, I believe so," she replied. "I will inform Caesar this evening."

That was as much as they would discuss it. Pomponia moved on to mingle with other friends, while Octavian called for Livia to join him in a conversation with a visiting foreign dignitary.

No one on the emperor's balcony even took notice that the gladiatorial games were now underway below. Such things were, in every way, beneath them.

* * *

Soren was asleep in the lectica. Anchises sat across from him and wondered what his master's mood would be like once they arrived at his home. Since leaving the amphitheater, it had vacillated between pleased—or at least what passed for pleased with Soren—and outraged.

On one hand, Soren was gratified to see how popular Thracius, now Ignis, was with the Roman people. Once he healed from his wounds, his comeback boxing match would make Soren one of the wealthiest men in the city. And that was before the coin he'd make from all those Roman wives who wanted a personal look at the boxer's burns.

On the other hand, he couldn't stop raging about the Vestal Pomponia. About how she had spared Thracius but had refused to spare Dacia. Anchises didn't dare ask who Dacia was. He had a good enough idea of what had happened.

For his part, Anchises was trying but failing miserably to put the image of Thracius being set on fire out of his mind. Every time he thought of it, he saw it and felt it anew. He had been a breath away from running to the edge of the balcony and jumping off so that he could die in the arena with the only person he had ever loved. He didn't care what happened: he only wanted Thracius to know that he wasn't dying alone.

The lectica stopped in front of the house, and Soren jerked awake. To Anchises's relief, he said nothing but just tiredly stepped out and headed through the portico. It was past twilight, and the moon was rising. It had been a long day.

Anchises delayed a few moments so that Soren would be well ahead of him before he stepped out himself. As always, a slave met him at the side of the lectica and had him change into a rough tunica before entering the house.

The virtuoso walked softly through the portico and into the atrium. He could hear Soren barking at a female slave and ordering her to his bedchamber. The female slave's bad luck was Anchises's good luck: with Soren occupied, he could grab a loaf of bread or a few figs before descending the stone steps into the hateful basement.

He slipped into the kitchen and stuffed a piece of bread between his lips—it was stale but still edible—and walked down the steps into the cool basement, flinching in pain. One of his sandals didn't fit properly, and it had scraped the skin on his ankle raw. He removed both of his sandals and walked down the dirt floor of the narrow corridor until he reached his tiny room.

Anchises sat on the hard mattress and rubbed his temples. He laid his head back on his shoulders—and gasped at the sight of Soren's frame standing in his doorway, towering above him and blocking any light that had been filtering in from the few oil lamps affixed to the rough stone walls outside his room.

"Domine," breathed Anchises, "did you require me?"

The singer started to get up, but Soren took a step closer to him. "Stay where you are," he said. He glared down at Anchises who was now on his knees. "Why did the Vestal spare Thracius?"

"Domine, I do not know."

"Have you been communicating with her behind my back? Exchanging letters or messages, maybe?"

"No, Domine," said Anchises. "The priestess bade me sit with her at Lady Julia's reception, that is all. I have no reason and no opportunity to communicate with her."

"No opportunity?" asked Soren. "Does that mean you've been trying to?"

"No, Domine. I can assure you. I have not. I would not."

"I needn't remind you where your loyalties lie," said Soren.

"Of course not, Domine."

"Have you been communicating with Thracius in the ludus?"

"No, Domine. I would like to see him. I worry about him, especially after today. He will be in great pain, and if his burns get infected, I worry—"

"I'm the only person you need to worry about."

Soren leaned against the narrow doorway. Anchises prayed he would just turn around and leave. Wasn't he anxious to join his bed slave?

"Domine, is there something else I can assist you with?"

Soren hesitated and then took another step closer to Anchises. "Since you're already on your knees, you may as well do something useful."

Anchises held his breath. Soren had used this threat to intimidate him before, but he had not followed through, and to his knowledge, the master only ever took female slaves.

Kneeling on the hard bed, Anchises raised the bottom of Soren's toga and then did the same with the short tunica underneath. Soren grabbed onto it and held it up as Anchises unfastened his loincloth. It fell on the floor between Soren's feet.

Soren was already fully erect when Anchises reached out to touch him. When he did, Soren made a low groan, and Anchises knew the man's arousal and curiosity had crossed the threshold. He did his best to imagine a moment between him and Thracius, anything to get him through it, and then he began to fellate Soren. After several moments, Soren pushed the singer away and directed him onto the mattress. Anchises felt the man's weight press down on him and squeezed his eyes as Soren tore off his loincloth and penetrated him, releasing—mercifully—after only a few painful thrusts.

Afterward, Soren rested his weight on top of Anchises and steadied his breathing. Then he pushed himself up, straightened his toga, picked his loincloth off the floor, and disappeared down the stone corridor and up the steps.

Anchises collapsed onto the dirty mattress and pressed his face into it. He reached for his one ratty woolen blanket and pulled it over himself. After Thracius's horrific ordeal, after his own violation, he should have felt hopeless and full of despair. But he did not.

He was holding on to one hope.

Anchises had caught sight of that hope when he was leaving the stadium. Soren had stopped to chat up the wife of an absent magistrate, and Anchises, lagging behind at a respectable distance, had thought he heard a familiar voice mumble his name.

At first he wasn't sure it was really him: the revolting beard, grimy face, and straggly hair. The slumped shoulders and leaner frame. But it was him.

It was Scorpus the Titan, alive and still in Rome.

CHAPTER XXV

Id Agas Tuo Te Merito Ne Quis Oderit

Take care that no one justly hates you.
—PUBLILIUS SYRUS

The Vestal priestess Lucretia shook her finger at one of her two guards. His name was Oeneus, and he was stuffing a piece of honey cake in his mouth.

"Those are for the children," she said, trying to appear angry. "Look at them all waiting in line for a piece, and here you are, a grown man and soldier, exploiting your position for a sweet."

He shook his head apologetically but said nothing—he couldn't with a mouthful of cake—and brushed a few crumbs off his iron breastplate.

The high priestess approached Lucretia and cast the guard a grin as she spoke to her sister Vestal. "I haven't seen the Forum Boarium this clean in ages," she said. "Nor the people this happy."

"This was a good idea, Pomponia," said Lucretia.

"You can thank the empress," Pomponia replied. "It was her idea."

"I will thank her when I see her."

"Yes, do. And make sure you do it in front of Caesar."

Lucretia nodded. Pomponia wouldn't admit it, but all the Vestals knew that it was she and not the empress who was responsible for this celebration in the Forum Boarium, the great cattle market alongside the Tiber River.

With the gloom of the contagion now behind them, Pomponia had searched through the archives for an excuse to have a public festival during a time when the fasti didn't recognize any dates that would be joyous enough to celebrate the end of the long contagion. Plus, Pomponia knew something uplifting was necessary in the aftermath of Julia's banishment. The people needed to have a good time, something beyond the blood sports of the **ludi**.

She had found the perfect thing. It was an old and light-hearted tradition where the Vestals would bring embers and ash from the sacred fire and lay them on the ground in the Forum Boarium. People would then walk their cattle, pigs, or horses through the embers—it was harmless enough—and in so doing, they would purify the wombs of their breeding animals. To the amusement of those present, a group of young women also ran through the embers, throwing flirtatious looks at the unmarried men who watched, laughing.

The atmosphere in the Forum Boarium was precisely as Pomponia had hoped it would be. The market area provided a casual and open space for thousands of people to celebrate and interact: music was playing, vendors were selling goods, and friends were visiting each other. Under the shade of the Arch of Janus, hundreds of children were lining up to receive the free honey cakes that the Vestal order had commissioned from a grateful bakers' guild.

Best of all from Pomponia's perspective, the occasion allowed Rome's children to have some face-to-face interaction with the Vestal order's young novice priestesses, as it was they who handed out the honey cakes to the little ones. It was important to Pomponia that the public saw the priestesses as real people. Yes, Vestals took part in all public rituals and festivals and could often be seen moving between buildings in the Forum; an occasion like this, however—informal, good-humored—allowed the public to develop an affection for the Vestals as individuals.

A swell of applause and laughter caught Pomponia's attention, and she gravitated away from the arch and closer to the river, guarded as always by Caeso and Publius whose eyes darted here and there and whose hands rested on the hilts of their daggers. As she cut through the crowd, men and women lowered their heads in deference.

Near the banks of the river, she reached the Temple of Portunus and the round temple that was dedicated to Hercules but also used by the Vestals to consecrate water from the Tiber: it was near the spot where Tuccia had performed her miracle years earlier.

A large crowd was gathered before the latter temple, where an actor dressed as Hercules pretended to fight the Nemean lion—in this case, another actor wearing a lion skin and balancing a giant lion head on his own. The lion's head kept falling over, and the crowd shrieked with laughter as the actor tried to keep his head and avoid the mighty hero's spiked club at the same time. The play was being enacted in this spot for a good reason: it was said that Hercules arrived in Italy at this port along the Tiber, which was also the site of Rome's earliest gladiatorial fights.

Surrounded by legionary soldiers and lictors, the emperor and empress sat in comfort under a rich purple canopy adjacent to the temple to watch the play. Pomponia smiled to see that Quintina was sitting beside the empress. Livia was whispering something into her ear, and the Vestal was laughing dutifully. **Good**, thought Pomponia. She had feared Quintina's resentment at Julia's banishment would show, but it did not.

Pomponia passed through the guards under the purple canopy to take a chair beside Quintina. As she did, some children noisily escorted a parade of braying donkeys past the canopy and waved madly to the Vestals under it. The donkeys' backs were draped with strings of colorful flowers.

Both Pomponia and Quintina waved indulgently at the children. The donkey parade was a whimsical tribute to Vesta's sacred animal. It was said that a braying donkey had alerted the sleeping virgin goddess to the rapacious intentions of Priapus, the god of fertility, and so Vesta had afterward favored the animal above all others.

With the donkeys moving on and the Nemean lion safely dispatched, Octavian excused himself to go speak with Tiberius, who was leaning against a large bronze statue of Hercules and eating a honey cake. Quintina went with him.

"Priestess Quintina seems to be taking on more public duties these days," Livia said to Pomponia when they were alone.

"Yes," said Pomponia. "She has a diplomatic nature." Pomponia's eyes followed Septimus as he strolled past the canopy holding hands with his soon-to-be wife, Cornelia. "For most things," she added. She accepted a glass of cucumber water from a slave.

"I assume you are training her to work alongside Tiberius," said Livia.

"I am," Pomponia replied.

"It will be to both their benefits if they are friends, as you and Caesar are. I know that is Tiberius's hope." Livia watched some civic slaves work just outside the canopy, collecting garbage and scrubbing animal waste off the street. "I must thank you again, Priestess, for allowing me to suggest this festival to Caesar. He was pleased."

I know, thought Pomponia. **I read Despina's letter. It said that Caesar has been bedding you lately instead of his slaves.**

"That is good to hear," said Pomponia.

Livia opened her mouth to say something else, but the authoritative shouts of some soldiers behind them made both women turn in their seats to see what was happening.

Oh gods, thought Pomponia. **I was hoping this wouldn't happen in public . . .**

Four or five legionary soldiers had surrounded Septimus. The young man had his hands out in disbelief. "I have never touched Caesar's daughter!" he shouted to Octavian, who stood fuming before him.

Livia sighed. "Why must he do this in public?" she muttered. "Why thunder on a cloudless day?" She looked around. "Where is Priestess Quintina?"

"I don't know," Pomponia replied, "but I'd better find her."

Pomponia hastened out of the canopy so quickly that her guards had to scramble to catch up to her. "Where is Priestess Quintina?" she asked them.

Publius saw her first. "There she is, my lady."

Quintina was standing openmouthed beside Tiberius, watching the accusation unfold. She seemed to sense Pomponia approach and rushed to the chief Vestal's side. "Pomponia," she breathed, "we must stop this. Septimus was never with Julia."

"Lower your voice, Quintina," Pomponia scolded. "Whatever Caesar is going to do, there is no stopping it. Not this time."

"Caesar will kill him!"

"And if you speak for him, you will condemn your-self." Pomponia all but yanked on Quintina's arm to bring her closer. "Whatever you're thinking about doing, Quintina, don't. You are too close to these people . . . to Julia and to Septimus. Both are known to have been promiscuous. If you speak for him, if you intercede in any way, suspicion will fall on you."

Both Vestals jumped as Publius brushed by them, catching Septimus's betrothed, Cornelia, in his arms. She slid down onto her knees before Quintina. "Priestess," she begged with wild eyes, "I know you are friends with Septimus. Please do something!"

Dazed, Quintina stared down at the desperate woman at her feet. So, too, did Pomponia, although it was not Cornelia's face she saw. It was Valeria's.

"Take her away, Publius," ordered Pomponia. "Quintina, let's go. There is nothing you can do."

The guard dragged Cornelia away, but Quintina refused to move. Pomponia stood at her shoulder, and together they watched Caesar, red-faced with anger, order his soldiers to pull Septimus to the banks of the river.

Once there, they pushed him to the ground. While two soldiers held him down, two more tied the rope of a heavy anchor around his legs. The young man fought hard, fought for his life, screaming and kicking and pleading for Caesar's mercy. "I swear to the gods, I never touched Julia! Ask her, ask anyone! Who would say that I did? I did not!"

"Quintina," said Pomponia, "I beg you, let's go. Do not watch this."

"I cannot move," said Quintina, her voice thin and trembling.

Pomponia put her arm around the younger Vestal and urged her to turn around. She finally did, and in that same moment a heavy splash sounded behind them. Septimus's shouting stopped.

Pomponia led Quintina through the square of the Forum Boarium toward their waiting carriage. She pushed Quintina into it, all but dove in after her, and quickly pulled the curtains closed.

Quintina put her hands to her face. "He is under the water right now, he is drowning . . . We can still save him. He will die in another moment!"

"He dies today, or you both die tomorrow," said Pomponia. "It is done." Through Quintina's gasping sobs, the high priestess heard a hushed voice outside the curtains.

"Don't just stand there, you idiots. Take them back

to the temple." It was Livia, instructing the guards. The carriage shifted as the horses moved forward.

"He is innocent," Quintina sobbed.

"I am sorry," said Pomponia.

"Who would accuse him? Who would have reason to spread such a lie about Septimus?"

Pomponia licked her lips. "Caesar is easily inflamed these days," she said. "When it comes to Julia and her lovers . . ."

"He was not her lover."

". . . suspected lovers, then. Any appearance of guilt, any association with her lifestyle . . . it is enough to be condemned. It is why you must be careful."

Quintina gasped. "I know who it was!" When Pomponia only shook her head, the younger Vestal continued. "It was Tacita! He refused her when he learned she was my sister. That would be enough to drive her to it."

"It may have been her. We cannot be sure."

"I am sure! I swear to the goddess, I will have her head on a spike for this. I will have her thrown off the Tarpeian Rock! I will push her off myself!"

Pomponia moved from her seat to sit close beside the young Vestal. She embraced her tightly. Quintina wept. "Pomponia," she asked, "do you think it's over? Do you think he is dead now? I cannot stand to think of him suffering, gasping for breath under the water."

"It is over," said Pomponia. "The goddess is lighting his way." She kissed the top of Quintina's head. "I will send some temple slaves tomorrow, at first light. They will see if they can . . ." She searched for the right words. ". . . if they can find him."

They rode together in silence within the carriage, the only sound being the occasional burst of sobs from Quintina and the clip-clopping of horse hooves on the street.

By the time they arrived on the streets of the Forum Romanum, Quintina's grief had hardened into something else. "I will have my revenge on her," she said.

"Do not speak like that, Quintina."

"It is strange that you of all people should say so."

"What does that mean?" asked Pomponia.

"What happened to the empress's sister? What was her name . . . yes, Claudia."

Pomponia pulled away from Quintina. "How would I know what happened to her?"

"After she accused Tuccia of breaking her vows, and after Tuccia's innocence was proven. What happened to her? No one speaks of her, not even the empress. Why is that? A noblewoman disappears—completely—and no one mentions it?"

"'Disappears' is a dramatic way to put it, Quintina. She isn't here, but that doesn't mean she disappeared. Perhaps the shame of her false accusation was enough to drive her into self-exile. If so, it was the first bit of sense the woman ever showed."

"I am not a fool, Pomponia. You are a priestess of Nemesis as much as Vesta. You have exacted revenge on those you hate but would stop me from doing the same?"

"You are wrong," said Pomponia. "I would never stop you from exacting revenge." She stroked Quintina's hair. "I would only delay you until the time was right."

CHAPTER XXVI

Canis Caninam Non Est
A dog doesn't eat another dog.
—A ROMAN ADAGE

Scorpus often heard shouts and scuffles from the street below this third-floor apartment in the Subura. It was usually nothing too serious—some kids trying to steal something from a shop, a husband and wife bickering, a few drunken men arguing over an imagined insult or which one of them would get the prettier whore for the night.

Despite the Subura's reputation, its residents were mostly just people trying to get by, trying to save some coin, trying to eke whatever stability and happiness they could out of life. Scorpus had seen its residents come together several times. Whether it was a fire or a lost favorite dog, neighbors looked out for each other.

That's why the shouts and scuffles outside his

small window didn't concern him too much. Not at first. But then something made him sit up on his mattress and listen more closely. **That voice . . . is that . . . Pomponius?**

He crossed the room in three steps and stuck his head out the window. Three men were on the street below: one was in a defensive posture, backing up with his arms out, while the other two advanced on him. Scorpus squinted against the glare of the still-rising sun, and then his face fell. It was Pomponius, doing his best—which was awful—to fight off two attackers.

"You," Scorpus shouted down. "**Abite!**"

Scorpus turned and ran out of his room, stampeded down the rickety wooden stairs, and burst out of the door onto the street to confront Pomponius's attackers. He stood to his full height. Both men took an instinctive step back and exchanged glances.

"What's going on here?" Scorpus barked at them.

"None of your concern, friend," said one of the attackers.

"**Paedica te**," spat Scorpus. "I don't know you. Be on your way."

The two attackers looked at each other. Scorpus leaned forward. He had one man right in front of him, but he didn't like how close the other man, who held a short sword, was to Pomponius. He was just about to tell Pomponius to move, when the man pivoted his body and thrust the blade into Pomponius's chest fast and hard. Both attackers turned and ran in separate directions. They had gambled that Scorpus would run to the fallen man instead of running after them.

They were right. The charioteer rushed to Pomponius's side and without wasting time checking the wound, lifted him over his shoulders with the ease another man might lift a light sack of grain. He ran down the cobblestone street to the door of the tombstone maker and kicked loudly.

"Palaemon!" he shouted. "Get your ass out of bed, now!"

After a few moments of rustling from the other side of the door, it opened wide and the darkened, leathered face of the old man stared up at Scorpus.

"Jove's ass, man!" he said. But he didn't protest as Scorpus ran into his home and dropped Pomponius's body onto a table.

"I need help," said Scorpus. "Get some water and some linen we can use as bandages."

As Palaemon dashed off to gather supplies,

Scorpus looked at Pomponius's face. He suddenly realized that the man hadn't cried out, hadn't screamed at all. Pomponius was gritting his teeth and clutching his tunica at his chest. His face was white from pain. His blood streamed out of him so freely that Scorpus could hear it—**drip, drip, drizzle**—land on the wooden planks of the floor. He put pressure on the wound, but his hands only seemed to sink into Pomponius's body, making the blood gush out more profusely.

"I'm going to die, aren't I?" Pomponius asked through clenched teeth. His voice was thin and trembling.

Scorpus had heard that voice before. It was how men sounded when they were in shock and had only a few heartbeats of lifeblood left in them. He had a sudden memory of a chariot driver—he couldn't recall the man's name, but he remembered the injury. After a nasty wreck on the track, a broken spoke had pierced his chest in exactly the same place Pomponius had been impaled. The chariot driver was a bigger, stronger man but hadn't lived long enough for the medics to reach him on the far end of the circuit.

"No, you're not going to die," he lied.

"I feel like I'm losing consciousness," said Pomponius.

"You might pass out," Scorpus replied, trying to sound matter-of-fact. "But that's good. When you wake, we'll have you patched up, and we'll get drunk."

"Are you sure?"

"Of course I'm sure. I've seen this injury many times." He swallowed hard. "Why don't you close your eyes and try to sleep."

"Are you sure?" Pomponius asked again.

"Yes, I'm sure. Go to sleep. It'll be easier for us to fix you up if you aren't whining about it like a goddamn woman."

Pomponius's face and body relaxed.

Palaemon appeared at Scorpus's shoulder. "Is he dead?"

"Yes," said Scorpus.

"Who is he?"

"A friend of mine," said Scorpus. **Probably the only real friend I've ever had.**

"Do you know who killed him?"

Scorpus lifted a tipped-over chair off the floor and then sat down heavily on it. The man with the short sword. Scorpus had seen that weapon before. He recognized its crimson hilt. It had hung over a statue of Hercules in the home of Soren Calidius Pavo.

Palaemon put his ear to Pomponius's nose and mouth. He glanced at Scorpus. "Do you want me to take him to the undertaker?"

"No," Scorpus replied. "I want you to take him to the House of the Vestals."

* * *

Pomponia's day hadn't gone the way she thought it would. At first light, she had sent temple slaves to go see whether they could retrieve Septimus's body from the Tiber. They had no sooner exited the portico than a leather-faced man had arrived in front of it. A teenaged boy was with him. They pulled a covered cart with the words "Palaemon Makes the Best Tombstones" painted on both sides.

The leather-faced man had spoken to the guards, and Caeso had quickly stuck his head into the cart. He pulled it out just as quickly.

Pomponia hadn't looked at her brother's body. Caeso had said he was dressed in a rough tunica and covered in blood. He had died from one deep stab wound to his chest.

She had given the man coin and asked him some questions: he had answered dutifully, although he had fidgeted nonstop in her presence. He was not the type of man who ever expected to speak with a Vestal Virgin during his lifetime, let alone the Vestalis Maxima herself.

That done, and still holding off the tears, she had ordered Pomponius's body be taken into the House of the Vestals and placed in the clinic room. She called for Musa to come from Caesar's house so that he could clean Pomponius's wound and dress him in a toga. She did not want the slaves to do it, and she could not. While Vestals could prepare the bodies of their deceased sisters for the afterlife, they were not permitted to touch the dead bodies of others.

She had done all that and more without really thinking, without really feeling. Such was the training of a Vestal priestess: do what must be done, regardless of the circumstances, regardless of your fears or your feelings.

Now she stood with her sister priestesses in the sanctum of the Temple of Vesta, crying over the sacred flame. It was always the same when a Vestal lost a loved one. They would all gather in the temple with her to pray and present offerings or libations into the ancient hearth. They had been making so many offerings lately. The contagion had taken sisters, brothers, cousins, and parents from all the priestesses. But this—a murdered family member—was an unusual thing for a noblewoman to experience.

One of the bronze doors of the temple opened a crack, and Lucasta poked her head in. "I am sorry to disturb you, sisters," she said. "I was supposed to tell you when Lady Tacita arrived. She is here now. I put her in the tablinum."

Pomponia and Quintina exchanged glances. They had sent for Tacita over four hours earlier. The young woman's tardy response to an official Vestal summons was an irritation that compounded their respective grief.

While Cossinia and Marcella remained in the temple on watch, Pomponia, Quintina, Lucretia, and Caecilia descended the marble steps and walked to the House of the Vestals. The latter two returned to the novices' study, while Pomponia and Quintina calmed themselves in preparation for their meeting with Tacita.

They pushed aside a heavy, gold-embroidered teal curtain to enter the tablinum, where the very pregnant Tacita was reclining on a large chair next to a statue of Flora and ordering food from a slave as if she herself lived there.

"Hello, sister," said Quintina.

"Oh, Quintina!" Tacita rolled herself to a standing position. "I was beside myself with grief to hear what befell our poor Septimus. What a shock it must have been for you." She put her arms around Quintina—her distended belly kept them at a safe distance from each other—and then wiped an invisible tear from her cheek. "I know you were close . . . well, as close as you can be to any man, I suppose." She rubbed her pregnant belly.

For the second time in as many days, Pomponia saw the face of Valeria. After all these years, she could still hear Valeria's voice.

I don't know what it is about Quintus's children. They are as hard on my body as their father is.

"We are not here to discuss Septimus," said Quintina. "We have some unfortunate news for you, Tacita."

"Do you?" Tacita plopped back down on the chair.

The Vestals sat across from Tacita. "It is about Pomponius," said Pomponia. "My brother told me that he is the father of your child and that you are to be married, so I wanted to tell you in person . . ." Tacita looked like she was going to interrupt, but Pomponia continued. "His body was brought here this morning. He was stabbed and killed in the Subura."

"The Subura? What was he doing there?" asked Tacita. "Doesn't seem like the kind of place a decent citizen should be found, alive or dead."

"I don't know what he was doing there," said Pomponia. In an instant, her grief had dissipated and re-formed into anger.

"How did you find out he was dead?"

"A shopkeeper," said Pomponia. "He heard a fight in the street and found Pomponius bleeding on the ground."

"How did he know to bring him here?"

Pomponia exhaled heavily. These were not the questions that a grief-stricken pregnant woman should be asking. "Pomponius told the shopkeeper that I was his sister," she said curtly. "They brought him here hoping to find a physician, but he died on the way."

Tacita leaned back comfortably in the chair. "Maybe he was keeping a whore in the Subura," she speculated. "It's probably cheaper to keep one there than in one of the finer districts."

If Pomponius were keeping any whore, Pomponia thought, **it's the one I'm looking at**.

"Sister," said Quintina. "Are you not saddened? The father of your child—"

"Pomponius isn't the father," Tacita said plainly. "Soren Calidius Pavo is the father. We were married a few days ago. It was a private ceremony. I did not want to bother you, sister, as you have been so busy with your duties. But Soren and I wanted to make it official before the baby comes." She giggled. "We are old-fashioned like that."

Tacita waited for a response from the Vestals—congratulations seemed in order—but their faces were unreadable.

The curtain to the tablinum opened, and the novice Lauressa peeked inside the room.

"Yes, what is it?" asked Pomponia, grateful for the interruption. It had prevented her from calling Tacita either a liar or a madwoman to her face. She was still unsure which applied.

"Excuse me, High Priestess, but you asked me to notify you immediately whenever messages arrived from the temple in Africa."

"Good. Thank you, Lauressa." She stood, as did Quintina.

"No doubt you have much to do," Quintina said to her sister. "A new bride and an expectant mother. Would you like me to arrange for a litter to take you back to your home?"

"Thank you, but no," said Tacita. She again rolled onto her feet. "Soren spoils me so. He will not let me walk anywhere on foot but insists that I am always in a lectica. Ours is waiting on the street."

"Good," Quintina replied. "May Juno smile on the birth of your child."

"I pray so," said Tacita. "I cannot wait for you to meet your nephew or niece." She touched Quintina's arms as if they were the best of friends, the closest and most loving of sisters.

"The child will be welcome at our house," said Quintina.

"And the child's parents?" Tacita asked.

"Of course," said Quintina. "Most welcome."

"I am happy to hear that. I hope this child will bring us closer as sisters. We have had our strife, but our affection for the child will bury it, nay?"

"It will bury it deeper than Hades," said Quintina.

Once Lauressa had escorted Tacita out of the tablinum, Quintina widened her eyes. "My sister is as mad as a maenad."

"Then she is fortunate," said Pomponia, "because I am beginning to think there would be a certain comfort in madness."

CHAPTER XXVII

Igne Quid Utilius?
What is more useful than fire?
−OVID

It was late afternoon on the ides of June and the last day of the Vestalia. For the previous eight days, the Vestal priestesses had tirelessly performed public ceremonies and rituals, prepared and distributed sacred wafers, and blessed those who took sacred embers from the firebowls along the Via Sacra to burn in their own homes.

They also opened the sanctum of the temple to allow Roman women to enter and offer plates of food to the goddess. These women gazed on the sacred fire of Vesta and gave thanks not just to the goddess but to the priestesses who guarded her eternal flame. Many left gifts of jewelry, silks, ivory ornaments, or coin for the Vestals.

The novices worked as tirelessly as full Vestals

during the Vestalia. They entered the temple on behalf of men and boys who had lost wives and mothers and therefore had no woman to present offerings for them. They kept the firebowls burning and handed out the sacred wafers so people could offer to and commune with the goddess in their own homes.

Although Pomponia and Quintina were still feeling the aftershocks of the deaths in their lives, the festival was helping to ease their grief over Pomponius and Septimus respectively, largely because it demanded so much of their time and energy. It also reminded them of their true focus—the **ignis inexstinctus**. The eternal flame of Vesta.

The Vestalia was a celebration of the goddess, but it was also a celebration of Rome's long history and legends, its power and endurance. And when it was over, as with any celebration, there was a mess to clean up.

Quintina was scrubbing the white and black mosaic of the temple floor alongside Lucretia, while Cossinia, Lucasta, and Marcella cleaned the walls. They used sanctified spring water as only pure water could be used to clean Vesta's temple.

Pomponia and Caecilia were cleaning the hearth itself, scooping out ash from the bronze bowl and nourishing the fire with fresh tinder. All ash collected from the eternal fire was kept in the **favissa**, the sacred depository in the temple's floor, to eventually be disposed of in the Tiber River under rites. Every time Pomponia brushed a new panful of ash into the depository, she was reminded that she had put both Fabiana's and Quintus's ashes here too.

Pomponia wiped her forehead with the back of her hand and stood up. "It's not going to get any cleaner than this," she said. "It's getting late. Our guests will be arriving next hour. Marcella and Caecilia, you will keep watch. Quintina and I will relieve you early this evening, so you will have time to wash up and enjoy the party."

Leaving Caecilia and the younger Marcella to tend to the fire, the rest of the priestesses hurried from the temple back to the House of the Vestals and their respective quarters to wash up and change for the evening's gathering in the courtyard.

After Pomponia's slaves had scrubbed the last of the grime off her body and she had been dressed in a stola and a light veil, she went to her office where a letter from Despina was waiting.

High Priestess Pomponia,
Matters between the emperor and

empress remain constant. The empress continues to order virgins for her husband from the slave market, although he takes her as often as he takes them. Last night, he first called for a girl and then changed his mind after she was prepared and called his wife to his bedchamber instead.

Tiberius was here last night and stayed up working into the late hours, even after Caesar had retired. The emperor relies on him for more and more duties, and he seems to be performing them adequately. He stayed the night, as he often does, but last night there was a change in his behavior that you should be made aware of.

After he had signed the last document from the Senate, he did not proceed to his bedchamber with a bed slave, which is his habit, but rather went to visit the servants' quarters. He moved from room to room, randomly ordering slaves to lie on the floor and have intercourse in front of him, always in groups of three or more. As they did, he knelt on the floor beside them and instructed them how to proceed, sometimes ordering a slave to penetrate another in this orifice or that.

When he grew tired of this, he took three young slave boys into the servants' baths with him and had them swim underwater to pleasure him until he was satisfied. I have not seen this behavior from him before. I will keep you apprised.

No one speaks of Julia, although late yesterday afternoon her mother, Scribonia, again came to the house and begged Caesar to let her accompany her daughter in exile. Again, Caesar refused. At the insistence of the empress, he barred Scribonia from visiting his house in the future.

That is all for now.

Despina

Pomponia curled the papyrus back up tightly, dipped its edge in the flame of the candle at her desk, and watched it burn, shaking the ash into the same silver bowl as always.

The change in Tiberius's behavior was worth following. The more she and Quintina could learn about him, the better. Despina's letters were helpful, but these days Tiberius spent most of his time in his own home, not Caesar's. It would soon be necessary to enlist a slave in the house of Tiberius as well as Caesar.

The last of the papyrus turned to ash, and Pomponia's shoulders dropped just a little as she thought of poor Scribonia. It was just a matter of time until Julia's mother came to her and asked her to intercede with Caesar. She still wasn't sure how she would handle that, but no doubt the goddess would give her a way.

Having brushed the ash from her hands, Pomponia left her office, walking quickly downstairs to enter the courtyard, where the Vestals' guests—Caesar and Livia, Tiberius, and the usual assortment of senators, priests, wealthy landowners, and high-ranking magistrates—were already drinking, eating, and socializing within the decorated open-sky garden.

Garlands of flowers had been wrapped around the columns of the peristyle and had also been draped around the necks of the Vestal statues that bordered the rectangular courtyard. The white rosebushes around the central pools were in full bloom.

Pomponia chose a violet-cushioned chair next to Caesar and Livia. Octavian waved for a slave to serve her a cup of wine. As the priestess took a sip of the sweet liquid, Octavian put his arm around Livia, and she rested her head against his shoulder. The emperor rarely showed affection to his wife in public. It was a good sign.

"Priestess," said Octavian, "you will be pleased to know that I have settled an additional five thousand veterans in Carthage and Thysdrus, and I've sent yet another troop of engineers to expand the public offices, baths, and temples. Business thrives there, so I've ordered more olive presses too. The thing that seems to please the most, however, is the amphitheater in Carthage. Taurus would run himself through with envy."

"How do the priestesses Nona and Sabina like Carthage?" asked Livia.

"They say they are happy," said Pomponia, "and I am inclined to believe them. Nona would not complain even if all the wine were vinegar, but Sabina would never hold her tongue. If she says they are happy, they are happy. They speak highly of their sister priestesses too." Pomponia tipped her cup to take a sip but realized she had already emptied it. Octavian laughed and bade a slave to refill it. "Does Virgil make progress on your epic?" Pomponia asked him.

"His three lines a day have shrunk to three words a day," said Octavian.

"Ah," Pomponia replied. "I must remind myself to not bring it up again." Her good humor soured at the appearance of Soren and Tacita entering the courtyard, the latter carrying an infant. Tacita had delivered a baby girl two weeks earlier.

In keeping with tradition, the girl was named Calidia, after Soren's family name. As far as everyone knew, and as far as the laws of Rome were concerned, he was the child's natural and legal father, and he had patria potestas over her.

Had the child's true father been known, if it could be proven, the child's name would be different. She would be called Pomponia, and she would now be in the care of the chief Vestal.

Pomponia excused herself and joined Quintina as they greeted Soren and Tacita, both Vestals using every ounce of their training to remain civil. They had to. It was the only way, at least for now, that they could keep watch over their niece.

Soren rocked on his heels. He tried to smile at Pomponia, but as usual, it formed into a smirk. "Your guard holds a grudge," he said. "He must remember me from when I petitioned for my slave's life." He jerked his head toward the peristyle where Caeso stood rigid and alert, hand on the hilt of his gladius. "You must assure him that I bear no ill will."

"Why would you?" asked Pomponia.

Soren did not answer but instead changed course. "Tacita and I were shocked to hear of your brother's death in the Subura," he said and then added, "of all places." He slurped his wine. "Have you determined what business he had there?"

"It remains a mystery," she said.

A flourish of music and then applause rose up in the courtyard and resonated within the enclosing marble of the peristyle. Pomponia turned to see the virtuoso Anchises walking toward the large decorative pool in the garden, beside which a lyre player and a raised platform awaited him. He stepped onto the platform and bowed to the gathering.

With Soren still at her shoulder, Pomponia pretended not to notice the change in the singer's appearance. Anchises was thinner. His face was pale and drawn. She wondered for a moment if he had been unfortunate enough to have caught the last remnants of the contagion, but he didn't look diseased. He looked defeated.

"Emperor and Empress." Anchises bowed to

Caesar and Livia, and then to Pomponia. "Blessed Vestalis Maxima and priestesses, I am honored to perform on this holy day, the last day of the festival to the fiery goddess Vesta." He waited until another swell of applause subsided. "Now, I will sing for you the famous Orphic hymn to the goddess."

Anchises nodded to the lyre player beside him, and once the music began, he sang.

> **Daughter of Saturn, with the beautiful name**
> **The heart that holds the eternal flame**
> **With sacred rites we honor you**
> **Mystical, blessed, holy and divine.**
> **In you, the gods have fixed the place**
> **The unshakable basis of the mortal race**
> **Timeless, dancing, ever florid queen**
> **Laughing and lovely, your sacred mien**
> **Accept these rites, grant each our desire**
> **And strength and needful good inspire.**

Despite his strained appearance, which no one but Pomponia seemed to notice, Anchises's voice was as skilled and pleasing as ever. Smiling graciously amid applause, he stepped off the platform, and a slave approached him with a tray of wine and food. His eyes moved directly to Soren before he declined.

Pomponia did not allow herself to think about it. She just did it. She strode onto the platform that Anchises had just stepped down from and clasped her hands in front of her.

"Caesar and Lady Livia," she said, "and all our dear friends here today, I and my sister priestesses thank you for the honors and graciousness you have shown during the Vestalia." A round of happy applause. "But if you will permit me, I have a request on behalf of the Vestal order." She smiled genially at Soren, and all eyes turned to him. "I would like to ask that Soren, cousin to our beloved Tuccia, sell the boxer slave known as Ignis, so named in Tuccia's honor, to our order." She extended her arms to Anchises. "We will of course purchase him alongside Anchises . . . We would not want to break up Apollo's Pair, lest the god disapprove."

Anchises dropped his arms to his sides. Slowly, breathlessly, as if afraid to lay eyes on a malignant spirit that stood growling behind him, he turned around to look at Soren. He recognized his master's expression all too well—the flared nostrils, the tight lips, the narrowed eyes. Barely restrained rage. Had they been alone in Soren's basement and not surrounded by upper society in the Vestal courtyard, Anchises knew he'd be bleeding on the dirt floor by now.

Soren's lips twitched, and he raised his arm to say something, but Pomponia interjected. "Oh, do not worry, Soren." She smiled. "We do not expect a deal." The gathering laughed. Soren's frugal nature was well known. "We offer the sum of five million sesterces," she said.

Impressed murmurs of approval made their rounds through the courtyard.

Soren forced his lips into a sociable grin. He remembered how good it had felt at the amphitheater the day he had given Thracius the new name Ignis, how he had left the Vestal no choice but to publicly submit. He imagined the priestess was feeling that pleasure right now.

He repeated the number in his head. **Five million sesterces.** It was almost double what he'd paid Bassus for them, and that was when they were both fresh and fit. Then again, he was fooling himself to believe he had any choice here, not with Caesar and Rome's elite holding their breath for his answer.

"I agree," he said with a bow, "out of respect for my dear cousin Priestess Tuccia."

Several senators approached Soren amid the boisterous applause to slap him on the back and praise him. He thanked them all and bowed deeply as Caesar himself came over to show his approval. Pomponia soon joined them.

"It is a generous purchase, Priestess," said Soren. "I will have the paperwork prepared tomorrow, and both slaves delivered next week. I will need to have Ignis transported from the ludus—"

"Nonsense," Pomponia said lightly. "This courtyard is crawling with magistrates." She turned her head. "Look, here is one now. Plinius, are you sober enough to be official?"

The magistrate threw his head back in laughter. "Yes, but not for long." He grabbed the tunica of a passing slave. "Go get some papyrus and a stylus."

"Then pack the coin," added Pomponia, "and have Ignis collected from the ludus straightaway."

The slave bowed and ran off as the other Vestals gathered around Pomponia. "What a wonderful idea, sister," said Lucretia. "A fitting way to honor Tuccia, especially during the Vestalia. She loved sport and the games."

"Do you remember what foul language she'd use whenever someone mentioned Flavius the charioteer?" asked Caecilia. "She hated that man. She used to call him the most obscene names."

"I was so young, I didn't even know what some of those names meant," said Quintina. The Vestal smiled at the memory of Tuccia and forced herself to keep smiling even as Tacita closed the distance between them.

Tacita, who had loved to hook her arm around Septimus and lean against him. Tacita, who might as well have tied the weights around Septimus's legs and rolled him into the waters of the Tiber herself.

Quintina looked into the face of her niece, trying to focus on her sweet pink lips, trying not to picture Septimus's lips, blue and cold.

"Would you like to hold Calidia?" Tacita asked her.

Quintina accepted the infant and cradled her affectionately. She turned to Pomponia, only to find the chief Vestal had discreetly stepped out of the conversation. It was not surprising. She had many duties to attend to and many people to visit.

It took several minutes, but Pomponia finally found Anchises sitting on a step at the far end of the courtyard. He looked even weaker than he had a few moments ago. She sat next to him, holding his arm down as he instinctively moved to stand in her presence.

"Priestess," he said, "I do not understand what is expected of me."

"Nothing is expected of you," she said. "Well, that is not true. You will be expected to sing. We will not have Thracius fight, but we will find use for him. Maybe not the kind of use he's accustomed to. This is the house of the goddess . . ." She smiled warmly. "He will be retrieved from the ludus tonight. You will stay here in our house until we make other arrangements, but you will not be parted again."

Anchises began to weep. "I have been so afraid, Priestess. I have lived in fear every day since coming to Rome. Soren, he will not . . . I cannot . . . I have not spoken to Thracius in so long. I have missed him. I worry about him. I don't know how he fares."

"You speak of the past, Anchises. It is nearly my watch in the temple, but for now I will have a slave get you settled." She stood up and then added in the virtuoso's native Greek, "**Pánta kalōs héxei.**" All will be well.

"Yes, Domina. Thank you. You will not be displeased with us. We will serve you well. We will do all that is asked of us. You will see, we will . . ."

"Rest," said Pomponia. She touched Anchises's shoulder. "The worst is behind you." She left the singer on the steps, still quietly weeping. She ordered a slave to bring him food and prepare a shared room for him and Thracius and then slipped out of the courtyard unnoticed. Everyone was having a good time. She didn't want to interrupt, not even to say good night.

Accompanied by Caeso and Publius, she moved through the house and atrium, out the portico, and then turned to walk the few steps along the cobblestone until she reached the temple. The guards stopped there, and she climbed the steps, opening the doors to the sanctum, where Marcella and Caecilia were tending the fire.

"I relieve both of you," she said. "Quintina will be here shortly."

Just then, Quintina brushed by her. "Quintina is here," she said, and they slipped into the temple together.

Once Marcella and Caecilia had gone, Quintina unwrapped two solid objects from her palla: terracotta figurines of the goddess Vesta.

"Votive offerings?" asked Pomponia.

"Votive promises," Quintina replied. "I want to do this together, the two of us, in the sacred fire."

Pomponia accepted one of the small figurines and stood before the white marble pedestal of the sacred hearth, atop which the perpetual fire burned in its gleaming bronze bowl. She watched the orange flames move and change shape as they swirled around the wood. She felt the heat radiate outward and heard the snaps and cracks of the fire, the voice of the goddess.

"Mother Vesta," said Pomponia. "**Do ut des.** I give this resemblance of your divine form to the fire that you may provide vengeance for my brother's death and bring his child home, to your sacred house. If you do this, we will make her your humble priestess." She placed the figurine in the fire. Flames curled around it, blackening the red clay.

"Mother Vesta," said Quintina. "**Do ut des.** I give this resemblance of your divine form to the fire that you will provide vengeance for Septimus's death and bring the niece of your priestesses home, to your sacred house. If you do this, we will make her your humble priestess."

They said nothing for a long time but only

watched the terracotta figures char and burn. "Will the goddess answer our prayers?" Quintina finally asked.

"She always does," said Pomponia. "But it may not be in the way we expect. I have learned that the gods have their own way of doing things."

* * *

When Pomponia was a young novice Vestal, she had always loved it when Fabiana would order their guards to remain at the temple and the two of them would stroll through the Forum Romanum after dark, after it had been closed to the public and the gates were safely shut and locked, when the only people who remained were the Vestals, the temple guards, and a few senators or magistrates working late in the Curia or basilicas.

She and Fabiana would walk along the cobblestone street, lit by moonlight and torches. They would wander past the Regia and the Temple of Castor and Pollux, along the columns and arches of the basilicas' arcades, and to the Senate house. Pomponia would climb the Rostra and run in circles atop the magnificent platform, looking up at the golden Eagle of Rome which shone bigger and brighter against the night sky than the moon.

No matter how many times she and Fabiana took their nighttime strolls, the novice Vestal had always been slightly amazed. How could the same space, the Forum that she knew so well, seem so different at night than it did during the day? It was a surreal experience. She could stand at midday on a certain cobblestone and look at the bronze doors of the temple, so familiar and expected. And yet when she stood on the same cobblestone at night and looked at the same bronze doors, it felt different.

Pomponia felt a touch of that now. She moved through her days and duties, but the absences in her life—Quintus, Fabiana, Medousa, Tuccia, Pomponius, even Nona and Sabina—were palpable. Life without them seemed different in the same way that the bronze doors seemed different after dark.

Yet she found comfort in one of her recent purchases—Anchises. Every night for the past week, the two of them had walked the Forum after dark. **Why is it**, wondered Pomponia, **that we always return to the things of our youth?**

The virtuoso and Thracius had now lived in the House of the Vestals for over a month. Pomponia had put them in Medousa's former quarters. Thracius was largely recovered from his burns, although they had left him with scars over most of his body. The guards still saw him as a celebrity, though, and he could often be found chatting on the street with them about Rome's biggest matches.

It was a moonless sky tonight. Torches flickered along the Via Sacra, throwing light on the columns of the temples, basilicas, and monuments as Pomponia and Anchises walked over the cobblestone. They stopped to chat for a moment with the guards in front of the Basilica Aemilia and then kept going.

"Tacita came for dinner tonight," Pomponia said to Anchises.

"Did she bring the child, Domina?"

"Yes, she always does. Poor Quintina. It is hard for her to smile at her sister after all of it. It is hard for me to be welcoming to Soren as well. Will he never stand before Justitia?" She faced Anchises in the dark. "You must feel the same way."

"Yes, but I have learned to accept the uncertainty of life," he replied. "I lived for a long time never knowing what would happen to Thracius, but I endured." He pointed his chin to the Palatine Hill, toward the house of Augustus. "Caesar fought Antony for years, never knowing if he would win the war. There are no certainties. We must just persist. Even if you do not get revenge for your brother, even if your niece grows distant from you, you must still live your life and do your duty. That is the vow you took, is it not?"

"Fabiana speaks through you, Anchises."

"I am a singer," said Anchises. "People always speak through me."

They wandered along the Via Sacra to stop before the Lacus Curtius. Enclosed on all sides by a low marble wall, the Lacus Curtius was a mysterious pit, now covered by a heavy slab of rich red marble with thin white veins crisscrossing its surface.

"When I was very young," said Pomponia, "before any Caesars ruled Rome, the marble over the Lacus Curtius was yellow."

"What is down there?" asked Anchises.

"Since you are fond of uncertainty," said Pomponia, "you will like my answer. No one really knows." She pointed to a square relief carving on the marble enclosure. It was illuminated by torchlight and showed a soldier on horseback falling into the pit. "One story is that in our earliest days, Rome was under attack by our enemies. A chasm opened right here, and a priest said that the gods were asking for a sacrifice. A brave soldier named Marcus Curtius drove himself into the pit. The gods were pleased, and so they saved Rome." Pomponia continued as they turned to walk back to the temple. "Many years ago, when I was a novice, the marble covering over the pit cracked. Fabiana let me climb over the wall and peek through the crack, down into the pit. It was blacker than this night, and for a moment I thought I saw two yellow eyes looking up at me. For months afterward, whenever I walked by, I would imagine a wolf was about to jump out and tear out my throat."

"Ah, well there is always a wolf waiting in the dark, is there not?" asked Anchises. "That is why we mortals lit the very first fire, and why you keep it burning still."

"Is that why?" asked Pomponia. "I love the goddess and have done my duty well. But I have lost people. I miss them, and sometimes I wonder . . .'"

"Domina, all those people who have gone before us are within the eternal flame, just as you and I will be, one day." He looked at the Temple of the Divine Julius. "In the end, the flames consume us all, Caesar and slave alike. That is how we come together again." In the torchlight, Pomponia could see the flash of his smile. "Do you see how poetic my trade makes me?"

"Unbearably poetic," she said and grinned.

They took a few more steps to reach the Temple of Vesta. It was time for Pomponia's watch.

"Bonam noctem, Priestess," said Anchises, bowing.

"Bonam noctem, Anchises."

The singer walked past the temple to the House of the Vestals. Caeso pulled one of its red doors open for him, and he disappeared inside.

Pomponia stood on the bottom step of the temple. Lucretia would emerge any moment, and they would pass by each other, one stepping up and one stepping down, as Vesta's priestesses had been doing for centuries in this very spot.

As she looked up into the darkness, the familiar bronze doors of the temple opened, and a slant of orange light from the ancient hearth fire—Vesta herself—slipped out of the sanctum and into the night, illuminating the cobblestone at Pomponia's feet.

EPILOGUE

Festina Lente
Make haste slowly.
—CAESAR AUGUSTUS

The Vestal lectica stopped in front of Pomponius's large house on the Caelian Hill. Pomponia pulled back the curtain and looked at the estate, the yellow wall that ran around the house, and the tall cypress and waving green palm trees that stood just inside the wall.

It was a short trip here from the Forum, yet she had not visited this house in many years. The last time was shortly after her father had died.

Even when Pomponius had said he was returning to Rome from his wanderings, she had charged a senior slave with preparing the house and stocking it with goods and servants. Many times she had intended to visit Pomponius here, but it had always

516

seemed easier for him to visit her at the House of the Vestals. She tried to not hate herself for it.

"Are you coming in with me?" she asked Anchises.

"Yes, I just need to fix my sandal," he said. His eyes lingered on the house's portico. "I will follow in a moment."

She nodded and stepped out of the lectica, careful not to drop the box in her hands. Caeso was already unlocking the heavy wooden door. He pulled it open and moved to step inside, but Pomponia stopped him.

"It will be safe enough," she said. "Wait here."

"Yes, Priestess."

Pomponia stepped into the vestibule and walked through into the brightness of the atrium. Pomponius had made some improvements. A brilliant peacock was painted against a deep orange wall. It was very beautiful.

She crossed the atrium to stand before the home's lararium, noticing the small bronze statuette of Vesta that sat on it. She looked up at the scarlet wall behind the lararium.

The death masks of her ancestors were there: her father, his father, and his father before that. She opened the box in her hands and removed Pomponius's death mask. A hook was already waiting for it, and she reached up high to place it securely on the wall.

The sight of her brother's face on the red wall looking down at her with such realism didn't make her sad. It made her angry. Why had Pomponius been in the Subura? Why had he been dressed in a freedman's rough tunica?

Soren was behind it. She knew it. Somehow, he was responsible for Pomponius's death, and it wasn't because he had to have Tacita. The man had nothing but contempt for his wife. It was the baby he wanted. It was revenge that he wanted. And all for some bed slave that probably wouldn't fetch a single sesterce at market.

Pomponia moved deeper into the house. There had to be a clue here somewhere, some kind of proof that Soren was not what he seemed and that Pomponius was the true father of Tacita's child.

She turned into his study. Shelves of scrolls lined the red and yellow painted walls. His desk was against the backmost, and she walked straight to it. A chair was tucked neatly under it, but its surface was scattered with scrolls and wax tablets, maps, coins, and what looked like a few lines of the epic Virgil was writing for the emperor. Nothing unusual, though.

She turned to leave the office—and stopped in her tracks.

A man was sitting on a chair against the far wall. He held a jug of wine to his lips and drank straight from it like some kind of barbarian, not caring that it dribbled down his sticky beard and over his dirty tunica. He wiped his mouth with the back of his hand.

"Gods, who are you?" Pomponia demanded.

"I am Scorpus the Titan," he said. "Have a seat, Priestess. We have a lot to discuss."

AFTERWORD

In **To Be Wolves**, book two in the Vesta Shadows series, my goal was to again bring the ancient Vestal order and religion to life in an exciting and informative way. I think it's important to position the Vestals within the larger Roman world they lived in, from its politics, punishments, and people's daily habits to its mythology, medicine, and monuments.

Yet, this is historical fiction, and I have taken some artistic license by simplifying complex ideas, adjusting timelines, and tightening up genealogies. My goal was to convey the major themes, accomplishments, and spirit of the period while remaining reasonably focused on Pomponia's arc and the Vestal order—and telling a fast-paced story in the process. For example, Agrippa and Julia had a number of children, including the notable Gaius and Lucius, but to Octavian's despair, they did not survive to become his successors, and he made Tiberius his heir as a last resort. Agrippa's posthumous son lived to adulthood, although he was then killed to secure Tiberius's position. Those versed in the subject matter will know where I have taken creative liberties.

As I mentioned in the afterword of book one, because so little is known about the personal lives of the Vestals, this series's Pomponia Occia is a fictionalized composite of two real Vestals: Occia and Pomponia. The second names of Nona Fonteia and Caecilia Scantia are also the names of actual Vestals. You'll find references to other real Vestals in this book as well. At the beginning of chapter XXIV, some of the names engraved on the walls of the novices' study are the names of legendary and documented Vestals. Cossinia was a real Vestal Virgin who served—as in the book, although later than depicted—at the Temple of Vesta in Tivoli, not far from Rome. You can still visit her tombstone and her temple in that pretty city.

There are countless resources and books on ancient Rome, but I again mention those modern works I've found particularly useful **Rome's Vestal**

Virgins by Robin Lorsch Wildfang; **Excavations in the Area Sacra of Vesta (1987–1996)**, edited by Russell T. Scott; **Mythology** by Edith Hamilton; and **Augustus** by Pat Southern. Any deviations from what is accepted as fact in this story are mine, for artistic reasons, and not theirs. As for the ancient sources—Livy, Dio, Gellius, Ovid, Tacitus, Suetonius, and so on—you'll see their inestimable influence throughout, adapted as necessary for the story.

A few last notes that may interest readers: Just as Flamma in **Brides of Rome** was the name of a real gladiator, Scorpus was the name of a real charioteer ("the Titan" is my own addition). Taurus's eulogy to him in the amphitheater is based on words the Roman poet Martial spoke of the real Scorpus. A pestilence did strike Rome around this time, and Octavian was often ill with a host of ailments. Livia had her own ailments, including a miscarriage and the "beauty pageant" with Terentia. A couple lines of the funeral oration that Octavian delivers for Agrippa were inspired by a fragment of a Greek translation of the actual speech. The adulterous Julia was exiled to Pandateria—indeed without wine or men.

I truly hope you enjoyed **To Be Wolves** enough

to read the third book in this series, **Empire of Iron: A Novel of the Vestal Virgins**. I also hope that you will visit VestaShadows.com, where you will find more history on Vesta and her priestesses, as well as a gallery of images from my personal collection plus blogs, videos, and other resources.

Thank you for reading, and all the best.

DRAMATIS PERSONAE

BOOKS ONE AND TWO

Aelina Wife of Mettius

Agrippa Marcus Vipsanius Agrippa, general and friend of Octavian

Agrippina Daughter of Julia and Agrippa

Anchises Slave, famed singer, and partner of Thracius

Ankhu Egyptian freedman in the employ of Pomponia, former messenger slave of Quintus

Bassus Owner of Anchises and Thracius in Capua

Brutus Senator and assassin of Julius Caesar

Caecilia Scantia Vestal priestess

Caeso Bodyguard of Pomponia

Cassandra Slave, intimate partner of Scorpus

Cassius Senator and assassin of Julius Caesar

Cicero Marcus Tullius Cicero, Roman orator and statesman

Cleopatra Cleopatra VII Philopator, Queen of Egypt

Cossinia Vestal priestess from Tivoli

Crassus Marcus Licinius Crassus, Roman general

Dacia Bed slave of Soren

Despina Chief slave in the house of Octavian and Livia

Diodorus Greek friend of Livia's first husband, Tiberius

Drusus Younger son of Livia with her first husband, Tiberius

Fabiana Former **Vestalis Maxima**, or high priestess of the Vestal order

Flamma Famed gladiator

Gaius Roman soldier

Julia Caesaris filia Daughter of Octavian and his first wife, Scribonia

Julius Caesar Gaius Julius Caesar, Roman general and dictator

Laelius Flamen Martialis, or high priest of Mars

Lauressa Vestal novice

Lepidus Pontifex Maximus, or chief priest of Rome

Livia Livia Drusilla, wife of Octavian and empress of Rome; mother of Tiberius and Drusus by her first husband

Lucasta Vestal priestess

Lucretia Lucretia Manlia, Vestal priestess

Maecenas Gaius Maecenas, close political adviser to Octavian

Marc Antony Roman general

Marcus Julius Caesar Agrippa Postumus Son of Julia and Agrippa

Manius A wealthy Roman living in Capua

Marcella Vestal priestess

Marcellus Octavian's nephew; Octavia's son from her first marriage

Medousa Greek slave, formerly owned by Pomponia

Mettius Owner of Scorpus the Titan in Capua and friend of Soren

Musa Antonius Musa, Greek physician of Octavian

Nona Nona Fonteia, Vestal priestess

Octavian Great-nephew and adopted son of Julius Caesar; Rome's first emperor, Augustus

Octavia Sister of Octavian

Palaemon Tombstone maker in the Subura district

Perseus Fabiana's dog (named after the hero who slew Medusa)

Pollio Wealthy Roman landowner and merchant

Pomponia Pomponia Occia, **Vestalis Maxima**, or high priestess of the Vestal order

Pomponius Brother of Pomponia

Publius Bodyguard of Pomponia

Quintina Quintina Vedia, Vestal priestess, elder daughter of Quintus and Valeria

Quintus Quintus Vedius Tacitus, former priest of Mars and soldier of Caesar

Sabina Vestal priestess

Scorpus the Titan Slave and famous charioteer

Scribonia Mother of Julia and previous wife of Octavian

Septimus Young priest of Mars

Soren Soren Calidius Pavo, Roman citizen, cousin of Tuccia

Spartacus Slave and leader of a slave revolt

Tacita Tacita Vedia, sister of Quintina; younger daughter of Quintus and Valeria

Taurus Senator and wealthy patron of the amphitheater

Terentia Wife of Maecenas

Thracius Slave, famous boxer, and partner of Anchises

Tiberius Tiberius Claudius Nero, son of Livia by her first husband of the same name

Tuccia Vestal priestess

Valeria Former wife of Quintus

Virgil Renowned Roman poet

ROMAN GODS, GODDESSES & MYTHICAL FIGURES

Aeneas A Trojan hero who fled the burning city and became the ancestor of Rome's founder, Romulus

Apollo The god of the sun and the arts

Athena The Greek goddess of wisdom; the Greek equivalent of Minerva

Atlas Titan that held the heavens on his shoulders

Atrox Fortuna Goddess of fate; an aspect of the goddess Fortuna

Bacchus The god of wine

Basilisk A snakelike monster

Cerberus The three-headed hound of Hades that guards the entrance to the underworld

Ceres The goddess of grain

Charon The ferryman of Hades; carries souls across the River Styx

Clementia The goddess of clemency and leniency

Clytemnestra The sister of Helen of Troy

Concordia The goddess of harmony and agreement

Cronus A Titan who ate his own children to avoid being overthrown by them

Cyclops A one-eyed monster from Homer's **Odyssey**

Diana The goddess of the hunt

Dis Pater A god of the underworld

Discordia The goddess of discord

Edesia The goddess of feasts

Europa A woman who fell in love with Zeus, who came to her in the form of a bull

Fates Three goddesses who determine human destiny

Flora The goddess of flowers and spring

Fortuna The goddess of fortune and luck

Fortuna Virilis An aspect of Fortuna that dealt with virility; a woman might pray to her to make her husband virile so she could conceive

Gorgons Three sisters with snakes for hair; their gaze turned all who met it into stone

Hades The underworld; also the Greek name for Pluto

harpy A terrifying mythical creature that is half bird and half woman

Helen of Troy A beautiful woman whose supposed abduction by the prince of Troy angered her husband, a Greek king, and started the Trojan War; credited with being "the face that launched a thousand ships"

Hera The Greek equivalent of Juno

Hercules A legendary hero famous for his strength

Isis An Egyptian goddess

Iuppiter Jupiter, in the original Latin spelling

Janus The two-faced god of beginnings and endings

Juno The wife of Jupiter; goddess of marriage

Jupiter The king of the gods; god of thunder and the sky

Justitia The personification of justice; also known as Lady Justice

Juturna The goddess of fountains, wells, and springs; in Rome she was associated with the Spring of Juterna, which was located in a corner of the Forum Romanum

Laocoön A Trojan priest who tried in vain to warn his people about the dangers of the Trojan horse

Luna The goddess of the moon

Lupa The she-wolf that nursed Romulus and his brother, Remus

Mars The god of war

Medea The enchantress who helped Jason and the Argonauts find the Golden Fleece

Medusa A snake-haired Gorgon; looking at her face turned one to stone

Mercury The messenger god

Midas A legendary king with the power to turn whatever he touched to gold

Minerva The goddess of wisdom

Minotaur A monster with the head of a bull and the body of a man

Narcissus A vain youth who was so enchanted by his own reflection in a pool of water that he fell in and drowned

Nemean lion A giant lion with an impenetrable hide; killed by Hercules as one of his twelve labors

Nemesis The goddess of revenge

Neptune The god of the sea

nymph A female nature deity intimately connected to a particular place or thing such as a tree or stream; nymphs usually appear as beautiful maidens

Pandora The first woman, whose curiosity released all the evils that beset humanity, save the lack of hope

Pegasus A white, winged horse belonging to Zeus

Penelope The wife of Ulysses

Perseus The legendary hero who slew the Gorgon Medusa

Pluto The god of Hades, the underworld

Proserpina The queen of the underworld

Quirinus An early god of Rome, likely originating as a Sabine god of war; Romulus was said to have been deified as Quirinus and was worshipped as such

Remus One of the twin sons of Rhea Silvia; brother of Romulus

Rhea Silvia A Vestal Virgin; mother, by Mars, of the twins Romulus and Remus

Romulus The legendary founder of Rome; brother of Remus

Scylla and Charybdis Two sea monsters in Homer's **Odyssey**

Spes The goddess of hope

Tantalus A figure punished after death (for stealing ambrosia and nectar from the gods) by the eternal torment of having to stand in a pool of water that would recede whenever he bent down to take a drink

Tiberinus The god of the Tiber River, often called Father Tiber

Titans A generation of gods that came before the Greek Olympian gods or the Roman **Dii Consentes**

Trojan horse A massive wooden horse presented as a gift to the besieged city of Troy by the attacking Greeks; hiding inside the horse, however, were Greek soldiers who, once the gift had passed through the gates, exited and destroyed the city

Typhon A giant serpentine monster from Greek mythology

Ulysses The Roman name for Odysseus, a legendary Greek king and the hero of Homer's **Odyssey**, who tried for ten years to reach his homeland after the end of the Trojan War

Venus The goddess of love

Veritas The goddess of truth

Vesta The goddess of the hearth and home

Vulcan The god of fire; blacksmith of the gods

Zeus The Greek equivalent of Jupiter

GLOSSARY OF LATIN
AND IMPORTANT TERMS AND PLACES

Abite! An expression meaning "Get lost!"

Aedes Vestae The sacred building that housed the sacred flame; that is, the Temple of Vesta

aere perennius "More lasting than bronze" (Horace)

aeterna flamma The "eternal flame" of Vesta

apodyterium The main entrance to a bathhouse; a changing room

Aquila The Eagle of Rome

atrium The central open hall or court of a Roman home, around which were arranged on all sides the house's various rooms

Attat! Latin expression of surprise, fear, etc.

augur Priest who interprets the will of the gods via the flight of birds

ave A word of greeting or farewell. When addressing more than one person the form **avete** was used.

balineum The washing or bathing room in a **domus**, often with a latrine

Black Stone The Black Stone, or **Lapis Niger** in Latin, was a mysterious and revered stone block in the Roman Forum, a monument thought to date back to the earliest period of Roman history

Bona Dea The "Good Goddess" whose rites were overseen by the Vestal Virgins

caestus The leather straps worn around the hands of boxers

calidarium A very hot bath in a bathhouse

Campus Martius The Field of Mars

Campus Sceleratus The "Evil Field," where Vestals were buried alive

Capillata tree An ancient tree so named because Vestals would hang their cut hair from it—**capillata** means "hairy, or having long hair" in Latin

captio The "seizure" ceremony, where a girl is taken as a Vestal

Caput Mundi "Capital of the world," meaning Rome

Carcer The notorious structure where prisoners were incarcerated

catamite A pubescent or adolescent boy kept by a man for sexual purposes

causarius A soldier discharged after being wounded in battle

cellae servorum The slave quarters in a **domus**

chaste tree A small tree native to the Mediterranean that was considered sacred to the virginal goddess

Vesta. Its fruit has long been believed to quell sexual desire.

Circus Maximus A large stadium in Rome that was used for chariot races, public games, mock battles, and gladiatorial combat

compluvium An opening in the roof of the atrium over the impluvium

cornu A type of Roman horn

crimen incesti The crime of **incestum**, where a Vestal is accused of breaking her vow of chastity

Curia The Senate house of Rome, located in the Roman Forum

curule chair A special style of wooden seat with curved legs that was reserved only for those of the highest rank, such as Caesar or a magistrate who held the power of imperium

decimation Type of military punishment, typically for desertion, in which every tenth man in a group was killed by members of his own unit

Dii Consentes The twelve major gods and goddesses of Rome: Jupiter, Juno, Vesta, Mars, Neptune, Mercury, Diana, Ceres, Venus, Vulcan, Minerva, and Apollo

divi filius Son of the Divine Julius Caesar (i.e., Octavian)

Divus Julius The Divine Julius Caesar

Do ut des. A petition to the gods: "I give that you might give."

Domina The deferential name a slave would use with his or her female owner

Domine The deferential name a slave would use with his or her male owner

domus A Roman home

dormouse [**pl.** dormice] A special type of mouse eaten as a delicacy

Elysian Fields In the afterlife, a beautiful place of rest for the good

Equus October The October Horse, annual sacrifice to Mars on the ides of October

exploratores Roman military scouts

fasces A bundle of wooden rods symbolizing a magistrate's authority; the rods may be bundled about the haft of an ax whose blade protrudes from them

Fas est et ab hoste doceri. "It is right to learn even from one's enemies." (Ovid)

fasti The calendar of religious festivals and events

fatale monstrum A "deadly monster"

favissa Underground temple depositories where sacred items no longer in use were placed. The favissa of the Temple of Vesta was where ashes from the sacred fire were stored.

fibula A brooch or pin used to fasten clothing or a cloak; on Vestals, it secured the **suffibulum**

Flamen Dialis The high priest of Jupiter

Flamen Martialis The high priest of Mars

Fordicidia An annual fertility festival held in mid-April

forum A public square or commercial marketplace that often included important judicial, political, historical, and religious structures

Forum Augustus A new forum built by Octavian

Forum Boarium Rome's cattle and animal forum near the Tiber River

Forum of Julius Caesar A forum built by Julius Caesar near the Forum Romanum; also known as Caesar's Forum

Forum Romanum The Roman Forum was a rectangular forum in the heart of Rome which contained many official and religious buildings, as well as monuments

frigidarium The cool or cold bath in a bathhouse

Futuo! Literally, "I fuck"; used here as a vulgar expression

gladius A type of short sword; the primary sword of Roman foot soldiers

Gratias vobis ago, divine Jane, divina Vesta. A thank-you to the gods Janus and Vesta, this phrase was used at the end of a ritual or ceremony

haruspex [**pl.** haruspices] A person who reads the entrails of sacrificed animals

ides The middle of the month, which was considered to be the fifteenth day for "full" months and the thirteenth day for the shorter, or "hollow," ones

ignis inexstinctus The "inextinguishable fire" of Vesta

imperator The title given to a citizen, such as a magistrate or general, who held **imperium** (great governmental or military authority); later, this term became nearly synonymous with **emperor**

impluvium A shallow sunken pool in the atrium of a Roman house, where rainwater collected

incestum The legal charge against a Vestal who was suspected of having broken her vow of chastity

infula The ceremonial woolen headband worn by Vestals

Insanos deos! "Insane gods!"—an exclamation of dismay, disbelief, or bewilderment

insula [**pl.** insulae] A Roman apartment block

jure divino An expression meaning "by divine law"

kalends The first day of a month

Lacus Curtius A deep and mysterious pit, chasm, or pool in the Roman Forum

lanista The manager, trainer, or owner of a gladiator or gladiatorial school

lararium A household shrine to the gods and ancestors

lectica [**pl.** lecticae] A covered or enclosed couch-like mode of transport used by the upper classes and carried on the shoulders of slaves

lecticarius [**pl.** lecticarii] A man, typically a slave, who carried a **lectica**; a litter-bearer

Liberalia The annual celebration of Liber, god of wine, fertility, and freedom

libri pontificales The records and books kept by the religious collegia

lictor An officer that accompanies magistrates or important officials

litter A **lectica**; also used for a horse-drawn carriage that transported important people

ludi The public games—gladiatorial combats, beast hunts, chariot races

ludus A gladiatorial training camp; also the singular form of **ludi**

Lupercalia An annual fertility festival honoring Lupa, the she-wolf that suckled Romulus and Remus

lustratio [**pl.** lustrationes] A ceremonial purification

lyre A stringed musical instrument not unlike a harp

maenad A female follower of Bacchus; the name literally translates as "raving ones," and they were known to behave wildly

Mala Fortuna! An exclamation meaning "Evil Fortuna!" or "Bad luck!"

manumission Release from slavery; the termination of a slave's servitude, at which point a slave becomes a freedman or freedwoman

Mare Nostrum The Roman name for the Mediterranean Sea

Mea dea! An exclamation meaning "My goddess!"

Mehercule! An exclamation meaning "By Hercules!"

Milliarium Aureum The "golden milestone," a monument in the Roman Forum from which all distances in the empire were measured and all roads were considered to originate

mola salsa A ritual salted-flour mixture prepared by Vestals

ne serva clause Contractual provision stating that a slave could not be sold into forced prostitution

Nemo supra legem est. "No one is above the law."

Nota res mala optima. "A known evil is best." Taken from a larger expression: **Habeas ut nactus; nota**

mala res optima est—"Keep what you have; a known evil is best" (Plautus).

obstetrix A midwife

Paedica te! A vulgar insult: "Go fuck yourself!"

palla A woman's shawl which was worn when out of the house and which could be pulled over her head

panem et circenses A famous Latin expression meaning "bread and circuses" (i.e., things used to distract or pacify the masses), attributed to Juvenal

patera A shallow bowl that held libations

patria potestas The legal power that a man held over his household, including his wife and children

Pax Deorum The peaceful accord between humanity and the gods, which was ensured only by proper religious observance

penus The hidden innermost chamber in the Temple of Vesta, where sacred objects and important items were kept

poena cullei The "penalty of the sack," where an offender was put in a sack with live animals (e.g., a snake, dog, rooster, and monkey) and drowned

Pontifex Maximus The chief priest of Rome

posticum The rear door to a Roman **domus**, often the slaves' entrance

quaestio A secular tribunal

quaestor A public official; a position that could lead to a political career

Regia The building that served as the office of the Pontifex Maximus and which had been the home of the early kings

retiarius A type of gladiator that fought with a net and trident

Rex Sacrorum A high-ranking priest

Rostra A large, decorated speaker's platform in the Roman Forum

rudis A wooden sword given to a gladiator upon manumission

salve A Roman greeting

scutum A type of Roman shield

secutor A type of gladiator that carried a shield and a short sword or dagger and was trained to fight a **retiarius**

seni crines A braided hairstyle worn by brides and Vestal Virgins

simpulum A long-handled ladle-like vessel that held libations

spina A low barrier wall that ran down the center of a circus. The Circus Maximus had a decorated spina with conical posts at each end, around which the horses and chariots turned.

SPQR An initialism of the phrase **Senatus Populusque Romanus**—"the Senate and the People of Rome"

stola A type of dress worn by married women and Vestals

strophium A band of cloth wrapped around the breasts; an early bra

stultus A fool

subligar A type of loincloth worn by a woman

suffibulum A short ceremonial veil worn by Vestal Virgins

supplicatio A day of prayer, usually a public day of prayer

Suum cuique. an expression meaning "To each his own."

tablinum The office of a Roman house, where business might be conducted

Tabularium A public office building in the Roman Forum

Tarpeian Rock A tall cliff overlooking the Forum that was used as an execution site: criminals were thrown from it

tepidarium The warm bath in a bathhouse; typically used after the **calidarium** and before the **frigidarium**

thermae Large public bath complexes

Tiberinalia The annual festival honoring Father Tiber, the god of the Tiber River

tibia a reeded Roman pipe, a type of wind instrument

toga The traditional garment of adult male Roman citizens. The color of the toga's stripe or border denoted a man's status; for example, a reddish-purple stripe was reserved for high-status men, while a toga of solid purple could be worn only by the emperor. A dark-colored toga was worn for funerals and during periods of mourning.

toga virilis The common white or off-white woolen toga of adult male citizens

triclinium The dining room of a Roman house, furnished with couches for reclining on while eating and socializing

tunica A garment worn alone or under a toga or **stola**

Twelve Tables The very earliest laws of Rome

Veneralia An annual religious festival to celebrate Venus

Vesta Aeterna "Eternal Vesta"

Vesta Felix Vesta, who brings good luck or fortune

Vesta Mater "Mother Vesta"

Vesta, permitte hanc actionem. An appeal meaning "Vesta, permit this action."

Vesta te purificat. "Vesta purifies you."

Vestalia An annual religious festival to celebrate Vesta

Vestalis Maxima The head, or high priestess, of the Vestal order

Vestam laudo. "I praise Vesta."

Virgo Vestalis A Vestal Virgin; a priestess tasked with keeping the sacred flame of the goddess Vesta burning in the temple

vitia Mistakes, especially those made during a religious ritual

vittae A type of ribbon or band worn in the hair; on Vestals, loops hung down over the shoulders

viva flamma The "living flame" of Vesta

Ancient terracotta votive offering, similar to the ones used by Pomponia and Quintina.

Ancient Roman coin showing the heads of both Augustus and Agrippa. This is the same coin that Pomponia mentions to Octavian.

Ancient bronze statuette of Vesta, first–second century CE, similar to the one Tacita gives to Pomponius.

A Vestal Virgin being condemned for bringing the plague; this is Pomponia's recurring nightmare. Engraving print of the Vestal Urbinia by Tardieu, 1798.

ABOUT THE AUTHOR

DEBRA MAY MACLEOD is an author of historical fiction focusing on the ancient Roman religion of Vesta and the Vestal Virgins. She is privileged to have been invited to participate in research excursions in the Forum Romanum, the Forum of Caesar and Imperial Fora, including places inaccessible to the general public, and informs her writing and work with this invaluable perspective. Debra has a bachelor of arts (English, classics) as well as a law degree. She lives in Canada with her husband and son, visiting Italy often for research (and sun).